1/12 40p

I'M
HER
MOTHER

BOOKS BY LAUREN NORTH

My Word Against His
She Says She's My Daughter
The Teacher's Secret

All the Wicked Games
Safe at Home
One Step Behind
The Perfect Betrayal

I'M
HER
MOTHER

LAUREN NORTH

bookouture

Published by Bookouture in 2024

An imprint of Storyfire Ltd.
Carmelite House
50 Victoria Embankment
London EC4Y 0DZ

www.bookouture.com

ISBN: 978-1-83525-541-4
eBook ISBN: 978-1-83525-540-7

For my editor, Lucy

PROLOGUE

Darkness surrounds us in the empty car park. The dim glow of yellow from a single row of streetlights provides the only light, but it's enough to illuminate the gun and the steady hand holding it.

My heart stutters at the sight of the barrel; that black hole. How did it come to this? I drag my eyes away, looking left and right, but there is nowhere to run. No escape. Petrol fumes carry on the cool breeze from the open water. A hundred metres away the engine of the large white ferry rumbles into life.

The sight of the gun has silenced us. An electric charge ripples through the air, and I'm certain I can hear the thudding pulses of the group. Racing and panicked.

'You deserve everything that's coming to you.' My voice is stronger than I feel inside, but I refuse to show my fear any longer.

The emotions of the last few days come rushing back. They are hands gripping my body, dragging me into the depths of a pitch-black sea. I've barely slept, barely eaten, barely breathed.

Someone shouts, but I don't hear the words. The barrel of the gun moves from one person to another. There's a gasp.

'Let's all calm down, shall we?' a voice calls out.

'No, let's not,' comes the reply.

All I want is to keep my daughter safe.

My daughter. Mine. I'm her mother. The words repeat over and over in my head. After everything I've done, we're still here at this point in time. I wonder now if we've always been moving towards it. All the years that have passed, all that's happened to us, and here we are.

'This ends now.' The voice thrown at me is hateful and angry.

'I was trying to protect her,' I cry.

I shift a little to one side, my gaze never leaving that barrel. The wind drops suddenly. It's one of those moments when it seems as though the world has paused and we're all statues. It passes in a heartbeat and then everything happens at once.

The gun swings towards me. I'm going to die. I see it in the glint of fury. Those eyes that have haunted me for so long.

There's a flash of light. The gun is firing. Once, then twice. The noise deafening. I don't think as my body moves, instinct taking over.

I'm too late.

All I wanted was to protect my daughter.

The bullet hits. Pain screams through my chest. My lungs, my blood, my body is on fire. The concrete rushes up to greet me as my legs give way.

I don't move from where I've fallen. I can't. I'm pinned down by the searing burn of pain. There are footsteps and noises around me. Someone is taking my hand. Calling my name.

'I'm her mother.' I try to say the words aloud, and maybe I do. My lips move, but I don't hear my voice. My thoughts are being dragged down into that black murky water. It's too late. It really is over.

I've failed.

DAY ONE: 4 P.M. SUNDAY 30TH JULY

ONE

ISOBEL

As Isobel looks over the endless cars and people at the M3 services, she wonders if holidays with all the packing and organising and driving are actually worth it. The longing to be home is acute. An hour to go, if they're lucky.

'Mummy, Daddy, can we stop now? I need a wee,' Lola's voice calls from the trappings of her car seat in the back, her words still a little lispy despite the hours of speech therapy Roly's mother insisted on this year.

Isobel paints on a bright smile and turns to look at her three-year-old daughter. The familiar rush of love hits her chest. 'I know, darling. We're just finding somewhere to park.'

Lola frowns, wriggling beneath the straps, cheeks red and blonde hair messy from sleep. She looks as dishevelled as Isobel feels after the four hours they've spent in this car.

She turns to Roly and thinks – like she always does – how handsome he is, despite the scowl and the constant tapping of the steering wheel as he watches a car ahead of them reverse slowly out of the space they want. The space they're holding up a line of cars to have. It really isn't fair that he's still so good-looking. The same rugged, youthful man she met a decade earlier. Sometimes she feels too old for him, even though she's three years younger. Only forty-four. That's still young, isn't it? Some days she's not so sure.

He sighs and hits the controls on his door. A split second later all four windows slide down, letting in air tinged with the smells of petrol and fried foods. There's a breeze, too. More April than July.

'When,' he starts to mutter as a car beeps from behind, urging them on. 'When,' he begins again, 'Dante wrote about his nine circles of hell, he forgot to mention roadside services on Sunday afternoons.'

Such a Roly comment. Just this week, the Italian philosopher also forgot to add poor restaurant service and supermarket self-checkouts to his Inferno. Any other time, Isobel might have laughed, but she can tell by the frown pinching Roly's brow that he is as fed up with their drive home from Cornwall as she is, and they really need to get Lola to the toilets before an accident and the awful tears that will follow.

'Maybe Lola and I should get out here and leave you to park,' she says.

'Good idea,' he replies. 'I need to make a quick phone call anyway, and who knows how long this bloke is going to take. Would it be too much to offer to reverse his car for him?' The frustration strengthens his accent, making him sounds every bit the public school boy – Eton-educated man – he in fact is.

'Don't you dare.' She smiles, hoping he's joking. Sometimes with Roly it's hard to tell.

He grins back at her, laying a hand briefly on her thigh. A look passes between them and she can tell he's thinking like she is of last night. Nine years of marriage and she still burns for this man. Maybe holidays are worth it. Great sex, family time, not to mention a week without her mother-in-law calling every day.

'Just checking in on my only grandchild,' Margaret always

says. Checking *up* more like, Isobel is sure. At least the phone calls are preferable to the numerous occasions Roly's mother turns up on their doorstep with a suitcase.

'Mummy?' There's an urgency to Lola's call.

'Coming, baby girl.'

Isobel ignores the stiffness of her legs and lower back and the discomfort of her own bladder as she hurries out of their Borasco Grey Range Rover and around the car to get Lola.

'Let's go,' she says, unclipping the straps and scooping Lola into her arms. Her yellow T-shirt is creased and there's a chocolate smear down the front Isobel isn't sure will come out. 'Do you want to bring Barnaby?'

Lola looks at the tatty and much-loved bear that rarely leaves her side before shaking her head. 'He's sleeping.'

'Are you sure?' Isobel asks in a sing-song tone, knowing how quickly Lola can change her mind.

'Hurry it up, Iz,' Roly calls out, and then Lola is scrambling down, wanting to walk, and there's no time to get Barnaby anyway.

'Hold my hand,' Isobel says, casting her eyes around the heaving car park before giving an apologetic wave to the woman in the car behind. The woman makes a gesture Isobel pretends not to see. Why do people have such issues with Range Rovers? They're just waiting for a space like everyone else.

'Meet us outside the toilets,' she calls to Roly before guiding Lola carefully through the car park.

Inside is chaos. The circular-shaped dome with its eatery kiosks around the edge and tables and chairs in the middle is heaving, the air stuffy with the smell of noodles and coffee. There are people everywhere. Groups of teenagers, shouting kids, exhausted faces. She tugs gently at Lola's arm, weaving them around a long queue for McDonald's. Isobel spots the line for Costa and sighs, wondering if the hit of caffeine Roly is desperate for is worth the time spent shuffling forward in that never-ending line.

It seems impossible to Isobel that no one has thought to establish some kind of first-class roadside services for those willing to pay the upgrade fee for clean and quiet and... and just not this. It wouldn't even be that hard. An annual charge. A building tacked on to one side. A discreet turning for those who know where to look. Would it be any different from the first-class lounge at Heathrow?

God, she sounds like a snob. She sounds like Margaret, she thinks with a grimace.

'Ducky.' Lola's shout is filled with delight as she points to a hideously bright-yellow stuffed animal strategically placed at the entrance to WHSmith. Isobel is momentarily distracted by a display of newspapers and Scarlett Peters' face staring back at her. That glossy, unmistakable red hair. There's a new appeal for information about the missing woman. Isobel only met her once – a brief shared smile from across the room at a dinner party years ago, but she's found herself quite obsessed with her disappearance since it hit the news nearly four months ago. How does a beautiful young woman just disappear into thin air?

'Mummy, can I get that ducky?' Lola's voice cuts through Isobel's thoughts.

'Toilet first,' she replies, already knowing there is no space for a new toy on Lola's bed but picturing the love and joy on her daughter's face when the duck is placed in her arms anyway.

'You spoil her. My grandchild needs boundaries.'

Whiffs of cleaning products and excrement hit Isobel as they make their way into the toilets.

'I want to go on my own,' Lola says, letting go of Isobel's hand and stepping towards a cubicle, and even though Isobel worries about the germs and potential for accidents and wet knickers, she doesn't protest.

Margaret's voice plays in her head again. *'Really, Isobel?*

She's nearly four. She should be going to the bathroom on her own.'

They've made such progress this holiday with Lola's independence; something Isobel is both proud of and a little heartbroken about too. It's not like she thought their only child would fall asleep in her arms every night for the rest of her life, but she misses it more than she can voice.

She hates to admit it, but on this one and only thing, Margaret is right. Lola's fourth birthday is only a couple of weeks away. She's starting school in September. Isobel shouldn't keep babying her.

'I'll be right next door,' she says, knocking on the plastic divide. Lola knocks back, a tap, tap, tap-tap-tap that makes her smile.

The need to relieve her bladder is suddenly urgent. Isobel wriggles out of her skinny jeans – a terrible choice for a five-hour car journey, especially after so many three-course dinners on holiday and none of her usual gruelling gym sessions, but Roly does love them on her and they've had such a nice week together. It has felt wonderful to have his attention. Those blue eyes on her when she walks into a room. Just like it was back at the start when he'd wake her up in the middle of the night just to kiss her and talk to her, hands roaming every inch of her body.

There have still been calls to his phone at all hours. *'It's a client wanting to check on an investment,'* he'd say, and she tried to believe him as he'd stepped out of the room before answering.

Yes, she thinks as she sits on the toilet, the relief instant. This holiday was worth the long drive and the packing and unpacking and packing again. It's just what they needed. A chance to reconnect after the strange mood that first came over Roly earlier in the year.

She still doesn't know what caused the sullen cloud to hang over her husband, stripping him of his energy and his boundless optimism. *'To be is to do, Iz. Let's do something fun,'* he always said. Roly had been short-tempered, snappish with her, and Lola sometimes too. Or retreating into himself, existing in a world where he barely noticed them. At one point she'd feared it was her. That the jibes from his mother had finally worn him down, or he'd met someone else and he was going to leave the family they'd both wanted so badly.

But slowly, it started to lift – good days began to outweigh the bad. And the holiday has helped. Everything is perfect again. They are perfect.

Quickly, while she has a moment to herself, she unlocks her phone and opens Instagram, smiling at the likes and comments from the photos of their holiday in Cornwall she uploaded that morning. She swipes through them, admiring her toned arms and slim figure. It was worth every hour at the gym while Lola was at nursery.

She never used to enjoy working out. It was always a chore she had to fit in between long hours at the office when she'd worked in the City. Then they'd started their family and Isobel had given up the career she'd worked so hard for, and exercise was something to be fitted in around nap times instead.

But then Lola had started nursery – another one of Margaret's ideas – and Isobel had needed a distraction; a way to burn off the constant anxiety of leaving her child. She quickly grew to love the gym and the way Roly's hand would linger on her toned body whenever he touched her.

The deep whisper of his voice from last night rolls over her thoughts. *'I'll never stop wanting to be inside you, Mrs Huntington.'*

She lingers on a photo of her and Roly arm in arm; his broad shoulders and the lopsided grin that never fails to stir something inside her. Their matching blonde hair – his natural, hers the result of a trip to a salon in Knightsbridge every six weeks – blowing gently in the wind, the sandy Cornwall coastline in the background. She swipes to the next photo. The three of them this time; Lola in a white sun dress, all of them grinning at the camera.

The perfect family.

If only people knew the truth.

The thought leaps out at her from nowhere, like always. An ambush she's never ready for despite their frequency. A familiar wave of nauseating anxiety pushes through her body. She swallows, fighting it back. Lola is fine. She's just next door.

Isobel tugs up her too-tight jeans, thinking suddenly of the huge pregnancy bump and then Lola as a tiny newborn.

She knocks on the cubicle again. 'OK, Lola?' she calls out.

There is no reply.

TWO

EMMA

The blasting roar from the hand dryers hits Emma as she steps into the toilets. She looks around the tight space by the sinks and sees her little girl standing on tiptoes, fingers stretching out to reach the soap dispenser.

Emma steps up beside her to wash her hands. They shake beneath the cool water, a juddering nervousness that has been zigzagging through her body for days now. Weeks. A lifetime? Her heart is hammering in her chest. The rush of blood around her body makes her feel unsteady, but she's here now. She's found her daughter. That's all that matters.

The water stops automatically, and Emma glances to the mirror as she wipes her hands on her jeans, avoiding the huddle by the dryers and the noise, that childish desire to cover her ears. Why do they have to be so loud?

Two wet streaks darken the denim across the tops of her thighs. They used to be her favourite pair of jeans once upon a time. It was the year before she'd left for university, when her head was buzzing with A-level revision and the glittering possibilities of the future ahead of her. All optimism and the sky's the limit. A fairy-tale life, just around the corner.

She'd wear the jeans all week and then wash them on a Thursday after college, draping them over the radiator in the hall to dry, ignoring the complaints from her mum about it damaging the wallpaper. The wallpaper – a busy and hideous floral design – was already ruined. It was older than she was, for one thing, and scuffed from her older brothers and the hundreds of times they'd lugged their sports bags around the house. Not to mention peeling at the seams where the glue had given up for as long as Emma could remember. And so she'd roll her eyes and hang them in the hall anyway.

They'd always fit best after a wash and she'd liked them for Friday nights when Damien would pick her up after her shift at the supermarket and take her to whatever party one of his mates was throwing that weekend.

She'd found the jeans in the back of her wardrobe a few months ago. The denim was faded, the shape not quite the same, or perhaps it was her that had changed. Inside and out. There were no thoughts of glittering futures anymore. Just a desperation to escape her present. But she still likes the jeans, and the bagginess does a good job of hiding her figure.

She looks up to her reflection in the mirror. She read online the other day about facial recognition cameras embedded in glass now, catching a million unsuspecting faces to watch and remember, but there's rust at the edges of the frames and so she decides this one is safe.

The face staring back is young; innocent, even with the ridiculous amount of eyeliner rimming her eyes. She still gets asked for ID everywhere even though she'll be twenty-five next month. It's her eyes – big Disney princess eyes – that make her seem younger. That and her hair; thick and a rich brown in colour with just the right amount of wave to it as it falls down her back.

Except today her hair is hidden, scraped back and tucked under a long blonde wig with a fringe she bought from a website that promised easy to fit and natural looking. Neither were true, but she'd made the best of it, and no one seemed to be staring. She can take it off in a few minutes anyway. Just as soon as they get out of here.

She touches the fake ends as casually as she can, making sure to nudge the pink strap of the *Dora the Explorer* backpack from her shoulder so it falls down her arm.

'Ducky,' Lola says from beside her, reaching out to touch the newly purchased yellow duck toy sticking out from the backpack.

Emma turns and takes in her beautiful girl with her blonde shoulder-length hair and cute button nose. Hers! Her daughter standing alone by the sinks. The tremble moves from her hands along her arms and through her entire body. Is she even breathing?

She waits until a noisy group of teenage girls huddle around the dryers before crouching down so they're face to face and talks quietly to Lola. She doesn't want anyone to overhear them. 'Hi,' she says, trying so hard to smile the kind and friendly smile she'd practised so many times. 'Do you like my duck?' She pulls out the yellow stuffed animal from the bag. Inside, a voice is yelling at her to hurry, to snatch and run, but she forces herself to keep things slow. If Lola starts crying now, this is all over. 'I've just rescued him from a life stuck on a shelf and I'm looking for someone who can take care of him. Do you know anyone who can help me?'

Lola's face lights up, a big smile stretching wide, dimpling her cheeks, as her hands bury themselves in the soft fur. 'I will,' she whispers with a pleading look to Emma.

'Great. Come on then,' she replies, her voice coaxing and fun, the kind of voice a child would trust. She slips her hand into her daughter's. It's warm and still a little damp but the perfect fit too. Emma takes a step and for a single heart-stopping moment, Lola is rooted; stuck. She looks towards the closed cubicles, her expression hesitant, before her gaze lands on Emma once more. Her head tilts to the side, taking her in, it feels like. Then she's nodding and they're moving. Away from the toilets and noisy hand dryers, around the groups of people waiting for food.

Hurry! Hurry!

Eyes down, always down. Mustn't look or they'll see her.

Walk quick but not fast. Don't draw attention. Her heart continues to lurch in her chest. Are they here?

Any second; any step now and one of them will stop her. She keeps her head down, hoping the blonde wig and make-up will be enough.

Lola's hand slips a little, and Emma slows her pace a fraction. 'Ducky was telling me how much he likes sweeties,' she says. 'And I've got some of his favourites in my car. They're Haribo.'

'I like Haribo,' Lola says, hugging Ducky to her body. 'So does Barnaby. He's my teddy.'

'I know all about Barnaby Bear. He's waiting in the car too. Let's be quick before he eats all the good sweets.'

Her daughter giggles at this. The final nudge to acceptance, and they're hurrying again, through the doors and to the small blue Peugeot. There's a dent in the front bumper that causes a small pang of something in the pit of her stomach. Guilt or doubt, she's not sure.

She remembers Haz telling her about the bump. *'Honestly, Em, the bollard was possessed. One minute it wasn't there, the next it was leaping in front of the car.'* He'd been jumping on her bed at the time, skinny arms pinned to his side; his dark hair sticking out like a young Einstein as he'd mimicked a haunted bollard, and making her laugh until her sides had ached. *'Malik almost killed me,'* he'd added, falling serious at the mention of his brother. *'He told me he'd never lend me his car again.'*

She wishes her best friend was here right now. She knows it had to be this way, but still, she wishes.

Emma opens the passenger door and lifts Lola into the special seat she'd bought from a car boot sale last week. She fumbles with the straps as a voice screams in her head to go faster.

Nearly there.

Footsteps behind her. Loud and heavy. She flies around but it's just a teenage boy being pulled along by a shaggy golden retriever.

'Sweeties?' Lola says as Emma jumps into the driver's seat.

'Just a second. Let's get going first.'

The engine starts first time. They join a line of cars crawling towards the exit. She looks left and right, then behind her, always with her head dipped low. No one is looking at them. No one is running after them.

Lola whines; a little whimper as though perhaps she's just realised something is amiss. They make it to the exit and the traffic clears, and Emma pushes her foot to the accelerator and they're away. Free.

Finally, she can breathe again. Relief whooshes through her at the same speed as the car. She desperately wants to call Haz and tell him she's made it. She thinks of the unregistered phone buried in the bottom of her bag. It's just for emergencies. She promised she wouldn't use it unless she really had to.

When she's sure they're on the right road, heading east, she reaches one hand across to the passenger seat beside her, picks up the tatty old bear she'd stolen from the Range Rover and passes it to her daughter.

'Barnaby.' Lola snuggles the bear beside Ducky in her arms.

'And the sweeties too,' Emma says, passing back a small packet of Haribo. 'Make sure you share them with Ducky though.'

'I will,' her little girl replies with a solemn nod, content now with her bear and her sweets. 'I promise.'

Emma swallows down the fear suddenly burning in the back of her throat. A hundred different outcomes fly through her head. So many ways it could all go wrong. And only one way they'll ever get away – running. As far and as fast as she can.

She had to do this. Had to! Her daughter is in danger and Emma is the only one who sees it; who can save her.

And I promise, you're mine now. I'm your mother. I will save you.

THREE

ISOBEL

Lola isn't by the sinks or the hand dryers. She isn't by the big mirror at the entrance to the toilets, pretending to do her lipstick like she's seen Isobel do a hundred times or more. A flutter of worry moves through her. Isobel knocks and then bangs on the cubicle she last saw her daughter walk into. 'Lola? Lola, are you in there?'

The seconds move slowly. She catches her breath. She imagines Lola struggling to pull up her knickers or lost in a daydream, singing to herself. But then the door opens and it's not Lola.

'Do you mind?' A large woman in a green tracksuit stands in the doorway to the cubicle Lola disappeared into.

'Sorry, I...' she starts to say, but the woman pushes by and Isobel can't get the rest of the words out anyway.

It's happening!

The crippling fear that has locked her muscles, tremored through her body, kept her locked inside her house day after day after day, is suddenly a reality. Lola is gone, just like she's always feared.

Isobel spins away from the empty cubicle, calling out. 'Lola?'

The rational part of her mind – the critical-thinking, logic-solving part that had made her so good at her job in the wealth management company she'd worked for before Lola – tries to speak up, to tell her that her daughter will be standing with Roly outside the toilets, but she can't stop herself knocking into people, desperate to get by, to get out and see for herself.

The main building feels busier than before. The putrid smells of cheap food hit her again. She's going to be sick. There are people everywhere. No Roly. No Lola. No cheeky smile, no little hand with chipped pink nail varnish held out for her to take. Her heart judders too hard and too fast. She can't catch her breath.

Isobel remembers a time a year ago with a two-year-old Lola in a sticky-tabled soft play in Shepherd's Bush. It had been a birthday party for a boy in Lola's nursery class and Isobel hadn't wanted to go. Wouldn't have gone in fact, if the mum hadn't been a friend of a friend of someone Margaret knew, and of course her mother-in-law had got wind of the party.

'You really must go, Isobel. How do you expect Lola to make friends if you keep her locked in that house all day?'

'She's only two. I think—'

'It will do you both good. I'll speak to Roly.'

That had been the end of it.

All through the night before the party, Isobel had lain awake; her mind racing with every possibility. Lola falling from a piece of equipment and breaking her arm, or worse, her neck. Lola being bullied by a group of older children. Lola getting ill. And of course the fear that was never far from her thoughts – Lola being taken. A hand covering her mouth, arms scooping her up and carrying her out of the back door.

But they'd gone and it had been OK to start with. She'd followed Lola through the squishy assault course, held her hand down the bright-yellow slide. Then one of Lola's friends had asked her to play hide-and-seek, and Lola had pulled her hand out of Isobel's.

'*Too big, Mummy. You watch.*'

So she had done; standing back and watching from the café area, tracking her daughter around the equipment until her phone had rung. She was no longer working for the wealth management company, moving client's money to offshore accounts, keeping their income low and their unrealised assets high, avoiding huge tax bills, making the richest one per cent richer. But she'd kept one client. Not because they needed the money. Roly's trust fund and his own position at the same firm had always been plenty, but because the client was a friend of Roly's and only trusted Isobel.

And on that day in the soft play centre, he'd barked down the phone, wound up about a tax letter and a filing deadline she was already on top of. She'd stepped away from the echoing yells of the children and had taken a minute to calm him down. She might only have one client, but if he needed her, he expected her to drop everything. He wasn't the kind of man anyone said no to, and if she was honest, he scared her sometimes. Not often, but enough for her to always answer when he called.

By the time she'd calmed him down and turned back to the bright purple netting, Lola was gone.

There'd been a mad scramble over and under squishy pillars with the same frantic energy she feels now, until she'd found Lola half buried in the ball pit and playing with a new friend.

This will be that, the logical part of her brain tells her as she scans the crowds. A nothing moment that will steal her sleep and play on her mind until the early hours of the morning. A reminder to take more care. A reminder of why they're safer and happier inside their home.

And yet, the alternative is grabbing and scratching at her

chest. Isobel yanks her phone from her pocket and calls Roly. He doesn't answer. His phone is glued to his hand but of course he doesn't answer this time, when she really needs him.

She blinks back the tears, pushes down the panic and turns in a full circle, searching for a flash of yellow T-shirt. 'Lola?' she shouts again, her voice lost to the echoing noise of the building.

The nausea returns. The insides of her cheeks ache, and it's a fight not to double over.

She'll be here.

But she's not. She's not by the overstuffed yellow ducks or the pink magazines with their plastic tat. She's not sitting on the chairs in the middle or choosing her favourite doughnut. She's not stroking a dog she's met by the entrance or climbing in the playground. She's nowhere.

A sob shudders through her body.

'Isobel?' She spins around to find Roly. 'What's going—'

'Is Lola with you?'

'No.' He frowns, eyes moving to the playground then back to her. 'Where...'

'I can't find her.' Isobel flings herself at him, blurting out a hurried explanation of coming out of the toilet and Lola being nowhere. His strong arms are around her and then his hand in hers as they rush to all the places she's just been. It takes longer for the panic to catch Roly in its grasp. Only when they've raced across every inch of the car park and they're back at their car, voices hoarse from shouting Lola's name, does his complexion drain of colour.

Isobel's eyes fly to the cars queuing to exit. There are so many vehicles, so many people, so many directions to go in. A boulder-sized lump cuts into her airway but still she manages to sob as the realisation truly hits her. This is happening. Lola is gone.

It's her fault. If they'd have been at a fair or a show or in the middle of a city, she'd have held on to Lola's hand, never let go, but here, among the ordinary and the mundane, Isobel didn't see the dangers.

Oh God, what has she done?

'Call the police, Roly.' Her voice shakes. The words hammer home a sickening reality. Her baby girl is gone. This is no longer in her head. It's not crippling anxiety or panic attacks that left her physically sick. Oh God, all those times she'd climbed out of bed to double- then triple-check all the windows and doors are locked. Every time she's cried to her GP and begged for another prescription of anti-anxiety medication. Everything she's feared and now it's real.

'I'm doing it now,' he says, opening the passenger door. 'Sit down for a second, Iz, while I make the call.'

She sinks into the seat of the Range Rover, hot tears racing down her cheeks, barely listening as he keeps talking, trying to reassure her it will be OK when it won't. She wants to apologise as he puts the phone to his ear. He is Lola's father too. This is as bad for him as it is for her, but it doesn't feel like the same. Isobel's heart has been ripped from her body.

She listens to the urgency in Roly's voice, and even though she's glad of it, relieved now that it's not just her in this state of panic and fear, it shakes her too. Roly is infuriatingly calm. He's breezed through the events that have bookmarked her life. Their marriage; everything they did to have a child; then Lola; first words, first steps. But this has shaken him.

'Just hurry,' Roly says. 'Please.'

She turns to look out the back window to watch him pace, but her eyes snag on the car seat where Lola should be, asking to watch something on the iPad with the chunky pink case, which is never far from her hands.

The space is achingly bare. The thought jolts – a prod to her ribs. It isn't her daughter missing from the back seat; it's the fact that the pink backpack and Barnaby Bear are missing too.

In a flash, Isobel is scrambling across the leather armrest and into the back. The pink iPad is on the floor along with a scribbled-on colouring sheet of Princess Elsa. A sick kind of knowing is squeezing her insides, and yet still her eyes scan the back seats.

Barnaby is gone and so is Lola's bag with all her favourite toys in that she likes to take with her wherever she goes – to nursery, and to restaurants when Roly is with them, and to Huntington Hall to see her grandmother in the huge country estate.

'Just in case there's time to play, Mummy.'

'Roly?' she calls out.

No reply.

'Roly?' Louder this time.

The door by Lola's car seat opens and Roly crouches down to look at her, his brow furrowed with concern. 'Iz, what are you doing?'

'Did you lock the car?' Her breath is coming in short gasps, her chest heaving up and down with the effort. The edges of her vision blur.

'I... er... what are you doing in the back seat?'

'Barnaby is gone and so is Lola's bag.'

'She probably took them with her to the toilet.'

'She didn't. Roly, she didn't. We left them. Did you leave the car unlocked?' Another sob catches in her throat.

'No,' he says, but a realisation is pulling on his features. It's his frown-like grimace, the look he gets when he's messed up. Like the times he's forgotten dinner reservations they've made, anniversaries, her birthday once too, or just the times she's asked him to be home in time to kiss Lola goodnight.

'Roly?'

'I stepped away from the car to make the call. I think I left the windows open. It was a minute tops. Someone must have taken her things then. But why?'

The question hangs between them, neither willing to

answer. To put a voice to the realisation pounding through Isobel's body.

She sinks into the seat as a dark foreboding seeps through her. She knows, deep inside her bones, that Lola is gone. Her beautiful baby girl has been taken. But it was not a random, spur-of-the-moment decision. This was planned.

FOUR

EMMA

Emma pulls off the blonde wig and loosens the tie in her hair as the jiggety drum and tooting trumpet of Baloo's 'Bare Necessities' fills the car. There is nothing she can do about the eyeliner and make-up yet, but she can wash it off when they get to the caravan in a few hours.

She sings along, the words coming back to her in that way long-forgotten lyrics do. '... and your strife.' She smiles to Lola in the mirror. Her little girl is hugging Ducky and Barnaby to her chest and murmuring along with the song. There's the tiniest pinch of worry to her face that Emma tries not to see.

She imagines, like always, a grand courtroom in her mind. Sometimes she's the barrister firing off the questions, other times she's the judge. Today she is the accused, sitting in the witness box.

'Why did you take Lola Huntington from Winchester services?' She pictures the stern glare and hooked nose of her old law teacher, Mr Kelp, as the barrister.

'Because I'm her mother.'

'Liar.

'I am her mother. And this was the only way.'

'Liar.'

'I'm not lying. I'm her mother.'

A storm begins to swirl and rage inside her. Fear and worry and guilt and doubt. It's furious and unrelenting. She is Lola's mother, she tells herself again, speaking the words loud and clear in her mind. This was the only way.

'We're on our way now,' Emma calls out, tone impossibly light, reassuring herself as much as Lola. She glances to the mirror and the road behind her. There's a dark-blue BMW and a red Sedan. She makes a mental note. No sirens yet. No convoy of police cars, no helicopter. But that doesn't mean they're not chasing her.

The police will give Lola back to those people. She won't be safe with them. No one will listen to Emma. They won't help. They'll send her to prison or back to the hospital, and... no, she won't think about the rest.

Sometimes she wants so desperately to travel back in time to the girl who wore these jeans the first time around and tell her to run a million miles in the opposite direction. But then she wouldn't have Lola. Emma can imagine herself in her made-up courtroom in a life that never happened. She can imagine a thousand ways what she's doing could go wrong. But she can never imagine life without Lola.

'... simple bare necessities,' she sings.

Emma checks the clock on the dashboard. They've been driving for six minutes on the main road. They'll know Lola is gone by now. The police will be on their way to the services. The CCTV will be checked; they'll see her and Lola – two figures racing to a blue Peugeot. They'll have the licence plate. The car is registered to Haz's brother, Malik. Eventually they'll connect him to Haz and then to her, but like the wig and the make-up, it'll buy her time, and that's all they need.

As if her fears have projected onto the road ahead, Emma catches sight of the almost invisible grey box to the side of the road. ANPR – Automatic Number Plate Recognition. It's not just knowing who a car belongs to; it's knowing where that car is. All the police have to do is type in the number plate and any time this car is captured on one of the thousands of cameras positioned on main roads and in towns and cities across the country, an alert will signal on a computer somewhere; a call made. The police will be on her in seconds.

She has to get off this road and dump the car like she'd planned.

The BMW pulls into the outside lane and overtakes them. Emma remembers to breathe, counting the inhale all the way to five and blowing the air through her lips. 'Four, five, six,' she whispers to herself.

It was Haz's idea to learn the breathing exercise. *'You've got to chill sometimes, Em,'* he'd said from across the table of the cafeteria, glancing behind him to check they weren't listening in, *'or you'll never get out of here.'*

She wishes Haz was sat beside her now. Already she knows she'll break her promise and use the 'just for emergencies' phone to call him later. They might only have known each other for a few years, but meeting in the worst possible circumstances, in the most hellish place on earth, forged an unbreakable friendship between them.

From day one it felt like Haz was the only person who could help her to see things clearly. She remembers the first time she saw him. He'd plonked his lunch tray down beside hers on her first week in the hospital she'd been locked in and had declared in a voice dancing with mischief, *'Any day now.'*

'What?' she'd replied, startled by the presence of the tall skinny boy about her age with limbs like sticks and dark curly hair he'd tell her later that his older brother was nagging him to cut shorter.

'Any day now, they're going to slap two Michelin stars on this restaurant food and everyone will want to come here. We'll

be queueing for hours for it.' He'd waved his hand over the rubbery-looking chicken and splats of overcooked vegetables.

She'd laughed and they'd joked for a few days about nothing in particular, seeking each other out whenever they were free until it seemed like they'd always had each other, and Emma couldn't imagine a world without his friendship. When Haz had asked why she was there, she'd told him, and he hadn't laughed or called her crazy. He'd squeezed her hand and told her he'd help keep her safe.

Thinking of Haz, taking the deep breaths, it helps. Panic is still whipping through her but her chest no longer feels like it will split open from the fury of her heartbeat.

This is the plan. She has to trust in it.

A turning appears ahead. It's sharp and curves onto a small B road that streaks across the countryside.

'Mother nature's...' she sings as she indicates, eyes on the mirror again. The red sedan is right behind her now, following her onto the quiet road. Up close she sees it's an old-style Volvo.

She picks up speed. Eyes on the road. Eyes on the mirror. Checking on her daughter. Checking the cars. The red sedan is still there. Is it following them? Is it— No, she cuts the thought down again, won't think about that. She won't go back to that place. Never, never. The memories crowd her thoughts. The screams. Locked doors. Numbing medication.

No.

Never again.

She takes a sudden left onto another winding lane and picks up speed. The red sedan carries on straight, but she watches the mirror anyway. It could be a bluff.

The trumpets fade and in the quiet before the next song loads, Lola speaks. A barely there whisper. 'I want my mummy.'

'It's OK, Lola,' Emma says. 'We're almost there.'

A new drumbeat begins. It's a song from *Frozen*. Emma hadn't heard it until last week when she'd made the playlist on an old, unregistered iPod, learning every word for this moment in this car with her little girl so she could sing along and make Lola like her, help her feel safe. That's her job now – keep her daughter safe. It's the job she should have been doing for the entirety of Lola's life. The thought scalds her insides.

Another turning appears ahead. Another lane. She stops the car, engine idling. They are completely alone on the road now. There is no one following them, no cameras here to track them. Emma takes a moment to gather herself and find her bearings.

'I want to go home,' Lola whimpers above the music.

'Have you ever been on a bus before, Lola?'

The little girl shakes her head. 'No.'

'Buses are very exciting. We'll do a little bit more driving and then we'll go on one. It will be the start of our adventure.'

'I want Mummy to come too.'

'It's all going to be OK.' Emma grits her teeth, pushing back a rush of frustration that comes from nowhere, and starts to drive again. She needs Lola to understand what's happening and stop asking about her mummy. 'I'm your mummy,' she mouths, forcing herself not to say the words out loud. 'Don't you know that?'

Another new song begins. Emma tries to sing, to be bright and merry, but she can't find the words above the memories in her head.

Already she can hear the screams. She'll die before she goes back there.

FIVE

EMMA

An hour of winding roads later, Emma pulls over. They're on an unmade lane with crumbling concrete and deep potholes; a little hideaway leading nowhere that she'd found two weeks ago when she'd poured over maps and spent hours driving around the countryside, memorising as much as she could.

'They're smart, Em, but you're smarter.'

Oh, Haz. She needs her friend so desperately. She needs him to tell her over and over that she is brave and she is someone, until she starts to believe it.

The lay-by is almost hidden by an overgrown willow tree with vine-like branches hanging low and brushing the dusty road. Last week on her way to Cornwall, she'd sat here for nearly half a day, watching the still farmland, making sure it really was the perfect place to leave the car, back when this had felt like a hypothetical what-if, a dream-like plan.

She cuts the engine, and in the quiet that follows, she finds her best happy voice. 'Let's go find our bus, shall we? It's just across that field.' Emma points to a metal kissing gate.

'Mummy?'

That again. She grits her teeth, bites back the words she wants to scream. *I'm your mummy!* 'It's OK, Lola. I promise.'

Things are far from OK, and she hates lying to Lola, but the red Sedan following them off the main road and the pulsing adrenaline of the services, it's made her feel brittle. She'll be better when they're on the bus, when they're further away from the services and the police and the monsters who thought they could call themselves Lola's parents.

She checks her watch. It's an old style with a white face and silver strap she'd found in the back of a drawer. Like the jeans, it's a relic from another time when the world had made sense and she'd trusted that people were good. When she'd believed the police and the law would protect her from those who weren't. That's why she'd loved studying law. There were grey areas in some parts of it, but not criminal law. She'd thought it was black and white. If you did bad things, you'd be punished.

Christ, was she really that naïve? She'd once thought she'd be a great barrister – the best. That dream seems so stupid now.

The watch isn't fancy, but it is untraceable. No GPS, no Wi-Fi, no app pinging a location. Just the ticking hands.

They have eight minutes until the bus arrives. *Be on time*, she wills it, pushing the thought out into the universe. *Be on time*.

The need to keep moving is eating at her again, biting and chewing – a monster inside her. Another thing people never understand, especially not the doctors.

'There's no such thing as monsters, Emma. No monsters inside you either.'

It had always amazed her that people so smart, so qualified, could be so stupid.

Emma grabs the wig discarded on the passenger seat as she climbs out of the car. Then she opens the boot, scooping her backpack onto her shoulder. Only one bag for both of them – a change of clothes each and a few toiletries, a bottle of water and a bank card just for emergencies she knows she won't use. An unregistered phone. Nothing that can track them. Just her and Lola. She has a plan for them. She just has to stick to it. Lola is hers now. And no matter what, she'll never let Lola go back to those people. Whatever it takes.

She stuffs the wig into a side pocket and picks up the hats – a black Adidas baseball cap for her and a yellow *Peppa Pig* bucket-style one for Lola. She'd watched her point to it at a beachfront shop in St Ives two days ago. The kind of place that sold buckets and spades and inflatable rings. The people who pretend to be Lola's parents hadn't bothered to look up from their phones, but Emma had been watching.

'Look what I got you,' she says, opening the passenger door and holding out the hat to her daughter.

Little fingers reach for the fabric rim. Lola gives a small smile that eases something in Emma. She places the hat gently on Lola's head, covering the fine white-blonde hair. But as Lola shuffles out of the car seat, Ducky under one arm, Barnaby the other, Emma realises her first mistake.

The hats are supposed to disguise them, but they're useless. People will not remember a woman and a little girl, or the colour of their hair, their age or any other features, but they'll remember a large and very yellow duck.

Damn it!

It was an impulse purchase – a split-second decision as she'd followed Isobel and Lola through the services. A way to coax Lola to come with her because all her planning and dreaming meant nothing if her daughter didn't trust her in that one moment.

'Let's pop Ducky in your bag and Barnaby in my bag, just until we get off the bus. They'll be easier to carry that way.'

Lola's grip tightens on her teddies, her expression hardening. A mini standoff.

Emma can feel the muscles of her jaw tightening; the

urgency pulsing in her veins. Five minutes until the bus is due to arrive and they haven't even made it across the field yet. 'Please, Lola? I've got more sweeties,' she sing-songs, unable to stop the desperation from leaking into her tone this time.

Lola hesitates, and in the pause that follows, Emma shoos her along. 'Here we go.' She crouches down and opens her back-pack. It's already full, but she takes out a jumper for Lola to wear.

She thinks of the police alert that might already be out there. A little girl in a yellow T-shirt, a woman with blonde hair. Not a brown-haired woman with a baseball cap. Not her daughter in a light-green jumper.

'Why don't you pop this on?' she says. 'It's a little chilly, isn't it?' Then she takes Ducky and squishes him inside the backpack. It barely shuts, but it will do for now. Barnaby slips into Lola's bag next, and then they're away again, half running as Emma wills the bus to be late now.

Just before the end of the field, when the bus stop is in sight, she turns, lobbing the car keys into a hedgerow of nettles and brambles. She says a silent apology to Haz's brother, Malik. She's not sure how or when or if the car will ever be returned to him. But in twenty-four hours she'll be in another country and no one, not even the police, will be able to find them. That's all that matters.

'Think about it, Em. We just have to get out of England and then it's safe.'

You'd better be right, she thinks as they reach the road just in time to see the bus trundling slowly towards them.

SIX

ISOBEL

'Iz.' Roly's voice pulls Isobel back to a reality she does not want to be in. She blinks and sees the familiar outline of their house, looking over the green expanse of Ham Common in Richmond. It's a grand London town house. The kind of building that looks like it belongs in a *Bridgerton* series. All pale-grey stone walls and huge windows on each of the three floors.

She loves this place. Sometimes it feels like she isn't herself, isn't really breathing, until she's stepped into the airy entrance hall and shut the huge wooden door. But the longing she'd felt in the services to be home has disappeared. She doesn't want to be here. They can't be here. Not without Lola. Fresh tears prick at her eyes. Leaving the car park in Winchester had been a wrench. She'd wanted to stay, but then the police had arrived and the detective had convinced them they were better off at home. The detective's name was DI Frank Gardner. He had a deep Mancunian accent and no clue who'd taken Lola or where she was.

'*Better to be at home and wait for news there,*' Roly had said, coaxing her into the car. They'd driven home in silence, and she'd lost herself to a smothering darkness that cloaked her thoughts until she thought they might choke her. Will she ever see her daughter again?

'I don't think I can go in,' she says, her gaze fixing on the darkening sky. It's gone seven. Lola should be having her bath and choosing her bedtime story. How can she... how do they exist in a world where those things aren't happening?

'You can, darling. You'll feel better when we've had some-thing to eat and a cup of tea. We have to be strong and stay positive.'

The thought of eating turns her stomach. She's not touched a thing since breakfast. Her mind races back to earlier that morning in the Cornwall house when she'd made maple syrup pancakes and crispy bacon – Roly and Lola's favourite. Roly had cut his pancake into a smiley face and held it up like a mask, sending Lola into fits of giggles.

'Stop encouraging her to play with her food,' she'd berated, laughing too. She'd almost told him her secret then. Lola had climbed down from the table to pack her toys, and Roly had pulled Isobel onto his lap and kissed her, and she'd felt the sweetness of the moment take over and the words rise to her lips. But it was too soon and so she'd swallowed it back, telling herself that there'd be another perfect moment. She isn't sure she'll ever find the words now.

The normality of that memory is enough to cause the tears to blur her vision.

'I'll get the cases in later,' Roly says, opening the car door. 'I need to call my clients and the office and tell them I won't be available.'

'How can you think about work right now?' A sob catches in her throat and she regrets the question the moment it's out. Roly looks stung, eyes wide with hurt.

'I just need to tell people I won't be around, Iz. That's all. So my phone isn't ringing constantly,' he says.

She nods. 'I'm sorry.' She knows how much Roly's job means to him, even if she sometimes thinks it's a ridiculous nothing job. As Client Relationship Director for the same wealth management company Isobel used to work for too, Roly's role is to keep the clients happy. Whatever it takes. Sometimes that means lavish dinners at London's most exclusive restaurants. Sometimes it's golf. Sometimes it's phone calls in the middle of the night.

He reassures, he pampers, he encourages more investments. He comes and goes from the office as he pleases and is accountable only to the other members of the board.

It took Isobel a few months of dating Roly to understand why he bothers to work when he doesn't need to. His trust fund is big enough that he could do as he pleases, like his sister Felicity does. But Roly is driven with a need to please and a need to be adored. Which means pleasing his mother by working in the same company his father had worked in before he'd died. And what better job than one all about pleasing the clients and making sure they adore him?

Roly slips his hand into hers, and it's warm and filled with the strength she needs, and she gives in and climbs out of the car. Before they're even halfway up the four steps that lead to the house, the front door is flung open and Margaret is standing there in her usual white linen trousers and cashmere cardigan. Isobel's body freezes. The same dread she felt in the car park returns, and she longs to rewind the last thirty seconds and refuse to get out of the car.

'Oh, Roly, darling. How are you?' Margaret calls out, flapping her hands and beckoning her son into a hug. 'I can't believe this is happening. Our poor Lola.'

'We're OK,' he says, even though it isn't true. He releases his hold on Isobel and steps forward, leaving her alone and unsteady as he gives his mother a quick embrace.

Isobel shouldn't be surprised that Margaret is standing in

her doorway, but the sight is so unwelcome she can't stop the question from spilling out. 'What are you...' she starts to say. 'Why...' She can't find a polite way to ask what the hell Margaret is doing here.

'Are you forgetting this is my house?' The older woman gives a tittering laugh that does nothing to mask the sharp edge that always seems to carry in her words towards Isobel. It's the tone that tells Isobel day after day that Margaret believes she's not good enough for her son. Not good enough to be a Huntington.

How could she forget? Isobel wants to retort. Margaret never lets her. The house was supposed to be a wedding gift. *'I want you to have it, my darlings. I hardly use it anyway, and it's far too big for me.'*

A few months into her marriage, Isobel had realised that 'have' had meant 'live in'. The house was still in Margaret's name and she would come and go as she pleased, making sure that Isobel felt like a guest in her own home as often as she could.

It's always been a sticking point between her and Roly. The one thing they've bickered about aside from the long hours he spends with clients doing God knows what. She'd tried to convince him that they should buy their own place, but Roly seemed oblivious. *'Why?'* he'd always say. *'This house is going to be mine one day anyway, and Mother will visit us no matter where we are.'*

She swallows down the bitterness rising inside her. She doesn't have the energy or the mental space to deal with this right now. She'll have to talk to Roly later. Margaret can't be here. 'Of course,' she says. 'Sorry. I meant, how did you get here so fast?'

Margaret raises a thin eyebrow. Her skin is taut in places and saggy in others. The facelift she'd had some years back isn't aging well. She doesn't look her seventy-one years, but she doesn't look fifty either. She looks like someone who's had too much plastic surgery. 'I jumped in the car as soon as Roly called me. Now come in. Tell me everything that happened.'

Isobel glances to Roly. *You called her*, she wants to say. *Why?* But then she knows why, doesn't she? Roly tells his mother everything. Almost everything, she corrects.

Her mother-in-law steps back, and even though Isobel hates that she's here, there is still the sense of relief at seeing the Victorian-style Pamplona black-and-white floor tiles and the gleaming white walls. The sound of the front door shutting. She is home.

'Put my bag in the guest wing on the top floor, please, Roly,' Margaret says, waving to a suitcase far larger than is needed for an overnight visit.

How long is she planning to stay? Isobel wonders as knots form in her stomach.

Margaret pats Roly's arm. 'I'll make us all some tea.'

He nods, doing as he's told, reverting to the obedient schoolboy. 'Thank you, Mother.'

'Where's Zeen?' Isobel asks, looking towards the open door that leads to the kitchen and wondering why Margaret isn't telling her housekeeper to do these things.

Isobel thinks of the Filipino woman Margaret sent them in the early days of Lola's arrival. Isobel had been resistant at first. She hadn't wanted another person in their home after everything that had happened, but Zeen is quiet and unimposing and has slotted into their lives as though she's always been part of it. Plus she's a fantastic cook, and always seems to know exactly what Isobel needs from her each day. Sometimes it's just someone to talk to. Other times it's to lend a hand with Lola when Isobel is finishing the monthly accounts for her client or answering one of his urgent calls.

'How on earth am I supposed to know where your maid is?'

Margaret replies. 'The house was empty when I got here. Those police officers beat you to it as well.'

'The police are here?' Isobel asks, pushing thoughts of Zeen to the back of her mind. She'll think about where her house-keeper is later. 'You should've said.' She takes a step towards the kitchen. 'Have they got news?'

'They were here but as soon as it became clear they had nothing to tell us regarding Lola's whereabouts, I sent them away. I told them to come back in the morning or when they have something to tell us. I couldn't have them cluttering up the house,' she adds as though she's referring to tacky ornaments instead of the police officers tasked with finding her grand-daughter.

'But—' Isobel starts to say.

'That's a good idea, Mother,' Roly jumps in, perhaps sensing the start of a disagreement between her and Margaret. 'Better they're out there doing their jobs than trying to reassure us. Isn't that right, Iz?'

She gives a slow nod, hiding the scream that's threatening to break out. She can't do this. Her daughter has been abducted. There should be people everywhere, urgent and fraught. Phones ringing, orders being given. And if anyone should decide whether the police are here or not, it's her and Roly. Not Margaret.

Unease begins to trickle through Isobel. It's not the clanging alarm of panic for her missing daughter, but it's there none-theless. It's the same feeling she often has whenever Margaret is with her. The sense that Isobel is being pushed aside; ignored. Except this isn't plans for Christmas or what Lola is going to wear to Margaret's summer tea party she holds every year in the grounds of the Huntington estate. This is her daughter's abduction.

Isobel thinks again how quickly Margaret got here. It's nearly a two-hour drive from Huntington Hall in Buckinghamshire. Plus packing that huge suitcase. It's doable, but only just. She wishes Zeen was here so she could ask her what time Margaret arrived but then wonders why it matters. It's not as though her mother-in-law had anything to do with Lola's abduction... What reason would she have to take Lola?

'Now, let me put the kettle on while you take my bag upstairs.' Margaret disappears into the kitchen in a whirl of cashmere and expensive perfume, and Isobel finds herself frozen. Unable to follow. Unable to retreat.

'Iz?' Roly's voice is filled with concern. She looks up at him, taking in the deep lines of worry on his brow and the pleading in his eyes, begging her in his silent way to accept his mother.

'Why did you call her?' Isobel asks in a hissed whisper.

'I don't know.' He shakes his head. 'I was freaking out and wasn't thinking.'

'She can't be here, Roly.'

He closes his eyes for a moment, and she knows he's struggling just as much as she is, but they have to talk about this.

'I know,' he says after a pause. 'But it's OK for tonight, isn't it? I'll talk to her in the morning, I promise.'

'OK, but you have to do it. She doesn't know about—'

'I realise that,' he cuts in before she can put a voice to the time before Lola they don't speak of. She wonders sometimes if what they did has been erased from Roly's mind somehow, or if he ever lies awake with a gnawing guilt like she does? Does he ever have that voice in his head jump out at him, reminding him in his happiest moments that they don't deserve any of it.

'Don't worry,' Roly says. 'I will talk to her. Do you want something to eat?' he asks, signalling he's done with their conversation.

She shakes her head. 'I'm not hungry. I think I might have a shower.'

He reaches out and touches her arm. 'It will be OK, Iz.

We'll find her.' Then he turns, disappearing up the stairs with Margaret's suitcase.

She follows slowly. Their bedroom is on the middle floor. A spacious white room at the front of the house, overlooking the common. The wardrobes are built-in and take up an entire wall. The furniture is white oak, and there's a king-size bed dominating the room.

Isobel strips off her clothes and steps into the white en suite with its large walk-in shower. She doesn't know how long she spends under the spray, only that her fingers are prune-like by the time the water runs too cool to carry on. She pulls on her robe and finds Roly in the doorway of their bedroom. He looks as lost as she feels.

They step towards each other without speaking, and he wraps her in his arms.

'I'm sorry,' she whispers through the emotion blocking her throat. He'll have told his mother everything by now. The full turn of events. No doubt she'll have commented on Isobel's part in losing their daughter.

'No,' Roly says, voice fierce as he cups her face in his hands. 'Don't do that, Iz. It's not your fault.'

It is, she wants to tell him but can't find the words.

His eyes search hers and then suddenly they're kissing. They fall in a tangle onto the bed, and her robe is open and his lips are roaming her body. He barely shrugs off his clothes before he's entering her so fast it takes her breath away. His movements are hard and furious; all-consuming and everything she needs.

Afterwards, Roly sleeps and she lies awake, feeling guilty for that moment of wanting sex with her husband when their daughter is missing; guilty that it's her fault Lola is not tucked in her bed right now.

The hurt threatens to engulf her. Lola is her daughter. Her

world. Her everything. She will not survive in a world that Lola is not part of.

The same voice from earlier whispers in her mind. The one that ambushes her all hours of the day and night, reminding her that beneath the surface, her perfect family is rotten at the core because of what she did all those years ago. *You deserve this.*

SEVEN

EMMA

It's gone seven by the time Emma encourages Lola to press the
bell to stop the bus and they've walked the half mile to a
caravan on the outskirts of Worthing on the south coast. The
park is quiet as they weave through rows of identical caravans.
Emma can hear television shows and the muffled voices of
people talking, but she's glad for the cloud cover and cool air
keeping the holidaymakers inside.

She finds number 281. It's smaller than the other caravans
they've passed and tucked away at the back of the complex.
Emma finds the lockbox on the side and puts in the code she's
memorised. The caravan was pre-booked with cash two weeks
ago. No inquisitive check-in clerk seeking answers that will later
be relayed to the police. Just Emma and Lola slipping inside the
small three-roomed container.

It is far from ideal. The rooms smell of apple air freshener
and damp dog, and it's only seventy miles from the services.
Not far enough. The thought threatens her with a wave of panic
and a need to run and run and never look back. The decision to
stay here feels like a gamble – a balancing act on a wire-thin
tightrope. She has to get as far away as she can from the services

and the police search, but she had to ditch the car too. The second the licence plate is in ANPR, Malik's car might as well have a tracking beacon on it. Besides, Lola needs time to rest and adapt to her new life.

Emma takes a breath, imagining Haz's calming hand on her arm. Tomorrow, they'll be gone forever – out of the country and safe. The thought should make her feel better, but she can't stop herself from wondering, then what? She hasn't allowed herself to spend too much time thinking about what her life will be like – hers and Lola's; mother and daughter.

Little snippets of normality run through her head sometimes. Holding Lola's hand on a walk. Getting ice creams. Playing I Spy. It isn't a plan, but it's been something to hold on to for all these years of emptiness.

'I just wanted to see her.' Emma remembers the screech of her voice. The desperation. *'She's my daughter.'*

'You can't.' Roly's tone had been firm. *'She's not yours, Emma. When are you going to realise that?'*

She'd tried to make them all see how special Lola was to her, but no one listened, and then she was forced into that hospital. She'll never let them take Lola from her again. She'll never be apart from her daughter again. Never, never. Only Haz's friendship saved her from dying in that hospital.

They spent hours talking, daydreaming about their futures.

'We'll go to America. New York or LA. You'll be a kickass lawyer, and I'll be a waiter or something until a Hollywood producer recognises my talents and I become a star.'

'Sounds great, except for the kickass lawyer part.'

'You are kickass,' he'd cried. *'Or at least you will be. That man has made you think you're worthless and it's not true, Em. You have a top law degree and you are the smartest person I know. You just have to visualise your dreams and go out and get them.'*

'*Sorry, but if I'm the smartest person you know then you need more friends. I've been so stupid.*'

'*You've been human. Stop beating yourself up and decide how to get your life back.*'

Haz had been right. And she does have a plan now – a series of steps to follow to a new life. She'll think about it tomorrow once they're further away from here. Only then will she believe it's really happening.

Lola gives a whimper, pulling Emma's thoughts back to the caravan. 'I want my mummy,' she says, sitting on the faded floral sofa and pulling Barnaby from her bag, hugging him in her arms as wide eyes take in her surroundings.

'How about some toast?' Emma asks.

'With jam?' Lola's voice is quiet. 'Strawberry jam is my favourite.'

'Of course. But no butter. Right?'

A small nod. 'Butter and jam is yucky.'

Emma laughs and even though the fear is circling her like a pack of wolves on the hunt, she feels herself glow. '*Look,*' she wants to shout, '*I am taking care of Lola. Only I can save my daughter.*'

'Have you stayed in a caravan before, Lola?' Emma asks as she opens the welcome pack of bread and jam and cereals ordered at the same time as the caravan.

Lola shakes her head.

'It's like a mini house. It's fun, you'll see.' She thinks of the dozens of holidays she had as a child in a caravan park on the Essex coast. The sense of freedom she'd felt as she'd run off with her older brothers to make friends and have adventures, while her parents stayed inside, watching TV like always.

Quiet holidays that matched their quiet existence in the small semi-detached in Tooting Bec at the bottom of the Northern Line. Her father a mechanic. Her mother a sales assistant in a clothing store. Emma had felt their lack of ambition from a young age. Not just for themselves but for their children too. It had never seemed to bother her two older brothers. Eddie went to work with their dad, and Anthony joined a window cleaning company.

Only Emma had wanted more. She'd been the odd one out – dreaming of university and a big dazzling career as a barrister – wearing that wig and gown and getting justice for her clients in the hallowed halls of the Old Bailey criminal court. Her family couldn't understand her dreams. They'd never been outright mean to her, never cruel or callous or uncaring, they'd just... never understood her. It was always them and her. When she was little – eight or nine – she used to think that if her family woke up one day and she wasn't there, they wouldn't notice. It turns out she'd been right because years later that exact thing happened.

It shouldn't surprise Emma that Lola has never stayed in a caravan before, but the realisation comes with a pang of guilt she doesn't expect. She's taken her little girl away from a life of wealth and privilege Emma has no idea if she'll ever be able to make up for.

'Don't be an idiot.' Haz's voice echoes in her mind, and she almost smiles.

He's right. Being with Lola is all that matters. Only Emma knows the danger her daughter is in, and only she can keep her safe.

A sudden exhaustion threatens to overwhelm her, as much from the constant racing of her mind as the events of the day. She turns on the TV and finds a channel of cartoons; bright colours and shrieking American voices. It's a far cry from the gentle tones of CBeebies, but it's enough to keep them both distracted while she finishes making the toast.

The tears come after three bites. Fat droplets that roll down Lola's cheeks. 'I... want... Mummy,' she says with a wail so loud that Emma has to fight not to put her hand over Lola's mouth.

The caravan walls are thin. Anyone passing will hear. Would they call the police?

'Shhh, Lola, please don't cry,' Emma begs, wrapping her arms around her.

'I want to go home,' she sobs. 'I want my mummy. I want my daddy.'

'*I'm your mummy,*' Emma says in her head as she hugs her little girl. 'I know you do, but remember I said that we're going on an adventure?'

Lola doesn't reply, but there's a pause in the cries; a hiccup.

'Well, that's because Mummy and Daddy can't look after you right now,' she says, hating the lie but knowing the truth – those words she desperately wants to speak – will only confuse and upset Lola more. 'There's a... a bad man after us. He's a monster, and he's trying to hurt you. I have to protect you, and I'm the only one that can do it.'

'A monster?' Lola's face scrunches up, another wave of emotion flooding to the surface in a loud cry.

'Please don't cry,' she soothes, wishing she'd said something else. The glow she felt only minutes ago at caring for Lola slips from her grasp. What is she going to do? 'It's OK. I can protect you. I promise. You're safe with me. Lola and Emma safe together.'

Lola doesn't reply, but she pushes her face into the top of Barnaby's head, and Emma feels her body relax and the crying subside. She forces herself to stay still until Lola's breaths deepen and she's sure her little girl is asleep. Only then does she scoop her into her arms and carry her carefully to the small bedroom before tucking her under the covers.

When she's alone in the main part of the caravan again, Emma feels a wildness swoop through her – an unstoppable panic. Everything has gone to plan so far and yet it doesn't feel like she thought it would feel. There is love of course. So much love for her daughter. But no relief, no sense that she's doing the right thing. Because she is. She meant what she said to Lola. Emma is the only one who can protect them.

The doctors, the police, her family – they don't get it. They don't see the danger.

There's a noise. The low rumble of an engine; a vehicle stopping outside. Emma drops to the floor out of sight and crawls to the window. Slowly, she moves herself into position and peeks out.

The sight causes a bolt of terror to shoot through her. She gasps, throwing herself back to the floor so fast the carpet tiles scratch at the skin on her face and arms. Outside, driving slowly past the caravan is a red sedan. The same car that she saw on the road behind her earlier.

She thought she'd been so careful, but they're here. They've found them.

DAY TWO: 7 A.M. MONDAY 31ST JULY

EIGHT

ISOBEL

Isobel is sure she doesn't fall asleep, and yet she jolts back to herself to find the window behind the curtains is bright and Roly's side of the bed is empty.

Her first thought is Lola. Her daughter's name is a scream in her head, and she's out of bed and throwing on a pair of leggings and a T-shirt in seconds.

Is there news?

Have they found her?

A part of her knows that Roly would've woken her, but she can't stop the fear and hope wrestling inside her as she hurries down the stairs, following the sound of voices to the kitchen on the ground floor.

Whatever Roly and Margaret are discussing, they stop when she appears in the doorway. Does she imagine the flash of guilt on Roly's face as he turns to look at her? She thought it was them keeping secrets from Margaret, and her little secret she's keeping to herself too. But for the first time, she wonders if the Huntingtons are keeping things from *her*.

She thinks again of Roly calling his mother at the services. What was he thinking? And Margaret getting here so fast, and where the hell is Zeen? Her housekeeper should be here this morning. And does any of this matter? All she cares about is getting Lola back. She swallows down the questions and the feeling of being pushed out and discarded by these people. Roly is her husband. He's not like his mother. He loves her.

Her eyes move to the three long chandelier lights that hang over the island. Bare bulbs visible through glass domes that remind Isobel of upside-down goldfish bowls.

'Can we get fishes, Mummy? Like the ones we saw on holiday. Pink ones.'

Longing claws at Isobel's chest and she looks away, focusing on the narrow garden and the grey morning. The kitchen, like the rest of the house, is very Margaret. The units are white. Cupboards and floor tiles and walls too. The counters are black granite with a gloss finish, showing every smear and smudge when the sun hits in the afternoon. Completely impractical. Poor Zeen is forever rubbing at them with a microfibre cloth.

'You look quite dreadful, Isobel.' Margaret voice drips with sympathy, but her expression is unreadable as she takes a sip from her coffee cup. She's wearing another floaty silk ensemble in a pale cream today. She looks immaculate from head to toe. Isobel looks to the large station clock on the wall. It's barely seven in the morning.

'I was just about to wake you,' Roly jumps in before Isobel can find the strength to reply to her mother-in-law. 'The police are on their way. I just got a call.'

'Have they found her?' she asks, holding her breath as she waits for his reply.

'I don't know. It sounds like they want to ask us some more questions.'

She feels the weight of fear and hope pulling her down. All she wants to do is crumble to the floor and cry for her daughter.

'Perhaps you should change?' Margaret nods to Isobel's creased T-shirt.

She grits her teeth, desperately wanting to snap a reply, to scream at this spiteful woman that her daughter has been stolen from them. What does it matter what she looks like?

But she has known Margaret for long enough to see that this is exactly the response she wants. No doubt if Isobel were to say those words, Margaret would find a way to remind her and Roly that Lola's abduction happened while Isobel should've been watching her. It's another example – another piece of ammunition – her mother-in-law will use to show Roly how unfit she is as a mother. It's a slow but unrelenting campaign that started the day Margaret set eyes on Lola.

'Why does Isobel never take Lola out?'

'Why is Isobel so anxious? Roly, you must get her help.'

'Why is Isobel keeping Lola from socialising? What does the poor girl do all day stuck in the house? It really won't do.'

At Christmas, Margaret had mentioned the boarding school one village along from the Huntington estate. The same one Roly started at when he was five, only coming home every other weekend, and then each half term after he turned eight.

'You remember how happy you were there, Roly? Don't you want Lola to experience that same happiness?'

'We don't want her to be away from her family,' Isobel had been quick to jump in before Roly had a chance to agree. *'And Lola is already enrolled to start in the reception class at Holmwood Hall in September. It's where her friends are going, and we can walk there.'*

'But I'm so close here. She can visit any time she wants. Just something to think about next year.'

Isobel can't give Margaret any more reason to whisper in Roly's ear. If she survives this, if she gets Lola back, she will never let her out of her sight again. Even before this nightmare began, she's barely been able to think of Lola starting school full-time in a few short months. She's not even turning four until the second week of August. So instead she nods. 'You're right; I will.'

As she turns to leave, her eyes meet Roly's. A split-second look passes between them, where she's asking silently if he's told his mother to leave. A frown pinches his brow and there's a slight shake to his head that makes her want to scream all over again. Surely he sees why Margaret can't be here? The woman likes to believe she knows everything that happens in her children's lives, but there are some things she can never find out about them and Lola.

Isobel turns away and hurries up the stairs. She changes quickly, wriggling into a pair of jeans that feel too tight around her waist. She adds a loose blouse in light pink and the new pearl earrings she got a few weeks ago. By the time she's stepping out of the bedroom, her hair in a bun at the nape of her neck and concealer under her eyes, Roly is showing two men into the living room on the middle floor.

Introductions are made, hands shaken. Detective Chief Inspector Owen Watkins is a stocky man with broad shoulders and dark eyes. A clean shave, grey hair cut short and a sharp suit adds to the formidable presence Isobel feels as he shakes her hand. Beside him stands DI Frank Gardner, the detective with the Manchester accent that met them at Winchester services yesterday. He's thinner and younger than his boss, but more weathered somehow. He's wearing a shirt but no tie, and the same leather biker jacket he was wearing yesterday.

'This is my mother, Mrs Margaret Huntington,' Roly says. 'She's worried about her granddaughter and has come to support us.'

Isobel grits her teeth and forces her expression to remain impassive. She knows how important his mother is to him. Roly's father died when he was eight. A fun man who never took life too seriously, according to Roly and the few memories he has of his father. From that point on, Margaret assumed the role of matriarch, ensuring Roly and his younger sister, Felicity, were living up to the Huntington name. Roly loves his mother and will do as she asks without question. But surely now, with Lola stolen from them, their world crumbling around them, Roly will find a limit to how much involvement in their lives he can take from her. He knows as well as she does that Margaret can never learn the truth.

'We met briefly yesterday evening,' DCI Watkins replies with a slight nod to Margaret. 'Please call me Owen.'

Isobel watches the detectives take in the space. The white walls and the large windows overlooking the common. DCI Watkins motions to the tan leather Chesterfield, and she and Roly sit down, while Margaret continues to stand. There is a nervous edge to all of them, but Margaret especially is pacing back and forth as though unable to sit still.

The sofa is uncomfortable. Too big, too hard. She prefers the fabric sofa in Lola's playroom on the ground floor. The only room in the house aside from Lola's bedroom that Margaret allowed them to decorate. Isobel prefers the bright colours and clutter too. The thought causes pain to stretch across her chest.

Lola is gone. It doesn't feel real. She'd do anything, give anything, to have Lola home safe, to be playing tea shops or schools or any of the hundred imaginary games her daughter so loves to play.

'What can you tell us?' Margaret's clipped voice is first to speak. 'Have you found my granddaughter?'

Isobel holds her breath and prays to a god she didn't believe in yesterday that the answer forming on DCI Watkin's lips is not of high-speed chases or dumped bodies or a hundred other dark unthinkable things that raced through her mind last night. She reaches out to fiddle with the pearl of one of her earrings as her heart beats too fast before forcing herself to sit still, hugging her arms to her body so Margaret doesn't tell her to stop fidgeting.

'We haven't found Lola yet,' the older detective says, and she's glad he's straight to the point. 'I've assembled a team of cyber intelligence officers. We have boots on the ground too of course. We will find her.'

'What about the press?' Isobel asks, already imagining Lola's face on every newspaper tomorrow morning.

DCI Watkins starts to nod, but Roly is leaning forward, pulling his hand away from hers. 'Actually,' he starts to say, looking first to Isobel and then to Margaret. His mother gives the slightest nod. 'I wonder if we should hold off on involving the media.'

'What?' Isobel shakes her head. Is this what he and Margaret were discussing in the kitchen when she walked in earlier? 'We have to involve them, don't we?' She looks to the detectives.

'In a child abduction case, the press can have a huge reach,' DCI Watkins says carefully, his gaze moving between the three of them as though trying to figure something out. Perhaps he's wondering who's really in charge. They are Lola's parents, she wants to remind him, but stops herself.

Roly nods. 'Yes, of course. I understand that, but I'm just thinking about who's done this. What if it's a ransom situation and we involve the press? If they get wind of it, then it could make it harder to get Lola back.'

'And it would make us targets for the future,' Margaret adds, and it's crystal clear that they've discussed it.

'You think this is about money?' Isobel asks. 'You think we can buy Lola back?'

'I don't know,' Roly says. 'That's the point. We don't know anything yet. I wonder if we just pause on involving the press, just for a few hours, half a day tops, and see what happens.'

'We feel it's better to keep the Huntington name out of this,' Margaret says.

We? Isobel shakes her head. She is not part of any 'we'. Why has Roly ambushed her like this? Why didn't he talk to her?

'Surely finding Lola is all that matters?' Isobel forces herself to speak out.

'Absolutely it is.' Roly takes her hand again. 'But we should think about Lola's future too. If we involve the press before we need to, then she'll always be the child that was abducted. She'll be constantly reminded of it. She'll never have a normal life.'

'But we have to find her,' Isobel cries.

'I know,' he says in that pleading *'I'm stuck in the middle'* tone he uses with her on the rare times she tries to stand her ground against his mother. 'And we will. And we will go to the press. I'm only suggesting we give it a few hours.'

Hot, angry, desperate tears burn at the edges of her eyes before spilling onto her face. Roly tightens his hand on hers, willing her to understand. She thinks of the promise he made last night that he'd tell Margaret to leave. Already she can see it's broken like all the rest.

'I promise I'll be home for dinner.'

'I'll take Lola to the park this weekend, I promise.'

'I promise you're the only woman for me, Iz.'

The last one stings the most, but she can't allow herself to think about it now.

'Roly makes a good point about a possible ransom,' DCI Watkins says, sharing a look with DI Gardner. 'We can hold off on alerting the press right now, but it's perhaps something I think we will need to consider in the next twenty-four hours.'

'And we don't want a family liaison officer or whatever they're called either,' Margaret adds in the voice she uses when speaking to the hired staff at Huntington Hall. 'You come to us. I don't want a go-between getting under my feet in my own home.'

Isobel stands suddenly, needing to be somewhere else. She can't stay in this room another second. She can't be this person.

The floor tilts for a moment before righting itself – a ship lost in a storm. Nausea churns in her stomach. She should really eat something.

Her eyes are drawn to the window and the early morning light pushing through the trees. From this floor, she can see a woman in a pink running set, stretching her legs by a bench. The world is waking up, carrying on without them. She wonders if Lola is still sleeping. Her daughter has always been a good sleeper. Twelve hours, sometimes more, even with the odd nap in the daytime. Other questions start to prod at the edges of her thoughts. Where is her daughter? Is she sad? Is she crying for them? Does she think they've deserted her?

And the other question, the one she's not allowed herself to think about. Who has taken her? That's what they really need to ask, isn't it? Who would do this to them? Who would target Lola? She desperately wants to ask them what they know so far, if they have a name, but the words don't come.

The detectives look at Isobel as though expecting her to say something. And she wants to. She wants to ask who would do this. She wants to tell them that Lola is her everything, and they need to do whatever it takes to get her back. But the words won't come.

'I'll... make some coffee,' she says instead, because deep down she knows any kind of media involvement would be bad. Not just for the Huntington name, like Margaret is worried about. Or about Lola's future, as Roly pointed out. But because of the secrets their family is built on. Isobel's heart has been ripped from her chest, every fear finally realised. She's been telling herself that her life has crumbled without Lola, but it's nothing compared to what would happen if the world knew what they'd done.

How long would it take one curious journalist to unravel their lies?

NINE

ISOBEL

Isobel makes her way to the stairs on legs that feel weak and untrustworthy. The staircase runs through the centre of the town house, curving around and around from one floor to the next, wide at the edges and getting narrower and deeper in the middle. Instinctively, she turns to look behind her to the space where Lola should be, following behind with her constant stream of chatter.

'Can we go see a panda, Mummy? A baby one? I like pandas. They will give good hugs like Daddy does.'

'Be careful on the stairs, Lola. Concentrate. Always hold on to the banister.'

'I am, Mummy. What are we doing today? Can we go to the swings?'

The space is empty of course. The little voice is in her head. Memories swirling with the imaginings of a world where her daughter is home and she is safe and all is right with the world, and she'll never ever, never again let Lola out of her sight.

They've been away from her only once before. Isobel and Roly had spent a long weekend in Nice when Lola was eighteen months old. Three nights and four days. Roly had booked it as a

surprise – an unspoken apology after that woman had banged
on their front door in the middle of the night and told Roly she
loved him.

'*It was a drunken snog in a nightclub,*' he'd told Isobel after
he'd got the woman to leave. '*I promise you, Iz, nothing more.
You're everything to me. You and Lola. That woman was crazy.
She's been calling the office non-stop. Some idiot must have
given her my address. Please believe me, I love you. I wouldn't
do anything to jeopardise us.*' There'd been tears swimming in
his eyes, and even though she wasn't sure she believed him,
she'd forgiven him. What choice did she have? They were a
family. He wasn't perfect, but neither was she, and she
loved him.

God, they'd adored Nice. Sleeping in, going anywhere they
wanted, never having to think about packing snacks and
changes of clothes or being back for nap times. Freedom, they'd
called it, clinking cold, fizzing glasses of champagne and
promising themselves they'd do it again the following year.

How stupid they'd been.

How wrong.

It wasn't freedom at all.

She'd missed Lola on that trip, worried about her staying
with Margaret, getting lost toddling down one of the corridors
of the huge country house nestled in the English countryside.
Or getting too close to one of the horses in the stables, but their
housekeeper, Zeen, had gone too, another pair of hands, and it
had all been fine.

At the bottom of the stairs now, Isobel stops. Something
about Zeen snags in her thoughts, but it's gone before she can
grab hold of it. Her mind blanks. She can't remember why she
was on her way to the ground floor. She takes a step into the
entrance hall. The black-and-white pattern of the floor tiles
seems to move beneath her feet. Isobel puts her hand to her
stomach, willing the fresh wave of nausea to pass.

Then she remembers the detectives. She's come to make coffee.

Keep it together.

Another movement catches her eye. Not the tiles but the silver-framed mirror and a woman who looks just like her mother did near the end, before the cancer finally got her. It's not her mother but her own reflection – grey and haunted. Unrecognisable to the grinning photos uploaded on her Insta feed yesterday morning. A different woman. A different life-time. Her face is deathly pale, her eyes swollen and red. She should've stuck with the leggings and T-shirt. Her outfit looks ridiculous. As though nice clothes and a pair of pearl earrings could disguise how awful she looks and feels.

Isobel drops her gaze from the mirror and focuses on moving forward. There are so many steps, and she falters outside the playroom. Tears threaten. The door is closed. She won't open it. She won't look in. Instead, she keeps going into the kitchen.

'Iz?' Roly's booming voice carries from the first floor. 'You OK?'

No, no she's not. But that's not what he's asking. Really he's asking where the coffee is and gently telling her to hurry up. A prompt from Margaret, no doubt.

'Be up in a second,' she calls back, pulling out the bone china cups and saucers that Margaret gave them as a wedding gift, along with the house.

She's halfway up the stairs with the tray and the cups rattling in their saucers from her shaking hands when she remembers the sugar. It's on her lips to call to Zeen to bring it up, and that's when she realises how odd it is that her house-keeper isn't here. Isobel had expected to see her last night. She doesn't normally work on Sundays, but she'd often be waiting for them on the day they returned from a holiday, even if it was a day off. Zeen seemed to know exactly when Isobel needed that extra pair of hands. Normally when they returned from holiday, Zeen was there to welcome them back, to unpack their cases, cook the dinner and put the first load of washing on; knowing Isobel would be too tired to want to do any of it herself.

It was unusual that she wasn't here yesterday, but her absence today is very strange. Every Monday without fail, Zeen has slipped into the house at 6 a.m. and begun her day with cleaning the kitchen. Isobel tries to think beyond Lola and the nightmare they're living in to remember if Zeen told her she wouldn't be in today, but there's nothing.

Where is she?

Her thoughts return to Margaret opening their front door yesterday. Arriving before them. Turning the police away so quickly. Isobel knows that it would've been Margaret's idea to hold off on alerting the press to Lola's abduction. She'd have convinced Roly to be the one to suggest it, no doubt. And Margaret hired Zeen all those years ago. Is there something else going on here? What is her mother-in-law up to?

Isobel pushes the thought away as she steps into the living room with the tray of coffees, spilling one of the cups she's over-filled as she slides the tray onto the coffee table. She trusts Zeen. There will be a reasonable explanation. She'll call her later to check she's OK and ask her to come. She needs someone to take care of them right now in the quiet, kind way Zeen has done for her and Roly and Lola for years now. It certainly isn't the kind of care she will get from Margaret.

She hands the detectives a coffee each, before giving a cup to Margaret and then Roly; saving the spilled one for herself.

As she takes a sip, a drop lands on the white-and-pale-green rug.

'Really, dear,' Margaret says in a voice meant to be heard by everyone in the room. 'You should take more care. This rug is an original Milano.'

Isobel's cheeks flame, but she bites back a reply and stems the tears threatening to fall as she places the cup back on the tray. She didn't even want a coffee.

Margaret has always been critical. Sometimes Isobel is surprised she even let the wedding go ahead. But then her and Roly had been such a whirlwind. He'd proposed after only three months of dating while Margaret was visiting her sister in South Africa. By the time she'd returned, the save the dates were already out and there was no way for Margaret to stop the wedding without causing a scandal. Something she'd never do. And so now she nitpicks and pokes and does all she can to wear a hole in Isobel and Roly's love.

Having Lola had made it easier on all of them. Margaret had a new focus – a grandchild to dote on; an heir to the Huntington name. And with the all-consuming love Isobel felt for Lola, it was easier for her to ignore the jibes.

'It's too soon to tell what the motive might be,' DCI Watkins says, breaking the awkward silence and shooting her a sympathetic look. 'The first thing we need to establish is who would do this. Roly has just given us a list of friends and family and those in your inner circle that we'll look into. It is possible this is someone you know looking for a payout.'

'I gave them Zeen's details too,' Roly adds.

Isobel shakes her head. 'No. She has nothing to do with this. She wouldn't. Margaret, you hired her. You can tell them they don't need to worry about Zeen.'

'I can do no such thing. One can never tell with the help.' The reply drips with entitlement and a world Isobel sometimes struggles to believe she's part of.

It isn't Zeen they should be worrying about, Isobel is sure. And even though there is one person she can think of who'd want to cause them harm, to destroy everything they hold dear, and even though she knows now is the time to mention it, she can't bring herself to say the name out loud. She and Roly never speak of that time.

'We're exploring every possibility. In the meantime—' The detective gestures to the Chesterfield, and only as she sits beside Roly once more does she realise DCI Watkins has something to tell them. Do they have a lead?

Please let her daughter be OK. She pushes the words out into the universe as her heart starts to pound in her eardrums.

'What is it, DCI Watkins?' she asks, unable to call him Owen like he's asked. It feels too informal when he's tracking down the person responsible for taking their daughter. 'Do you know who's done this?'

'We don't have an identity for the person who abducted Lola yesterday, but we do have the CCTV from the services,' the detective replies, perching on the edge of the armchair opposite. Even Margaret sits now, taking the space the other side of Roly. Only DI Gardner remains standing. His large hands make the coffee cup he's holding seem toy-like. She feels him watching her and wonders if Margaret said something while she was in the kitchen, something about the time when Lola was so little and Isobel had struggled with anxiety and panic attacks. Frustration pounds along with her racing heart. How dare Margaret insist on inserting herself in the worst moment of their lives?

DCI Watkins reaches into the inside pocket of his jacket for his phone. 'This is the car that was used to drive Lola away from Winchester services.'

He taps the screen and a video starts to play. She watches a small blue car move slowly through the car park and join the line of cars heading to the exit. There are people everywhere, but no one is paying attention.

Tears spill from her eyes. 'Oh God.'

'You can track the car, right?' Roly asks. 'With the licence plate?'

The detective nods. 'Last night we used Automatic Number Plate Recognition retrospectively, which told us where this car went after leaving the services. We know Lola was driven east before the car disappeared. We're targeting a search in the area where it was last seen.

'We also know the whereabouts of the car last week.'

'Last week?' Isobel frowns. 'Is that important?'

'You told DI Gardner yesterday that you were driving home from a holiday in Cornwall.'

They nod.

'This blue Peugeot was logged on an ANPR camera in St Ives last week.'

'That's where we were.' The words burst out of Roly, shocked and indignant.

'We believe whoever took Lola was targeting her specifically and they may have been following you for some time, looking for an opportunity.'

Margaret makes a noise in her throat, shooting a look at Isobel. 'Which they never should've had,' she says.

'Mother.' Roly's voice is firm, and it surprises Isobel. He rarely stands up to Margaret, especially when Isobel is the target. 'That's not helpful,' he adds, tone softer.

'I'm sorry, darling, but I'm struggling to wrap my head around this. I cannot understand why someone would take Lola. What possible reason would they have?'

He shakes his head. 'I don't know.'

'What if someone wants to hurt her? Or... or it's a trafficking group or... someone wants to kill her?'

Margaret's comment makes Isobel feel sick. She can't imagine never seeing Lola again, can't imagine her not in this world. She waits for Roly to reply. Will he mention revenge as a motive? Or is that a can of worms he won't want to open?

'We can't think like that,' Roly says. 'It's bound to be someone targeting our money.'

Is it?

She's desperate to know what's happening, where her daughter is. If she's OK. But what good can speculating do them? 'So you don't know where the car is now?' she asks DCI Watkins.

'No. But we have an alert on the plate. The next time it passes a camera, we'll know immediately.'

Then he taps his phone again and another image appears. She and Roly lean forward. It's a photo this time – a shot from above the doors overlooking the food court. It's so clear that Isobel wants to reach into the photo, climb back to that moment and sweep the little girl in the yellow T-shirt and pale-blue shorts out of the photo and into her arms.

'Lola,' she whispers. The feeling of missing a vital part of herself returns. She isn't sure how she'll survive one more minute without Lola in her arms let alone another hour, another day, a week. A lifetime?

Her daughter has one arm wrapped tight around the stuffed duck teddy Isobel was going to buy her, and one hand being held by a woman with long, straight blonde hair and baggy clothes.

'Do you recognise this woman?' DCI Watkins asks, his gaze moving from Roly to Isobel.

She shakes her head and looks to Roly. He stares at the image for a long moment and for a second, she thinks he might be about to nod. Bile burns in her throat. She can't bear the thought that he recognises this woman, that he knows the person who would take their little girl. Isobel's mind races back to the night on the doorstep and the woman banging on their door.

She wonders again about revenge. And about all the nights Roly is late home, always telling her he was with clients. But then he shakes his head and sighs, blowing out a long puff of air. 'No,' he says at last. 'Who is she?'

'We're looking into that now,' DI Gardner answers. He steps forward and there's a small notebook in his hands. 'The car this woman used is registered to a Malik Kahn. Does that name mean anything to you?'

They both shake their heads.

'We have visited Malik Kahn's address this morning, but there was no one home. Locating this person is our top priority.'

'Does this man have a criminal record?' Margaret asks. 'Is he involved in anything that would explain why he's taken my grandchild?'

'No.'

'Who are these people?' Isobel can't stop the tremor in her voice. 'What do they want with our daughter?'

'We don't know yet,' DCI Watkins replies.

'Well, perhaps,' Margaret begins with an icy tone Isobel knows all too well from the hundreds of times she's said the wrong thing to her mother-in-law, 'you should be out there finding out instead of sitting here drinking coffee with us. Unless you have anything else to tell us, that is.'

'Not at this time.' DCI Watkins stands and, for the first time, Isobel is glad Margaret is with them, shooing these detectives away to do their jobs.

Roly shows the men out, and Isobel hurries along the corridor to the bathroom. She needs to speak to Roly soon. They must decide how much they tell the police about their past, especially with Margaret here, but first she needs to be alone.

Her pulse is juddering, her head spinning with all that she's been told. Malik Kahn. A woman with long blonde hair. Being followed in Cornwall. And they still have no idea where Lola is. What's going to happen to her?

It's been sixteen hours since she last saw her daughter. Isobel's thoughts leap suddenly to Scarlett Peters – the woman on the front page of the newspapers yesterday. The police have been searching for her for four months. Isobel is quite sure she will not survive even one more day of this.

She reaches for her phone and finds Zeen's number. She needs her housekeeper here. She needs to know why she's not. The phone rings and rings, but there is no answer. No voicemail either. Isobel cuts off the call. Where the hell is she?

She stares at her phone. There is another person she should be calling. The one person who can help them find Lola, but the thought scares her nearly as much as losing her daughter forever.

Her cheeks throb; her mouth fills with saliva. She drops to her knees in front of the toilet and gives in to the nausea.

TEN

EMMA

The scream from a nightmare catches in Emma's throat, and she wakes with a gasp. She pins her lips together, head shaking from side to side. It only takes a beat for reality to catch up with her and the walls of the hospital to fade away, leaving her to blink in the grey-and-pastel-pink surround of the caravan.

They are still here.

Still hidden.

But for how long? A breathless panic rushes through her. It feels alive – a pummelling beast of a thing. They have to leave. They have to keep moving. Away, away.

She slows her breathing, in for three, out for five, focusing on the lingering hints of apple air freshener, the quiet. How long did she lie on the prickly carpet tiles last night, waiting for the red sedan to come back?

Hours, she thinks. Before she'd crawled on hands and knees to the sofa and fallen asleep, half wondering if it had been a different car or if it had even been there at all.

'There's no such thing as monsters, Emma. It's all in your head.'

But it isn't. She doesn't care how many people tell her she's unwell, using every medical term they can, dancing around that one word, like the game of Taboo she'd played at school with her classmates sometimes, when it was too wet to go outside.

But she knew what they meant. *Crazy.*

Even her family think it. She sees the wary looks they give her. Only Haz believed her. He's always been there to listen, shooing away her concerns for him, pulling his sleeves over his wrists, hiding the scars they both knew were there.

'*The question is,*' he'd always say when she'd cry and rage, '*what are you going to do about it?*'

She reaches for her phone – a lifetime habit she wonders if she'll ever break. It's not there. It's hidden in the drawer of the nightstand in her childhood bedroom. She remembers turning it off last week before the journey to Cornwall.

She stands, reaching for the backpack and unpacking two outfits. Leggings and T-shirts and clean underwear. One set for her and one set for Lola. Then her fingers touch the hard plastic of the cheap unregistered phone at the bottom of her bag. Emma knows the dangers the phone carries – even an unregistered one she'd bought with cash miles away from her home or anywhere connected to her life. If she calls any number the police are monitoring, they can find the location of the phone.

But she needs to hear Haz's voice. To hear that reassurance that she's not crazy. Before she can talk herself out of it, the phone is on and she's tapped in his number. It rings and rings. She's not surprised. He's always been rubbish at answering. Then the ringing stops and Haz's voice fills the silence.

'Hey, this is Haz. Leave a message, or better yet, send me a WhatsApp.'

There's a beep, and she hangs up, tapping out a message instead. *I'm scared.*

She doesn't wait to see if the ticks turn blue before powering off the phone. Somehow reaching out to him is enough to soothe her fears. She's scared she's done the wrong thing by taking Lola. Scared she's as crazy as everyone thinks. But Lola is her daughter. And only Emma can save her.

The thought spurs her on, and she hurries to get dressed before brushing her teeth and washing herself in the sink as quietly as she can. She pulls her brush through each section of her hair until it's smooth and shiny and lying down her back.

Emma breathes deeply again, taking the last few moments of alone time to gather the broken pieces of herself and stick them back together, hoping the glue holds for another day. Then she goes to wake Lola.

Her little girl is sleeping on her back, diagonal on the bed, head off the pillow, arms flung out. The sight of her warms something inside Emma. She steps into the room and sits on the side of the bed, stroking the silky blonde hair away from her sleeping daughter's face.

'Hey, Lola,' she whispers.

The little girl stirs and, with her eyes still closed, her hands pat the mattress until she finds Barnaby and pulls him close.

'Lola, it's me, Emma. It's time to wake up and have breakfast now.'

Her eyes open, instantly curious.

'Morning, precious girl,' Emma says again. 'I have Coco Pops.'

'I'm not allowed Coco Pops unless it's a special day,' Lola says, her voice still slow with sleep, face buried in Barnaby's head.

'Today *is* a special day,' Emma replies. 'It's our adventure day, remember? Today we're going to take another bus, and then we're going to collect our new car, and tonight we'll be far, far away and safe.'

Lola sits up, reaching for Ducky. 'Will we see Mummy and Daddy?'

The word 'mummy' slices through her, sharp and easy – a carving knife through butter. She feels a flash of anger. Not at

Lola. Never Lola. But at them – Isobel and Roly and the doctors. All the people who've crushed her dreams over and over. And... and... there is one name she's thinking of, one person who terrifies her, but she tries so hard not to think about it.

I am your mummy. She bites back the reply and forces her friendliest smile. 'Come and see your new clothes and eat some Coco Pops. We need to leave soon.'

Very soon, Emma thinks as she coaxes Lola into clean clothes and fights back the pulse of fear that comes with knowing that soon she'll be unlocking the caravan door and stepping outside.

She wishes there was another way out of this. She closes her eyes and thinks of her and Lola leaving their bodies behind, flying up and away from the fear, the constant looking over her shoulder, all the people chasing them. Just her and Lola. Together forever. Safe.

ELEVEN

EMMA

They are on another bus. Heading north now. Emma pictures their journey on a map. East from the services to throw off the police search. Then south to the caravan park. And finally, north. Finally, the direction they need to go in.

The bus is slow, trundling through one village and then another.

Hurry! Please, please hurry!

The words rush around and around her mind at the speed she wishes they were traveling at. It's early – not yet nine – and she watches men and women in bright polo shirts and office wear step through the doors. Ordinary people. An ordinary day. Sitting beside Lola, listening to her talk about a city farm she likes to visit to feed the animals, and pointing out fields of sheep and cows, she can almost believe they are ordinary too. If it wasn't for the words in her head and the thumping beat of her pulse in her ears.

Emma wants to believe in safety in numbers, in blending in and being invisible. She is just another mother taking her daughter on a trip. Except the bus is so slow. If they know she's here, they'll be able to get ahead, stop them, snatch them.

Hurry. Please hurry!

The bowl of cereal she forced herself to eat feels as though it's sloshing in her stomach, curdling, unmoving. They just have to make it into town, she reminds herself. Then they can disappear down back roads, collect the car waiting for them and be away. Safe.

She allows herself to think ahead to tonight and the ferry that will take them out of the country. From there, they will keep moving for a while more, until they find a corner of the world somewhere tucked out of the way. A beach, a sea, a little house with a picket fence she'll paint white. At weekends they'll meet friends in the park and have movie nights. She isn't sure where that place is yet. She hadn't wanted to search in case she left a trail online, but she's certain they'll know the right place when they see it.

She'll find work. Maybe in law, although she no longer believes in justice – in laws that protect the good and punish the bad. Maybe she'll open a florist. For the last few years, she's loved working in the flower shop on the high street near her home in South London. It feels like that job saved her when everything else in her world had fallen apart. Yes, a flower shop. A beach. The life she should have had with Lola for all those years. It's almost in reach.

Except there's a man three rows ahead of them who caught her eye as he'd stepped on at the stop after theirs, looking from her to Lola and back again. He's shifted in his seat and glanced at her twice since then. Does he recognise them? Are their faces already on posters being shared on news sites and online? She doesn't want to check for herself. It'll only make what she's doing harder. Then there's the black dome with the grey surround on the ceiling at the front – an all-seeing eye. Is someone tracking them from a surveillance room somewhere?

She has no idea how good her disguise was yesterday. Do the police know who she is yet? She imagines them showing a photo of the blonde woman with the heavy make-up to Roly and Isobel, and a fierce hate burns beneath her skin. They do not deserve Lola. She's not theirs. They can't keep her safe like she can. How can they when they don't even see the dangers?

She has a sudden urge to leap from her seat and smash the camera from the ceiling, yank out the wires, block the feed. But that would be the quickest way to draw attention. And it's not the cameras that are the problem. There are over five million of them in this country. For the most part, their feeds go unmonitored. It's only when the police begin searching a particular area that they'll rely on the cameras. If they don't know who she is or where, then they won't know which CCTV feeds to look at.

She wishes she knew how close the police are to finding them. The not knowing is eating her up inside. Are they seconds away from capture, or can she breathe? Have they found her dumped car? Are they at the caravan already? She thought the fear would be easier to manage today as they covered more ground, but it's the same feeling pummelling her. Like trying to stand upright in a hurricane.

There's a movement from the seat behind them. Emma jolts and turns, coming face to face with a woman with long white hair hanging loose around her face. She's wearing a purple smock and dark lipstick. She smiles at Emma and Lola with yellowing teeth. 'What a cute teddy,' she says.

Emma nods but doesn't speak. She can't find her voice.

'What's its name?'

'Who?' Emma asks, her heart already starting to race. She means, who are you? What do you want? Why are you talking to us?

'The bear of course,' she says, pointing to the teddy on Lola's lap, smiling still but uncertain too. 'I do like bears.'

'Barnaby,' Emma replies before turning away and pointing at a field of cows, distracting Lola before she can tell the woman that she herself is Lola and this woman stole her from the only parents she's ever known.

She senses Lola shrink further into her seat, and Emma hates that she's scared and that it's her fault. *'Remember, Lola,'* she'd said as she'd unlocked the caravan door and stepped into the grey morning. *'We must be secret. We can't talk to anyone, OK? We don't want them to find us.'*

Tears had built in those crystal-blue eyes. *'The monster?'* she'd asked with a trembling bottom lip, and Emma had nodded, hating herself for it.

'I want to stay here.'

'We can't. I'm sorry, Lola. I know it's scary. I'm scared too. But we have to keep moving or they'll find us.' Any minute. Any second, they'll be here. Hurry!

It had taken promises of ice creams and adventure and a dozen other lies Emma hoped Lola would forget before she'd nodded and taken Emma's hand.

Emma points to the window now. 'One... six... eleven...'

A small smile, a tiny shake of her head before her little girl counts them properly, voice a whisper. The woman tuts but says nothing. She was only after a bit of small talk to pass the time in that way people like to do sometimes. Emma knows that. And yet, she has no space in her head for chit chat. She wishes they'd sat further back. Now the woman will remember them if she's asked. *'They seemed like a normal mother and daughter on their way to the shops. She was quiet. A bit rude actually, which makes sense, doesn't it?'*

The bus jolts to a stop outside a parade of shops. Passengers get off instead of on. Another few minutes pass, and then the town centre appears, still quiet, still sleepy. It will pick up when the shops open soon. The morning quiet was always Emma's favourite time working in the florist. When the air smelled earthy and sweet, and the bouquets were ready, but the doors still locked for those final few minutes of peace.

It was always in those still moments when she'd thought of all the ways her life could've been different. Sliding-doors imaginings of standing in a courtroom in a wig and gown, presenting her argument. Or picking up her daughter from nursery, walking hand in hand to the playground to play on the swings. One life, then another. Then neither.

The bus rounds a corner, and Emma sees a pedestrianised area to the left that leads down to a mall. To the right are the cheaper shops – a Cash Converters and a Poundland, wedged in between a kebab shop and a greasy spoon.

The bus stops, and the doors open with a 'shuuuush'. It's the end of the line. The passengers file off, an orderly line that Emma wants to barge through. She loses sight of the man who was staring at them. Where did he go? Is he hiding? Waiting to follow? Outside, a chill lingers in the air. She catches the mutterings of two women ahead of them.

'Call this July?'

'I know. Where's our summer?'

Emma is grateful for the cool day. Her skin already feels clammy, her T-shirt damp from wearing the backpack. She takes a moment to get her bearings, pulling up the maps app on the phone just to be sure. She thinks she remembers the route from her visit two weeks ago but doesn't want to get them lost when they're so close to escape.

'This way, Lola.' She takes her daughter's hand and is about to guide her away from the shops when she sees the man from the bus. He's leaning against a wall, a vape in his hand; watching them.

There's something about him that causes a scream to build in Emma's throat. She can't keep the terror from consuming her, eating her whole. Is this man following them? Does he know who they are? Is he... is he working for the one person who will kill Emma if he finds her? The person she's tried so hard over the last three years to forget but who still barges into her night-mares every night.

She imagines this man with his vape catching her arm, holding her tight, hissing in her ear. *'Jonny sent me. He wants a word.'*

TWELVE

EMMA

The thought of Jonny launches a bolt of fear that catapults Emma forward. 'Come on,' she says, dragging Lola and running around a corner then another, little legs, little shoes, running, running, until Lola is crying noisy sobs and Emma is breathless with the terror of the vaping man and Jonny and what he'll do if he catches them.

'I'll kill you. I'll kill everyone you love, including Lola, and no one will even notice.'

Emma wants so badly to believe it's just the police after her. Just those people who call themselves Lola's parents. But there is Jonny too. She knows he'll never let her go.

She remembers him stroking the side of her face, looking at her with an intensity she once thought meant he cared and knows now it was possession. Control. *'There is nowhere you can go where we won't find you, Emma.'*

Then the sneer of his face. The mask falling to reveal the monster beneath.

'You're nothing to me. Nothing to anyone. When are you going to realise that?'

'I'm sorry.' Emma remembers the desperation in her voice. *'Please, Jonny, I'll be good.'*

'Yes, you will be. And I have just the place to put you to make sure.'

A sob catches in her throat. She won't go back to that hospital. She should never have been there. But Jonny had drugged her with sedatives and told a pack of lies to the Accident and Emergency staff. She'd been locked in the secure ward before she'd been able to string a sentence together.

It wasn't even the worst thing he did to her. Not by a long shot.

How could she have ever thought he cared for her? The handsome man with his expensive suits and his money. It wasn't just the gifts he lavished on her. Those beautiful dresses. It was the way he looked at her when she talked, like she was the only person on earth he wanted to be with in that moment. He'd made her feel seen in a way no one had ever done before.

It was all a lie. From the very first second Jonny had laid eyes on her, she'd been nothing but a possession to him, something to be used and thrown away.

Tears fall down her face, and she finds her feet stopping. It's useless. They are too slow. They can't outrun someone on foot. She stops and scoops her little girl into her arms and crouches in a doorway to an office building, hugging Lola tight and staring back down the road, watching for any sight of the man with the vape. He's not following them. Was he ever? She isn't sure. Can't trust her own judgement.

'I'm scared,' Lola cries. 'I want to go home.'

'I'm sorry, Lola. I'm so sorry. It's OK. Everything is OK.'

'Is the monster still chasing us?'

Emma has no answer. She blinks the memory away. How can she explain that now she doesn't think it was a monster after all but her own paranoia snapping at their heels? And yet Jonny and his friends are still out there, and she knows him well enough to know he'll never give up. The police will be searching too. And Lola's so-called parents. They want her back, but they can't have her. Emma is her mother. Lola is hers now. Only she can save her.

Instead Emma soothes her daughter for a minute more, rubbing her back as she watches the street. The man doesn't appear. She takes a breath. In for five, out for six. She wishes Haz was with them. She knows exactly what he'd say. *'Some people are monsters, and yes they are out to get you, but there are good people too. Not everyone is bad. Try to remember that, Em.'*

He's right. Not everyone is out to get her. It just feels like it.

'OK,' she says, pulling her hair into a high ponytail and away from the damp skin on the back of her neck. 'Let's get walking. Once we find our car, everything will be fine.'

She has to believe it. The car, the drive, the ferry, the different country. A new life. They're almost there.

Lola sniffs, cuddling Barnaby tight in her arms. Ducky is wedged in the pink backpack on her back, and Emma takes a moment to make sure the zip is secure after their dash. The last thing she needs is to lose one of Lola's teddies. They start again. Emma's legs feel wobbly from the rush and the adrenaline. Lola is quiet, but Emma soon gets her talking.

'It's my birthday soon,' she says, as though Emma doesn't know, could ever forget. 'I'm having a farm party with ponies and goats.'

'And pandas?'

Lola giggles. 'Pandas don't live on farms.'

They pass a big school with tall metal fences, closed up for the summer, then a park, and then it's sprawling roads of houses. Her eyes flick up to lampposts, searching for CCTV. She sees nothing and tries to calm down her racing heart and concentrate on the route they are taking and Lola's chatter.

'Are we nearly there?' Lola asks as they turn down yet another road of houses.

'Not far,' Emma says brightly. 'About five minutes and then we'll find our car, and then we can listen to the music again. What's your favourite song?'

'I miss Mummy.' There's a wobble to Lola's voice, and it's enough to send a stream of tears falling down her face. Each one is a knife in Emma's chest. However much she tells herself this is right, however fervently she believes deep in her core that she is the only one who can keep her daughter safe, Emma can't ignore the fear and uncertainty she is putting Lola through.

She has to focus on why she's doing this – to keep them both safe from Jonny. When he said he'd kill her and everyone she loves, including Lola – especially Lola – it wasn't a threat. It was a statement.

'Don't cry.' She hugs Lola tighter.

Across the road, two teenagers stroll by hand in hand. The girl laughs at something her boyfriend is saying. She is pretty. Her hair is bleached and dyed a pale pink, and she has a piercing in her nose and one in her lip. She must be sixteen or seventeen and seems to Emma to be unfathomably cool. So much cooler than she was at that age. The awkward invisible teen who hadn't found yet where she belonged in the world but knew she didn't.

It had taken a boy to bring Emma out of her shell back then and to stop hiding in her studies and dreaming of a future she couldn't wait to get to. Damien had been a few years older. Nineteen to her seventeen and had seemed so worldly to Emma when he'd come into the supermarket she'd worked in part-time while studying for her A levels, buying cigarettes and bottles of alcohol.

'Got a party tonight,' he'd always say. 'You should come.'

She'd smiled, shaken her head, dropped her gaze, but as the months passed, she'd found herself looking forward to seeing Damien on those Friday evenings. And then one day, her exams were finished and results day had rolled around, and she'd achieved all As and been offered a place at University College London to study law. It had felt like her dreams were one step closer, and she'd so badly wanted to celebrate. Until she'd realised she had no one to celebrate with. She'd never been good at making friends and had been too busy studying and working part-time to find any real friends on her course. And even her parents had been cautious instead of proud.

'It's all very well, Emma, but remember – the bigger the mountain you set out to climb, the further there is to fall. And you know we can't afford to help you.'

So when she'd gone to work that Friday and Damien had winked and said, 'You should come,' she'd shrugged and said, 'OK.'

The party had been more of a gathering. Ten or so lads in a grubby flat filled with a haze of cigarette smoke. A baseline of music thumping against the walls, reverberating through her.

They'd dated for a few years before Damien's worldly feeling had petered into something small and stifling and she'd found him too like her family, dreaming too small, too safe; nagging her to spend time with him instead of at the library.

She wonders sometimes where Damien is now. Is he still chatting up girls in supermarkets and working as a delivery driver? Is he even still alive or did Jonny get to him too? It was Damien who'd introduced Emma to Jonny – a chance meeting at a party when her relationship with Damien was all but over. Jonny had made her feel so special. Introducing her to his friends, listening when she talked about law and her plans. In those early days, there had been no hint of the world of trouble that Jonny would drag her into. Trouble she's still scrambling to escape from.

Escape. The word echoes in her thoughts. They must keep going.

'Hey, guess what?' Emma says, pulling away from their hug

and looking into Lola's wide, fearful eyes. 'I've got a present in the boot of the car for you. A friend for Ducky and Barnaby.'

There's a moment of quiet. Lola sniffs then pulls away. 'What kind of friend?'

'Why don't you guess?' Emma says, standing up and coaxing them on.

'What colour is it?'

'It's two colours.'

'How big is it?' Lola asks, the tears forgotten.

'In real life, it's very big.'

'Bigger than my daddy?'

Emma nods. 'Yes. But your new friend is a smaller version. Smaller than Ducky.'

The questions keep coming. Emma pictures the soft fur of the panda teddy in the car, excited to see Lola's face when she gives it to her.

They round another corner, and finally the road she's been looking for appears. She's about to whoop and tell Lola they're here, but something is wrong. Her feet falter. She's aware of Lola, silent now, looking up at her. But all she can think about is the car – their freedom, their safety, their escape. The car that is supposed to be parked on the road ahead of them.

The car that is not there.

The road is closed by two large orange barriers, and there are no cars. None at all. Her eyes dart to the road name, praying she's wrong, but no. This is the road. Everything collapses inwards like the nursery story of the little pigs and their house made of straw. The big bad wolf coming for them. Panic surges through her – a fireball, an explosion.

How could this have happened? The car isn't here. What the hell is she going to do now? Her thoughts spiral. No car means no supplies, no money and no transport – no way to outrun the police or... or Jonny. No escape.

Emma isn't sure she's ever felt so completely and entirely alone.

Except that's not really true, she reminds herself. She does have one person helping her. And maybe now is the time to reach out.

THIRTEEN
ISOBEL

Isobel runs the brush over her teeth, replacing the acidic tang of vomit with mint. She can still feel the ache of her abdominal muscles and knows if she looks at the toilet bowl, she'll be on her knees retching again.

She must get a grip! Telling herself she can't do this isn't helping.

But even as she dabs fresh concealer on the shadows beneath her eyes, she knows getting a grip is an impossible task. Her daughter is missing. She can't begin to comprehend how scared her little girl must be. But if Isobel allows the horrors of her worst nightmares to crowd her mind, she will crumble to the marble-white tiled floor and never get back up. And so she readjusts her hair, checks her earrings are still in place and steps out of the bathroom. There's an unnatural quiet to the house. She has been in the bathroom for nearly an hour. Where's Roly?

She turns down the hallway and there he is, standing motionless in the doorway of Lola's bedroom. It's strange to see him so still. He is a man who is always in motion. Hands flying wildly about as he tells a story or rubbing at the stubble on his jaw; pacing too, and always tapping or talking or scrolling on his phone. Isobel didn't think it was possible to feel any more hurt or broken than she already does, but seeing Roly like this, it's like she's taking on his pain too. This is her fault.

'Roly,' she says, voice barely above a whisper.

He starts and turns to face her, and she spots the phone gripped in his hands. 'I... I was just messaging... my boss,' he says, before slipping the phone into his pocket.' She has a sudden urge to reach into his pocket and look for herself. She wants to ask him about that woman who banged on their door in the middle of the night. She wants to ask him why his mood had changed so suddenly in the spring and what had kept him out late so many nights. And she wants to ask him if he really didn't recognise the photo of the blonde woman who has taken their daughter.

But it's not his fault Lola is gone, is it? It's hers. She was the one who wasn't watching Lola properly yesterday. She is the one keeping a secret. They need to stick together right now. They need each other.

'Are you OK?' she asks instead.

He nods to the open doorway and the bright-yellow walls of Lola's room. It's a large square space with a bed in one corner and a beautiful polka-dot teepee in the other. She'd bought it last Christmas from a hideously expensive toy boutique, and Lola had slept on cushions inside it for a week. Now it's filled with all her teddies.

'It's like, if I stand here, I can still feel her in the air, and I don't want to go in and disturb it.' His voice breaks, and she reaches for him.

They hold each other for a long moment before Roly pulls away.

'I'm sorry about Mother,' he says in a quiet voice. 'I know I should ask her to leave, and it's completely crazy that she's here talking to the detectives, but I don't know how to tell her to go. She's Lola's grandmother.'

'I know it's hard,' she is careful to reply, wanting him to see she understands, but they don't have a choice. 'But, Roly, what if she finds out about... what we did? We could lose everything.'

'She won't find out,' he hisses. 'We've come this far, haven't we? We're good parents, Iz.'

She wants to push him again. Margaret is smart and astute. One wrong question, one comment is all it would take for the world they've built to fall apart. Not to mention the lingering suspicion that Margaret is up to something. Would she really not want to involve the press because of the Huntington name? Is that more important than her own grandchild? But then what else is going on? Maybe her and Roly really do believe Lola is being held for a ransom. A chance for someone to get their hands on Roly's trust fund and Margaret's money too.

Roly sighs, and the look of desperation makes her stop. She won't win this battle. Roly knows the risks with Margaret finding out the truth as well as she does, maybe more even. Besides, there is something else she needs to ask him.

'Roly,' she says, watching his face as she finds the words. She didn't make a second call in the bathroom just now, but she knows Roly will have done it. 'What's Jonny going to do?'

He glances behind her, checking Margaret isn't coming up the stairs, no doubt. 'Let me call him now.' He beckons Isobel into the living room and closes the door before pulling out his phone and putting it on speaker as it starts to ring.

'Chum,' Roly says in his usual greeting when Jonny answers, as though he's about to invite his friend for a round of golf. 'I've got Isobel here too,' he adds. 'What's going on?'

'Nothing right now, mate. I'm doing everything I can,' Jonny replies in his usual brusque tone. 'But look, I'm sorry, I need to go. I'm right in the middle of this, but I'll be in touch very soon. Trust me, she won't get away. I'll get you your daughter back.'

He's gone before Isobel can say a word.

'What does he mean, everything he can?' She shivers,

hugging her arms to her body and feeling torn between wanting
to know and wishing she didn't.

'You know what it means.' Roly gives her a pointed look,
and she fights back the urge to cry.

'Why is he helping us?'

'Because he's my friend, Iz. He probably feels a bit responsible that it's come to this. I trust him, though, and you should
too.'

Does she have a choice?

Isobel remembers so vividly the first time she heard of
Jonny. It was the same day she met Roly. He'd burst into her
office, halfway into a conversation with her before their eyes
had even met. *'Now look,'* Roly had said. *'I have a friend who
needs a bit of help with his business. He's a good egg, Bobby. I
told him you'd help. And before you say you're too busy, you owe
me for that lap dancer thing I covered up for you.'*

She had raised her eyebrows. *'What lap dancer thing?'* she'd
asked, wondering what kind of dirt this blond hulking man
who'd strolled into her office like he owned it had on her boss.

'Oh, you're not Bobby,' Roly had said with a bemused smile.
He'd looked back to the door, reading her name in silver lettering. *'Not Bobby at all. I do apologise.'*

He'd held her gaze as he'd started to back away, and she
could've let him go, carried on with the accounts for the Dubai
businessman she'd been working on all morning, but she'd been
more than a little amused at the prospect of picking a handsome
stranger's brains and getting one up on her boss in the process.

'Don't worry about it.' She'd smiled. *'Maybe I can help your
friend? I'm better at my job than Bobby, although don't tell him I
said that.'*

Roly had grinned. *'Your secret is safe with me. How about
we discuss this over lunch? I'm positively parched.'*

Their lunch had rolled into cocktails and then dinner, and
in between talking about themselves, he'd told her about Jonny.

'He's one of those with fingers in every pie. He's built a... er... property portfolio, shall we say. He wants some help keeping the tax man happy. Needs everything transparent and all that.'

Isobel had been happy to take on the work. Keeping track of cash payments. 'From my landlords,' Jonny had explained in their first meeting, giving her a wolfish smile that made his eyes shine. He wasn't classically good-looking like Roly, but there was something about him. She could see he wouldn't be short of dates, although Roly had told her he was picky and careful with whom he trusted.

She and Roly had married the following year in the little chapel on the Huntington estate, and when they'd first had trouble conceiving, Roly had suggested she give up her job, only keeping Jonny on because he was Roly's friend and because she enjoyed the work, and if Isobel was honest with herself, because a part of her knew Jonny was a man you didn't say no to.

She'd known, of course, that it wasn't all above board the moment she'd seen the fluctuating cash payments and the PO box addresses and named directors who were just that – names. A landlord paying a letting agent. The agent paying a cleaning firm. All businesses owned by Jonny. All money zigzagging back to him.

She didn't know the full extent of Jonny's businesses, although he'd once let slip that drugs were involved. But she didn't need to know any more to do her job. She'd always liked it that she was important to him. In this world of wealth and privilege where Margaret, and sometimes even Roly, looked at her like she didn't belong, Jonny had made her feel like she'd mattered.

It was at one of Jonny's dinner parties where Isobel had shared a smile with the missing woman, Scarlett. Maybe that's the real reason the disappearance had got under her skin. The secret knowledge she held about a businessman who earned his money doing bad things they all pretended not to see. Trying not to wonder if the bad things included making women disappear.

Roly tucks his phone into his pocket, and Isobel pushes the memory of Jonny aside. Maybe it's best not to know what he's planning. All that matters is that she gets Lola back. She catches the time on the clock on the wall, surprised it's only ten thirty. Not even lunchtime. It feels more like midnight. Like they've lived a whole day in just a few hours.

'I think I might have a quick nap,' Roly says after a pause, as though he too is feeling drained from the talk with the detective and the worry about Lola. 'I didn't sleep well last night. I don't know if I'll be able to sleep now, but I can't think straight. You should too. You look—'

She shakes her head. 'Don't.'

'I was going to say exhausted. You know you have to ignore Mother. I've told you, she doesn't mean what she says.'

She does, Isobel is quite sure, but she lets it go too. Exhaustion doesn't come close to how she's feeling right now. She thinks about climbing into bed beside Roly. But what kind of mother would that make her? To sleep while her daughter is missing.

'I think I'll go for a walk on the common. I need some fresh air.'

'OK.' Roly kisses her cheek. 'We'll get her back, Iz.'

She offers him a small smile and wishes she could feel the same certainty he does. But then, everything has always worked out for Roly. The right school, the right family name, the right connections. Always enough money. No one stands in the way of that.

She watches him disappear into their bedroom and lets the guilt overwhelm her. As much for Lola as the other secrets she's keeping. Isobel places her hands on her abdomen, feeling a new softness where toned skin had been. If she closes her eyes, she can remember the tiny weight of her daughter in her arms. That first moment when a wriggling, bloody body had been placed on her chest and she'd burst into tears and kissed the soft downy white hair on her Lola's head.

It hadn't been easy. Months of fear – that constant worry that something would go wrong. And so much of that time spent housebound too. And before that, all the disappointments. She knew what people thought. That she'd left it too late to find love and start a family, not meeting Roly until her mid-thirties when her career was well-established. They were wrong. Aren't they always? She'd tried dating, searching for the elusive 'one', but until Roly stepped into her office that day with his blond hair and teasing half-smile, she'd thought herself unlovable or perhaps unable to love.

After the whirlwind romance and the wedding at the little church on the Huntington estate, and the honeymoon on the private island in the Caribbean, they'd started trying straight away. Roly had wanted a child just as much as she had. A Huntington heir, as Margaret so loved to say. Trying and trying. Fun at first. Then not as the months rolled into a year. Roly pretended he was fine, but he didn't understand that the forces of nature didn't bend to his will. Then being poked and prodded and tested. Worn down by failure.

'It's highly unlikely you'll ever conceive,' a doctor had told them after another failed round of IVF. Her fifth cycle. It had left her body feeling swollen, hormonal and not her own.

But then a miracle had happened. The most precious gift – her daughter. It should've been the happiest time of her life. Except all those months being stuck at home alone, quitting her job in the city and keeping Jonny as a client. Because he trusted her and she didn't know how to quit. Plus she'd owed him by that point. He'd been right beside them in all the things they did to get their perfect family.

She'd been so isolated. Worrying constantly that something

would go wrong. Until that worry had latched on to her, burrowing deep into her core, making her constantly anxious. She'd tried to ignore it. To tell herself it would be easier after the birth, but it wasn't. If anything, having her daughter in the world made it worse. The fierce need to protect her from harm, the fear of all that could go wrong now that she finally had the perfect family after everything they'd done, added to her anxiety. It created a dark foreboding that was never far from her thoughts. Some days it got so bad she couldn't leave the house.

Isobel touches her stomach again now as she moves to the stairs. Things will be so different this time. If she can just get Lola home safe, she'll be different, she swears it.

FOURTEEN

ISOBEL

Isobel finds Margaret in the kitchen, sipping a cup of hot water and lemon. She has a leather diary open in front of her, and an iPad open with the gridlines of a spreadsheet visible on the screen. She mutters to herself as Isobel steps into the room. 'This isn't right.'

'Is everything OK?' she asks. 'Do you want me to take a look?'

Margaret's hand flies out, shutting the tablet and closing the diary before Isobel has the chance to take another step. 'Oh, you'd love that, wouldn't you? No. You're not getting your hands on my money that easily.'

'I wasn't trying...' she starts to say. 'I was offering to help. Forget I asked.'

Isobel reaches for a glass and pours herself some water. 'I was thinking about Zeen. I tried to call her, but she didn't answer. I was wondering if you used an agency to find her. Perhaps they have another contact for her. It's so unlike her not to turn up to work.'

'I couldn't possibly remember. There may be some paperwork about her at the house, I suppose, but it will be years out of date. She's been with you how long? Three years?'

'Closer to four.'

'And you don't know any more about her?'

Margaret has turned this back on her. A classic move that Isobel has fallen for. The truth is Zeen has always been quiet. What does she really know about this woman who has been in and out of their house nearly every day since Lola was two months old? Nothing. 'I didn't hire her,' she replies, standing her ground.

'Leave this be, Isobel. If the police think Zeen is involved, they will find her. It's not your job to be digging into things that have nothing to do with you.'

Nothing to do with her? Except Zeen is her housekeeper. And Lola is her daughter. Isobel bites back a retort. There is no point arguing with this woman. She takes a sip of water. It's cold and fresh, and she suddenly feels more awake than she has done all day. When she turns back to Margaret, the woman is staring at her with her favourite narrow-eyed expression.

She points her index finger, tapping the countertop in the way that never fails to rile Isobel. 'There's something you're not telling me,' she says.

Isobel freezes, her heart jolting in her chest. There are so many things Margaret could be alluding to. Has she already guessed that they're both hiding something from her? She told Roly this would happen. This woman is no fool and even a sniff of what they did all those years ago and she'll be digging. Not stopping until she has the truth. 'I... don't know what you mean,' she lies, wondering if it's simpler than Margaret guessing the truth. Is the woman trying to change the subject from Zeen?

Her mother-in-law removes her glasses and fixes a steely gaze on her. 'Your problems. They're back?'

Isobel almost laughs at the woman's choice of the word 'problems' to describe the unbearable days of anxiety that kept

Isobel shut away in the house with Lola when she was little. Panic attacks that made her physically sick. It got so bad that Margaret stepped in and insisted on a nanny to help. Of course that made everything worse. But at least she hasn't guessed the truth.

'I'm worried about Lola. I think that's understandable,' Isobel replies.

'I heard you in the bathroom.'

Her cheeks flush. 'It's the anxiety,' she lies. 'But it's not like before.' Isobel is relieved Margaret has jumped to the wrong conclusion. It's no surprise. After the years of failure and then the miracle of Lola, Margaret would never expect her to fall pregnant, especially now she's forty-four. Even she didn't believe she could be pregnant at first. But she doesn't want Margaret to think the panic attacks are back either. If Roly's mother thinks she's struggling, she'll use it to undermine her even more than she already is.

'In fact, I'm going out to get some fresh air.' Isobel turns quickly, hurrying to the cupboard to find her trainers before pulling open the front door. She will tell Roly and Margaret about the pregnancy when she's ready. Isobel only has space in her head for Lola and what's happening right now.

Outside, the sun is struggling to push through billowy clouds and the expanse of the common is all but deserted. Isobel takes the tree-lined path that cuts through the centre of the grass, feeling out of place without a pushchair or a little hand to hold. She isn't sure she's ever walked the common without Lola.

'*Can we feed the ducks today, Mummy?*'

Fresh tears form in Isobel's eyes.

She walks to the opposite side of the green, to another road of houses just as grand as her own, before looping around the edge towards the pond. The fresh air helps. She feels more awake and less sick now she's out, putting one foot in front of the other.

She passes a woman with a floppy sunhat and a wagging-tailed dog. It looks like a poodle mixed with something, and exactly the kind of dog Lola always likes to stop and stroke.

'Can I, Mummy? Can I say hello? Can we get a dog? Please, please, please.'

Her feet stop dead as pain slices through her body. She misses Lola so much, she can't draw in her next breath.

'Excuse me.'

Isobel jumps, looking up to the face of the woman.

'Sorry,' the dog walker says. 'I didn't mean to make you jump. I just wanted to check you're OK.'

Isobel realises what a state she must look. Dishevelled and pale and crying too. She forces herself to nod. 'Yes. Thank you. I'm fine. Everything is fine.' She dips her head and keeps walking, hurrying now to be home. What if DCI Watkins has called with news and she's missed it?

The house is silent when she returns. There is no sign of Margaret in the kitchen now. She wonders if her mother-in-law has gone out on an errand or to lie down like Roly has. The Huntingtons do like their naps.

Isobel roams the house, room by room, unable to sit still. She feels like a ghost haunting a house that was once a home. Questions circle her thoughts like vultures. Where is Lola now? Why have the detectives not called? What will happen to her daughter?

She thinks of Roly's suggestion that Lola's abduction is a ransom. He thinks someone will call soon asking for money. Margaret was so quick to jump in with her own feelings on the press. That desire to keep their name out of the papers. She thinks of Margaret closing her tablet as she'd walked into the kitchen, her snappish reply to a question about Zeen. There is more going on here – Isobel is sure of it.

It feels wrong that the entire world is not searching for her daughter. She knows it's a risk, but maybe they can keep their secrets safe even with Lola's face on every newspaper in the country. When Roly wakes and DCI Watkins calls again, she'll push it. They can't carry on like this.

Isobel makes a decaf coffee she doesn't want just for something to do before finding herself in Lola's playroom with its soft-lilac and dark-teal walls, clashing with the red stripy rug on the floor and the colourful toy boxes stacked in a unit below the window.

'This room gives me a headache. I cannot be in here,' Margaret had declared as soon as she'd seen the changes they'd made. Another reason it's Isobel's favourite place in the house.

She curls up on the playroom sofa and turns on the TV just to hear the sound of voices that aren't in her head. She flicks to a news channel, wondering for a stupid moment if the police have ignored Margaret's demand for privacy. They could do that, couldn't they? They won't, she's certain, but the thought is still there, and with it the uncomfortable knowledge that they're not doing everything in their power to find Lola and bring her home.

'In other news,' the presenter is saying in a sombre voice, 'police have been searching woodland in the Chingford area of Essex today, searching for the body of Scarlett Peters, a missing woman from the Islington area of London, who has not been seen since leaving to meet a friend in West London on the night of the first of April, earlier this year.'

Isobel sits up so fast that coffee splashes onto her blouse. Her mind flashes again to the photo on the front page of the newspaper yesterday. Have they finally found something? She hates herself for caring when her own child is missing too, but this story has been under her skin for months. It feels different when you've met the person, even if it was just the once, and so brief.

'According to police sources, an anonymous tip has led police to search the woodland.'

The screen changes to another photo of Scarlett. She looks in her mid-to-late twenties and is wearing a black choker necklace and a silver sequined top. But it's the hair that Isobel stares at – long and dark red, like Julia Roberts in *Pretty Woman*. So distinctive. So memorable. The thought makes her shiver.

She thinks back to that one look across the room at Jonny's dinner party. Roly had drunk too much – another promise broken. It was just after the last round of failed IVF. She remembers because her clothes felt tight, her body bloated with hormones, her emotions a wreck. She'd told Roly she'd drive, knowing that alcohol would only send her spiralling into the dark heartbreak of her failure to conceive.

As the evening had worn on, Roly's endearing, jovial nature had tipped towards idiotic. And the louder he'd become, the quieter she'd been, sitting back and watching the guests and counting down the hours before they could go.

She'd looked across the table, hoping to see someone standing to leave so they could follow without being the first and risking upsetting Jonny. It was then that Scarlett had caught her eye. She'd smiled with deep-red lips that should've clashed with her hair but somehow didn't. It was a 'we're in this together' smile, and Isobel had looked to the man beside Scarlett, seeing he was just as drunk as Roly. She and Roly left ten minutes later, Roly staggering towards the car, telling her over and over how much he loved her.

That look she shared with Scarlett had been a nothing moment Isobel could so easily have forgotten, but it's been replaying in her head for months, ever since that first news story broke. And no matter how many times she told herself it was nothing to do with them and the events that keep her awake at night – the ones that she and Roly pretend didn't happen, the bad things they did – she still found herself wondering if Scarlett's disappearance was somehow connected to Jonny and, through him, to them.

Her head spins with her past and the present nightmare. Isobel snatches up the remote, and with a shaking hand, she plunges the room back into silence. Tears well in her eyes, fat and hot as they roll down her face. There is more they should be doing to find Lola. The guilt is a dead weight pulling and pressing, always there. She will not be able to live with herself if anything happens to Lola because of the decisions she's made. She will not be able to live without Lola.

'We'll get her back, Iz.'

Roly is so sure. She wishes she could feel the same. Her shoulders slump, defeated, exhausted. Her breathing snags in her throat and she sobs, a loud, anguished sound.

Please, please, please let Lola be OK.

FIFTEEN

EMMA

What is she going to do without a car? The question echoes through Emma's mind. No answer comes. What the hell are they going to do?

She looks down at Lola. Her little girl's blonde hair is windswept from their run earlier, her face still streaked with the remnants of her tears. All morning, and all day yesterday, Emma has jollied her daughter along, promised treats and safety and adventure just to get them to this place. And now it's all gone wrong. She has failed Lola again. She couldn't stop those people from being her parents for nearly four years, and when she finally does something about it, she can't keep her safe.

A mounting sense of panic and dread build up and up inside her. She can't do it. She can't do this alone. Emma pulls out her phone and stares at the blank screen. She wants so badly to call for help.

'Memorise my number. Don't write it down anywhere. Don't save it in the new phone. There can be nothing that connects us so don't contact me.'

'Why do I need to memorise your number if I can't call you?'

Emma had asked, feeling out of her depth. Their plan had seemed easy when that's all it had been. But as they'd taken those first tentative steps – booking the caravan, borrowing Haz's brother's car – it hadn't felt easy. It had felt impossible. She'd ignored her worries, squished them down to a dark corner in her mind, telling herself the plan would work. Finally, she had a chance of a new life with her daughter.

'It's just in case. Don't contact me until you've got Lola somewhere safe or it's an absolute emergency. Life or death! And message. Don't call.'

'You think it's going to go wrong,' Emma had said, unsure if it was a question or an observation.

'Of course not. I've planned for everything. But I can't help you until you're out of the country. I won't be able to do anything while you're on the run.'

'I know,' she'd replied with more confidence than she should have done. *'I can do it alone.'*

Life or death.

Emma wonders if this is it and knows it's not. They are not caught yet. They're not even being chased despite her earlier fears about the man on the bus. But the plan for their escape feels suddenly far away and utterly impossible. What is she going to do without that car? She'd thought they'd planned for everything, but already it's falling apart.

The ferry leaves tonight at ten thirty, and they still have hundreds of miles to travel to reach the port. There's no way they'll make it without the car. No way they can leave the country tonight. And... and if they can't leave, it means... Emma's thoughts tumble towards her new reality at the same speed as her racing heart. The police will find Malik's car on the quiet lane, if they haven't done so already. They'll trace her movements to the caravan park, the bus, here. And then there's Jonny. He'll be looking for her too. There is no way they can make it across the country and to the ferry port without a car, and no way they can stay on the run for another day without being caught.

'Emma, where's the car?' Lola's voice drags her back to the road.

'It's not here,' she says, and even though Emma knows she has the right place, knows the car isn't here, she still finds herself stepping closer, hoping she's wrong.

There's a large Road Closed sign sitting in the middle of the street in front of the two orange barriers. For a second, the worst moment, Emma wonders if it could be Jonny. Did he somehow find out their plan and get ahead of her? Did he set this up? A trap she'll blindly walk into just like the last time.

No. Jonny and the friends he uses to help him are sneaky. They're black SUVs with tinted windows pulling up beside her. They're strong hands snatching. Blink and you'll miss it. He is coercive. Talking her into things without her realising. Even convincing her that destroying her life, obliterating her dreams, had been her idea.

'I'll be watching, Emma. Remember that. I'm always watching.'

This – here – is busy and noisy. There are workmen in orange safety wear beside a cement lorry with the mixer on the back. Lola pulls her hand out of Emma's and covers her ears to the sound of a jackhammer drill. Emma wants to do the same and thinks of the hand dryers in the toilets at the services. Was that only yesterday?

They've reached the barriers now, and Emma can see the drill and the broken-up concrete. She sees it all. All except the small burgundy Ford that was supposed to be here waiting for her.

'Get to Vale Road in north Crawley on Monday. I'll leave the car there for you. It's a residential street with lots of cars parked on it, so no one will notice an extra one.'

'Can't you leave it at the caravan park?'

'It's too risky. We have to be careful, remember? They're smart. All cars are parked beside the caravans. It will look suspicious if I leave it somewhere in the area. Someone might think it's an abandoned vehicle and call the police. Besides, we don't know how quickly they'll find the dumped car. If they track you to the caravan, someone might remember the licence plate and then they'll have you on the traffic cameras in minutes. This way, it's not connected to you, is it? Anyone who looks twice at the car on the residential street will just think one of their neighbours has a visitor. It'll be easy for you to get a bus to Crawley first thing in the morning. You'll be out of the country that night.'

'And what about you?'

'Don't worry, Em. It's like I said – I'll meet you in Belfast.'

Her fingers tighten around the useless key fob in her pocket.

'You all right, miss?'

Emma jumps, grabbing Lola's hand too fast, too tight, as she turns to face the voice. It's one of the workmen. He has a long wiry beard, the hair scraggly and a mix of ginger and brown. Beneath it is a young face, not much older than she is, with friendly eyes.

'My car,' she says above the drilling, the desperation blocking her throat.

'Oh no,' he cries out with genuine dismay. 'Was it parked on this road this morning?'

She nods, fighting back tears.

'Sorry, miss. The notices have been up for weeks. Anything here at five a.m. this morning was towed away. We're laying a new water pipe network across the whole area. It's been on the calendar for months.'

She bites her lower lip, trying to hold it together, but it's too much, and her eyes brim with tears. She wishes so badly she could take the plan back, like the cross-stitch patterns she'd get in her Christmas stocking every year, unpicking the thread and starting over any time she made a mistake.

'Hey hey,' the workman says with a cheery smile at Lola before looking back to Emma. 'It won't be too hard to get your car back. It'll be at the impound.' You only need your driver's licence and they can look up your car.' He pauses, pulling another face. 'Might be a fee though.'

'Thanks,' she whispers. 'I'll do that.' She won't of course. She can't. Her name and driver's licence aren't connected to the car. That was the whole point.

She turns around, taking Lola's hand again, and they start walking back towards the town.

'I'm tired,' Lola says.

'I'm tired too. I'm so sorry, Lola. The car has gone.'

'My present?'

She nods. 'It was in the car. I'm sorry, Lola. We can get you a new present.'

Lola falls silent, but Emma can feel the weight of her daughter's sadness on her shoulders, pulling at her along with the backpack she's been carrying all morning. When they're around the corner, away from the noise and the watching eyes, she sinks to the edge of the pavement and pats the space beside her. Lola plonks herself down and takes off her backpack to stroke Ducky's head.

'Let's rest for a minute and have a snack,' Emma says, unzipping the front pocket of her bag and wishing she had the cereal bars and sweets and stash of food sitting in the boot of the car, alongside all the other things they need – more clothes, toiletries, money. All she has with her is a Wispa bar, warm and soft.

The chocolate is sticky goo, but the sugar helps. Emma draws in her five-count breath and exhales slowly. She can't break down with Lola relying on her. But her head is spinning with a hundred racing thoughts and questions. How close are the police? How close is Jonny to finding them? She can't think about him. She can't let him get into her head again or she'll panic, make mistakes. That's what he wants. Out of nowhere, his laugh fills her head. That callous sound when she'd told him she thought it had been love.

'You're more stupid than I thought you were then.'

She cuts the thought dead. No! She won't allow him in. She's spent years trying to keep him out of her thoughts; keeping her life small and unnoticeable so he wouldn't come back. She can't let him win now. She is Lola's mother. Only she can save them.

Her eyes draw to the empty residential street, and she wonders again if hers and Lola's faces are on the front pages of every newspaper in the country. If they haven't figured out who she is yet, they surely will soon.

'What we need,' she says, dropping a kiss on top of her daughter's head, 'is a new plan.'

'Like Daddy Pig when he lost his car keys.'

'Exactly.'

'Miss Rabbit took him to work in her helicopter.'

Emma manages a smile and hands the last of the chocolate to Lola. This is what she knows: no matter what, they need to leave the country. It's the only way they'll be safe. Which means they have to get to the ferry port near Liverpool. It's nearly two hundred miles to travel, and they're being chased by a monster who wants to kill them both and the police who will only delay the inevitable.

Deep breath in. Long exhale.

They need to keep one step ahead and hidden, which means staying away from main towns and cities and CCTV as much as possible. The journey ahead of them will be slower. It's already midmorning. They won't make it all the way to Liverpool today.

But they might make it tomorrow.

'Breathe, Em. Remember to breathe.'

They'll need supplies – all the things in the boot of the car they can't access. Food, clothes and, most importantly, money. She thinks of the cash in her purse. Fifty pounds. Not enough to stay anywhere tonight. Plus the cost of travel, food, water. Plus the ferry tickets. Thank God she's got the passports in her backpack.

Her pulse starts to race with the impossibility of what she's doing.

She'll have to use her only-for-absolute-emergencies bank card that's zipped in a hidden pocket in her backpack. It's dangerous. If they've figured out who she is already, then they'll be monitoring everything. The moment she slots the card into the cash machine, an alert will be sent. They'll know exactly where she is. They'll be able to track her on CCTV, follow her every move. They'll be on her in minutes. Sirens and road-blocks. Her pulse quickens.

Emma remembers stepping off the bus earlier and the vape man she'd thought was following them. Trying to run with their backpacks and Lola's little legs. She can't outrun anyone, least of all the police. Another wave of loneliness hits her; cavernous, all-consuming and sickeningly familiar. She longs for Haz to sit down beside her, take her hand and tell her it's all going to be fine.

She pulls out the phone, and before she can stop herself, she's calling him again. Ringing fills her ears. She waits for the click of the voicemail and to hear his voice, but instead the ringing stops early. 'Hello?'

She gasps, almost dropping the phone in her hurry to hang up. Haz is her best friend. Her only friend, but she'd expected his voicemail and the reassurance of the recording. Hearing that 'hello', she knows she can't really talk to him. Haz knows better than anyone that only she can save her daughter, but there is no way to explain all that she's doing now. No way for him to understand just how far she's gone.

She thinks of her family again. Her parents and brothers

with their small lives. They've never understood her dreams, and they certainly wouldn't understand this. She remembers phoning them from the hospital ward when the drugs had worn off and she'd been able to think clearly. They'd come the next day, clutching hands, wide-eyed. She'd told them everything – the truth of where she'd really been when she'd told them she was going to do volunteer work abroad. Lola. Jonny. Roly and Isobel. The words spilled out through angry, heaving sobs.

Her parents had been horrified. But then the staff had called them all into a meeting and used words like 'delusional' and 'breakdown', and her parents' horror had transformed to pity and mistrust. They hadn't believed her of course, and in the end, she stopped calling them.

The hospital released her eventually. Four months of daily counselling and being called a liar; forced medication and locked rooms. She thought she was free when they finally let her leave, but as she stepped out of the hospital, she found Jonny leaning casually against a wall, waiting for her.

'Have you learned your lesson?'

She nodded, unable to speak through the fear grabbing her in a chokehold. She'd glanced back to the rising floors of the hospital, wishing just one of those stupid doctors could see what was happening. *'There is a monster and he's right here,'* she'd wanted to shout.

'Good, because this is the one and only time I will say this.' He leaned towards her, so close his breath was hot in her ear. *'If you step out of line again, if you try to contact me or Lola or anyone connected to her, I'll kill you. I'll kill everyone you love, including Lola, and no one will even notice. So stay away from her and stay away from me. I'll be watching, Emma. Remember that. I'm always watching.'*

She'd run all the way to the Tube station and cried for the entire journey on the Northern Line, hating herself for ever being so stupid. Hating how easily she'd fallen for his gifts and his charm. How easily she'd trusted him. Hating Jonny too. And Isobel and Roly. Those people. They call themselves Lola's parents but they're no different from Jonny. Monsters, all of them.

She hadn't wanted to go back to her parents, but she had nowhere else to go. And so she climbed into her old single bed and tried to shut out the world. Her mum made her instant hot chocolates every afternoon, leaving them on the nightstand beside the bed. Only once did she sit down beside Emma, patting her leg. *'I'm afraid this is what comes from reaching too high, darling. You've burned out. You see that now, I'm sure. But you can still have a nice life. Just look at us. We're happy with our lot.'* And even though Emma hadn't thought it possible, she'd felt the emptiness in her balloon, engulfing the last vestiges of her dreams.

A month after coming home, her dad called in a favour with one of the clients whose vans he fixed and got her a Saturday job working at a florist on the high street. She dragged herself out of bed at first, barely able to put one foot in front of the other. But the work had helped, the tranquillity of being around flowers all day – that sweet earthy smell – and she'd been grateful when she'd been offered more hours.

Giving her notice last month was harder than she'd thought it would be, and she'd cried on her last day. But she hadn't told her parents. She'd left a note on the kitchen table last week, telling them she was leaving but not to worry, sneaking out of the house before dawn. She hadn't wanted to lie like the last time she left, spinning a story of travelling the world when really she was only a few miles away in another part of London.

Emma feels a sudden stab of guilt. The police will be knocking on her parents' door as soon as they figure out it's her who's taken Lola. She hates that they'll have to go through an interrogation, endless questions, but what choice did she have? She isn't sure she'll ever see her mum and dad again. Despite

how distanced she's always felt from her family, the thought is
unnerving and squeezes her chest tight. She looks down at Lola.
There is melted chocolate smeared on her fingers and around
her lips. Emma smiles and pulls out a wipe. This here, her love
for her little girl, is all that matters. It is her job to keep her safe.

Emma stands then, brushing off her leggings and her disappointment; pasting on a wide smile. 'Let's get cracking,' she
says.

'Where are we going?' Lola asks, and Emma is grateful that
her voice is curious rather than sad.

'Well, that's a good question. The answer is – I don't know.'
Lola giggles at that, and it makes Emma laugh too. 'Adults are
supposed to know everything, aren't they?'

Her little girl gives a firm nod of agreement. 'My daddy
knows everything.'

A flash of Roly's giant frame elbows to the forefront of her
mind. That voice – too posh and too ridiculous to be fake.

'We're her parents, not you. You're no one to her.'

She shuts it down. She won't allow those memories in.

She is Lola's mother. She knows she is.

'I think he just pretends. Grown-ups are good at pretending. What I do know is that we're still going on an adventure,
and I will keep you safe.'

'From the monster?' Lola asks, and there is a wobble this
time.

'That's right,' she replies as the guilt returns – a hard knot in
her stomach. 'We need to be smart and very careful so they
won't get us. But we can do that, can't we? We can be brave
warriors.'

'Like Mulan? She was a warrior.'

'Yes,' Emma says, grinning, remembering the fierceness and
determination of the Disney character.

Lola slips her bag onto her back and holds out her hand for
Emma to take. 'I like Mulan. We can walk now.'

Emma leans down, kissing the top of her head, and wishes she felt half as brave as Lola.

They start to walk. Slowly now, giving Emma time to plan. She needs money, which means she has to use her bank card. But then they'll need to disappear because if the police already have her name then they'll be on her in minutes. It will be the same frantic run from the services yesterday, except there is no element of surprise, no head start. This time, they'll be waiting for her.

SIXTEEN

ISOBEL

Something has woken her. The thought floats lazily across Isobel's mind. She stretches. Her neck is stiff as she moves; her hand knocks against one of the sofa cushions. She draws in a long yawn, and feels the emptiness of sleep pulling her back into its depths and the dream she was having about Scarlett Peters. They were at a party in Jonny's house, and it was so busy. Lola was there too, and she kept losing sight of her. Pushing through the crowds, calling her name, seeing a flash of her before she'd disappear again.

Isobel is so very tired, but she's not in her bed. The thought is strange enough to keep sleep at bay, and even though it wasn't a nightmare, the dream was unpleasant. She doesn't want to return to it.

There's a noise – a chiming bing-bong. The doorbell. That's what woke her. The remnants of sleep disappear for good. Her eyes fly open. Reality crashes in like the propulsive explosion of a bomb detonating. Lola. Lola is gone.

How long was she asleep? What's happening? The speed of the questions is as dizzying as the sudden movement as she leaps up. She's about to call out to Zeen, to ask her to answer the door, but remembers her housekeeper isn't here. She must try to call her again. Isobel wishes there was an explanation for Zeen's absence, but the more hours that pass, the stranger it is that she's not here.

She reaches for her phone and checks the time. It's only 1 p.m. She's barely been asleep an hour. Time is moving slowly and yet every hour that passes feels like a tightening vice around her chest. She must speak to Roly about involving the press. The world is continuing to turn outside these walls, but people have no idea her daughter is missing.

She has a sudden urge to call Jonny herself. To plead and beg and shout, to tell him that whatever he's doing, he needs to do more. It's his fault Lola is gone as much as it is theirs. Hers.

It's been nearly twenty-four hours since the roadside services and Lola being snatched from them. Surely if there was going to be a ransom demand they'd have had it by now? No. This is something else. Dark scenarios crowd her mind. Things that should be unimaginable but are told in shocking news stories far too often. It can't happen to Lola. Not her precious daughter. Her whole reason for existing. She won't think about it. All she can focus on is getting Lola home safe.

'Iz?' Roly's voice shouts from somewhere in the house, and thoughts of Zeen and calling Jonny are pushed aside. Floorboards creak above her. 'Can you get that?'

'I am,' she calls back as she rushes down the hall, smoothing out her hair and checking her earrings before straightening her top.

The front door is heavy wood and set in a frame with narrow windows on either side, but she doesn't stop to see who is on her doorstep as she yanks at the handle and the door flies back. Her daughter's name is on her lips, her gaze already looking down to where Lola would be if she was there, cuddling

Barnaby in her arms; her face lighting up at the sight of her mother.

The space is empty. Isobel's gaze moves to the path beyond, before settling on DCI Watkins, alone on the doorstep. The sight makes her heart stutter in her chest. Fear and sadness wash over her, all-consuming.

'DCI Watkins,' she says. 'Come in.'

Be good news! She repeats the words twice more in her head as the detective steps through the doorway just as Roly is hurrying down the stairs.

'What's happening?' he asks, reaching his arm around Isobel's waist. His hair is damp at the edges, and he smells of soap from a recent shower. She leans into his warmth, feeling unsteady, half-broken.

Please let Lola be OK.

'Have you found her?' she asks, her voice suddenly too high.

'No, but I do have news.'

'What is it?' she asks at the same time as Margaret's voice carries from the kitchen doorway.

'Don't just stand there then. Let's be civilised and sit down, shall we?'

Isobel feels a scream build inside her once more. She does not want to be civilised. She wants to shout and cry and plead with this police officer to find her daughter. But Roly is already waving DCI Watkins down the hall. Isobel closes the front door before following them into the kitchen. Margaret resumes her seat at the counter and motions for them all to sit down around the large island.

'I hope you feel better after your sleep, Isobel,' she says with an arched eyebrow as though echoing Isobel's own disbelief that she could sleep when her daughter is missing.

'Yes,' is all she can think to say. If the detective wasn't here, she might have pointed out that Roly slept too. Lola's father.

Her son. Why is he allowed to sleep without comment, but she is not?

'You look better for it at least.' Her eyes fix on Isobel and it's as though she's saying with that look, *'You're hiding something from me.'* Isobel turns away and sits beside Roly.

DCI Watkins looks as though he'd rather stand, but he eventually pulls out a stool too. She wonders how many times he's knocked on a door like this and updated a family about a loved one. How many times they've screamed and shouted. How many times he promised their safe return.

'We'll find Lola.'

How many times the promise was broken.

'I have several things to tell you,' DCI Watkins begins, leaning his forearms on the counter, looking every bit as focused and in control as a detective should. His gaze moves from Isobel to Roly and then Margaret. 'Since our conversation earlier this morning, the investigation has progressed.'

'How?' Isobel asks, willing him to speak faster. The detective is so calm, every word so measured. She wants to leap up, grab him by his shoulders and shake the information out of him.

'We've connected one of the names Roly gave us this morning to Malik Kahn, the registered owner of the car that was used to abduct Lola. We were able to speak to Malik an hour ago. He'd just landed from a business trip in Dubai and called as soon as he got our messages. He confirmed that the car is his but that he'd loaned it to a friend of his brother's. His brother is Hussain Kahn, known as Haz. Do you recognise the name?'

They shake their heads.

'Malik confirmed that the friend is one of the names on the list.'

'Is this a game of Guess Who?' Margaret snaps suddenly. 'Or are you going to tell us who exactly has taken my grandchild?'

Isobel thinks she catches a flash of tension tightening across the detective's jaw, but his reply when he speaks is just as calm. 'We believe the woman in the services yesterday and the person responsible for Lola's abduction is Emma Jacobs.'

'No.' The word is loud and echoes around the kitchen. It takes Isobel a beat to realise it came from her. 'After all this time... I thought... I thought she'd moved on.'

She looks to Roly. He is staring at her with wide disbelieving eyes that mirror her own. She blinks away the tears, but one escapes, rolling in a line down her face until she wipes it away.

'Is someone going to explain to me who this Emma Jacobs is and what she wants with Lola? Roly?' Margaret asks.

A silence settles over the kitchen. DCI Watkins raises his eyebrows as though he's also asking the question. Isobel was in the kitchen making coffee earlier this morning when Roly gave the names of anyone connected to them. She's surprised he gave Emma's. He's always refused to talk about what happened.

'Roland?' Margaret's tone is harsh, making him jump.

'Mother,' he says, the word coming on an exhale so he sounds a little breathless. A little panicked. He looks from her to the detective. 'Emma is...' He pauses, struggling to find the words. He glances at Isobel, but she can't help either. How can they describe everything that happened?

'She is...' Roly tries again. 'I mean, she was... our... our nanny,' he says at last. 'She was here in the house when Lola was a newborn.'

Roly finds his stride then and carries on, and the way he speaks makes Isobel realise he's not forgotten about that time at all.

'She was great at first. Doing whatever we needed. She was a second pair of hands as Isobel recovered and found her feet. But then she developed a bit of an... obsession, I guess you'd call it, with Lola, and we had to ask her to leave. She caused us a bit of trouble after that. She came back to the house a few times until we got the police involved. Then it all went quiet. We haven't seen her for years. It was so long ago I almost didn't tell you about her this morning.'

DCI Watkins slides his phone across the table. 'Using the ANPR information from the whereabouts of the car in Cornwall last week, we were able to find this CCTV footage.'

The three of them lean forward and watch the images play. It's her and Roly and Lola strolling together along the quaint and narrow high street of St Ives. Lola is in the middle, holding a hand each, and she's laughing at something Roly is saying.

They are so crystal clear that Isobel gasps at how perfect they look. They pass the camera, and a few seconds go by before another figure comes into view. It's a young woman with long brown hair flowing from under a black baseball cap. Recognition is a bullet shooting straight into Isobel's chest. Her throat closes. Not enough air.

'Yes, that's Emma.' Her hands fly up to cover her mouth.

Bile burns the back of her throat, and she's sure that if there was anything in her stomach right now, she'd be heaving it up.

Emma has her child.

This is bad. So very bad.

'Why on earth would this woman do this?' Margaret asks. 'What does she think she's doing?'

'I have no idea,' Roly mutters.

Isobel drops her hands and shoots him a look. 'Isn't it obvious?'

'She doesn't still think...' Roly's voice trails off. 'She's not still...'

'Of course she does,' Isobel half shouts, unable to wait a second longer for Roly to find the words. She looks first to DCI Watkins and then to Margaret, breathing through the jagged lump in her throat and swallows. 'Emma Jacobs is the nanny you wanted us to hire, Margaret, remember? When Lola was born and you didn't think I could cope?'

The words fly out. Margaret's mouth gapes. She looks as though Isobel has slapped her.

'Emma is completely crazy, and she thinks she's Lola's mother.'

SEVENTEEN

ISOBEL

Isobel stares at Roly. She's waiting to see if he'll say anything else about Emma's time nannying for them and how he'll do it without talking about Jonny and everything they did. Shock is pulling at Margaret's features, distorting the composed, unflappable expression Isobel is so used to. In that moment she looks old and just a little frail.

Roly has said more than she expected – peeling off the lid to a poisonous can of worms. Emma was their nanny, hired at Margaret's insistence they have help. She did become obsessed with Lola, but there is so much more lurking in their past.

'I cannot possibly understand why I'm only just hearing about this now,' Margaret says, and it's clear from the clipped tone she usually reserves for the staff at Huntington Hall that she's recovered her composure. 'If my grandchild was in danger, I should've been informed.'

Of course she's making it about her. Isobel wills Roly to stand up to his mother. It's so rare that he does. His need to please this woman is woven into his DNA, and the more time he spends in her presence, the worse it becomes. She's sure Margaret knows this too, and it's one of the many reasons she drops by for visits so often, always outstaying her welcome. Isobel tries to calm the hot anger racing through her blood. They can't keep doing this.

'We didn't want to worry you.' Roly's voice is quiet as he lies to his mother.

'Well, that may be, but as you are fully aware, I always prefer to be in the know. And might I just add that we would not be in this situation right now if Lola was at St Martin's where myself and the school staff could keep a careful eye on her.'

'Margaret!' Isobel cries out. Her mother-in-law is lashing out, angry and maybe even hurt at being the last to know, but Isobel doesn't care. Her words find their mark. She has simultaneously told her that she isn't a fit mother, while also suggesting a three-year-old child would be better off at a boarding school than with her parents.

'Mother, please,' Roly sighs, rubbing the back of his neck. 'I've told you, Isobel and I will discuss St Martin's when Lola has turned four. Now can we please talk about this later?'

Four?

The smallest noise escapes Isobel's throat. A yelp too quiet for anyone to notice as Roly and Margaret continue to bicker about Lola's schooling. Isobel tunes it out. She is sure what little colour she has in her cheeks has drained away as Roly's words sink in. He can't really be thinking of sending Lola away? Never! Not after everything they went through to have her. And especially not after this. She is so young. So precious. She needs her mother. She needs Isobel.

'Lola is four in a couple of weeks,' Isobel says, her voice quiet now. This is madness. Are they really arguing about schools when Lola might not come home? 'She already has her school place for September. There's nothing to talk about.'

'All I'm saying—' Margaret says.

'All you're saying...' Isobel cuts in, her voice shaking with a quiet fury directed at her husband and his mother in equal measure.

She loves Roly beyond words. Why else would she turn a blind eye to all the secrets he thinks he keeps from her? The women. The business investments. Not to mention how weak he is with Margaret. But Lola is her priority. When she is home safe, there is no way on this earth Isobel will allow her daughter to be sent away.

If you ever see her again. The voice whispering in her head is taunting. She won't listen.

'... is that you don't think I'm a fit mother,' Isobel continues. 'Has it ever occurred to you, Margaret, that my anxiety about something happening to Lola, my "problems" as you like to call them, all stemmed from Emma being in our house, which would never have happened if you hadn't insisted that we hire a nanny?'

It's only half true. Isobel's anxiety started with her struggles to conceive, but she wants her mother-in-law to share in this guilt.

'Darling.' Roly reaches out and squeezes her hand, and she's sure he's urging her to stop rather than offering comfort. 'We should talk about this later.' He looks at the detective. 'I'm sorry, DCI Watkins. Please continue.'

He gives a single nod. 'How long was Emma your nanny for?'

'Only a few weeks.'

'Two months,' Isobel corrects. The nausea returns, an acrid bitterness to the back of her throat. As if she could ever forget that time.

She'd been so excited about the birth and having a baby at last. She'd been worried – what new mother wouldn't after all they'd been through? – but she'd been coping. Until Margaret had got involved.

'*Of course you must have help,*' she'd told Roly. '*My grand-*

daughter is a Huntington heiress and should have the best. Get on it, please, Roland.'

And so they'd hired Emma. Young but capable and so caring towards Lola. She wasn't just another pair of hands for the night feeds and the nappy explosions; she was company too when Roly was out entertaining clients all hours of the day and evenings.

Every afternoon in those early weeks, Isobel and Emma would put Lola into her pushchair and walk the common, burning off the baby weight and the fog of sleepless nights. Despite their differences and the employer–employee awkwardness they both pretended wasn't there, Isobel had thought of Emma as a friend. Right up until she'd overheard Emma that night when Lola was only two months old.

She'd been out at a work function of Roly's. A black-tie event that she'd loved dressing up for, finally able to wear one of her favourite dresses. But the night had been long and dull, the wine giving her a headache instead of a buzz. When Lola had woken in the early hours of the morning, crying for a feed, Isobel had already been awake, and even though Emma had offered to do all the night feeds, Isobel couldn't resist climbing out of bed and tiptoeing down the dark hallway to see her baby. In the glow of a nightlight, she'd seen Emma already in the nursery, scooping Lola into her arms, talking so softly that Isobel almost didn't catch the words. Almost.

'Shush now, my baby girl. Mummy's here. I won't let anything bad happen to you.'

The words had stung – salt in an open wound – and she'd wanted to shout out, rush forward and snatch her daughter away, but it was like a hand had been covering her mouth, a body holding her back, and instead of doing those things, she'd moved silently back to her bed, lying awake as Emma's words had played over and over in her mind.

By morning, the shock had settled, and Isobel had told Roly.

He'd sent her out for a walk with Lola, and by the time she'd returned, Emma was gone. To this day, she doesn't know what Roly said to Emma, or what he told Margaret about the nanny she'd insisted he hire, but her mother-in-law had sent Zeen to work for them the following week – a housekeeper rather than a nanny – and Isobel had pushed thoughts of Emma to the back of her mind, certain she'd never see the girl again.

Until a few months later, when all the trouble had started.

'When did you last see her?' The detective's question drags Isobel from the memory. She looks to Roly, and he shrugs.

'We asked her to leave after a few months when it became obvious she'd developed strong feelings for Lola. I saw her again in the January a few months later. She was waiting for me on the common.'

'She tried to attack you, didn't she!' Roly jumps in. 'And take Lola.'

DCI Watkins fixes his eyes on Isobel, and she nods. 'Emma is dangerous,' she says as her vision blurs. She wipes at her eyes with a shaking hand. 'She believes she is Lola's mother. She also believes she is the only one who can save our daughter from some kind of monster only she can see. That day on the common, she was frantic and rambling. And she said... she said, she'd rather die and Lola die too than for the monster to get them.' A shiver races down Isobel's body. Goosebumps rage across her skin at the memory.

'It's been so many years, Iz. She can't still be obsessed with Lola.'

'You didn't see her that day,' Isobel replies. 'You didn't see how desperate she was.'

'Christ,' Roly sighs. 'I think she might try to harm Lola. If she's still obsessed with our daughter after all these years, then I don't think she'll ever let her go. If she can't have her... I don't know what she'll do.'

Fresh tears spill onto Isobel's cheeks. She squeezes Roly's

hand, wishing there was some reassurance she could offer. But there's nothing.

Roly puts an arm around Isobel, and she buries her head in his shoulder as old hurt and new battle to cause the most pain.

'Do we have any idea how long she's been planning this for?' he asks.

'Not yet,' DCI Watkins replies. 'It'll be one of the questions we ask when we have her in custody.'

When. Not if. Such confidence. It flutters through her, not able to settle. She tries to imagine Lola falling asleep last night without a kiss goodnight and an extra hug.

'*One more squeeze, Mummy. Squeezy pleasy.*'

'*An extra squeezy just because you said pleasy,*' Isobel would always reply, hugging her daughter tight one more time, breathing in the smell of strawberry bubble bath and the coconut detangling spray she used in Lola's hair.

The memory, the reality, they crush against her, squeezing her body and her chest until each breath feels shallow and strained. Lola is her whole world. If anything happens to her... She forces the thought back before it destroys her.

'We're monitoring ANPR and public transport in the area of the services,' DCI Watkins continues. 'Rest assured, modern technology makes it near impossible for anyone to completely disappear. She will slip up, and we will find her.'

A clawing desperation scratches beneath her skin. It's a fight not to rush down the hall and out of the front door, to pound the pavements and run and run and not stop until Lola is in her arms.

'What about the press?' Isobel looks from the detective to Roly then back again. 'You said this morning that we'd reconsider it in a few hours, and now we know it's not a ransom, don't we? Emma doesn't want money. She wants our daughter.'

'For what purpose?' Margaret asks. 'What is she going to do?'

'She's crazy,' Roly replies. 'Like Isobel said. She's probably got it in her head that she can run away with Lola. What worries me is what she'll do if she feels cornered or trapped. I don't think she'll let Lola go.'

'Which is why we need to find her now,' Isobel says. 'We need to go to the press.'

The detective nods. 'I agree. We can't wait any longer. I'll release a statement and photo of—' The trill of a ringtone cuts him short, and he picks up his phone. 'DCI Watkins.' He turns on the stool, putting his back to them so he faces out to the garden. The clouds have won, the sky a blanket of white-grey. 'Right... good work. Send me a recording of the footage.' He hangs up but doesn't turn back to them.

'What is it?' Margaret asks. Impatience carries in her voice, but the detective already has his phone to his ear again.

'Frank,' the detective says, 'we've got a location.'

The words cause a bolt of something to shoot through Isobel's body – electrical; charged. They know where Lola is right this second. Roly catches her eye. He smiles his lopsided smile, eyes shining with hope.

'It's going to be OK,' he whispers, kissing the top of her head.

DCI Watkins is silent for another moment and then: 'The withdrawal was two minutes ago... I've sent you the address... yes... yes... call me as soon as you get there.'

Finally the detective faces them, a broad smile stretching across his face. 'An hour ago, we placed an alert on all of Emma's social-media accounts, her emails, phone and bank card. We've got lucky. My cyber team tell me she's just withdrawn £250 from a petrol station in Crawley. We're getting the CCTV from the cash machine now.

'A local police unit is en route, and DI Gardner and his team are also on their way.'

'A police unit?' Roly looks stunned for a second. 'Just one?'

he adds, squeezing Isobel's hand again, reminding her that he is right beside her in this nightmare.

'DI Gardner is also on his way,' DCI Watkins repeats. 'And the cyber team can track her movements on CCTV in the area.'

Isobel's heart skips a beat. They've found them. They've found her daughter. *Please, please let her be OK.*

Even as she prays for her daughter, memories of that cold January day on the common circle her thoughts. Emma had been so desperate, acting so strangely, a shadow of the young woman who'd lived in their home. How far will she go to keep Lola to herself? Isobel is not sure of the answer, but she knows one thing with razor-sharp clarity – Lola is not safe with Emma.

EIGHTEEN

EMMA

Emma yanks the bank card free from the machine and tucks it into her back pocket. Her heart is pounding so hard it feels like her ribs will crack. 'Come on,' she whispers, staring at the money slot.

Have they stopped the transaction?

How will they survive without this money?

Do they know who she is yet? Has she given away her location?

The questions pummel her head as the seconds stretch out. She can feel the lens of the camera on her. Imagines the police watching. Officers running towards cars. Engines starting. Sirens and speed.

Will Isobel and Roly see this video too? Another question that comes from nowhere, dragging with it years of bitter hurt – a sharp stone moving through her veins.

'Come here, Lola.' She beckons her daughter close, and her little girl pushes up against her, thumb in mouth. No Barnaby in her arms now. They've tucked him carefully into Emma's backpack. Her shoulders hurt from the weight of it again. She's carrying Lola's bag too, freeing Lola to run.

They've been walking for hours now. After finding the car gone from the road, they'd walked back into town, and Emma had scoped out the cash machines at the train station. She'd thought about grabbing the cash and jumping on a fast train. Getting into London and out again, travelling north. The speed had appealed to her. They could be in Liverpool by evening if they took trains. But trains also had locked doors and no way off. If they're tracking her bank card already, then they'll easily find the train she's on and be waiting at the next stop. She shivers as a memory pushes up into her thoughts. Those hands grabbing her away.

'Jonny sent us. He wants a word.'

She can't let them take her again. Away from escape and freedom. Away from Lola.

The cash machines on the high street were no better. Too many cameras. Too easily tracked. But this cash machine is on the outskirts of town. There are fewer cameras here, less ways to watch her. Beyond the petrol station and the busy road is a golf course. A huge sprawling eighteen holes of lush green land and trees. Lots of trees. If she can make it across the road and the golf course before the police arrive, they'll have no way of knowing where she went.

Thoughts of roadblocks – a net closing in around them – fill her head, but this is the only way. If only the car had been parked waiting for her this morning like they'd planned. God, if only she'd driven straight to it last night before if had been towed. But there's no point dwelling on it. She must concentrate on the present. Whether she reveals her location or not, she has no choice but to use the card. She needs money to get them to Liverpool and the port in Birkenhead, the ferry out of the country where help and her new life is waiting for her. The longer she leaves it before withdrawing the cash, the more likely it is they'll know who she is and be waiting. She imagines the police closing in again – a rope tightening a noose around her neck. If they're quick, if she's smart, they might be able to slip away. She has to try.

Her pulse drums in her ears, barely distinguishing one beat from the next.

Come on! She wills the money to come, hand hovering ready to grab.

She did not want to do this.

Any of it.

She didn't want to snatch Lola from the only family she's ever known and cause her daughter so much hurt and fear. But Jonny is a monster. He has killed before – she's sure of it. He's left her no choice but to take Lola and keep her safe, be part of her life, always there to protect her.

She puts a protective arm around her daughter. *Her daughter.* Let her so-called parents see. Let them feel the same tearing pain she has felt all these years.

Another second passes, and just when she feels an anguished scream catch in her throat, the slot finally opens and the stack of money appears. She snatches at it, twisting around to zip it safely into the side pocket of the backpack.

Run!

'OK, Lola. Remember what we said?' Emma's voice is high and urgent.

Lola pulls her thumb from her mouth and nods. 'We walk that way.' She points to the back of the petrol station. 'And then we cross the road and we run.'

'Yes. As fast as we can.' The panic rises. It's an effort to walk slowly, normally, away from the camera she knows is still watching, tracking their every step as they walk towards the back of the petrol station in the direction of town.

She checks her watch. Time is racing ahead of them. They need to hurry. The taxi will be waiting. She thinks of the call she made from her burner phone an hour ago to book it. She'd found the number for an out-of-town firm, hoping it will take the police longer to check.

Hurry!

They have ten minutes until the taxi arrives. She can't be late and risk the driver leaving. A distant siren cuts through the air. She jumps at the sound, gaze flying around her. They know! The police have connected her to Lola somehow. From Haz's brother's car perhaps, or maybe Roly and Isobel saw through her disguise. It's been years since she was in their home. She wonders if they ever even think of her.

'Quick,' she hisses, taking Lola's hand as they reach the busy dual carriageway that circles Crawley. No time to look, listen and look again. No time to wait for a space or an understanding driver.

Emma scoops Lola into her arms. The weight of her along with the backpack is almost too much, but fear is snapping at her heels again. She is risking both their lives, but anything is better than staying here. The siren echoes in the air, closer this time. She catches the first flash of blue in the corner of her vision and darts to the middle of the road. A horn blasts, but she doesn't stop until she's stepping over the metal barrier between the lanes of traffic.

She pauses, just for a second, feeling like Frogger from the computer game her brothers used to play. That tiny green frog crossing the busy road. Emma tries not to think about how many times the frog failed as she dashes the final few metres.

More horns sound and the whine of brakes, lost to the wailing siren. The noises blend in a frenzy in her head. But they make it across and onto the grassy outskirts of the golf course. Five hundred metres away, across two holes and crops of trees, is a little road of houses Emma found earlier. The taxi will be there any minute.

'Well done, Lola,' Emma says, taking her hand again. 'Let's see how fast we can run to those trees.' She points ahead. A hundred metres away, maybe two, is a line of oak trees, trunks wide and bushy with leaves. The perfect cover if they can just make it.

She risks a glance back. In the distance, the traffic is parting for the police car. The wail of the siren drowns out the rumble of the cars and her shaking breath.

Then she sees beyond the police car. The world seems to falter around her. She stops breathing, thinking; existing.

A voice is screaming at her to run, but she's frozen, unable to look away as a black SUV with tinted windows moves through the traffic.

Jonny!

He's found her just like she knew he would. She won't go back to that hospital. Never, never. She'll die before that happens. Whatever it takes to keep them both safe.

'Emma.' Lola tugs at her arm, and she is back in her body and horribly aware that they're still standing opposite the petrol station. So close. So exposed.

'Quick.' The word comes out as a sob, and it must sound terrifying because Lola screams, a yelp of a sound, and she runs so fast that for a second, it is her pulling Emma.

The open grass seems to go on forever, the trees moving no closer, but they keep on running. The backpack jumps up and down on her back, yanking at her shoulder muscles with every step. Sweat pools under her arms, and her hair falls loose from its tie. She can't stop herself from looking back again. The police car is stationary outside the petrol station, the siren has stopped, but the blue light continues. There is no sign of the black SUV, but it was there. She saw it. Didn't she?

'*There are no monsters, Emma. You know that.*' The voice is monotone and a little bored. She can't picture the doctor it belongs to, just that voice and that unwavering belief in themselves and their world of black and white.

Emma turns back, pushing on. They reach the trees, breathless and panicked. Lola's little chest heaves in air. Emma looks to where they've run, expecting to see a figure sprinting towards them, but the green space is empty.

'OK,' Emma gasps. 'We're almost there. We still need to go quickly but not as fast.'

Lola nods, freeing two lines of tears from her eyes. A sickening wave of guilt presses down on Emma, threatening to drown her. All she wants is to comfort her daughter, but there's no time.

They start moving again, keeping the treeline behind them, hiding them from the view of the petrol station. She can see the edge of the golf course and a street of houses. There's a silver car pulled to the side of the road with a yellow logo on the side. The relief feels like a whoosh of air rushing through her. It's there. The taxi is there.

Don't go, she wills it, starting to run again, tugging on Lola's hand. The thought of being this close and missing it is too much. Her mouth is dry, but her insides feel like liquid, sloshing and useless.

The driver is shifting in her seat, looking around her. Emma shouts out a, 'Hey,' and gives a frantic wave. And then they're at the door, diving into the back seats, both struggling to breathe.

'Wow,' the woman chuckles. 'Where's the fire, kids?' She catches Emma's eye in the back mirror and smiles.

'No fire,' Emma says, forcing herself to laugh. 'Just didn't want to miss you.'

'Where to then?'

She names a village she found on the maps app earlier, walking another tightrope between wanting to get as far away as she can, as fast as they can, but also conserving money and wanting to keep hiding.

Emma clips a seat belt around Lola before hugging her close and kissing the top of her head. Her hair is windswept and tangled. They both are. Inside and out. Emma stares out of the window, scouring the road ahead for any sign of police cars and cordons. The driver pulls away, and Emma sinks into the seat, feeling the weight of their escape lifting from her shoulders. She can't stop herself glancing out of the back window at the disappearing petrol station. How long until they realise she cut across the golf course? How long until they find her?

'Did we make it?' Lola asks before dropping her voice to the tiniest whisper and shrinking into herself. 'Is the monster still chasing us?'

'Not right now,' Emma says, unsure how true that is. 'We're safe.'

But for how long? The journey ahead feels impossible.

NINETEEN

EMMA

'We did it, Lola.' Emma kisses the top of Lola's head as the train pulls away from the station. She opens the cheese sandwich she'd bought from the little station shop and hands it to Lola before piercing a straw into a carton of Ribena. There are two packets of crisps and a KitKat on the seat beside her.

'My daddy calls them dig-dogs,' Lola had said in the shop, making the shop assistant smile. Emma had smiled too but not at the mention of Roly, but that her daughter was OK. The mad rush, the fear, it had all seemed to wash over her. Except now Lola is so quiet. She takes a bite of sandwich, chewing slowly, her gaze distant.

'We're OK,' Emma says as much to Lola as to herself.

The relief is a skittish, wriggly animal she can't keep hold of. It's mixing with the heart-racing desperation she's felt since finding the car gone this morning. It's a tumultuous concoction. Part of her wants to sigh and cheer and grin from ear to ear. The other part of her wants to cower and cry and scoop Lola into her arms and run as far and as fast as she can until her legs give way.

Lola swallows and looks like she's about to take another bite then pauses. 'I'm tired,' she says in a small voice.

'That's all right. Eat what you can and we can save the rest for later.'

Lola takes one more bite before handing the sandwich back to Emma and resting her head against the seat.

Exhaustion is tugging on Emma too. It feels like a week has passed since they left the caravan to begin their 'adventure', as she'd called it, all cheery-voiced and jollying along in a way she doesn't have it in her to be right now. It was all she could do to get them to the station and buy food and tickets for the first train out, even if that meant travelling in the wrong direction.

The thought worries away at Emma's relief. They need to travel north to Liverpool, but instead the train is taking them to Brighton on the south coast. Any semblance of the plan has gone. There are no steps to follow, no reassurances. She is alone, and she is scrambling. There was another train fifteen minutes later that would've taken them in the right direction. Except it was going to Crawley. From there, they'd have had to change for a train to London. She couldn't do it. Couldn't stand on the platform waiting, straining to listen for the sound of sirens. She couldn't risk going back into Crawley either.

This morning, she'd been desperate to know how close the police and Jonny were to catching them. Now she does. They were only minutes away from the cash machine. They'll probably be waiting at Crawly station by now.

And so, even though it causes a lurching unease, going south is her best chance of escape and keeping her daughter safe today.

'Can I see Mummy and Daddy now?' Lola's voice is a sleepy mumble.

Emma wishes she couldn't hear the hope in that question; wishes she wasn't about to destroy it. 'Not yet,' she says. 'We have to keep you safe, remember?'

The mention of Isobel and Roly causes a memory to flash in her thoughts. Lola so very little, so helpless. They couldn't see the danger she was in. But from the moment Emma had first held Lola, she'd known how precious she was, how much she needed protecting. And so Emma had stayed close, ignoring her degree in law and her own future, and becoming a nanny for that family.

She'd lived in their house. She'd done their chores, she'd smiled and she'd pretended not to hear the arguments. All to be close to Lola and keep her safe. Until the day Roly had called her into the kitchen and sat her down.

'I'm sorry, Emma, but this isn't working. We've decided we don't need a nanny anymore.'

'Oh,' had been the only word she'd managed to say through the crushing sense of loss she could feel coming her way. 'I understand,' she'd lied, keeping up the pretence of the perfect nanny for this perfect family. 'I'm happy to stay on until the end of the month.'

'It's best you leave now actually.'

'Now?' She'd shaken her head, her eyes wide with disbelief and pleading.

'Right now. I've already packed your bags. They're by the door. I just need your key, please.' He'd slid an envelope of cash towards her. 'This is your wage until the end of the week.'

She'd stared at the money, not wanting to take it. This wasn't about money. It never had been. 'I... I don't understand. Why?'

He'd sighed, pinching the bridge of his nose before looking at her. 'You need professional help, Emma. Isobel heard you. We're her parents, not you. You're no one to her.'

'But I love her,' she'd stuttered, realising then that she must have slipped up somewhere, given herself away.

'Yes, and that's why you must leave. You're not her mother.' He'd stood and motioned to the door. All the things she'd wanted to say, all the warnings, all her fears and love had lodged in her throat.

Emma can feel tears building behind her eyes now. It hurts to think about that time and all that happened afterwards. She looks down at her daughter and is overwhelmed with how much she loves her. Lola is staring out the window at the blur of landscape rushing by. Golden crop fields surrounded by bushy green trees. A distant church spire, a narrow road with a line of cars trying to pass a cyclist.

Emma draws her eyes away and looks up and down the train. What's left of the relief from their escape disappears in another spark of worry. What if someone on this train recognises them? There's no doubt the police are onto her. She is no longer being hunted by them and Jonny and his men but by the whole country it feels like. How long before her photo is everywhere? Maybe it is already.

She reaches into her bag and pulls out her baseball hat, positioning it low on her head as she stares around her. The train is a small local service with three interconnecting carriages that creak and rattle on the tracks. It's almost empty. There are a group of teenage boys in the carriage ahead and a noisy family with boisterous children in the carriage behind, jumping from seat to seat. Emma and Lola are alone in the middle and she wishes she could use this time to calm her nerves, but they are not safe, nowhere close.

'Emma?' There's a tug at the arm of her T-shirt. She looks down to find Lola is no longer staring out the window but up at her. 'Where are we going?'

'We're...' She doesn't know how to answer. 'We're going on an adventure, remember?'

'But where? When will we see Mummy and Daddy?'

'Mummy and Daddy can't look after you right now. I'm keeping you safe.'

'Will the monster get them? Can they come with us?'

Emma shakes her head as the guilt scours her insides. 'No, Lola. They can't. But they're fine, I promise.'

I'm your mother. The words are there but she keeps them in. Lola is only three years old. Her life is about pretend tea parties with her teddies and watching episodes of *Peppa Pig* and singing to Disney music. Emma has already turned her world upside down; there is no way she's going to make it worse by destroying everything Lola believes in.

Her thoughts return to their future and the house with the white picket fence and the movie nights. All of a sudden it feels less like a plan and more like an imagined dream.

'*We'll have plenty of money.*'

'*How?*' she'd asked.

'*Don't worry about that now. Just get Lola out of the country. You can do it! I know you can.*'

Maybe she should've asked more questions. Except, if Emma is honest, she's not sure she'd wanted the answers. Perhaps deep down she'd known how impossible this whole thing was.

Haz's favourite expression pops into her head. '*Blind faith, Em. That's how we're going to survive this. Blind faith and our big-boy pants. Girl pants for you though, yeah?*'

She'd always laughed. '*Yes. Blind faith and big-girl pants.*'

He'd said it every day, right after a breakfast of cereal with milk that always tasted a little off or cheap bread never quite toasted enough. He'd hook his arm through hers and they'd walk to the day room like two Victorian aristocrats taking a stroll on the promenade.

The hospital stay had dragged on and on. One month, then two. She'd asked to leave again and again, sometimes calmly, laying her reasons out one after the other. Sometimes screaming and shouting, although not often. It only made things worse, and they'd up her dosage of sedative, keeping her spaced out and useless.

'*We can't let you leave until we're certain you're not a*

*danger to yourself, Emma. Or anyone else. You were in a very
bad way when you came in.'*

'*I was drugged.'*

'*I realise that's what you've convinced yourself happened,
but all the evidence points to you taking an overdose. You
confirmed it to staff in A&E on arrival.'*

Had she really said that? Or had Jonny had a quiet word
with one of the staff, paid someone to say it? In the end, it didn't
matter. The more she'd talked about him and the monster he
was, the less they'd seemed to believe her, and so eventually
she'd stopped trying to explain about Lola and Isobel and Roly
and Jonny too. She'd stopped telling the story of being dragged
off the street by Jonny's men a day after seeing Isobel on the
common outside her house that January, when all she'd wanted
was to see her daughter and warn Isobel that Lola wasn't safe.

After four months, the hospital had finally let her go. Haz
had squeezed her so tight on her last day.

'*I don't want to leave you here alone,'* she'd said.

'*Don't be daft. I'll be out of here tomorrow. I was just
waiting for you.'*

She'd laughed, only realising when he'd shown up at her
parents' house the following week with chocolates and trashy
magazines that he might have been telling the truth. Even with
the hours they'd spent talking, she knew so little about why he'd
been on the ward. The scars on his wrists told part of the story.
The way his face darkened with any mention of his brother told
her more.

'*I can't possibly talk about it,'* he'd said more than once. '*It's
too much of a cliché – I'd die of embarrassment.'*

Only much later when she'd met his brother, Malik, in
person, had she realised the full extent of what Haz had gone
through growing up in the shadow of his parents' perfect son.
And Malik was such an arsehole too. Beneath the charm and

faux sympathy was a homophobic bully, she's sure. It's why she doesn't feel too bad about ditching his car.

She wonders if they've found it yet. Have they spoken to Malik? What will he have told them about her? Do they know about her and Haz's friendship? Are her parents being grilled by officers right this second? A new worry starts to form. The police have a lot of resources, but they follow the law. The same can't be said for Jonny. She'd been so careful to make sure none of her family or anyone she knew caught even a hint of what she was planning. But Jonny doesn't play by the same rules, and he has just as many ways to find her as the police. Perhaps more.

She shoves the thought aside and focuses on her breathing and what happens when the train reaches the end of the line in Brighton. The day is slipping away from her, and she has no idea where they'll sleep tonight or whether they'll still be safe come morning.

TWENTY

ISOBEL

Time seems to slow to the speed of a snail crawl. Desperation hangs in the air too like a bad odour clinging to her clothes and her skin. How many minutes have passed since DCI Watkins took that call? Ten? Twenty? The detective's phone remains infuriatingly silent.

What's happening? Is her daughter safe?

Emotions push up and up until she's not sure if she's going to scream or cry. She can't just sit here. She wants to tear at her skin, pull back the layers just to let the feeling out, but it's trapped inside her. A wave of nausea washes over Isobel so quickly that she leaps up from the stool, the legs scraping the tiles and eliciting a tut from Margaret.

'Are you all right?' Roly shoots her a worried look.

She nods, swallows, forces herself to speak. 'I just... I can't just sit here. I'm going to' – she thinks for a second then remembers something she should be doing – 'call Zeen again. I tried earlier, but she didn't answer. I can't understand why she's not here today.' She swallows again. Her cheeks ache with the familiar need to retch, but she turns to the detective. 'Is that OK?'

He nods. 'Yes. Good idea. We've so far been unable to locate your housekeeper. If she does answer your call, please ask her to get in touch with us. I'd like to rule out any involvement in Lola's abduction.'

'Involvement? But we know it was Emma,' Isobel says.

'We can't rule out that she's not working with someone else. And even if Zeen is innocent, it may be that she saw something in the run-up to the holiday that could help with the investigation.'

'What kind of thing?' Margaret asks.

Isobel doesn't wait to hear the answer. Her stomach cramps, and she grabs her phone and hurries from the room, barely making it to the upstairs bathroom in time to dry retch over the toilet bowl. There is nothing inside her since the last time, and it's a reminder that she needs to eat and drink. She doesn't have the space in her head to think about caring for herself while Lola is out there somewhere, but it isn't just about her anymore. She is ten weeks pregnant. And if she isn't ready to share this secret with Roly and Margaret, then she needs to do a better job of hiding it. Starting with eating properly. It will boost her energy levels, even if it doesn't stop the sickness.

When the retching is over and she's brushed her teeth and splashed cold water on the heat of her face, Isobel calls Zeen. The phone rings five times before there's a click and then more ringing, as though the call has been transferred abroad. She's about to hang up when it's answered to the sound of roaring traffic and distant shouts.

'Hello? Zeen?'

'Iso—' Zeen's voice cuts off.

'Are you OK?' Her voice is loud, bouncing off the tiles of the bathroom.

'I'm sorry.' There's a crackling sound, and Zeen's voice trails off.

'Zeen? What are you sorry for? Where are you?'

'Lola—'

'What about her?'

There's silence and then the sound of an engine.

'Zeen?'

The line goes dead. Isobel stares at the blank screen of her phone before trying again. There is no ringing this time, just an electronic voice message asking her to leave a message. She rattles off a rambling plea for Zeen to call her. 'What were you trying to tell me about Lola?' she asks before begging her again to call back.

Isobel slips her phone into the back pocket of her jeans and stares at the wide-eyed, fearful woman staring back at her from the mirror above the sink. There is a haunted expression on her face that reminds her of Emma that day on the common, and she can't stop her thoughts returning to the memory.

It was a bitingly cold January; the grass shimmering white. But the buttery yellow sun was out that Tuesday, and the first daffodil stalks had pushed through the hard ground. Lola had been nearly five months old and teething. By mid-afternoon they'd both been fractious. So Isobel had wrapped Lola in her white fleece-lined snow suit, tucked her in the pushchair and thrown on her own winter coat, and they'd gone out to walk the common.

She remembers feeling lonely. Every week, she'd meant to take Lola to the baby massage group that runs in the church hall around the corner; make the mum friends she'd always imagined she'd have. But every time she'd gone to leave the house, a bubbling anxiety had pushed its way up. It was that all-too-familiar fear that something bad would happen to Lola. But it was more than that too. She'd been unable to shake the feeling that those other mums would be able to see beneath the tired eyes of night feeds and sleepless nights to the woman beneath it. A woman who'd so desperately wanted a child but didn't deserve one.

If Roly wasn't with her, then walking the common in sight of her home was all she'd been able to manage in those months after Emma had left them. Being in sight of her home and a locked door had made her feel almost safe. That day, Isobel had made it all the way around to the duck pond before she'd seen Emma. The younger woman had come out of nowhere, stepping in front of the pushchair and blocking Isobel's path. It had taken Isobel a beat to recognise the woman who'd lived with them all those weeks. She'd been so skinny, strung out. Hair limp and tangled.

'*Emma? What are you doing here?*' The unease had been instant. A jump in her heart rate that caused her to shift position, moving the pushchair, putting herself between it and Emma.

'*I just need to see her,*' she'd replied, the words strangled by a sob.

'*You can't. She's not yours.*' Isobel's gaze had flicked from Emma to the path beyond, but the common was suddenly so empty; her daughter so vulnerable.

'*Please,*' Emma had sobbed. '*Please.*'

There was something fidgety about Emma's demeanour, something off. She kept looking over her shoulder, flinching as she took in a passing car or a runner on the opposite path.

'*How is she?*' Emma asked.

'*She's good. Really well.*'

Isobel had felt the world shrink, disappear to all but her and Emma and Lola.

'*I...*' Isobel had faltered, her own tears falling. '*We... love her. She's our daughter, Emma.*'

Something had hardened in Emma's face. Anger flashed in her eyes alongside an unpredictable wildness that had caused Isobel to take a step back. A cry from Lola had pierced the silence.

Emma's gaze had shifted to the pushchair. *'I have nothing left,'* she'd said. *'Lola is all I have.'*

'She's not yours, Emma. Please understand that. You're young. You have your whole life ahead of you. Move on.'

'I can't.' She'd taken a step closer. *'You don't understand. She's not safe. He'll come after her. I have to protect her.'*

'What are you talking about? She's safe with us.'

'NO! Only I can protect her from that monster. I'd rather we were both dead than he get her.'

'Stop it,' Isobel had cried. *'Don't say that.'*

Emma had lurched forward suddenly, and Isobel hadn't known if she was leaning in to look at Lola or trying to grab her baby, or attack Isobel, and she'd panicked and shrieked and pulled back. Then a group of dog walkers had rounded the corner and Isobel had breathed a sigh of relief that she was no longer alone.

'Please go,' she'd said. *'Lola is our daughter. We have the DNA test to prove it.'*

To Isobel's surprise, a look of defeat had crossed Emma's face and she'd nodded.

TWENTY-ONE

ISOBEL

Isobel forces the memories aside and hurries back to the kitchen. She won't let Emma get under her skin again. Months and years of her life have been spent thinking of that woman and what she tried to do.

It wasn't just how she'd overstepped as a nanny, or that time she'd spoken to Isobel on the common, but everything that had happened in between. After they asked her to leave their house when Lola was two months old, Emma had gone to a solicitor and demanded a DNA test for her and Lola and Isobel and Roly. They'd agreed, just to end the madness. But it hadn't helped. Emma's appearance on the common that day in January was the final straw. Roly had called Jonny and only then had it all stopped, and Isobel had allowed herself to believe that Emma had finally moved on. But really, she'd just been waiting for the right time. There was no amount of DNA evidence, no amount of help that Emma could have, that would convince her Lola wasn't her daughter.

The sinking dread she felt at the services yesterday returns. Emma has waited nearly four years to take Lola. How far will she go to keep her? The thought spins in her head as she enters the kitchen to find Margaret is still quizzing the detective on what they're doing to find Lola. She doesn't want to listen. Anything short of an army – a million soldiers knocking on every door – blocking every road, searching every corner of this earth, will not be enough.

The realisation is a reminder that they should be doing more. They should be doing everything to stop Emma, and they're not. Should she mention going to the press again? It's been nearly twenty-four hours since Lola was taken. How much longer are they supposed to go on like this?

Roly is no longer at the kitchen island but standing by the open fridge, a chopping board and a loaf of bread already out.

'I'm making you a sandwich, Iz,' Roly says as she steps into the room.

'Thank you.'

He looks at her, and there's a frown pinching the space between his eyebrows. For a split second, she wonders if he's guessed about the baby and wants to make sure she eats properly. She drops the thought. Roly is many things. He is fun and generous – always buying her the latest designer bag or clothes, always telling her to treat herself – and he is smart. Beneath the entertainer, the pleaser and the charmer is a savvy businessman, with one eye always on the markets and another on opportunities to grow his wealth. But when it comes to relationships, he isn't intuitive. He takes things at face value. It's why he doesn't see all the snide ways Margaret undermines her.

'Mother?' Roly asks. 'Would you like a sandwich?'

'No, thank you, my darling. I had something to eat while Isobel was sleeping.'

Point proven, Isobel thinks, ignoring Margaret's dig and moving to stand beside Roly just in time to see him slipping his phone into his pocket. She wonders who he's messaging and questions like yesterday when he'd called his boss, how he can think about anyone or anything outside of this nightmare.

'How are you doing?' she asks quietly, placing a hand on his back, needing his warmth and his comfort as much as she wants to give it.

He doesn't look up from slicing the cheese, and she senses a stiffness to his posture, an anger maybe. He's upset about Lola, she tells herself, but still the fluttering insecurity comes. That question in her mind, wondering if she's done something wrong, something to upset him.

She never used to be an insecure person, but time has worn away her confidence, or maybe it's a side effect to the years of anxiety and always worrying something will happen to Lola. The insecurity has been worse this year, ever since that dark spell in the spring where it felt like Roly was a stranger living in their home instead of her husband, the man she loved, Lola's father.

Even now, she doesn't know what started his change in mood, but she remembers when it began, because it was the same week that Scarlett Peters' face was all over the news, the week the young woman left her home in Islington to meet a date and didn't show up.

'Roly, look,' Isobel had called to him one night as he'd stepped through the front door, an hour later than he said he'd be.

Silence had followed.

'Roly?' she'd called again.

'What?' The word had been snappish, but she'd been too caught up on the news to pay attention. He'd appeared in the doorway to the living room, tie askew, his features pinched.

'Did you see this?' she'd pointed to the TV. 'A woman in North London has gone missing. I'm sure we've met her. At—'

'You're spending too much time cooped up in this house,' he'd replied, barely looking at the screen and sounding so much like his mother. 'I've never seen her before.'

'Yes. We did. You remember. It was—'

'*Don't be ridiculous. Now leave it, Iz,*' he'd shouted, the words loud enough to wake Lola. Her little girl had padded barefoot out of her bedroom, snuggling into Barnaby and asking in a sleepy voice if it was morning.

Isobel had been as surprised as she'd been hurt by his outburst. He'd been the same one night the week before for no reason at all, snapping at her about there being no dinner left for him even though he'd told her he wouldn't be home.

It was rare for Roly to be moody, and each time he always apologised, blaming work and tiredness. And he was always so nice to her afterwards, taking her and Lola for lunch at the weekend. Sending her flowers when he was at work.

Then it changed again. He stopped being snappish and then loving, and instead there came a slow withdrawal into himself; barely speaking to her from one day to the next. Not coming home until the middle of the night. Locking himself away in his study on the top floor at the weekends.

'*What's going on?*' she'd asked a hundred times. '*Have I done something to upset you?*'

'*I've told you, I'm fine,*' he'd reply, always finding a reason to leave the room.

Of course, her mind had leaped to worrying about an affair. She remembers those weeks so clearly. Sniffing his shirts for the smell of another woman's perfume. Searching his pockets for receipts. Looking for any sign of what was going on inside his head. Maybe Roly had been right, and she spent too much time inside the house.

Then the weeks passed and news about the missing woman petered out, the papers moving on when there was nothing more to say. The old Roly returned eventually, and she'd put his mood down to a spell of depression or a midlife crisis of some kind.

It's on the tip of her tongue to ask him if he's angry with her as he closes the fridge. *Have I done something wrong?* She holds it in. Roly is desperate to find Lola, that's all.

He hands her a plate with a sandwich and a chopped apple.

'Thank you,' she says, fighting back a sudden need to cry as she eyes the fruit. He's cut the apple into slices rather than chunks, the way Lola likes it. She wonders if he even realises he's done it. They sit back at the island as Margaret asks another question.

'How much do you know about this Emma woman's mental state? How dangerous is she?'

'She thinks she's Lola's mother,' Roly sighs. 'And she's threatened to harm Lola if she can't keep her safe from whatever imagined danger she thinks is trying to harm her. What more do you need to know, Mother?'

'Emma spent several months in a secure unit,' DCI Watkins says, his voice so even beside Roly's. 'It was some years ago, and from what you've told us, it appears it was soon after her time nannying for Lola. We're interviewing her parents today in the hope they'll have knowledge of her plans.'

Roly rubs a hand over his face. 'You've got her though, right? You said there are police at the petrol station and DI Gardner. She can't get away?'

'It's very unlikely. We have CCTV and trained officers on the scene. By all accounts, she is a troubled woman who isn't thinking clearly. The reality of being on the run is very hard. Emma is likely to be in a state of extreme anxiety. And Lola will be slowing her down.'

They fall silent again. Isobel forces herself to eat, grateful her body accepts the food.

'This is becoming quite ridiculous,' Margaret says suddenly. 'Perhaps you need to call this DI Gardner.'

DCI Watkins starts to reply, but then his phone rings at last. Roly takes her hand in his and holds it tight.

'What's going on?' the detective says by way of hello.

There's a pause.

'Check again,' he barks into the phone before hanging up.

'You've... lost them, haven't you?' The words come out trembling, but she has to ask.

'We're still looking,' the detective replies with a sigh that feels like a yes. 'We'd hoped to pick Emma and Lola up on CCTV leaving the petrol station, but she's disappeared. The cyber team is widening the search. I've got units at the train and bus station in Crawley. She may be lying low right now, but she'll have to come out at some point.'

An icy chill pushes through her. Lola is gone. She tries to swallow, to breathe, to not cry out in pain, but it's impossible. She makes a noise, and they all turn to look at her.

'Iz, are you OK?' Roly asks.

She shakes her head. 'How can I be? Our daughter is missing and we thought the police had found her, but they haven't. She's gone, isn't she? And now we might never find her again. What if Emma doesn't use her bank card again? What if she's never spotted on another camera? Then what?'

'We'll find her,' Roly says, his words offering no reassurance.

'We have to do more.' She looks from him to Margaret and finally to the detective. 'You have to do more. We have to go to the press now.'

Roly doesn't shake his head this time but instead looks at DCI Watkins. The detective nods. 'I'll have a press alert released within the hour. We'll launch a social-media campaign as well. We've seen great success with them recently.'

'And our name – it has to be used?' Margaret asks.

'Margaret, please,' Isobel says. 'Lola is more important.'

'I'm only trying to think of the future. But I won't stand in your way if you feel this is the best course of action.' She sniffs. 'Now, what I want to know is where is this Emma woman trying to take my grandchild?'

'We're trying to determine that now,' DCI Watkins replies. 'We assume she will be trying to take Lola out of the country.'

'That's impossible, surely?' Margaret replies. 'She doesn't have a passport for her. You told me not five minutes ago that this was a girl with mental-health problems. And now you're suggesting she has the means to take her abroad?'

'That's not what I'm saying,' he replies. 'Emma may try to take her out of the country, but that doesn't mean she'll succeed. Does Lola have a passport?'

Isobel nods. 'It's upstairs.'

'You're sure?' DCI Watkins asks.

'Yes. I mean, I think so. I wouldn't have moved it.'

'Even so,' Margaret continues. 'She'd be stopped, wouldn't she? You can put a stop to her passport? You can alert all the customs agents or what not?'

There's a pause, a moment where the detective glances to Isobel and Roly before turning his attention back to Margaret. 'Of course. Unless—'

'What?' Isobel asks. All of a sudden, she can't catch her breath. What is she missing? What is he going to tell her?

He sighs. 'Not all links out of the country require a passport to be scanned. Journeys to other parts of the United Kingdom only require a photo ID to be checked. So while we can alert the customs authority, if Emma has Lola's passport, she could, while it's unlikely, take her out of the country.'

Isobel's heart is pounding so hard, she feels her pulse throbbing through her whole body. They found them, they had them, but somehow Emma has escaped and Lola with her. Will she ever see her again? If Emma is really trying to leave the country and fails, what will she do with Lola?

'I'd rather we were both dead than he get her.'

The same dawning reality seems to play on Roly's face. He stands and strides towards the hall. 'I'll check for her passport now.'

Emotion engulfs her. The longing to hold Lola in her arms is unbearable. Her heart shatters all over again at how close they'd come to having her back. She moves to the sink, needing a glass of water and a moment to fight back the tears before they can fall. Guilt is sweeping through her too; a gale force, hollowing her out. This is her fault. She is the one who should've done more back when Emma was staying in their house. She is the one who let Lola use the toilet alone yesterday. She is the one who sat for that precious extra moment on her phone when she should've rushed, finished first, been by the sinks waiting.

She is the one who was so desperate for a family that she did unspeakable things to get it. She is to blame for all of this. Because Emma might be crazy, but if she is, it's Isobel's fault.

TWENTY-TWO

EMMA

Emma looks down at Lola's angry red face and feels every shred of that frustration humming in her body. Beneath the grey clouds, the sun is starting its descent over the rows of houses around them. Emma checks her watch. It's 7 p.m. and they are lost somewhere in Brighton.

The worry inside Emma's body is flittering, coming in bursts, almost forgettable beside the urgency and the fear and paranoia she's felt over the last twenty-four hours, but not quite.

'Please, Lola,' she begs, and there is no jolly-along tone now; just a frayed pleading. 'Just a little bit further.'

'Tired,' Lola cries, tears rolling onto already damp cheeks. 'I want to go home.' Her voice is loud and wailing, making Emma flinch. Her gaze darts around them. She sees a dog walker pause on the opposite side of the road, staring for a beat too long. Does she recognise them? Their faces will be everywhere by now – she's sure of it.

Emma repositions the cap on her head and crouches down to Lola's eyeline. She's about to tell Lola again that they need to keep moving, but then the blue of her daughter's eyes stare into hers and she sees a little girl who is desperately tired, hungry and in need of rest. It's enough to quiet the panic. As though she's stepped into the eye of the storm, and she knows they have to stop.

'OK,' Emma says. 'Let's find a place to sleep.' She brushes the tips of her fingers over Lola's cheeks, wiping her tears before looking again at the street. Two lines of large, detached houses slope up a curved road away from the beach and seafront apartments. Among the older Victorian structures are new builds with grey rooftops and large glass windows that seem to have been placed in an unsymmetrical, haphazard fashion.

They've been walking for at least an hour, maybe two. Emma had picked a direction at random after leaving Brighton station and they'd started to walk, eventually finding their way to the seafront. It had been busy with families playing on the beach, splashing in the sea despite the whipping cold wind blowing through them. For a spell in the late afternoon, it had felt so normal to be strolling on the promenade. She'd bought them both whipped ice creams with Flakes and they'd sat on the sand watching the tourists. Blending in, hiding in plain sight.

But then Emma had seen two police officers in that familiar black uniform walking along the seafront. She'd looked up and seen the cameras positioned high and secretive on the lampposts, pointing down at them – watching. She'd no longer felt hidden but exposed. Their route from the railway station to the beach was suddenly so obvious, so easy to follow on the dozens of cameras outside shops and on street corners and lampposts. She'll never understand why people don't care that their lives are under a microscope. That they are being constantly watched and observed – on the streets, the roads and online too. Social-media posts, emails and texts and any bank-card purchases. Nothing is private. People think the cameras are for protection. Once upon a time she'd been stupid enough to think the same. Right up until the society and rules that were supposed to protect her turned against her, and suddenly CCTV didn't mean safety, it meant danger.

She'd grabbed Lola's hand and they'd hurried away, off the beach and up side roads, cutting through alleyways, making turns at random. Now they are away from the cameras – no way for someone to follow them from a dark room in the back office of a police station anymore – but they are away from the noise and the people too, standing out on this quiet street as Lola cries with the same exhaustion pulling at every muscle in Emma's body.

What is she going to do?

The voice inside her head is urging her on – *Hurry! Hurry!* – but to where? If only the car had been there this morning. Everything would've been different.

'You can trust me. I will help you in any way I can. You're not alone anymore.'

'I am alone,' she wants to cry. She wants to stamp her foot and wail like Lola is. But she can't. The police are so close. And... and that black SUV. That was there too at the petrol station, wasn't it? She didn't imagine it. She's sure.

A noise breaks through her thoughts. A humming that's coming from her bag. She jumps then shrugs off the backpack and pulls out the phone. She hadn't realised she'd left it switched on.

She stares open-mouthed at the screen. It's Haz's number. The sight of it causes a new barrage of emotions to whip through her. Why is he calling her? The longing to speak to her best friend is fierce, almost painful. She can just imagine what he'd tell her right now. *'Trust yourself, Emma. The moment you start second-guessing what you know is true, you'll go insane.'*

But she can't answer the phone. Her head fills with all the reasons why. The police could already be tracking the number. They could already be on their way. She should never have called him on this phone, except... Haz's phone is unregistered too. The only way they'll be able to track it is if someone tells them about it. Not Haz though. He'd never.

She can't talk to him though. She can't tell him everything that's happening, and it half kills her that it's his number on the screen.

Each breath in and out is quick and ragged as she rejects the call and powers off the phone. However much she wants to believe that help is there for her, she is alone right now. Only she knows the dangers her daughter is in.

'Emma, I'm hungry.' Lola clutches her stomach. 'I need the toilet.'

Emma forces the memories and fears aside. She must focus on finding them a place to sleep tonight. Food and a toilet.

'OK. Hang on.' Her eyes scan the street again, landing on a small black sign at the end of the road. It's like a For Sale board, but the word swinging from a hook at the bottom reads 'Vacancies'. She'd have preferred a youth hostel or a cheap hotel, somewhere with a bored check-in assistant who wouldn't look at them twice. But they've already walked so far out of town. There is nothing else. This bed and breakfast is a beacon of hope. They'll be away from the street and curious eyes, and it will give Lola a chance to eat and sleep. And will give Emma the time she needs to plan how the hell they're going to get to Liverpool tomorrow.

'Look.' Emma points to the sign. 'Can you see that? There's somewhere we can stay.'

'I want to go home,' Lola says, but it's quieter this time, and she doesn't protest when Emma guides her towards the bed and breakfast.

Please be a little old lady with poor eyesight. A kindly grandmother type who'll usher them in, give them help and support. Even as the thought lands, creeping unease travels over Emma's skin. By the time she's lifting Lola up to press her finger to the doorbell, her pulse is racing around her body and her breath is coming in ragged gasps.

The door flies open, and it's not a woman at all but a man in his sixties with large thick-framed glasses and a curiously amused expression as though a question and a comment are vying for attention in his thoughts. The look – the face – is it familiar? She's sure she recognises him.

Unease morphs into a dread that threatens to swallow her whole. She has met this man before. He is one of them.

TWENTY-THREE

EMMA

Her past is chasing her. Like the police. Like Jonny. Except she can't outrun her memories. Something jumps out from a hidden corner in her mind. The first time she met Jonny. She remembers the beat of music, the push of bodies, the sticky sweetness of cocktails. Her head spinning from the alcohol and Damien's clammy hand in hers. How he'd wanted to leave and she'd said no, and years later she'd wish she hadn't.

It wasn't like the first party Damien had invited her to with his mates and the cans of lager in that smoky flat, but a proper party. In an actual mansion in Belsize Park, right at the very top of the Northern Line. The kind of house she'd only ever seen on TV. The kind of place she'd thought only Premier League footballers lived in. They weren't supposed to have been there. But Damien had needed to pick up his wage packet from the boss, a man he'd rarely mentioned in the nearly two years they'd been dating.

'We'll just swing by,' he'd told her earlier that evening when he'd picked her up. His plan had been to collect the money then head back to their local pub to meet some of his friends. Her plan had been to slip it into conversation at some point in the evening that she thought they should break up. She was going to blame the workload of her law degree, and it had been that in part, but it had also been him. His nagging to see her. The odd hours of his job as a delivery driver, and that same stifling small-world mentality of her family that the life in front of him was enough.

When they'd arrived at the mansion, Emma's jaw had dropped. She'd been expecting a warehouse or a two-up, two-down. Damien was a delivery driver, not a chauffeur. It had only been when he'd killed the engine of his Ford Transit outside the huge gated property with a dozen sports cars and three limos parked in the driveway that she'd thought to question what it was exactly that Damien delivered.

The party was in full swing as they'd stepped through the open front door. A waiter had handed them two bright red-and-green cocktails, not questioning who they were. Emma was glad she'd worn the low-cut black dress Damien had bought her as a birthday gift in the summer because he was sick of her wearing those same jeans every time he saw her. She'd shrugged off her cardigan and let her hair loose from its bun so the thick waves of it fell around her face and shoulders. She hadn't felt like she belonged, but she hadn't felt out of place either.

'*Jonny, this is my girlfriend, Emma,*' Damien said, introducing her to his boss. She'd expected an overweight sixty-something, but Jonny was a good-looking man in his forties with a charming smile and an air of authority as though he understood his place in the world.

'*What's a beauty like you doing with this scruff?*' Jonny had asked with a wink, clapping Damien on the shoulder and handing him an envelope.

'*I've been asking myself the same thing,*' she'd quipped. And when Jonny had asked them to stay for a drink, she'd said yes.

The house was warm and so grand, so much more than Emma had ever seen before and would probably ever see again, and there were dainty canapés and champagne flutes. At some point, Damien was called away by someone he knew, and Emma had found herself chatting in a group with Jonny and some of his friends. They'd been funny and outrageous flirts, making her feel ridiculously important and nothing like the poor, overworked student she really was.

Later she'd wonder if a part of her had fallen in love that night. With the house and the money and the life, all those stories of boarding-school antics and private planes. It had never been about Jonny, despite what he'd always wanted to believe.

Stupid!

Waltzing into the monster's den with a cocktail in her hand and a smile on her face. Oblivious to the danger. Why hadn't she ever questioned Damien's job? Why hadn't the envelope of cash Jonny had given him set alarm bells ringing? She ended her relationship with Damien the next day. Jonny called the following week.

'*How did you get my number?*' she'd asked.

'*I have my ways,*' he'd replied, and she could tell he was smiling. '*I wanted to invite you to another party I'm having. My friends and I were quite taken with you, Emma. Will you come?*'

'*OK. I don't have anything to wear though. I'll have to—*'

'*I'll send you something.*'

He'd hung up before she could give him her address or size or question what he would send her. The dress when it arrived the next day was beautiful. Bright red and backless. She'd paid to have her hair blow-dried at a salon and her nails done too.

It had been a perfect evening. Jonny had been so attentive. His friends funny and sweet. Weeks later, she was head over heels in love. How Jonny had laughed when she'd told him. '*Well, aren't you in trouble then?*'

Nothing bad happened in those early weeks of parties and secret dates in anonymous restaurants and expensive hotels. That all came later. But if she thinks back to those men and their smiling faces from the first party, didn't one of them look just like the B&B owner taking in her bedraggled appearance and the tear-stained face of her daughter?

'Hello there,' the man says with a lavish sweeping of his hand, as though welcoming them into a grand castle. His eyes seem to linger on Lola for a beat too long, and Emma reaches a trembling hand out, pulling her close. 'How can I help you two ladies?'

She starts to back away, sensing a danger she can't voice but knowing that a thousand more miles of walking would be better than one step forward. Except even as she's thinking of leaving, something in the man's face softens, and Emma no longer feels that tug of recognition. She suddenly isn't sure if she knows him, if he's one of them, or if the fear and exhaustion thrumming in her head is making her paranoid. She studies his face again, searching for the fleeting sense that they've met before. There's nothing this time, and yet she still wants to scoop Lola into her arms and turn away.

But there is nowhere else. Lola is hungry, half asleep on her feet.

'H-Hi,' she stutters, when the silence goes on too long. 'I was wondering if...' She can't finish the sentence. What to do? The indecision is on her again. Is it safe? How far away are the police? What is Jonny planning? The not knowing eats away at her confidence.

'I'm hungry,' Lola whines from beside her, and the man opens his door wider, and Lola is pulling her hand out of Emma's and walking in, and the decision is made. All she can do is follow reluctantly behind.

'You'd like a room,' the man says, reaching for a burgundy leather notebook. 'One night, is it?'

Emma nods. 'Yes, please.'

'One room with breakfast is seventy-five pounds. The little one eats for free of course.'

She thinks of the money in her backpack that she risked everything to get today. The taxi, the train tickets and now this. So much of it gone already. She needs to save enough for the ferry.

'I've got some beef stew and dumplings I can warm up. Would you like that?' he asks, and she wonders if there's something suggestive about the way his eyes linger on her. She can't trust anyone, but she doesn't trust her own mind right now either.

Lola's face stretches into a long yawn, but she nods too. Emma is sure he could've told her it was raw Brussels sprouts and she'd still have nodded.

'Thank you,' Emma says.

'Come through. I'm Teddy, by the way.'

'Nice to meet you,' she replies, not filling the pause that follows as he waits for her to tell him their names. She would lie, but Lola is right beside her, and she didn't think to tell her in advance that they shouldn't use their real names. She can't trust that she won't stomp her foot and tell this man, clear and loud, that she is Lola Huntington and this woman is not her mother. Better to appear rude.

The house is large but dated. Dark wood furniture clogs the hall and the living room, making the place feel smaller than it should. Lola's face lights up, and she rushes to the cream sofa by the window. At first Emma thinks she wants to sit down but then something on the sofa moves. It's a small white dog that stretches and yawns.

'Be careful,' Emma says, darting forward.

'Oh, don't worry. That's Luna. Luna Wolfston. She was my aunt's dog originally, but then she passed away and Luna... well, we're making it work. She wouldn't hurt a fly, but she will insist upon ample belly rubs.'

The little dog opens her eyes, takes in Emma and Lola, and

then rolls onto her back as Lola reaches out to fuss her. 'I love her,' she says, a smile lighting her tired face.

'Shall we settle up now?' Teddy asks, and Emma sees that he trusts her as far as she trusts him.

'Of course. Is cash OK?'

'Oh.' A pause. 'I'm afraid I'm card only. I switched after some burglaries in the area.' His words are a weight sinking inside her. A minute ago, the last thing she wanted was to step into this house and now the thought of leaving makes her want to drop to her knees and cry.

In the pause that follows, she imagines the wails from Lola when she tells her they have to leave. The tearful walk back into town, searching for somewhere to stay that will take cash. Desperation claws at her – sharp and piercing.

'Is there a problem?' Teddy asks.

Emma swallows down her emotions; tells herself to act normal. 'It's just that my card stopped working earlier. I dropped it in the sea. So annoying.' She tries to give a friendly eyeroll, but the effort feels too much. 'Is there is any way you can make an exception, please? I have cash.'

He watches her for a long moment. She thinks again of the news and if their faces are splashed across the news channels. What lies are they saying about her? Does Teddy recognise them? Her eyes are drawn to a TV in the corner of the room. She's relieved to see that it looks old and is covered in a fine layer of dust. Teddy looks her up and down again and then his gaze moves to Lola. Her little girl is sitting on the sofa with Luna on her lap.

Teddy nods. 'I think I can make an exception if you have the correct money.'

'Thank you,' she replies with a long exhale. 'Thank you so much.' She turns her back and pulls out the notes, feeling his gaze on her bag and the money.

Their fingers touch as she passes it over and it's a fight not to flinch.

'I'll put you in room three. It's got a double bed and a single bed in it and a nice shower. But be sure to run the water for a few minutes before getting in as it takes a while to get hot.'

The thought of a shower and being clean and lying in a bed, it's all too much. Teddy steps back to the doorway but doesn't turn around. He just stares at them. Curious and assessing. Fears fly through her head. He knows. He knows who she is and what she's done. He'll call the police. He'll call Jonny. It's all over.

He smiles and something in it makes a scream catch in her throat. Instead of keeping Lola safe, has she dragged her straight into the den of another monster?

Run!

If they go now, if she pulls Lola away from the dog and they run to the door, then they might make it out. But then what? Where will they sleep? What will they eat? They won't be safe out there.

They're not safe in here.

Before Emma can make up her mind, Teddy returns with two plates filled with thick dark stew and fluffy dumplings and her stomach cramps with hunger, and she knows she's out of time; that they'll stay and she won't sleep a wink, listening out for him in the middle of the night. The weight of what she's doing is so much heavier than she could possibly have imagined. Lola is everything to her. But the responsibility to keep her safe suddenly feels too much to carry alone.

She closes her eyes for a second, imagining again the relief she'd feel if her and Lola could simply float up and out of this world and never be scared of anything again. Tears prick at the edges of her eyes. She reaches for the phone in her bag and wonders if now is that life-and-death moment where she should reach out for help.

DAY THREE: 9.21 A.M. TUESDAY 1ST AUGUST

TWENTY-FOUR

ISOBEL

'Come on,' Isobel hisses as she yanks open one of the drawers in Roly's antique mahogany desk in their top-floor study. 'Where is it?'

The drawer moves slowly, the wood scraping on the old runners. The desk had been a wedding gift from her to Roly. She'd found it in an antique shop in Richmond and had it delivered and carried up the two flights of stairs while he was out playing golf one Saturday soon after they'd moved in. It had been the first time she'd used the credit card he'd given her.

'What's the limit?' she'd asked the week before, and he'd laughed as though she'd told a joke.

'There is none.'

She hadn't known how to process that. How can a credit card have no limit? Isobel's upbringing had been good. Her parents had been loving and supportive. They'd both been doctors, taking her on exotic holidays every year and sending her to the nearby private school. She'd seen what obscene wealth looked like in some of her classmates, and she'd still grown up confident in herself and her abilities. It's why she'd never minded working for a wealth management company that focused on the obscene. She loved her job and she'd been good at it. Exceptional even. But she never thought she'd marry into that world – something Margaret likes to remind her of often. To her mother-in-law, Isobel is the wrong sort; an outsider. No royal lineage in her bloodline, and in Margaret's antiquated stance, that means Isobel could be crowned Queen of England and she still wouldn't be the right sort.

But Isobel has always tried to fit into Roly's world, tried to be a good wife, tried to spend money like it didn't matter, and so she'd bought him an overpriced antique desk and the matching chair and forced herself not to flinch when she'd handed over the credit card.

'I love it, Iz. Thank you.' Roly had run a hand over the dark-reddish wood before sweeping her into his arms and spinning her around, stripping off her clothes and having furious, noisy sex on the green leather top.

'At least we know it's sturdy,' he'd said, laughing afterwards.

The memory feels unreal. Two other people. Not her. Not them. Not the same universe where she and Roly are on their knees searching this same desk for Lola's passport. It should be here, but it's not. The search is pointless. Roly looked yesterday after Emma had escaped the police with Lola and found nothing. She'd looked too, because did men really ever know how to find anything? Still nothing. Between them they'd searched every drawer and cupboard and forgotten bag in the house.

And now it's morning again. Another sleepless night. Another day where Lola isn't home. Outside, the sky is pale blue and clear, and yet there is no warmth to the sun yet. When she'd given up pretending to sleep and opened the curtains this morning, the grass on the common had glistened with dew, and she'd watched the same runner in the pink outfit she'd seen the previous morning stretch by the bench.

Standing by the window, Isobel had slipped into a fantasy where Lola was home and padding into their bedroom in her yellow *Hey Duggee* pyjamas. A running jump onto the bed, snuggling down between her and Roly, Barnaby lofted in the air for them both to give him a good-morning kiss.

'Can we go to the park today, Mummy? And can we bake cupcakes?'

She'd almost been able to hear her daughter's laughter. Always so easy to please. Will she still be that same smiling, happy girl when this is over? *If*, she corrected. *If* it's ever over.

The drawer finally opens with a clatter as the ornate metal handle knocks against the wood. Isobel rifles through a pile of papers. Bank statements and Roly's trust fund portfolio, and the business investments he's made over the years.

'Any luck?' Roly asks from where he's kneeling. He's rifling through the other set of drawers, and she wonders if he's really looking, or if he too knows this search is a final futile attempt to delay their reality – Lola's passport is gone.

She'd cried heaving sobs last night when they'd first given up looking for it. She'd trembled and sobbed in Roly's arms, allowing all the what-ifs to spill out. What if Emma has it? What if she stays in hiding? What if she does get out of the country?

She shakes her head and sits back on the carpet. The jeans she's wearing are high-waisted and push uncomfortably against her growing stomach. 'It's not here, is it?'

He stops and turns to face her. He looks better than she does this morning. He's lost the rugged glow to his cheeks, that schoolboy-out-in-the-cold-playing-rugby complexion that never failed to make her smile when they'd first started dating.

'It never fades,' he'd said on their third date when she'd commented on it. *'I'm actually scarred for life from standing in the bloody freezing cold for most of my school life. I'm not the only one. There's a support group for us types, you know?'* he'd joked.

Yes, he's a little pale now, but not grey and washed out like she is. And he's sleeping too. She'd lain awake last night listening to him breathe, too tired and broken to get up and do something, too desperately worried to sleep.

For one crazy moment, she is consumed with anger. How can he sleep so easily? How can he look so normal? How is he not desperately fearful that something will happen to Lola? But the feeling is gone as quickly as it arrives. Blaming Roly for not worrying as much as she is is as pointless as blaming him for how he looks. The world of privilege Roly was born into is one where everything always works out for him and those like him. He has no concept of failure. His love for Lola is indisputable. He just has no way of comprehending that she might never come back to them.

'I can't understand it,' Roly sighs, rubbing the back of his neck. 'We've always kept the passports together. And it's not just Lola's that's missing. Ours are too. Which makes me think they've got to be somewhere. I always keep them with the certificates and stuff.'

'Certificates?' Isobel gasps and is back on her knees and yanking open the drawers once more.

'What is it, Iz?'

'The clear plastic folder with all our certificates in. Our marriage certificate and our passports, and... and Lola's birth certificate and the DNA test results. They're not here either.'

Roly moves back to his side of the drawers, and together they search again. Passports can be moved. It's easy to think of them as forgotten in a side pocket of a suitcase somewhere or thrown out in a neglected bag. She opens her mouth; tries to speak the thoughts forming in her mind. But there is rarely any reason to move a marriage or birth certificate, and the documents of their lives.

She heaves in a breath, and then another and another, but it's not enough. The air isn't going in. 'Everything,' she gasps, unable to continue.

'Iz, calm down. Come on. It's OK. Talk to me.'

She nods, forcing away the panic as best she can, and when the words finally come, they spill out in a rush. 'Everything that proves Lola is our daughter is gone. Someone must have taken it all. It's not just our passports.'

'Christ,' he mutters, scooping her into his arms and holding her tight. 'You're right.'

Neither speak for a moment as the enormity of the moment sinks in. There's only one person who would take Lola's birth certificate and the DNA results proving that Isobel and Roly are Lola's biological parents.

'It has to be Emma,' Roly says, echoing her thoughts. 'And I get taking the passport if she's thinking of going abroad, but why the certificates too?'

A headache starts to throb across Isobel's forehead. She swallows and her throat is dry, but at least the nausea has passed quickly today. 'Because she hates us for having them. She doesn't want us to have that proof.'

'But we can easily get it again.'

'That's not the point.'

'What is then?'

In the silence that follows, Isobel listens to the quiet of the house. There's a faint clink of china from the kitchen where Margaret is sitting, but she lowers her voice anyway. 'The point is, we ruined Emma's life in our own desperation for a child.'

'Lola is our daughter. We have the DNA test to prove it.'

'No, we don't. That's what I'm saying. I know you hate talking about this and I'm sorry, but us being good parents to Lola doesn't mean we didn't do something terrible. Everything Emma is doing now is only what we drove her to.'

'We can't think like that.'

'What we can't keep doing is pretending that this is an ordinary child abduction. It isn't helping us get Lola back. You need to call Jonny again. You need to find out what he's doing. If we want our daughter home, he's the only one who's going to get Lola back for us, and you know it as well as I do.'

'He's already messaged me this morning.'

'What did he say? You should've told me.'

Roly pulls out his phone from his pocket and shows her the screen.

Sending more friends to the south coast right now! We'll get her today!

She gasps, unsure whether she should be relieved or terrified and feeling both. She wants Lola home safe more than anything in the world, but what will happen if Jonny's friends do find Emma and Lola? Emma will not give in without a fight. What will happen to Lola if she's stuck in the middle? A crushing sense of desperation takes hold. Isobel wishes with every cell in her body that Lola was in her arms right now. She needs her mother.

TWENTY-FIVE

ISOBEL

When there is nowhere else to look for Lola's passport, when there is nothing but defeat facing them, Roly goes for a shower and Isobel pushes herself up from the carpet and makes her way to the kitchen. She has blow-dried her hair today, added a touch of make-up that is already feeling smeared and washed out, but a Huntington always looks one's best, as Margaret so often likes to remind her, and Isobel feels as though she needs that armour today.

'Good morning,' she says, finding Margaret at her usual stool at the island counter. There is a large pot of coffee in the centre and toast too, already cut into slices and placed in a silver rack beside a tall cafetière. She prefers her toast straight from the toaster, piping hot and slathered in butter, not bothering with a plate, but she says nothing. This is how toast is served at Huntington Hall. This is how they always eat toast.

Margaret lifts her head a fraction, eyeing Isobel with a look that could almost be approval. 'Your earrings,' she says.

Isobel's hands fly up to the circular pearls, checking they're in place. 'What about them?'

'They're new. I don't remember Roly telling me he'd bought you pearls.'

'I bought them for myself,' she lies, dropping her hand and reaching for a slice of toast as though she isn't holding her breath, fearing more questions.

Margaret raises a surprised eyebrow. 'I see.' She returns her gaze to her diary and her breakfast, and they sit in silence. Isobel finds herself reaching for the jam, but her hand falters midway. Her body reacting before her mind has caught up. The jam is strawberry. Lola's favourite.

'For my birthday, can I have a jam cake, please, Mummy?'

Isobel had laughed at the question. *'You mean a Victoria Sponge with jam in the middle.'*

Lola had shaken her head and grinned. *'No sponge. Just jam.'*

'That sounds a lot like a bowl of jam rather than a cake. The candles will sink.'

'I don't mind. As long as it's—'

'Strawberry,' they'd said in unison.

Isobel closes her eyes as fresh pain tears through her. It's the start of August today. Eleven days until Lola's birthday. Will she have her daughter back by then?

The chime of the doorbell dislodges the memory, and she leaps up, grateful for the distraction. It's less surprising today to find DCI Watkins is alone on her doorstep. The detective is wearing a dark-blue suit, and there's an alertness to him. She senses his energy, his mind working three, four, a hundred steps ahead, as she leads him into the kitchen.

'What's happened?' Roly asks, appearing in the doorway behind them as Margaret pours him a cup of coffee.

'I have some news,' he says before nodding a thanks to Margaret.

Roly huffs. 'If you've come to tell us you're really close, please don't bother. After yesterday—'

'Roly,' Isobel cuts in. 'Let him speak. Please.'

He pauses, nods. 'Sorry. I'm not at my best today. Have you got any new leads on Lola? Has the press stuff helped?'

Isobel bites her lip. She was the one who'd pushed for the world to know her daughter is missing, and yet she's been unable to look at the news or check online. Somehow it will make this nightmare all too real when Isobel is already struggling to get from one minute to the next. How much longer can they carry on like this?

'Not yet,' the detective replies. 'We have released a photo of Emma on social media with a helpline number to call, which we expect to yield results today.'

Isobel bites back a remark, a hissed 'What if you don't?' question. Her head fills once more with thoughts of Scarlett Peters. Her photo has been in the national press for four months and they still haven't found her. They're searching woodlands. It can only be for a body. They think she's dead. The thought hurts more than it should. She thinks of Scarlett's family. What must it be like waiting for that news?

'In the meantime, we've spoken to Emma's parents. It appears Emma left them a note to say she was leaving and that they shouldn't worry. They claim to have no idea where she is, and I believe them. However, we were also able to locate Emma's phone and have set up traces on all her contacts. If she reaches out to anyone she knows, we'll have her location. Emma's phone also provided us with her search history,' the detective continues. 'By the looks of it, she began planning this abduction in early April.'

'My God,' Roly mutters.

'Can you remember anything different happening at that time? Did you notice being watched?'

Roly shakes his head, and it takes Isobel a moment to think. Emma started planning this in early April. She tries to think back to that time. What was she doing? Lola was obsessed with hopscotch. They'd do it for hours in the garden or playroom when it was wet. They'd even hopscotched all the way home from nursery one day. The memory is painful and she forces herself on.

What else happened in April? Scarlett disappeared, she thinks suddenly. Roly withdrew into himself around then too. But those things are not connected to Emma's planning to take Lola.

'Why April?' she asks aloud. 'All those years where she did nothing. Why now?'

'We don't know,' the detective replies. 'We're also working on the assumption that someone may have been helping Emma.'

'Who?' Margaret asks.

'With Lola's passport missing, we're working on the assumption that it could be Zeen Garcia, your housekeeper. We've still not been able to locate her or make contact with her. Can I ask where you hired her from?'

'I hired her,' Margaret says. 'She came highly recommended from the family of a close friend. And' – she pauses, her gaze flicking briefly to Isobel before she continues – 'I had a private investigator do a thorough background check on her.'

The words are jolting. A private investigator for a housekeeper. She didn't mention this yesterday when she'd asked Margaret about Zeen. Isobel shouldn't be surprised by the lengths Margaret will go to for anything related to her family. This is the woman who flies a speech therapist down from Newcastle every fortnight to privately tutor Lola, because he's the best in the country.

'Anything and anyone can be bought if you know their price,' Roly had said once when Isobel had suggested that this man might not want to fly across the country every two weeks to tutor their daughter. The words had wedged themselves into a space in her mind like a splinter burrowed in the skin. Always there.

'She was going to be living in my home with my family, my grandchild,' Margaret adds as though sensing Isobel's surprise. 'Of course I was thorough.'

DCI Watkins looks at something on his phone. 'Are you aware that Zeen has a brother in prison in Manila?'

Margaret splutters a, 'No, I certainly was not.'

'Did Zeen and Emma ever meet that you're aware of?'

Roly shakes his head. 'No. Emma left and then Zeen started a week later. They were never in the house at the same time.'

More questions come. Margaret and Roly answer them, firing back their own to the detective, but Isobel is barely listening. She can't shake the strangeness of Zeen disappearing this week of all weeks after faultless care and kindness for over three years. The phone call she'd made yesterday plays on her mind. Those broken words. Zeen's apology. Mentioning Lola. What was she trying to tell Isobel?

And yet, the detective is wrong. Zeen can't be involved. She never met Emma. But there is someone else connected to this – Scarlett. Maybe the timings aren't a coincidence after all. Emma started planning to abduct Lola in early April. The same time that Scarlett disappeared.

Isobel met Scarlett across the room at a dinner party of Jonny's. Scarlett was one of Jonny's girls. Smart and beautiful. That was his type. Just like Emma had been. If Scarlett and Emma are both connected to Jonny, then it's possible they also knew each other. Maybe they were friends.

Goosebumps prickle her skin. She forces herself to focus on what DCI Watkins is asking them, but inside she is screaming that it isn't Zeen helping Emma.

She wants to tell them about Scarlett. But it's not something she can just blurt out. Because talking about Scarlett's connection to Emma also means talking about Jonny's connection to Emma and Scarlett.

And his connection to them.

TWENTY-SIX

EMMA

Emma settles into the back seat of the taxi, Lola beside her, eyes glued to the window and the bridge stretching over a sandy banked river winding its way inland from the sea. A plane flies low in the air, gaining altitude as it swoops above their heads as they leave Brighton behind them. Lola follows its path with wide eyes, and Emma wonders if she's wishing, like her, that they were on that plane.

She rubs at her forehead. The voice urging her to hurry is louder today, and heaviness presses down on her chest. Once, when she was ten or eleven, she went on a school trip to Hampton Court Palace to learn about Henry VIII and all his wives. She remembers nothing about the grandeur of the palace or the history, but she does remember the vast maze in the gardens and how she hadn't wanted to stay in the group she'd been given. There were two other girls and one boy, being guided by a parent helper, and all the children were being silly and scared of getting lost. Emma hadn't been scared.

She'd wanted to explore, to be free, and so she'd hung back, taken a left when the others had turned right. It had been so fun at first – the high hedges, the dead ends. And then it wasn't fun.

She was lost. The coach taking them home was going to be leaving, and that same fear she'd always felt at home reared up. Would anyone realise she wasn't there? She'd raced down path after path, trying to work out which turn she'd taken that had been the wrong one, and which one she should now take that would lead her to safety, all the while fearing she'd run out of time, would never escape.

She feels the same desperation chasing through her veins now.

'Where are you two heading then?' the driver asks.

Emma glances to the mirror, and as their eyes meet, she tries to smile. He's around fifty, she thinks, with thinning grey hair, deep-set eyes and a black shapeless T-shirt. He gives her a wide grin, and she catches the gap in his mouth where a tooth should be.

'Just a day out,' she replies before turning her head to stare out the window, hoping he gets the message. The road has widened into two lanes of traffic on both sides. They're on the outskirts of Brighton now on a road with bungalows on each side that look too close to the road.

She's so tired. Her eyes are gritty, eyelids weighing down. She hasn't felt like this since Lola was first born and those sleepless nights of a crying baby, her body unfamiliar and aching to hold her child. That sense of relief when she'd scooped Lola into her arms. Emma didn't care what that DNA test said. She was Lola's mother, and she would do anything to protect her daughter.

Last night she seesawed between snatches of sleep and being wide awake, listening to every creak of the house, convincing herself that Teddy was right outside their door, waiting to creep in and hurt them. Or thinking that any second she'd hear the thump of a fist on the front door, a shouted, 'Police,' and it would all be over, everything she'd done for nothing.

What then? Will Jonny have her locked up again, stripping her of her life and everything she is? Or will he simply kill her like he promised. She doesn't care. They can do what they like to her. But Lola? No. She'll be taken back to Isobel and Roly, back to a world where Jonny can smile his charming smile and they'd open the door and let him into their home with no concept of the monster lurking inside him.

This is why she'd had to take Lola now. All those years of keeping quiet, saying nothing. Doing nothing. Never daring to set foot near Richmond or anywhere else in London where she might accidentally see Lola or Isobel and Roly, no matter how much she yearned to see her daughter again.

If she'd had even a scrap of choice, she'd never have stopped trying to see Lola, to be part of her life, to get her back. Even after the horrors of all those months in hospital, after she'd tried to talk to Isobel and it had all gone wrong and Jonny had snatched her off the street, her first thought as she'd walked out of the hospital's revolving doors and felt the warm sun on her face was of Lola.

Except Jonny had been waiting for her on the corner, barely ten steps into her freedom.

'If you step out of line again... I'll kill everyone you love, including Lola, and no one will even notice. So stay away from her and stay away from me. I'll be watching, Emma. I'm always watching. Remember that.'

She'd understood then that in order to keep Lola safe, to keep her alive, Emma had to stay away, to shrink her life down. And she did. She has barely left the house other than to work in the florist, barely lived for fear of angering Jonny. She could've carried on like that forever. Accepted the small existence of her new life, just like her parents. She would've done it for Lola. Knowing that even if she couldn't see her every day, couldn't talk to her, couldn't shower her with a mother's love, her daughter was safe.

But then everything had changed earlier this year with a visitor to the florist. She'd been working alone on a funeral wreath when the bell over the shop door had dinged with the arrival of a customer, and she'd stepped away from the back and the funeral wreath she'd been making.

'*Emma?*'

The loneliness of the shop, the sound of her name had shot a bolt of fear through her veins. It was that day she'd realised that however small and insignificant her life was, it was over. She'd never be safe and nor would Lola. They were both loose ends that needed to be tidied up. The thought worries away at her along with all the others swirling in her head.

Emma's eyes flick to the meter, already nearing ten pounds and they've barely made it three miles out of Brighton. Watching the red digits tick upwards releases a different kind of fear bubbling in her stomach. But it was either walk out of Brighton or taxi, and walking meant risking being seen on cameras. It meant tired legs and tears too.

She feels them closing in again – lurking on every corner. Public transport felt too risky this morning. She'd been certain they'd still be watching mainline stations in the area. But in her waking moments last night, she formed a plan – something to cling to, to aim for. A taxi west to Arundel and then, when they are far enough away from the bigger towns, they'll catch a bus to Southampton and then another bus to Newbury, then Birmingham, avoiding London and the areas she's already been. If she can just get them away from the south coast, she's sure she'll feel calmer, less hemmed in; less trapped.

From Birmingham it's only a few hours to Liverpool. The ferry from Birkenhead to Belfast leaves in twelve hours. It feels an eternity and no time at all, but she has to believe they can make it. Sometime in the middle of the night, she'd sent a message to the number she'd memorised but not saved, explaining the roadworks and the towed car and being chased to the south coast. She'd stared at the blank screen for as long as she'd dared, but there'd been no reply, and she'd turned off the phone in case Haz's number appeared again. She misses him so much, but she has to do this without him.

Lola shuffles in her seat. She's holding Barnaby and Ducky up to the passenger window. 'Will we see Mummy today?' she asks.

Emma freezes. Doesn't breathe. Her daughter's words have broken the silence of the taxi. Did the driver hear? Her gaze darts to the mirror as heat floods her face. Then his eyes are on her, and she knows the answer. The silence draws out. She flounders, unsure what to say, and then the moment passes and she's left it too long to brush away.

'Where is your mummy?' he asks, doing that voice adults do when speaking to children. The same coaxing 'you can trust me' tone Emma had used in the toilets at the service station two days ago.

'She's on holiday,' Emma says quickly before Lola can reply, forcing her own sing-song tone. 'Isn't that right?' She squeezes Lola's hand, wanting her to know it's OK. Lola buries her head in Barnaby's fur and scrunches her eyes shut, and Emma is consumed once more with guilt of what she's putting this little girl through.

The taxi driver raises an eyebrow before turning his focus back to the road. There's a shift in the air – a silent tension that wasn't there before. She feels him glance back at them in the mirror, and when they stop at a set of traffic lights by a T-junction, he picks up his phone and taps something on the screen. Emma's pulse quickens – a galloping beat that has begun to feel almost normal over the last few days.

Don't be paranoid, she tells herself, thinking of Teddy, the B&B owner this morning. She'd been so certain he was bad, barely sleeping in fear of what he'd do. But then after a breakfast of eggs, bacon and sausages, and a second helping of jam on toast, he'd beckoned her to one side.

'It's obvious to me that you're in some kind of trouble. Please take this money back. I feel like you need it more than I do.' He'd held out an envelope, and even though she'd wanted to take it, she still shook her head.

'I... no... I couldn't. We have to pay.'

'No, you don't.' He placed the envelope on the hallway table and stepped back. *'My sister runs a women's refuge centre in the Romford area of East London. There's a number in the envelope.'* Then he'd turned away, busying himself with tidying the breakfast table and she'd picked up the money, whispering a 'thank you' she hopes he heard.

They'd been safe with him, but she'd been too wrapped up in her fears to tell the difference between peril and security, allowing her night-time imaginings to keep her from the rest she so desperately needed. After everything that happened to her, she knows she'll never fully trust anyone again, but that doesn't mean everyone is bad and out to get her.

'This weather is crazy, isn't it?' she says, filling the silence, trying to be normal. 'They say it's going to finally get hot this afternoon and be nice for the rest of the week.'

She waits for his reply. An 'about time too' comment that doesn't come. The traffic light turns green, but they don't pull away. The driver's attention is still on his phone. A horn honks impatiently from behind them, but instead of putting the car into gear and moving forward, he shifts in his seat and looks at them – a long moment of staring first to Lola and then to Emma before his gaze moves back to something on his phone.

Her mouth turns dry. 'Is... everything OK?' She forces out the question as she pulls her backpack onto her lap.

He nods but doesn't speak. Another horn beeps, and a car moves around them.

She casts her gaze around her for a way out. She wants to

open the door right here and take Lola's hand and get out of this car, get away, but there are vehicles everywhere, moving around them in both directions. It would be too dangerous. And now the driver is moving again.

'Would you mind pulling over?' She points to a parade of shops. 'I'm feeling a bit car sick.'

Without a word, he flicks on the indicator, and they turn into a lay-by. She feels a shaky relief nudge at the sharp corners of her panic.

'Thanks,' she says, opening the zip pocket of her backpack. Her focus is on the money she needs, so she doesn't notice straight away when he turns off the engine and opens the driver's door.

Before she can react, he's already out, the door shutting behind him. A 'no' starts to form in her mouth as she sees what's happening. Time is slow and fast all at once. She's reaching for the door, telling herself she's wrong, knowing she's not.

And then it happens. The soft clunk of the locking system. She grabs the handle, not believing it, but it flaps uselessly in her hand.

'No,' she shouts, banging the window.

'What's going on?' Lola whispers.

'It's OK,' Emma replies, taking her hand.

'Is the taxi man going to hurt us?'

How can she reply to that? 'It's going to be all right, Lola. I love you. Remember that, OK? All I've ever wanted is to protect you.'

The taxi driver steps to her window and lifts his phone so she can see the screen. It's open on Facebook, to a poster with a blue strip at the top. 'Police Appeal for Information' is written in white lettering. Just beneath it is a thicker band of red and a single word – 'WANTED' – and below it, a picture of her face.

The photo is one from the hospital. It must have been when she was admitted because she doesn't remember it being taken.

She's wearing a white-and-green gown, and her hair is unbrushed and greasy at the top. Emma's face is fuller now, her cheekbones less jutting. But it's undoubtedly her.

'I'm calling the number,' he shouts, pointing to the bottom of the screen.

'Please.' She bangs a hand on the glass. 'Don't do this. I can explain.'

He gives her a look that is somewhere between pity and disgust and steps away.

Emma's hands grab at the doors again – hers then Lola's then reaching into the front and trying them both. It's useless. He's locked them in. She falls back into her seat as the crushing reality of what's happening rushes through her.

The police will be coming for her. So will Jonny and his friends.

There is no escape.

Emma has failed. All the plans, the desperate rushing of the last few days – it's all been for nothing. She'd done this to keep her daughter safe, but all she's done is put her in more danger than ever.

TWENTY-SEVEN

EMMA

Silent tears stream down Emma's face. She grabs at the door again and again. 'No, no, no.' An anguished sob leaves her mouth.

'Please,' Emma shouts, 'you don't understand what you're doing. You can't keep us locked up. There are people after us.'

The taxi driver taps his index finger on the passenger window and with a look that sits somewhere between smug and annoyed, he shakes his head at her and wags his finger. Her panic is a wild, monstrous beast of a thing. She has to get them out. She can't go back. She won't. This is what it must be like to drown, she realises. Trapped under water, no air, no breath to take. No escape. She can almost feel the scream of her lungs, that same desperation to live.

Beside her, Lola whimpers, pressing her face into Emma's lap. She can feel the dampness of Lola's tears on her leggings and the heat of her distress radiating from her skin.

'It's OK, Lola,' she says, even though it's not and they both know it.

'Is he the monster?' she whimpers.

'No, he's not,' Emma says, wishing she could shield her

daughter from this fear. She should never have told her about a monster, but she needed her to see, to understand why they were doing this.

Emma reaches again for the handle, but the driver's face looms behind the glass. Another head shake. Less amused, more angry this time.

'I've already called the number. The police will be here any minute,' he says, exaggerating the mouthing of the words. 'They can sort this out.'

No, they can't!

She wants to beg and plead again, but there is no point. She twists to look out the back window. How long have they been trapped here? How long before that black SUV with the tinted windows arrives? The lay-by is at the edge of a busy T-junction with traffic lights and eight lines of stop-start traffic, two in every direction. There's a parade of shops to the left. A barbers, a Co-op supermarket and a butchers. Emma spots a couple leaving the Co-op. They're in their mid-thirties and the woman is pregnant, the bulge of her stomach stretching out the white T-shirt she's wearing. The man is tall and handsome with brown hair and a short beard. They look every bit the quintessential picture of a happy couple.

Emma leans across to the other side of the car and bangs on the window. 'Help,' she shouts at them. 'Help us, please.'

They look over, alarm registering on their faces. She bangs on the glass again. 'Help! He's locked me in here. He won't let me out.'

For the smallest of moments, it seems as though the couple are going to keep moving, look away, pretend they've not seen, but the woman's eyes meet hers and she's moving closer, calling out to the driver. Hope brims inside Emma. *Please make him see sense.* The driver moves quickly towards them, and the three exchange words Emma can't hear. His phone is in his hand and he's pointing at the screen. The man is nodding, but the woman is shaking her head, pointing at the car. Both men seem to be talking at the woman now, but she raises her hand and shakes her head before pulling out her phone and pressing it to her ear. She ignores their protests and the look of outrage on the driver's face and steps around them to the taxi.

'I'm calling nine-nine-nine,' she says, crouching a little to look at Emma. 'I've no idea what's going on, but no one should lock you in a car. Hold tight.'

Hot tears stream down Emma's face. She should feel relief, but there is only the burning, unspeakable knowledge that time is slipping away from her. They will be here any minute. She has to get out of this car. She has to run.

'Please,' Emma tries again when the woman hangs up. 'You have to make him unlock the car.'

'I'm trying. The police have a car in the area. They'll be here any minute.' She steps back to the men. The driver is shaking his head, but there's an uncertainty now that wasn't there before. And then he's pulling out his keys and turning towards the car, and finally there is relief – a wave of it that hits so hard she's sure it would knock her down if she wasn't already sitting. Then he stops, hand aloft but not pressing, not unlocking. A flash of blue and yellow catches Emma's eye.

It's too late – the police are here.

The sense of drowning returns, and the tears keep falling. Lola is crying too, head still buried in her lap, and all Emma can think about is the memorised phone number.

'*Don't contact me until you've got Lola somewhere safe or it's an absolute emergency. Life or death!*'

This is that moment.

Right here. Right now.

Except, there isn't time to pull her phone from her backpack and turn it on. And even if there was, what can anyone do to stop this scene from unfolding? The police car pulls to the side of the road, parking in front of the taxi. Two officers climb out.

Both are women with hair pinned in neat buns at the nape of their necks. One is in her thirties, and the other looks impossibly young and can't be much older than eighteen. Both carry themselves with confidence, as though they have absolute faith that whatever they are walking into, they'll be able to deal with it. How wrong they are, Emma thinks as reality gnaws in the pit of her stomach.

The officers split up. One to the taxi driver and the couple, and the other to the car and Emma. It's the younger officer who crouches down to look into the back seats at them.

'Hi,' she says, voice clear despite the glass between them. 'I'm PC Ravi Krishna. Can you tell me what's going on?'

Emma nods and wipes her sleeve across her face. 'The taxi driver, he... he's locked me and my little girl in here and won't let us out,' she says. 'Please let us out.'

Time has run out on them. She twists in her seat, searching the traffic. They'll be here any minute.

'Did he give you a reason?' PC Krishna asks. 'Was it an unpaid fare?'

Emma shakes her head. 'No, nothing like that.' She considers lying. Telling the officer that this is a case of mistaken identity. That the taxi driver has got it all wrong and she is not the woman on the police alert. But even as the thought forms, she's dismissing it. Her face has changed since that hollow-cheeked girl was pushed in front of a camera, but it is still very clearly her – her wide brown eyes, her long hair – and getting caught in a lie now will not help her get out of this car.

In less than a minute, they will realise she is a wanted fugitive. And yet she can't bring herself to tell this officer the truth either. Everyone has thought her crazy. The doctors, her family, the solicitor she'd hired – everyone – thought she was making it up when she'd told them what had happened to her. Trying to explain to PC Krishna what Jonny and Roly and Isobel did won't help either. 'Please...' she says instead. 'Let us out. My daughter is really scared.'

PC Krishna gives a reassuring smile. 'What are your names?'

'I'm Emma Jacobs, and this is Lola.'

The officer waves and gives a big smile as Lola lifts her head from Emma's lap. 'How old are you, sweetheart?'

'I'm three. I want to go home,' she says before burying her face back into Emma's body again. And even though it's an unpleasant thought, Emma is glad Lola is filled with such terror that she can't tell PC Krishna that Emma is not her mummy and isn't taking her home.

'We will be soon,' Emma lies, rubbing Lola's back and shooting another pleading look to the police officer.

A yell makes them all turn to the group outside the taxi. The couple are stepping away. They are no longer holding hands. The woman looks to Emma and mouths an apology.

'Look,' the taxi driver shouts, jabbing a finger to his phone. 'I was being a good citizen.'

Emma closes her eyes for a moment as her final chance to escape slips away. The officers have seen the alert. She is no longer a woman to be helped but someone mentally ill who deserves to be locked up. Desperate. Dangerous. Not to be trusted.

Emma doesn't catch the reply of the second officer. It's spoken softly, soothing, and the man looks like he grunts, but then he's reaching into his pocket and pulling out his keys. A second later there's another soft clunk. Emma launches herself at the handle, and the door swings outwards. 'Look, Lola,' she says, hugging her little girl, 'the nice officer has unlocked the doors. We can get out.'

Lola lifts her head and watches wearily as PC Krishna gives a welcoming smile. Emma can sense her daughter's hesitation.

Being locked in a car is scary, but being out in the world with the monsters is considerably worse. She is right to be wary.

'It's safe,' Emma says, hoping it's true as she climbs out, eyes scanning the roads again. An image flashes in her head. The vice-like grip of hands on her, lifting her up, dragging her away to the hospital.

'Thank you,' she says to the officer, weak with relief as she breathes in the fresh air.

'Now, I'm loath to put you back in a car, but would you mind sitting in our police car for a little bit, just while we speak to the taxi driver and take both of your statements?'

Emma's feet falter, her fingers tightening a little around Lola's hand. *Run now. Go!* 'I don't want to press charges,' she blurts out. 'We can just go. We're actually running late, so...'

The police officer offers a sympathetic smile. 'Don't worry, it won't take long, and I'm not going to shut you in. We'll keep the door open. It's just somewhere for you and your daughter to sit while we get this cleared up.'

Emma nods. What else can she do? They can't outrun this officer and trying will only add to her problems. They walk to the police. Lola shuffles in first, sliding across the leather seats. The presence of PC Krishna has calmed her, and she's turning in the seat to play with Barnaby; strapping him in with a seat belt, clipping it into place. 'Barnaby, you have been a naughty bear. You are going to prison.'

PC Krishna smiles before stepping back to her colleague. When she returns, a crease has formed on her brow and she's shaking her head a little.

'So,' she says, crouching down so she's level with Emma, 'the driver of the taxi has shown us a social-media post of a police alert for you.'

The world closes in. Emma is no longer locked in a car, but she is just as trapped. Any second now they will realise she has abducted a little girl and there is no way she can explain that.

Telling herself over and over that she is Lola's mother isn't enough.

'I...' she starts to say as PC Krishna continues.

'But the thing is – and this is what we're trying to get to the bottom of' – she pauses, and in the beat that follows, she searches Emma's face – 'the post looks real. Even fooled us at first, but there is no alert for you on the national database. The post the taxi driver saw is fake. You are not a person of concern or interest in any police investigation.'

Tears spill onto Emma's cheeks. She is not a fugitive. She is not wanted by the police. She wasn't sure if Roly and Isobel would call the police. She'd assumed they might, assumed their love for Lola would overrun their need to keep the police out of any investigation into the little girl they say is theirs. The relief is barely a whisper.

What difference does it make now? She is still being chased. Lola is still in danger.

There is so much she wants to tell this officer, but where to begin? It all started at a party of Jonny's, and Emma falling so stupidly in love that she didn't see the danger she was in until it was too late. 'The people doing this... they're bad. They think I know something about the woman who disappeared – Scarlett Peters.'

PC Krishna's eyes widen a fraction, and she nods for Emma to continue.

'They have a lot of money and resources, and they threatened to hurt my daughter, so I ran away, trying to hide from them, but—'

There's a flash of black medal in the corner of her vision. She spins around and there it is – the SUV pulling up alongside the taxi. Jonny is here.

Everything stops. All she can hear is the rapid thump of her racing heart. One thought sticks in her head.

She's as good as dead.

TWENTY-EIGHT

ISOBEL

A headache throbs across Isobel's temples. She craves caffeine but won't drink any more. She's only had two sips from her first cup, balancing the desire to push away the exhaustion fogging her mind and not wanting to hurt the baby.

For the last hour, they've sat in this kitchen and asked and answered questions with DCI Watkins about their lives and Emma and Zeen and a dozen other things that Isobel is sure are not important. And now even Margaret has fallen silent. They've just watched the CCTV of Emma at the cash machine yesterday. Seeing Lola's tear-stained face push up against Emma's body, gaining comfort from a woman who is not her, had decimated the last shards of Isobel's already broken heart.

'I'm her mother,' she'd wanted to scream. She would've done too, if Margaret hadn't been in the room. How long are they supposed to keep pretending this is an ordinary abduction, if such a thing even exists?

She isn't the only one frustrated. Roly is rubbing constantly at his neck, shooting looks at her she can't decipher before looking at his phone as though the answers lie inside it. *She's your mother*, Isobel wants to tell him. *You were supposed to get rid of her.*

Margaret breaks the silence, tapping her finger again on the counter and fixing her gaze on the detective. 'Don't take this the wrong way, DCI Watkins, but would your time be better spent with your team, directing the search from the police station? I'm certain you aren't being of any use here.'

'Mother,' Roly says at the same moment Isobel wonders what the right way to take that comment is.

'I'm sorry, darling, but it's been two days. This is quite ridiculous. I ought to be calling this man's boss,' Margaret replies, completely unaware of the grenade she has thrown among them. Any second now it will detonate, surely?

She glances to DCI Watkins. His face is unreadable, but there is no mistaking the tension clouding the air.

'Mother.' Roly's voice is loud and harsher than she's ever heard him use with his mother before. 'Please stop.'

Margaret's lips purse, and there's moisture glistening in her eyes as she looks at her son. 'I'm worried about my only grand-child. I'm only trying to help.'

'I know,' Roly sighs, his tone softening. 'Why don't you have a lie-down? I can come and get you if there's any news.'

Isobel doesn't dare look at her mother-in-law, doesn't dare breathe in case the woman might see the words rushing silently through Isobel's head. *Please go!*

The pause that follows drags on and on, and then Margaret is nodding. 'Yes, I think I will. You'll wake me if there's any developments?'

Roly nods. The relief in his face is unmistakable. No one talks as Margaret gathers herself and sweeps from the room. They wait as she walks up the stairs, remaining silent until the soft thud of a bedroom door carries through the house, and Isobel stands and shuts the kitchen door.

She turns to the men. Roly is rubbing his hands over his

face. He looks up as she moves back to her seat. 'I'm sorry,' he says, but she isn't sure if the apology is meant for her. 'Thanks for doing this, Owen,' he adds.

'You've always had my back, old chum, and you know I'm happy to help, but just to be clear, I'm putting my career on the line for this.'

'Of course, and we're grateful.'

And there it is. The truth at last. A truth Isobel has been longing to face ever since Margaret had opened the front door of their home two days ago and ushered them in, and they'd begun this ridiculous charade. She's hated the pretence. All those times she'd told herself she couldn't do it, couldn't carry on with the lies, but now the truth feels just as impossible. Maybe a part of her had been leaning into the fantasy they'd created for Margaret, pretending too that an entire police force is out searching for their little girl.

A memory of the roadside services rushes back at her. Shouting at Roly to call the police. And his reply. *'I'm doing it now. Sit down for a second, Iz, while I make the call. I'll ring Owen. He'll know what to do.'*

Not 999. Not emergencies and sirens, helicopters and road-blocks, but Roly's childhood friend, Owen Watkins. He is a police officer. A detective chief inspector based out of Scotland Yard. That is true at least. But there's nothing official about what he's doing here. How could they have ever called emergency services and reported their daughter missing? It would've brought a spotlight on them and everyone connected to them – including Jonny.

But he stepped in of course. A friend of Roly's. Favours owed. But more than that – he's as tangled up in this as the rest of them.

He tops up his coffee cup. 'It was a good shout to mention a ransom as a reason to keep the press in the dark, Rols. Although I could've done without you pushing it again yesterday, Isobel.

It meant I had to lie outright to Margaret about releasing a press statement. It puts me at more risk.'

'I... I'm sorry. I just want to find Lola.' Hurt spreads across her chest. There is no alert. No photo on front pages. No press conference. She'd known it was impossible, but she'd pushed anyway. Out of desperation perhaps. It's why she didn't want to check the news this morning. There would've been nothing to see, and that truth is almost unbearable.

'Iz was just keeping up the pretence for Mother, weren't you, darling? We know you can't really talk to the papers.'

'Well, the game would've been up if Margaret had pushed for a public statement.'

His flippant reply slices through her. *It's not a game*, she wants to cry out. This is not some schoolboy antic they're trying to cover up. Lola has really been abducted by a crazed woman. She bites it back, keeps it in. If they were any other people, they would've called the police. They'd have a team of officers in their home, the press camped outside. They'd have been making appeals and sharing photos of Lola.

But they're not any other people. They are Huntingtons. One of Britain's oldest families, descended from Edward VI. And part of their ongoing success is keeping just under the radar. Of course, that's not the reason Roly called DCI Watkins on Sunday instead of dialling 999. That reason is far more complicated and one she is still trying to wrap her head around. So no matter how she feels about what's going on, this man in her kitchen is one of only a handful of people who knows Lola is missing.

'Mother wanting the Huntington name out of the papers is always a given, thank God.'

'Lucky for us, she didn't want a family liaison officer in the house either,' the detective says. 'That would've been a hard one to pull off.' He gives a rueful smile. 'Although I could get used to you calling me DCI Watkins.'

'What's really going on, Owen?' Isobel blurts out when she can't stand the lightness to this man's tone anymore. And despite everything, it feels strange to call him by his first name after all this time. 'What are you really doing to find Lola?'

He turns to look at her, and she can't stop her hand reaching to fiddle with one of her earrings as her cheeks flush under the weight of his gaze.

'Please don't worry,' he replies. 'Everything you've heard me say when Margaret is in the room is happening. All of it apart from releasing any information to the national press. It's just not an official investigation.'

'But how?' she asks. 'How are you watching the CCTV cameras? Who's doing that?'

'It's been relatively simple, bar a few hiccups. I've used some of my training budget and assembled a team for what they believe is an exercise. They think Emma is an undercover detective also in training and using her own daughter to create a realistic abduction scenario. The team have created a social-media awareness campaign and used a photo of Emma from her time in hospital. So we have still got the public on alert for Emma.

'You know Frank is also a trusted friend of ours.' He nods to Roly. 'And he's taken some holiday days and is acting as our team on the ground with another... associate, shall we say. There's no red tape here, Isobel. We have just as good a chance of finding them as a real police investigation. And nobody is querying us. Her family were happy to cooperate with me. I genuinely believe they have no idea where Emma is.'

Isobel clings to the reassurance he's offering her.

'We had a challenge with the petrol station cash withdrawal yesterday,' he continues. 'Frank wasn't near enough to be on scene. Fortunately, I've got a friend on the Crawley force who owed me a favour and sent a squad car to hold Emma and Lola until Frank got there. Obviously, we underestimated Emma yesterday, but that won't happen again. Frank is staying in the area and ready for the next alert.'

'God, I almost put my foot in it yesterday when you said the police were on their way,' Roly groans. 'I should've known it was part of the plan.'

'Yes, you should've done. I'm calling in every favour I can for this. I'll say it again: I'm risking my career to help you both so please, think before you speak when Margaret is in the room.'

'We will, won't we, Iz? Thank you, Owen.'

She nods. 'You're assuming Emma hasn't already left the country with Lola?'

'It's highly unlikely.'

The men continue speculating. All the things they think Emma might do, places she might go. Isobel is only half listening. Inside, the dark foreboding returns. The familiar voice reminding her that she deserves this. Except it's worse. Now Margaret is no longer in the room and all pretence has been stripped away. Now there is nothing to shield Isobel from the truth, the guilt of what they're doing floods every cell in her body. Burning and hot.

What kind of parents call a friend instead of the police when their child is abducted?

What kind of mother doesn't do everything she can to make sure the world is searching for her daughter? The answer stares back at her from the mirror every time she looks at her reflection.

The insistent buzz of a phone pulls Isobel away from her panicked fears and back to the kitchen.

'Hello?' The voice is officious once more. There's a pause, and she watches his expression change. Eyes widening, a nod, a lifting of his posture. She holds her breath until he hangs up and a smile stretches across his face.

'We've got them. We've got Lola.'

TWENTY-NINE

ISOBEL

The rush of emotion is a tidal wave; crashing, pummelling. They've got her. The knowledge that she will hold Lola in her arms again causes a gasping relief, but it is short-lived, because the guilt is still there, sharp and unforgiving like the point of a knife held to her throat.

Isobel tries to imagine waking up tomorrow to Lola's shouts of, *'Mummy.'* A day of toys spread across the playroom. The familiar theme tune of *Peppa Pig* playing from the TV. A world of normal where they're all the same people they were just days ago.

No. The ripples from these nightmarish days will run too deep to go back to the people they were before. Those people pretended and ignored, lived in a fantasy that started long before the pretence of the police investigation Margaret believes is underway. Where does that leave them? She doesn't know, but she's certain there is no way back to the perfect family they'd pretended to be for so long.

'Thank God,' Roly says, jumping up from the stool and stepping over to kiss her; his joy so simple and uncomplicated.

'For real this time?' she asks, because the thought of holding Lola is almost too much to bear if there's even the smallest chance Emma could escape again. 'Is she on her way here?'

'She will be soon,' the detective replies.

'What—' Isobel starts to say, but Roly gets there first.

'What does that mean? Either you've got her and she's on her way or you don't.'

'It's fine, chum. Calm down. We've got Lola, and we're going to get through this whole thing unscathed and get back on with our lives. We just need to keep our shit together for a little while longer.' He says 'shit' like it's a normal event – a boring meeting, a dull family dinner – and not the abduction of her daughter, the implosion of their world.

Roly pulls an apologetic face. 'You're right. Sorry, Owen. I'm just bloody relieved this is almost over. What's happening?'

'The cyber team got a call half an hour ago to the number we've been using for the social-media campaign about Emma. We made the alert look exactly like a police alert and gave a helpline number that's directed straight to the cyber team.

'A taxi driver told us that a woman and a little girl got into his taxi at a rank in Brighton. He's absolutely certain it's Emma. He pulled over and has locked them in his car until we get there.'

'Locked them in?' Isobel repeats.

The detective continues, oblivious to the horror in her voice. 'He's parked in a lay-by on the A27 heading west out of Brighton. We told him to hang tight and that the police are on their way. Frank will be there any minute.'

They really have Lola this time. She tries to keep hold of that thought and not the image of her daughter terrified and trapped in the back of a taxi. Isobel pictures the Mancunian detective who stood in their living room in his leather biker jacket only yesterday morning. She's seen him a dozen times or so at a dinner or a party. Another one of Jonny's friends, except he's never looked comfortable sitting down at a table, eating delicate food and making small talk. He's never brought a wife or date like most of the men do, preferring to be up and working the room or in a corner watching. A cold chill shoots down her body. There's something about Frank she's never liked, never quite trusted, although she's not sure why.

It's all too easy to imagine Frank arriving at the lay-by. She sees him stepping from a car, holding out his ID. Not the type of man anyone would second-guess. A taxi driver has seen a social-media alert that he believes is from the police. In his mind he has called the authorities and is expecting them to arrive. He will see everything he wants to see and will unlock his car and hand over Emma and Lola without a second thought.

'I'm expecting Frank to call any second.'

'Brilliant,' Roly says. 'So we should have Lola back home in a few hours.' A smile stretches across his face, crinkling his eyes.

Isobel smiles too, but it feels as fake as everything else they've been doing this week. She wonders about Emma. When Lola is home and their life carries on, what will happen to Emma? It will be Jonny's decision, and that makes her think of Scarlett and where the missing woman is. Did she run away? Is she out there? Or will the next news story about her be about a buried body and grieving parents.

They wait. Impatience hangs in the air, stifling like Margaret's perfume. That heavy almost masculine scent her mother-in-law loves so much to wear.

Every minute that passes feels like an hour, and then the call finally arrives. Isobel holds her breath, waiting for him to tell her Lola is with his team, but his expression darkens. 'Damn it.'

'What is it?' Roly asks.

'Frank's there,' the detective says. 'They have eyes on Lola and Emma. But it seems a passer-by called 999 and two officers are already on the scene.'

The mention of the police – the actual police – causes Isobel's stomach to lurch. How much trouble are they in? How will they explain to officers why they didn't call the police when Emma stole Lola? There is no answer. They are terrible parents.

Emma is a desperate woman who believes with every fibre of her being that she is Lola's mother. Isobel doesn't know what Emma will do if she feels trapped with no way out, and that thought scares her more than anything in the world. More than explaining herself to the police. More than losing this life they've built. Even more than Jonny.

'What's going to happen?' Isobel asks. 'Can Frank show his ID and take Lola?'

'It's too much of a risk doing that. I highly doubt Emma told them anything. At the moment, they probably only have her name. Frank will be aware of this and will not want to start a paper trail that can lead back to him and us at a later date. The best thing is to wait. Eventually, the police will let Emma and Lola go. They've got no reason to hold them. They'll know the social-media alert isn't real. If they're diligent officers, they'll report the fake posters, but nothing will come of that.'

'So we do nothing?' Isobel asks.

'And what if Emma starts talking to those police officers?' Roly asks. 'And tells them what's really going on here?'

DCI Watkins raises his eyebrows. 'And says what? She's abducted a little girl from two loving parents because she believes she's her mother?'

The exhaustion of the last few days hits Isobel, pulling and pushing, giving the sense that she's falling, unable to right herself. Their lives are unravelling, collapsing around her.

She is Lola's mother. Her real mother. There is even a DNA test to prove it. Whatever has happened to that file, whatever happens next, Isobel clings to the knowledge that she is Lola's mother. But if Emma starts to talk, if an eager officer starts to scrape the surface of Isobel and Roly's lives, it won't be long before they discover that not everything is as shiny and bright as they make it seem.

THIRTY

EMMA

The SUV looks like a tank compared to the taxi it pulls up beside – a looming dark shadow. Emma could never quite wrap her head around the differences between all those doctors, the clinical psychologists, psychiatrists and counsellors. The only thing she was certain of is that they were all wrong. *'There's no such thing as monsters, Emma.'*

'There is. And he put me in here.'

They thought she was crazy and so they heard crazy thoughts. She could never make them see that she didn't mean the nightmare, bogeymen and mythical kind of monster. She'd meant evil and unnatural – something inside those that walked among them. Like the two men climbing out of the SUV right now. Sent to take Lola home and... then Jonny will get her. But how can she explain all of this to these two police officers when she's been silent for so long?

Emma's silence over all that happened to her was forced in two ways. The first, by drugging her and shoving her in a secure ward for the mentally ill. From that point forward, she was a woman who couldn't be trusted to tell the truth. Discredited and destroyed in one go. Even if she'd been prepared to risk her life by telling the police about Jonny and all his businesses, they'd never have believed her. But just to be sure, Jonny had put Lola on the line, making it clear that he would kill her little girl if she tried to speak out. There can't be many people in this world who could threaten to kill a child and mean it. Even fewer who would go through with it. But Jonny is one of them. She might have been blinded by love for so much of the time she'd spent attending his parties and dinners and enjoying a lifestyle that was so far beyond what she'd ever known, but even then she'd seen that Jonny's businesses meant everything to him. He'd never let anyone stand in the way of that. Child or not.

Those two factors had kept Emma pinned into her small life at the florist and sleeping in the single bed in her old bedroom, never daring to even think of reaching for more. But then Scarlett had come to see her earlier in the year. She was in trouble and wanted Emma's help.

But there'd been no time to help, no time to plan before Scarlett had disappeared and everything changed again. Emma's knowledge of Jonny's businesses and his connection to Scarlett was suddenly dangerous. Emma could connect him to a missing woman whose photo was on the front page of every newspaper.

The police might've laughed at her or ignored Emma if she'd told them about a ruthless businessman who'd destroyed her life, but they'd have listened if she'd mentioned Scarlett.

Jonny had a trusted circle of friends. Those who owed him, those too tied up in his businesses to ever dare cross him. But Emma was not one of his friends anymore, which made her a liability. She'd known the second she'd seen the news about Scarlett that he'd be thinking the same. Jonny was careful and meticulous and ruthless. He did not like loose ends or threats, and she and Lola were both.

'Do you know these men?' PC Krishna asks, dragging

Emma back to the police car. The officer nods towards the SUV.

She shakes her head as heat burns beneath her skin. Sweat prickles under her arms. She wants to say yes. She wants to tell this kind police officer all that has happened, to warn her not to trust them as they approach the taxi driver and the other officer, but memories are flying through her head. All she can think about is the last time a black SUV pulled up beside her. Those grabbing hands.

They'd come for her in the January when Lola was five months old and Emma hadn't seen her for three of those months. It was after the solicitor had shown her the DNA test, told her nothing more could be done, after she'd approached Isobel on the common, trying to appeal to Isobel's kindness, begging to see her daughter, warning her Lola wasn't safe. Emma had been so unhappy, so lost and lonely; hollowed out from the need she felt to be with Lola. But she'd made a mistake going to the common. There had been no kindness in Isobel. No female solidarity that urged her to keep their conversation secret.

Emma hadn't noticed the SUV at first. Her thoughts were so loud and raging that it had blurred the outside world, and so she'd paid no attention to the car that had pulled out of a space just as she was leaving her house on the way to a shift at the supermarket – right back to where she'd started, except worse because she could no longer spend those long hours dreaming of a bright, dazzling future.

Her head had been down against the cold, and she'd barely registered the slow speed of the vehicle as it had moved alongside her. Then the bang of a car door; footsteps on the pavement.

'Emma? Emma Jacobs?'

The voice had been friendly, as though the person might be an old school friend, surprised to see her. She'd spun towards the figure and found herself face to face with a giant of a man who was already upon her before she had a chance to react. Another car door had banged. Engine rumbling. The driver running around to help as strong hands had grabbed her, lifting her feet from the pavement as though she weighed no more than Lola. And before she'd even drawn breath, found the words to protest or scream, she'd already been shoved into the footwell in the back of the car, the driver pulling away, the strong hands not letting go.

'Don't try to move or I'll snap your neck. Jonny sent us. He wants a word.'

Jonny had turned from the front passenger seat and smiled at her. 'You've been causing trouble, Emma.' He'd given her his warnings, and she'd promised never to approach Roly or Isobel again, but he'd wanted to make sure his message had been received and so he'd given her such a strong dose of sedative and something else too that she'd been both high and half dead as they'd dragged her into the hospital. They told the doctor it was a suicide attempt, and she'd been committed to a secure unit. It was only later in one of the many long and pointless therapy sessions that a doctor had told her how close to an overdose and organ failure she'd been. She wonders if that had been their plan all along.

Emma blinks, looking around her now as the beat of her heart thrashes in her temples. Her body is tense, frozen. She has to focus, has to stay present. She can't allow the memories to drag her back to that time. All that matters is her future. Hers and Lola's – her daughter, her everything. Together always. The look of concern on PC Krishna's face – the frowning worry – is almost enough to make Emma nod in response to the question of whether she knows these men, but she can't.

'Will you be OK if I step over there and speak to them?' she asks.

Emma nods. 'We'll be fine here. Thank you.'

The hammering of her pulse has yet to subside, but all of a sudden, it's not fear causing the burst of adrenaline pumping through her body; it's the smallest window of opportunity opening before her. If she's quick, they might get out of this still.

'Lola, come sit on my lap,' Emma says quietly.

Her little girl slides away from Barnaby, strapped in and ready for his trip to Lola's imaginary prison. She clambers onto Emma's lap, her body firm and warm and everything that matters in the world.

'I'm scared,' Lola says, voice so tiny.

'Me too. But we have each other. I will do everything I can to keep you safe.'

'Where has the police lady gone?' Lola asks. 'I like her.'

'I do too.' And Emma is surprised to find that she feels a little bad about what she's about to do. Her eyes follow the officer as she moves towards her colleague, the taxi driver and the two men.

'See those people,' Emma says, pointing to a lanky man in a leather jacket and the one stood beside him with the shaved head and bulging muscles.

Lola gives a furtive nod before ducking down, hugging Emma tight.

'They want to take you.'

'No,' she whimpers.

The guilt hits so hard, Emma feels sick, but she has to make Lola see how important this is. 'It's OK. I won't let them get you.' *I'm your mother. I would never let anything happen to you,* she adds in her head. She holds her daughter tight, all too aware of the stakes. If she fails now, there will never be another chance. The thought is lighter fuel to the burning terror already scorching through her body.

'Get ready,' she whispers in Lola's ear.

'OK,' Lola says, the one word shaking with fear.

Emma tightens the straps of her backpack and slides the

pink bag onto her daughter's back. There is no escape in staying here. Either Jonny's friends will take them away now, or the police will. And however much that second option appeals over the first, it will only delay the inevitable. She can't tell them about taking Lola, and there'll be no reason to keep them in a police station. They'll let them go eventually, and she knows the men will be waiting. She tightens her grip on Lola, shuffling forward in the seat so her feet are out of the car. She's perched; ready as she watches the group no more than ten metres away.

Emma can't hear what's being said, but she sees the men smile with their 'we're here to help' expressions. Hands out, open, nothing to hide. The older officer smiles too, and it seems as though all is lost. One of the men – the taller one with the leather jacket she thinks she recognises from another lifetime – he pulls out his phone from his pocket and shows the screen to the officer and the taxi driver. She wonders what photo he is showing her. Is it the one of her in the hospital gown, or is it the perfectly posed photo of Isobel, Roly and Lola, the one that sits in the silver frame in their living room. The mother and father and their little girl – just as blonde as her parents.

No. She won't let them do this again. She won't let them convince the world she is crazy, that Lola is not hers. Emma's breath catches in her throat, rasping, panicked. Any second, any moment and the officer is going to let these men take her and Lola. More memories of the hospital leak into her thoughts.

'*Your brothers brought you here, Emma. Remember? You signed the paperwork.*'

'*No, no, they weren't my brothers. It's all a mistake. They're bad men. Monsters. You have to believe me. I need to get to my baby.*'

'*You don't have a baby, Emma. We've talked about this. Remember? You've never been pregnant. You've never given birth.*'

'*I did. I was. Please, you have to believe me.*'

Emma's hands tighten around Lola's body, and the little girl whimpers with the same fear pulsing through her.

The taxi driver waves his hands in the air. 'I'm losing money now.' His voice carries over to them. 'Why am I still here?'

The officer replies, too quietly for Emma to hear.

'I didn't kidnap them,' the driver shouts again.

One of the men steps towards the driver. PC Krishna moves between them, her gestures urging calm, but there is more shouting. Emma stops listening, focusing instead on the road ahead of them and the busy T-junction. There's a bus pulling up to a stop ahead of her. How far away is it? Twenty metres? Thirty?

Hurry!

Run!

This is her chance. Her one chance. She glances back at the group. They are all focused on the taxi driver, but any second now, one of those men will see the same opportunity Emma has, and he'll step away and move towards the police car.

It's now or never.

'We're going, Lola. Hold on to my neck really tight.'

And then she's up and out of the police car, legs moving. Running and running. Lola is heavy in her arms, but the weight is nothing to the fear snapping at her heels. She doesn't dare look back to see if anyone has noticed her bolt for freedom.

Fifteen metres. Ten metres. Ahead of her, the passengers have all stepped onto the bus and the doors are starting to close. Five metres.

Emma's shoulders and legs cry out in pain. Lola is so very heavy. Her lungs run out of air. She can't draw in enough breath.

Keep going!

If she can't get on this bus, then everything is lost. There is no way she can outrun the two men on foot. The bus is not a perfect escape. The second the men realise she's gone, they'll be on the phone to that dark room somewhere and she'll be tracked on the CCTV. They'll see the stop she gets off at, be minutes behind her. But those minutes are her best chance.

The bus doors shut with a thud and a whoosh of air, and she's still metres away. She tries to shout, but her voice is lost to the heaving of her chest. Tears form in her eyes. It's all over.

The bus moves, lurching forward. Now what does she do? She can't go back to the police car. Can't carry on running either. Then a woman is standing up from one of the seats on the bus. She's pointing towards Emma and Lola, and the bus jolts to a stop and the driver turns with a smile, and the doors are opening again and she's stepping on. Jelly legs, weak with exertion and relief.

Lola is crying in her arms, but it's OK. 'We made it,' she says before giving a breathless 'thanks' to the bus driver and the woman who called out.

She fumbles to pay, dropping coins into the tray beside the driver before falling into a seat. Every part of her body is shaking. She draws in a ragged breath, and as the bus pulls away, she risks looking back. Her heart skips a beat. She can't believe her eyes for a second. They are still standing by the taxi. Even from this distance, Emma can see the wild anger of the taxi driver. And even though it was him that made the call, him that locked her in his car, she is unspeakably grateful that he has allowed her to escape. No one has noticed she's gone.

She leans back into the seat, hugging Lola tight and shushing her tears and her silent, heaving sobs. Emma sweeps her soft blonde hair away from her face and kisses a damp cheek. 'We made it, Lola. It's OK. We got away. Look!'

Lola shakes her head against Emma's chest, releasing a keening wail that causes the elderly gentleman in the seat in front to turn to look at them in surprise.

'Barnaby.' Lola chokes out the name, and Emma's heart stops in her chest. Lola's bear! It's here. It's got to be here. She wouldn't have left it. She knows how important it is. Even risked sneaking across the services car park to snatch it from the back seat of the car when she'd watched Isobel walk with Lola across the car park and seen the bear hadn't been in Lola's arms. Emma's hands pat the seat, eyes already scanning the floor and the aisle. She yanks open Lola's backpack and there is Ducky, but not Barnaby. She tries her own bag next, scrambling with shaking hands, already knowing the answer. Barnaby is not here. He is still on the back seat of the police car with his seat belt on.

'Go back,' Lola cries, her body heaving against her.

'It's her teddy bear,' Emma says in reply to the concerned looks from the passengers. The last thing she needs is an entire bus full of people looking her way, recognising her from the fake police appeal just like the taxi driver did. 'We left it at home, that's all. I'm so sorry, Lola.' Emma fights back the despair and the tears.

'Go back?' Lola asks, tilting her head up and looking at Emma with her blue tear-filled eyes.

'I'm sorry; we can't. I'm so sorry.'

Lola's face scrunches up, bottom lip quivering. Another sob shakes her daughter's little body.

'The police will look after Barnaby for us,' Emma tries to reassure her. 'That nice officer – PC Krishna. She'll look after him until it's safe for us to get him.'

Lola cries into Emma's chest, and she lets the tears fall down her own face too. They've escaped. But they are broken, exhausted – a trembling mess. How much more can she take? How much more is she prepared to put Lola through? And the final question that haunts her thoughts – will they ever be safe?

THIRTY-ONE

ISOBEL

Questions and fears pummel Isobel's mind until she feels dizzy and sick. What's happening? Is Lola safe? The racing of her pulse reminds her of all the panicked times in this house where she'd been unable to leave, unable to trust that the world was safe. The anxiety started after the failed IVF. Her life had never been the doors-open, everything-easy world of Roly's, but she'd learned that working hard paid off. Good grades, a good university. She'd known she was beautiful and successful, earned a good living, fallen in love, married, happy.

Roly hadn't understood that the universe wouldn't bend to his will and give them their longed-for child. But Isobel had struggled with it too. Only for a different reason. Failure. She couldn't put the hours in, work her way to conceiving. The failure had been a sharp sting, an alien feeling she couldn't escape. That and the hormones that had been injected into her body again and again. Then negative pregnancy tests, doctors with sombre expressions and pity, and more hormones, and Margaret always there to whisper in Roly's ear that perhaps Isobel was not the best choice for a wife.

It was no wonder paralysing anxiety had attacked her mind.

Suddenly nothing had been easy. Getting ready for work, deciding what to wear, required gigantic effort and left her head spinning with the fear of what people would say, how they'd look at her. She'd lost her unflappable confidence and lived in constant fear of making a mistake.

She kept all her feelings in, hiding them behind a layer of make-up and the right smile, pretending to Roly she was fine. It had been a relief when Roly – at Margaret's prompting – had suggested she give up work. She'd thought the time resting and the pregnancy would help heal her. It hadn't.

But that anxiety, those fears are nothing to the untamed wildness coursing through her veins. Someone has snatched Lola away. Her little girl is in danger. And there is nothing Isobel can do to help. The men are talking quietly about a business deal of Jonny's that Roly is investing in. She can't listen. The normality of their chat grates at Isobel's insides. Besides, it was Roly's relationship with Jonny that dragged them into this mess, into a world where they can't call the police when their own child is abducted.

God, she never should've taken Jonny on as a client. And she should never have listened to Roly's reassurances on the drive home from the services that it would be better for everyone if they keep the police out of it.

A noise makes her jump. The kitchen door opens, and Margaret is stepping back into the room, her hair newly brushed, lipstick shimmering. She's changed her beige cashmere jumper for a white blouse.

'Mother,' Roly says, standing up and looking every bit the little boy being caught doing something wrong. 'I thought you were going to try to sleep?'

'I was,' she says, looking between them. 'I decided a freshen up would do just as well. Has something happened?'

A look passes between them all before Roly replies. 'There's been another sighting. The police have been sent to a location

outside of Brighton and we're waiting to hear.' The lie feels ugly
and obvious, and Margaret must sense something isn't right
because her eyes narrow.

Not on Roly though, her precious son who has just lied to
her, but Isobel. The woman who will never be good enough.

'You're hiding something.' She nods to Isobel. 'What are
you keeping from us?'

Isobel's mind leaps straight to what she's doing and then to
the baby growing inside her. Margaret is right; she is keeping
something from all of them, but there's no way her mother-in-
law can know that. And anyway, her question is not really about
an answer. It's about accusing and hurting.

The sudden attack feels off somehow. Margaret is usually
more subtle. A trickle of little comments designed to chip away
at her confidence and, she suspects, Roly's love for her. Except
now Isobel thinks about it, Margaret has been cruel and
outspoken towards her since they arrived back from the roadside services on Sunday. She'd put it down to her mother-in-
law's blame that Lola was abducted on Isobel's watch. But as
she takes in the pinched lips of the older woman, Isobel notices
a worry dancing in her eyes.

Is she attacking Isobel for another reason?

She remembers Margaret and Roly talking in the kitchen
without her. The look of guilt on Roly's face when she'd walked
in. With everything happening, she'd forgotten to ask him about
it. The woman had been evasive about Zeen too when Isobel
had asked, and again she remembers how quickly Margaret
arrived at the house after Lola was taken.

The feeling returns that there is something the woman is
keeping from her. Isobel asks herself again what possible reason
her mother-in-law could have for wanting to take Lola away
from them.

'Margaret,' Isobel says, shaking her head, 'I'm not hiding
anything from you or Roly. I'm scared to death something will

happen to Lola. As a mother, I'm sure you can understand that.'

'A mother,' she scoffs. 'What kind of mother are you? You're too selfish, Isobel. You constantly put your own little problems before your daughter. That's why St Martin's is the best choice for her. Everyone can see that. Even Lola told me herself that she wanted to live near her grandmother.'

The hurt is a prickling angry kind. A pit of stinging nettles. All too familiar. She opens her mouth to retort, to share her suspicions, but Roly gets there first.

'Mother, this isn't helping,' he says with a sigh and no conviction at all. Gone is his harsh tone of earlier.

'When did Lola tell you that?' Isobel manages to ask.

'Before your holiday, dear. I took her shopping while you were having your hair done, remember? She told me then that she'd be very happy to live near me.'

Isobel can just imagine the conversation. Margaret painting a magical picture, asking leading questions that a three-year-old could not possibly answer with anything but the desired response.

'She's three, Margaret,' Isobel says, forcing a lightness to her voice she doesn't feel. 'Last month, she asked for a panda for her birthday.'

'And a holiday to the moon,' Roly chips in with a huffing laugh, trying and failing to lighten the mood.

Margaret sighs. 'All I'm saying is that Lola disappeared on your watch. Perhaps you need to consider that.'

'I'm very aware of my role in what's happening,' Isobel snaps, wishing Roly would stick up for her more, or even a bit. But along with the familiar hurt she feels is the undeniable knowledge that no matter how many years they are married, no matter what Isobel does for Roly, no matter that they have Lola now, Margaret will always come first for him. And maybe not just Margaret. In Isobel's darker moments, she suspects the

Huntington family name and all that it comes with sits above her and Lola too. Because even though Roly denies it, tells her not to be silly whenever she brings it up, she thinks deep down that a part of him also sees her as the wrong sort.

'Well then. Something to keep in mind for the future.' Margaret glides back to her usual stool, the sense of victory in the tilt of her head. 'Make some coffee, will you, please, Roland.'

'Of course,' he replies, no doubt glad the moment is over.

Isobel fights back easy tears and the desire to flee. She needs to be in this room. She needs to know what's happening. The detective has busied himself with his phone during the exchange but glances at her with sympathy in his dark eyes. She isn't sure if it's for Lola and what's happening, or because of her mother-in-law. Either way, she doesn't want this man's pity; she wants this all to be over.

His phone rings then, the sudden burst of it making her jump. Each note in the ringtone fills her with hope and despair and a heart-stopping fear. DCI Watkins stands, stepping from the room.

THIRTY-TWO

ISOBEL

The moment DCI Watkins returns, Isobel knows they've lost Lola again. They were so close this time. Energy drains from her body so fast she isn't sure how she's still holding herself upright. The same hot liquid guilt returns. She did this.

'I'm afraid Emma and Lola have slipped away again. But we do have an exact location. They're in a busy, built-up area, and I have instructed the cyber team to monitor every camera. And obviously police are in the area too.'

She swallows bitter disappointment as she pictures not an army of police officers patrolling the streets, like he's telling Margaret, but Frank and a friend who've taken a few days' leave from the force to help out.

Isobel is suddenly terrified. It's not just Lola being gone but what could happen when she's found. These men are all connected to Jonny. Their motive isn't just to save Lola and return her to them, but to stop Emma too before she can tell the police or anyone else what happened to her. If it comes to a choice – save Lola or stop Emma – which one will they choose?

'I'm confident we're very close and we will get Lola home very soon,' the detective continues. 'But right now, I'm needed

218

back at the station.' He turns to Margaret. 'Mrs Huntington, please rest assured that everything is being done to bring Lola home safely. I'm the senior officer on this case, but I can put you in touch with my boss, if you'd like to talk to him.'

He tucks his phone into his suit jacket and they wait for Margaret's reply. It's a bluff of course. A way to placate Margaret, and it seems to work for now at least. She nods. 'Thank you, DCI Watkins. We'll continue as we are for now, but I'll be thinking about it.'

Roly leads the way to the front door, and Isobel follows behind the men, glancing behind her to check Margaret hasn't followed. Roly opens the front door, and both men step out. She remains in the doorway, close enough to hear them, one eye on the empty hall.

'What happened?' Roly hisses.

'The taxi driver kicked off. Made a bit of a scene by the sounds of it. Frank tried to calm him down, but the two PCs stepped in to de-escalate the situation. Emma used the opportunity to do a runner with Lola.'

Roly swears, and in the moment that follows, Isobel swallows, steeling herself for what she must ask.

'What if,' she begins, forcing her gaze to remain steady as she looks at the men, 'we involved the police? For real, I mean. And actually got a nationwide alert going and an entire country searching.'

The detective is shaking his head before she's even finished. 'We can't, Isobel. I'm sorry. I know this is hard for you both, but we've come too far for that. Imagine what you'd say. How would you explain that your daughter went missing two days ago and you've waited until now to call?'

'Please,' she croaks, tears spilling onto her cheeks. 'We have to do something.'

She senses a sudden anger rippling beneath the surface of

his calm demeanour, but she had to ask; surely he sees that. She has to do everything she can to get her daughter back.

'Remember I've put myself on the line for this. Because of our friendship.' His gaze fixes on Roly for a second then moves back to her. 'It would be impossible for me to explain my part in this, not to mention the training exercise I have the team doing to search for Emma and Lola. I would lose my job. But I'm here anyway because I understand the challenging situation your past has put you in. We've all got too much on the line to change course now.'

'I know, and I'm grateful,' she says. 'It's just, this has got out of hand. We have to call it in. Roly?' She turns to him, pleading.

He says nothing. It's as though he hasn't heard her. She knows that faraway stare. It's the same look he gets when Margaret starts talking about wanting another grandchild – a boy and heir, as though they're living in the bloody 1500s.

'Look at all the coverage that missing woman, Scarlett Peters, is getting,' Isobel says, pushing when she knows she should stop but needing to try anyway.

Anger flashes in the detective's eyes, but it's Roly who speaks.

'Isobel,' Roly snaps, her name hissed and angry.

'Don't we want that same attention for Lola? Won't it help us find our daughter?' Isobel pushes her hair away from her face. A strand is caught around her earring, and she pulls it free. 'I... I remember Scarlett. She's been to the parties. She must know Emma too. What if she's the one helping her? You said Emma started planning this at the start of April. That's when Scarlett was reported missing, isn't it?'

'Don't make connections where there aren't any.' Owen's reply is low and laced with warning.

Roly clears his throat. 'Isobel, take a moment, OK? Owen is our best chance of finding Lola.'

'Your only chance,' the man adds.

She falls silent. Whatever she hoped to gain from trying this has been lost.

'Iz, darling,' Roly says, 'can you check on Mother? I'll be right in.'

She nods, reality settling over her like a wet blanket on a wintry day – heavy and chilling. She's turned a blind eye to the truth about Jonny's businesses. Never asking questions or prying where she shouldn't. She's always taken the money and enjoyed the praise he lavishes on her. That gratitude for all the times she found another loophole to save him money. Smoke and mirrors hiding the truth from the government.

Isobel wonders now if not asking questions is why her beautiful little girl, her whole world, has been ripped away from her. She didn't ask about Jonny's business dealings, and she didn't ask him about Emma on that first introduction. She didn't ask what happened to Emma after that day on the common when Roly had called Jonny and asked for just one more favour.

In the kitchen, Margaret is sipping from a mug of steaming coffee and staring with narrowed eyes at a spreadsheet on her tablet again. She's opened the French doors, allowing in the fresh air and the smell of the roses that climb the garden walls. Isobel has a sudden yearning to be outside, heaving in mouthfuls of air. She should go for another walk. Clear her head. But then Roly appears behind her in the doorway, a strong hand comforting on her shoulder. She leans into him, wishing they could be alone.

When she looks up, Margaret's expression is fierce, her gaze darting from Roly to Isobel. 'I think it's time one of you tells me what is really going on here, don't you?'

THIRTY-THREE

EMMA

Emma glances around the car park of the roadside services, eyes landing on a woman in a black maxi dress and giant sunglasses walking towards her. It's not Winchester this time but a carbon copy near Portsmouth. People rushing to get to or from their holidays, barely noticing her on the warm August afternoon. For the last two days, it would have suited her to go unseen, but everything has changed and she needs people to stop and help.

Somehow, they have covered nearly forty miles today from that lay-by with the taxi. After the first frantic dash to the bus, and race across town, they'd found themselves walking by the side of the road, looking for another bus stop – Lola still crying over Barnaby, Emma just as sad, unable to decide what to do next, where to go, how to keep them safe. She'd messaged the memorised number, but it had been no help.

It's all going wrong. You have to help us.

There's nothing I can do. I'm sorry. Keep going!

Easier said than done, Emma had been about to reply when

a woman in her seventies with badly dyed red hair and thick-rimmed glasses had pulled over her baby-pink Fiat and opened the window.

'You two ladies look as though you need a ride,' she'd said with a wide smile.

'Oh, no. That's so kind, thank you, but we're fine.' The words had raced out before Emma had time to think, pulling Lola to her side, unable to consider climbing into another car.

'I don't believe that for a second,' the woman continued. 'If you were my daughter and granddaughter, I'd want someone like me to stop and offer help, so why don't you climb in just for a few minutes, and I'll take you a little further along the road.'

Emma had hesitated, but not for long. Lola needed to rest, and the lure of being off this street, out of sight, was too great to ignore. 'Thank you,' she'd said, opening the door and bundling them in.

The woman – Octavia – had told them she was seventy-nine, as fit as any thirty-year-old, still running half-marathons, and on her way to the wholesalers to 'stock up'. On what, Emma wasn't sure, or where it would go in the tiny car, but she was too grateful for the lift and Octavia's friendly chatter to care.

Octavia had dropped them at these services an hour ago. Emma had lied and said she'd call a friend to collect them. The woman's kindness had lifted her, and after a lunch of chicken nuggets and French fries, she'd realised that Octavia had shown them another form of transport. She can't believe she hadn't thought of it before. Hitchhiking was free and, more than that, it was untraceable. No CCTV. No ANPR. No way for Jonny or his men to find them. She just had to trust that there was good in people.

'*Not everyone is bad.*' She remembers the doctor. A skinny woman with a plain face and thin blonde hair that she'd tucked limply behind her ears. She wasn't the worst of them, but she didn't listen either when Emma had tried to tell her the truth.

'I think they are,' she'd replied.

'That is your paranoia because of your breakdown. The vast majority of people are good.'

Emma bites her lip and steps forward. 'Excuse me,' she says to the woman in the dress. 'I'm looking for a lift north with my daughter. Are you...' Her voice trails off as the woman shakes her head without looking.

It's the fifth person she's approached in the last twenty minutes, and every time she does it, her heart races with the fear that they'll recognise her just like the taxi driver did. She knows now that the police are not chasing her. Not in the real sense of the word. The thought does little to soothe the urgency still pulsing in her temples. Jonny has friends everywhere, including the police. Especially the police. There is no escaping the fact that she is being hunted right now.

'I might be able to help,' a man says with a strong Dublin accent.

Emma takes in the small man with thick black hair under a baseball cap and a broad smile.

'Where are you going?' he asks.

She can't tell him about the ferry leaving tonight from Birkenhead, across the river from Liverpool. She can't risk that at some point he'll connect her to the online photo, call the number and tell them her plans. She can't let him see the fear or desperation either, so she matches his smile. 'Anywhere that's up,' she says with a light laugh, breezy; easy-going, as though she is a drifter, happy to move from place to place and go where the rides take her.

Inside, every cell in her body feels tense – cement when it should be liquid. She doesn't want to hitchhike, to climb into a car with a stranger. The dangers are unthinkable. For her and Lola. She hates putting her daughter at such risk, and yet what choice does she have? They have to get away from the south coast, and they have to go now. Twice now they've been seconds away from being caught by Jonny and his friends. First the cash machine and then the taxi. She can't make it a third time.

'I've got a van and I'm driving a table and chairs to Edinburgh. I've got plenty of room. I can take you all the way if north is where you're going.' His voice rings with a suggestion she tries to ignore. He is just being friendly, she tells herself as icy fingers of fear trace a line down her back.

'And you're sure you have space for me and my daughter?' she forces herself to ask.

'Sure do.'

Her heart bangs a warning drum in her chest. Hard and thudding. He can take them north. She checks the time. It's early afternoon. There is still a chance they can get the night ferry to Belfast leaving at ten thirty this evening. Only a day later than they'd planned. Help will be waiting for them. She won't be alone anymore. Lola will be safe.

God, how she wishes there was another way out though. Somewhere closer to them. There are ferries from Southampton of course, but not ones that will take her to Belfast. And it has to be Belfast. It has to be Northern Ireland. As part of the United Kingdom, it only requires a photo ID to travel there. Emma has their passports of course – hers and Lola's – but the checks on their IDs and their names are far less when travelling within the UK. It's the safest way for them to get out of the country without anyone noticing. The night ferry will be quiet too. Tired staff and sleepy passengers. They can slip away unseen. And from Belfast, they'll travel to the Republic of Ireland and from there – with a little help, some fake passports that have been promised in Belfast, and some money – the world.

The thought is flimsy – a hologram she can't trust. Her gaze is drawn to Lola, playing with a boy that looks about her age. They are chasing around the little playground beside the entrance in a game of tag with the boy's older brother. Lola charges across a wooden bridge and taps the older boy on the back, shouting a delighted 'it', oblivious to the fact that he slowed down, allowed her to tag him. He grins and gives chase on his brother. Seeing Lola laugh lights her up inside.

It is the most normal thing. Simple, sweet and exactly what children should be doing. Not getting into vans with strangers, not racing across the country, being chased by men capable of every horror imaginable.

'OK.' Emma nods to the van driver, hating herself for it. 'Thank you. We don't need to go all the way to Edinburgh. Do you think you could drop us in Birmingham?'

'Sure can.' He grins, delighted, like the winner of an unexpected prize.

Then he winks at her, and she forces herself to smile too.

'Give me ten minutes. I'll meet you back here,' he says.

The man disappears inside, and Emma covers her face with her hands. There is a voice in her head screaming at her not to do this. But the urgency to move on is louder. Deep breath in. Come on. Count the seconds. Calm down. Long breath out. It doesn't work. She can't count away the panic any longer. Two questions battle for space in her head. Is she really doing this? What choice does she have? The trapped feeling from the taxi is still skirting the edges of her body. But the fear is nothing compared to the thought of the black SUV pulling into the car park. The two men... she can't... can't think about it. Not for the first time, she says a silent thanks to PC Krishna and her colleague for their distrust of the men. She wonders how things would have played out if the two PCs had been male.

'Emma,' Lola calls out, pulling her back to the services and her daughter, who is now hanging from the monkey bars. 'Look at me.'

'Very good.' She claps and smiles, pride welling inside her, reminding her of all the little moments she's missed out on with her daughter. 'We need to go in a minute, OK?'

Lola falls silent, the joy diminishing, but she doesn't shout or cry. She drops to the ground and runs back to the two boys. Emma is grateful for the playground and the distraction of the other children. She knows Lola will remember Barnaby again soon and the tears will start. She can't believe she left the bear behind. Of all the things, it feels like the very worst.

Emma glances to the glassed entrance, looking out for the van driver. She spots him in the queue for Starbucks. He twists around, sees her staring and makes a coffee gesture with his hand. She shakes her head and tries to believe that if he's offering to buy her a drink, then he must be a decent man. But no matter how she tries to sugar-coat it, she's jittery, wishing there was another way. Wishing herself and Lola out of here. Wishing Haz was with her.

Before she can stop herself, Emma is turning on her phone. He's not replied to her message, and the ticks are still grey. She taps the number and calls him. She holds her breath as she waits for the voicemail. But again, the call is picked up.

'Emma, don't hang up,' a voice tells her as she's pulling the phone from her ear. 'Emma?'

'I'm here,' she says.

'Why are you calling Haz's phone?' Malik asks, his voice gentle.

'I... I'm sorry.'

'What's going on, Emma? Where's my car? Some guy, a police officer, came asking about you. They said you'd used my car for something criminal and dumped it.'

'Are you sure he was a police officer? Did he show ID?'

Malik is quiet for a moment. 'He said he was, but I don't remember seeing his ID. Are you OK?'

No, she wants to say, but there's no point. 'Yes, I'm fine. I'm sorry about using your car. It will get back to you soon, I'm sure.'

'You know I don't care about that. I'm worried about you calling Haz's phone though.'

'It's nothing. I just wanted to hear his voice.'

She knows what Malik is going to say before the words come, and she suddenly wants to hang up, but she's frozen. 'He's dead, Emma.'

The words feel as all-consuming and world ending as they did the first time she heard them a year ago. Haz is dead. She knows this. Some days it's all she thinks about. But others, she likes to think of him still alive and out there somewhere, living his best life. But he's not and never will be. Her gaze drops to the ground, and she expects to see a cavernous hole forming, her falling.

'I know,' she whispers. 'But I miss him.'

'So do I, but calling and messaging his phone won't help.'

She looks back at Lola, still playing on the bridge and the slide, racing around and around. Emma remembers the funeral at the end of last summer. The devastation she felt mirrored on the expressions of his family. Malik crying to her at the wake. Telling her he felt responsible. All the times he'd pushed Haz to get his life together, to cut his hair, get a steady job. Give up on acting and be normal. *I said that to him once. I said, "Be normal," but I didn't mean it, Emma. I want him to know that. I loved him. He was my little brother. I was just looking out for him.'*

Emma had nodded and given comfort she'd barely had it in her to give. She couldn't tell Malik all the times Haz had complained about him. Or all the ways she knows Malik made his life so much harder than he had to. Who was she to judge anyway? When she'd last seen Haz, all she'd done was moan about her own life, her own problems. If she'd only asked him how he was doing, maybe she could've stopped him sending her that final message.

> *I've got to go now. I'm not meant for this world, Em. But you are, and you're a survivor. Don't stop fighting for what you know is true! Xx*

She'd seen the message an hour later, and by then it was already on the news. The jumper from London Bridge. A twenty-six-year-old man dead.

'Emma, are you still there?' Malik asks.

'Yes.'

'I have to go. I've got a meeting. I just wanted to tell you that we're cancelling Haz's phone contract. We should've done it months ago, but I knew you were calling and leaving messages, and I didn't want to make things worse for you. His voicemails were forwarded to me, but I'm going to stop it all now. I only turned his phone on today to tell you.'

She shouldn't be surprised, but it still hurts. 'OK,' she replies.

'Look, I don't know what's going on here, but Haz loved you. I know you helped a lot when he was... when he was in that place. If you need any help, you can call me.'

'Thanks.'

They say goodbye, and Emma turns off the phone. She can't ask Malik for help any more than she can ask Haz. Whatever amends he's trying to make now, she can't forgive him for his part in Haz's death. Or herself for her own part, for that matter. If only she'd paid more attention to him, pushed him more on the times he'd waved her concerns away. She'd give anything to tell him how sorry she is for not helping him when he needed it. And there are other things she wants to tell him too. Like how she wouldn't have survived without his belief in her. She wants to tell him how much his friendship still means to her. She wants to tell him so many things. And it hurts unbearably that she can't.

Malik is right. She needs to stop calling and messaging Haz's phone. But she'll never stop talking to her best friend in her mind and imagining his replies. Like how she knows if he was still alive and she'd told him about the visitor to the shop in April and the plan they'd made to take Lola, he'd have warned her not to trust the help being offered. And she'd have known he was right.

But it was the only way to keep Lola away from Jonny and keep her safe. And so she had to trust that Haz was right, that she's smart and capable. With him gone, all she can do is trust in herself and in the plan.

'I've planned for everything. But I can't help you until you're out of the country. I won't be able to do anything while you're on the run... Don't worry, Em. It's like I said – I'll meet you in Belfast.'

Just like she's going to trust this van driver with his knowing smile to take her towards Liverpool. There is no other choice.

THIRTY-FOUR

EMMA

Emma slips her phone into her pocket before stepping to the railing that surrounds the playground. Behind her, an exhaust rattles as a car pulls out of its space and drives towards the exit of the services. The trapped feeling from the taxi returns. She wants to leave too. They shouldn't stay in the same place too long, especially now she's used her phone. She doesn't think Jonny will be tracking Haz's phone. Jonny is smart and ruthless, but there is nothing sentimental about him. It would never cross his mind that she'd phone the number of someone who is dead just to hear their voice.

She glances at the main building, scanning the crowds for any sign of the delivery driver who promised to take them to Birmingham.

'Hey.' A hand touches Emma's arm. She cries out, already cowering, a scream lodging in her throat. But it's not Jonny or one of his men, or the police. It's a woman in a faded green T-shirt and denim shorts.

'Sorry,' she says, dragging the word out and making a face that ends with a sympathetic smile. 'I didn't mean to scare you.

I'm Jenny. The little boy your daughter is playing with belongs to me. He's Toby, and his brother is Josh.'

'Oh, hi.' Emma gives a shaky smile and tries to act normal. She has seen mums gravitate towards each other in play-grounds, searching, she thinks, for a connection to someone else in the trenches of parenting. She should be friendly or it will set alarm bells ringing. 'I'm Emma, and that's Lola.'

'Hi,' Jenny says again, waving a hand as though she's not standing right beside her, and then laughs at herself.

They stand side by side. Emma searches for something to say. 'How old is—' she starts, but Jenny is talking too.

'Look, it's none of my business— Oh sorry, Toby, he's three. He'll be four soon.'

'The same as Lola,' Emma replies, and for a single moment she looks ahead to a future where it is Lola's birthday and they are somewhere safe. It feels too dream-like.

'Sorry if I'm being out of turn,' Jenny says. 'My husband is always telling me not to stick my beak in, but it's just who I am. Anyway, I overheard you talking about needing a ride to Birmingham?'

'I...' Emma drops her gaze, unable to muster the breezy go-with-the-flow act as the shame burns hot on her cheeks.

'It's just, I'm heading home to Bridgenorth with my boys. We can drop you on the outskirts of Birmingham if you want?' she adds.

Emma looks up, startled by the offer. Out of nowhere, a wall of tears forms in her eyes. She doesn't know how dangerous the van driver really is. She can't see past her own warped view of the world, but even with her paranoia, she knows Jenny is the safest option for hitchhiking.

'You really have space? You'd really do that for us?' Emma asks.

'Sure. It's just me and the boys. We were visiting my mum this week and now we're heading home. It will be nice to have some adult company,' she adds as though it is Emma about to do her a favour. 'We even have a car seat for Lola. Josh grew out of his this week so Toby is having his, and I've still got Toby's old one in the car. And' – she pauses, throwing a glance towards the services – 'I don't think you really want to get in a van with that man, do you?'

Emma shakes her head, freeing the tears to roll down her face.

Jenny throws her arm around Emma, rubbing her back. 'Hey, don't cry. Say you'll come with us. I can drop you wherever you need to be.'

Emma thinks of the journey ahead. Ten minutes ago, she had visions of getting out of the country tonight, but she sees that's stupid now. Lola will be tired and hungry by the time they reach Birmingham. They'll need to stop and rest. However much she wants to escape, she must put Lola's needs first. If she can just get near enough that they can leave tomorrow, that will be enough to ease the urgency thrumming in her body, surely.

But the thought of wandering the streets of an unknown city, looking for somewhere to stay, or worse, trying to hitchhike again, it's too much. 'Actually, I... I know somewhere I can stay in Bridgenorth,' Emma lies.

'You have family there?' Jenny asks, a smile lighting her face.

Emma hesitates before nodding. It's another lie. She has no one but Lola in her world right now. But she remembers the quaint British town west of Birmingham where she'd holidayed with her family for a few summers before her father had said it was too far to drive and *'what was wrong with Southend-on-Sea anyway?'*

The memory of Bridgenorth is from a lifetime ago. It's more a feeling of having people around her, being loved. Playing, reading, exploring. No responsibilities or fears. She knows she won't find those things in Bridgenorth now, but it is quieter than the city, and they'll find somewhere to stay, she's sure.

'It was totally meant to be.' Jenny grins and turns back to the playground. 'Boys,' she calls out. 'Time to go.'

'We're going too, Lola,' Emma adds, and the three children pile out of the playground together. Emma crouches down to Lola's level, tucking Ducky back into her arms. 'This nice lady is called Jenny, and she and her boys are going to give us a ride.'

'Are we going home?' Lola asks with such hope in her voice that it almost breaks her.

'Not long now,' Emma whispers. The answer is vague, but she can't bring herself to upset Lola again, and even though Jenny is kind and lovely, she is also a mother who has her own children to protect. Emma understands that feeling better than anyone. If she suspects Emma is in trouble, being chased by bad people, she might change her mind.

Jenny touches the top of Emma's arm. 'How about we get going now? I don't know about you, but I don't fancy seeing that man again. He gives me the heebie-jeebies.'

Emma's gaze turns back to the glass entrance. The van driver is at the front of the coffee queue now. A few more minutes and he'll be back. She nods. 'Me too. Thanks.'

'Don't mention it. I warn you now, our air conditioning is broken so it gets a bit warm.'

Emma's throat tightens as they weave through the cars towards a dusty silver Volvo; the emotion of the last few days welling up at this woman's kindness. For the first time in her life, she feels the solidarity of motherhood, that sense of belonging that was stolen from her by Roly and Isobel.

Five minutes later, she finds herself in a car that smells a little of gone-off bananas and Play-Doh, and is listening to Jenny talk about her jewellery-making business and her husband, who works as a GP and couldn't get the time off to go with them to visit her mother.

Every so often, Emma turns to check on Lola, but her daughter is asleep in the middle seat, Ducky in her arms and her two new friends either side of her, watching iPads. The lure of sleep tugs at Emma too, but she fights it. She feels almost safe with this lovely mum and her children.

Almost.

They are finally heading away from the south coast, finally moving in the right direction after two days of scrambling and panic and running. She draws in a breath, and it shudders in her chest.

'Are you all right, Emma?' Jenny asks, her eyes still on the road ahead and the slow-moving traffic. 'Tell me if I'm talking too much, won't you?'

'You're not at all. It's nice. Sorry, I'm probably not the best company. I... Thank you for doing this. You have no idea what a lifesaver you are.'

'Honestly, I think I do.' Jenny pulls a face. 'That man looked proper creepy.'

'He did, didn't he?' she replies, glad it wasn't just her paranoia this time. 'It's... we're... er...' Emma falls silent, searching for the words. *Desperate. Alone. Running for our lives.* She doesn't know whether to tell this woman a lie or a half-truth or if there is anything that can explain why she'd risk putting herself and Lola in such danger by hitchhiking.

'You don't have to tell me,' Jenny says. 'You're clearly in some kind of trouble, but you seem like a mother who loves her daughter, so whatever it is, I don't need to know any more than that.'

'Thank you,' she whispers, the emotion catching her in its grasp again.

'Will you tell me one thing though?' Jenny continues. 'Where are you going? Only I have family everywhere. If I can help with lifts or places to stay, I will.'

Suspicion rears its ugly head – a sense of wanting to withdraw. She tries to push it aside. 'We're going...' She hesitates, but then she thinks about the kindness of this woman, and how trust is how she made it out of Brighton in Octavia's Fiat, and trust is how they're finally on their way north. 'We're going to Liverpool. We're getting a ferry to Belfast.' Saying the words aloud makes it seem almost real, and for the first time since they turned the corner in Crawley and found the car towed away, she wonders if they might make it after all.

'Oh,' Jenny replies, sounding disappointed. 'I was hoping you'd say Aberdeen or Newcastle. I'm sorry, Liverpool is probably one of the only places I don't actually know anyone.'

'That's OK. We'll be fine.'

They fall silent. Jenny doesn't ask why Emma is so desperate to flee the country, but the question hangs between them nonetheless. The truth is, Emma isn't sure anymore why leaving the country is the answer she's been clinging to for so long now.

She remembers the elicit meetings. Huddled on a London bench on sunny spring days; heads bent. *'Let's say I pull it off and grab Lola. Where will we go?'* she'd asked. *'They'll find me. I know they will.'*

'If you stay in this country, yes. But they'll have no reach to track you outside of England. It's the only way. I'll be there to help you once you're away. I promise.'

So the plan had formed. A ferry to Belfast where they'll meet and travel south together. Then they'll catch a flight from Dublin to anywhere in the world. It still feels so impossible – out of reach – but this time in a few days, her toes could be slipped into warm sand and Lola could be dancing in the shallows of a sea far away from Jonny and danger and black SUVs.

'Tell me about your holiday?' Emma asks, wanting suddenly to fill the silence again.

Jenny laughs. 'Eventful,' she says before launching into a long story about the strained relationship with her mother.

Emma tries to listen, to follow the dramas, laugh in the right places, but the journey and dangers ahead of them consume her thoughts.

Bridgenorth is only a few hours from Liverpool. Tomorrow they will reach the ferry port and escape to Ireland. One more day without being caught. That's all she needs. As soon as she's out of the country, she'll no longer be alone.

As though the thought triggers a chain reaction in the universe, her phone buzzes with a message.

Where are you? Are you OK?

Emma fires off a reply. *We're fine. We won't make tonight's ferry. But we'll be on it tomorrow!! Will you be there to meet us from the ferry?*

The reply comes a second later. *Change of plan. I'll meet you at the port in Birkenhead.*

Another message lands straight after the first, and the words swim across Emma's vision. She tries to absorb what she's being told, but it doesn't fit. The plan she's been blindly following has felt near impossible, until now. This new plan is ten steps beyond crazy, even with everything she's already done. She's still heading to the port in Birkenhead, but everything else is changing, and there's no way she can do what's being asked of her.

THIRTY-FIVE

ISOBEL

Isobel hugs Barnaby to her body, breathes in the musty smell of his fur and kisses the top of his head, just like she's done a thousand times before.

'Barnaby wants a night-night kiss too.'

'Has he brushed his teeth?'

'Bears don't brush their teeth. They don't like minty toothpaste.'

Isobel remembers kissing the bear and then flopping onto the bed. *'Noooo,'* she'd cried.

Lola had giggled. *'Mummy, what is it?'*

'Bear breath. It's fatal.'

'Oh, Mummy,' Lola had admonished before kissing Barnaby and hugging him tight, whispering something in his ear – the worn one that she rubbed with her finger when she was tired, holding the bear close to her face so she could suck her thumb at the same time. This bear is so much more than a lump of polyester and wool. This bear is loved so fiercely by her daughter that it feels almost a part of their family.

How is her little girl coping without Barnaby in her arms? Isobel knows the tears and distress this forgotten bear can cause.

The times they'd left it in the car while shopping in the farmer's market, only for Roly to run back and get it while Lola sobbed in Isobel's arms beside the organic fruit stall. Or the time Lola left Barnaby at nursery and hadn't realised until bedtime, and Isobel had called the manager and begged her to go back and unlock the doors so they could get him.

There is something so precious about holding Barnaby now. As though the stuffed toy is a bridge between her and her daughter. Except this bear is here with Isobel, swiped out of a police car by Frank and driven back to London, handed over on the doorstep an hour ago, like Lola should've been.

'*Did you see her?*' she'd asked.

He'd shaken his head. '*She was in the back of the police car, and then she was gone.*'

'*Are you going back to Brighton later? What if they turn up again?*'

Another headshake. '*We've lost her from CCTV. She could be anywhere in the country by now. We need to wait to see where she crops up next. But don't worry, she will turn up somewhere. They always do.*'

Isobel closes her eyes and tries not to think about Frank. After today, it's impossible to pretend to herself even for a second that they are anything but terrible parents. Bad people. Margaret is right: she is selfish. They all are.

Even Margaret, who sees herself as elevated from them all, including her beloved Roly, can only think about herself. Her precious family name. When she'd accused them of hiding something earlier, Roly had been quick to reply. 'We're considering a press appeal with Lola's photo.'

The lie had come so fast and so smooth that it had surprised Isobel for a second that her husband, the man she thought she knew, flaws and all, had it in him to deceive so smoothly and easily, especially to his mother, a woman he worshipped. An uncomfortable thought had sprung into her head, and she couldn't believe it had never occurred to her before. They've both being lying to Margaret for years. And yet there was something in the way Roly had lied so easily to his mother then that she'd wondered if he could do the same to her too.

The thought had hounded her as she'd walked the common in the afternoon. She'd seen the same dog walker again, and they'd said hello, walking in the same direction for a while. The distraction had been nice for a minute or two before Isobel's thoughts had returned to Lola, and she'd said goodbye and hurried home.

Now, her whole being aches with the loss of her daughter. The pain is as real as any physical injury – a slice through the skin, a shattered bone. Her eyes are sore. She is exhausted and too broken to do anything but tuck the duvet around Barnaby's body and lie down beside him and cry.

Time passes in that hopping and jumping way it does sometimes when she doesn't think she's slept but time has been lost.

'Iz,' Roly calls from the upstairs hall. 'Where are you?'

She lifts her head from the now damp pillow and wipes the tears from her face. 'I'm in Lola's room.' Her voice is croaky, not her own.

He appears in the doorway a moment later. 'Are you sure you don't want some dinner? There's plenty left,' he says. She shakes her head, unable to contemplate food, even if it is from her favourite Thai place on Kew Road.

'What's Margaret been saying about me?' she asks, unable to stop herself.

'Nothing important.' He gives the briefest shake of his head. She doesn't believe him.

A frown forms on Roly's face, that upside-down smile. When he speaks, his voice is caring. 'Are you OK?'

She shakes her head. His voice is the same soft tone he uses when it's Lola lying in this bed, unable to sleep or unwell, and he has stepped through the front door from a day of meetings, kicked off his shoes and taken the stairs two at a time to catch the last few minutes of her day before she sleeps.

'*Princess Lola, what can I do to make it all better?*' he'd say when she was poorly with a cold or the time she'd caught the sicky bug from nursery and was so pale and feeling so yucky.

'*Ice cream would help,*' she'd replied in a small voice, a smile twitching at the sides of her mouth.

'*I think Mummy will say it's too late for ice cream.*'

'*A unicorn then. That would help me feel better.*'

'*A unicorn. Crikey. I'm not sure about that one. Perhaps I can rustle up some ice cream after all,*' he'd relented like they'd both known he would.

Roly steps to the bed and lies down beside her, pulling her to him. The mattress is small, squeezing them together. She relaxes into his warmth, taking in the smell of fabric softener and the understated woody scent of the Clive Christian after-shave she buys him for his birthday every year. God, she loves this man. Even now, with everything that's happening, she loves him.

'What are you doing in here?' he asks.

'I... just feel so lost without her,' she whispers, emotion quivering in her voice.

'Me too.'

'We can't carry on like this,' she says, feeling Roly tense beside her. He doesn't want to talk about the reality they're living in. He wants to continue telling her and himself that it will all be over soon.

She hates pushing him, but she can't escape the feeling that they're running out of time. They're not doing enough. She's not doing enough. He didn't back her up in her pleas to involve the police earlier, and while a part of her understands, it's just the two of them now.

'It's been over forty-eight hours, Roly. What if they can't find Emma again? How long do you think we can continue this search for? How long before the cyber team gets moved on to something else? This fake investigation can't go on forever, can it?' The fears rush out, quickening her pulse, leaving her feeling worse not better. 'Where does that leave us?'

Roly is quiet, the motion of his hand pausing on her back. Then it starts again and he says, 'If that happens, if Owen can no longer continue to help us, then we'll hire a private detective.'

Isobel remembers Margaret's comment about hiring someone to check Zeen's credentials, and it reminds her again that their housekeeper has still not been in touch. Isobel is certain the woman who's spent nearly every day of the last three years in their home is not involved in Lola's abduction, but that doesn't explain the call she had. Zeen's distant voice trying to tell her something. But what? She'll try and call her again later.

She sits up, staring down at Roly, willing him to see the pain she is in and the reality of their situation. 'A private investigator could take weeks, months. We need Lola back now—' Her voice breaks, the final word ending in a sob.

'You can't seriously be considering going to the police?' he asks.

'Would it really be so bad?'

'Yes,' he says quickly; decisively. 'We've broken the law ten times over, Iz. I don't need to explain that to you. There is only so far the Huntington name will stretch, and even if we escape prison, the family reputation would be mud. I can't do that to my family. You know I can't.'

'We are your family too,' she cries as a pressure hits her chest. The need to scream whips around her throat. What does it matter? Names, money, reputation – what does it all matter when their daughter isn't with them? Why does he not see that? 'And let's not pretend that all of this, us not going to the police when our daughter has been taken from us, isn't just as much about protecting Jonny as it is the family name.'

'What does it matter what the reasons are? This is the situation we're in. We need to stay positive. We'll get Lola back.'

'Have you spoken to Jonny?'

He nods. 'He's got some friends going out tomorrow to help. He'll be there too.'

'Doing what?'

'He doesn't want her to slip away a third time. As soon as there's another sighting, he's going to be there.'

A cold chill travels over her body. It's Jonny's involvement but it's also the mention of the word 'friends'. They aren't friends; they are business associates, people who do Jonny's bidding. And however much Isobel tries not to think about what that means, she can't pretend she hasn't seen these men coming in and out of Jonny's house when she's been there. Those muscular frames and watchful eyes. Like Frank, although at least Frank is a detective for the Met. Surely that means there is some moral compass within him. She doubts the same can be said for the others.

For a second, Lola's happy, yellow walls close in around her, the panic freezing her body. Jonny and his world is so far away from the shiny, perfect life they have in this house with all their nice things and their nice views. How can this be happening to them?

Roly tightens his hold on her as though sensing her fears. 'We have to trust Owen to do this. He won't let us down.'

She nods, but the fragility of their situation is sickeningly clear. Roly would never do anything to damage his family name. Jonny will do anything to protect his businesses. No one has put Lola first, not even her.

They are silent for a moment, but there is more to say. 'Roly, did you know Scarlett Peters?' She holds her breath and waits for him to reply.

His body tenses just for a second. 'Yes. She came to a few of Jonny's parties and dinners.'

'Did you talk to her?'

'Maybe once or twice,' he says after a beat, and she hears the sudden tension in his tone, making each word sound clipped. 'Why are you asking?'

'Because... because it feels like there's something we're missing here. Who is helping Emma? There's no way she's doing this alone. She started planning this at the exact same time another one of Jonny's... I don't even know what to call them – female friends? Girlfriends? Whatever you call them, Scarlett knew Jonny. Emma knew Jonny. Emma starts planning to abduct Lola at the same time as Scarlett is reported missing. Could Emma and Scarlett know each other? And...' She pauses, forcing herself to make the connection she hasn't wanted to see. 'And at the same time you disappeared on me too. Not physically. I know you were here, but you were so moody and so withdrawn—'

'Don't be ridiculous. I was having a bad spell. Some stupid midlife crisis thing about turning forty-seven. The same age my dad was when he died. It had nothing to do with Scarlett. I barely knew her. Like Owen said, you're making connections where there aren't any.'

Last week, she might've believed him. But after seeing him lie so easily to his mother earlier, she can't stop herself from wondering if she knows Roly as well as she thinks she does.

'Iz,' Roly says, his lips close to her ear. 'We'll get Lola back. It's all going to be OK, I promise.'

She forces herself to nod. 'I... just... I just wonder if this is what we deserve.' There, it's out. She's finally spoken the words they've been dancing around since the roadside services.

'What?' Roly leans back to search her face; his expression is one of disbelief. 'What are you talking about?'

'We've never spoken about it, and I get that—'

'I don't want to hear it.' He pulls his arms out from under her, leaving a cold void where his body had been. The sudden anger in him takes her by surprise, throwing her back to those first weeks in the spring when Roly's mood had been so dark and troubled. The stony silences, the unpredictable anger. The feeling of walking on eggshells.

'Roly, please,' she says as he stands and moves away from the bed. 'We can't continue to ignore what we've done.'

'We've not done anything. Emma has. She has stolen our daughter.'

Isobel shakes her head. 'But—'

'No. Stop this, Isobel. Lola belongs with us. She's a Huntington.'

'I just want to—'

'Isobel.' His tone carries a warning, but it only makes her even more determined to push forward. The guilt over what they've done has clogged her body – a blocked artery – for so many years, but worse is the guilt of what they're doing now. Roly wants to believe they are good parents. And they have been. But good parents don't call a friend instead of the police when their child is abducted.

'We did this,' she whispers.

'Emma did this.'

'Yes, Emma took Lola, but that's because...' Her throat squeezes shut. One second then another. She can't breathe or talk beyond the truth she has fought so hard to keep pushed into a tiny corner of her soul.

Roly jumps in, words quick as he reaches the door. 'Because she's a sick woman who needs professional help.'

Isobel can't stop now. She's trembling all over, a sobbing mess, but she needs to say this. 'No. It was because—'

The door to Lola's bedroom slams shut, and she hears the thud of his footsteps moving away so she has to shout the final words, not caring if Margaret hears.

'—we destroyed her life!'

THIRTY-SIX

EMMA

Bridgenorth is exactly how Emma remembers it. A quaint English town west of Birmingham, built on two sides of the River Severn and connected by an old bridge built of large stones with picturesque arches looping underneath.

As they weave through the narrow roads of the old market town in the early evening sunlight, the shopfronts look almost fake, like Emma and the car she's in have shrunk to the size of the little Borrowers she used to love reading about, and they are passing through one of those tiny model villages that tourists walk through, cooing at the minute details.

There is something comforting about being in a place that only holds happy memories for her. She pictures a world where she and Lola take the Victorian railway to the top of the cliff and explore the ruins of the old castle, buying overpriced stationery in the gift shop and eating scones with jam and cream in one of the many tea rooms. The image disappears as Jenny pulls the car into a space outside a small supermarket with navy awnings. This is not a holiday, she reminds herself. She must not relax, not for a second.

Jenny turns in her seat and smiles at Emma, eyebrows

already rising in a question. 'Are you sure this is OK? I can drop you anywhere, or you can come back with us and sleep on our sofa.'

'Yes,' Toby shouts from the back. 'Lola can sleep in my room.'

The thought of going home with Jenny, being among the noise and chaos of a family, fills Emma with a sharp longing, and yet she holds back. She isn't sure if it's trust that stops her or the thought of the black SUV and those men at the door – not wanting to put Jenny and her family in harm's way.

'That's so lovely of you,' she replies. 'But this is perfect. You've already done so much. I can't thank you enough.'

There's a bang of doors and the rustle of bags as she and Lola climb out on legs stiff from the long drive. The evening air still holds the warmth of the summer sun as she stretches and loops her arm through the strap of the backpack.

Jenny pulls them both into a tight hug that makes Emma want to cry. 'Take care of yourselves.'

'Thank you.' The emotion catches in her voice. 'You've saved our lives.'

Only when they drive away does the looming fear creep back into her body. As though Jenny and her car were a force-field protecting them, keeping them hidden, and now it's gone and they're exposed, in danger. Terrified. She has a sudden urge to race down the road, wave her hands in the air and beg Jenny to stop, to take them with her. The feeling lands too late, the car already disappearing around a corner. Emma closes her eyes and swallows down the panic pushing up from the depths of her being.

One more day.

She breathes in air that smells of fresh-cut grass and flowers from the hanging baskets by the supermarket, and counts her five beats in, six beats out. Only after two more breaths does she slip her hand into Lola's.

'Come on then,' she coaxes.

'I want to go to Toby's house. Please can we go there?' Lola begs. 'Toby has a dinosaur game, and he said I can play it with him.'

Emma isn't sure if she's relieved that Lola is not asking for her mummy and daddy and to go home, or she's saddened that she is so far removed from it now, she doesn't ask. It is another reminder of the hurt she is causing her daughter and the long-term damage this journey must be doing. A wave of desperate sadness floods through her. She crouches down and hugs Lola. The little girl's arms are already wrapped around Ducky, but she leans her head against Emma's shoulder, and Emma takes comfort in that.

'I know this is really hard,' she says. 'And I know you're scared. I am too. But I promise you, this is almost over. Tomorrow night we'll be safe.'

She hopes with every fibre of her being that it's true, and yet standing on this street, they are so very, very alone. Help feels like a million miles away; safety an unreachable place. Was this really the only way? With the hours that have passed, the risks they've taken, the danger she has put Lola in, it's getting harder to believe it.

'Where are we going now?' Lola asks with a long yawn. She rubs her face on Ducky's fur then freezes. The question is forgotten as her bottom lip trembles. 'I miss Barnaby,' she cries.

'How about we get some food? We'll have a picnic,' she says, hoping the upbeat, jolly-along tone will make up for the fact that she has no answer to Lola's question, no way to offer the comfort Barnaby gives her.

The truth is, Emma has no idea where they're going or where they'll stay tonight. When Jenny had mentioned Bridgenorth, Emma's first thought had been the holiday cottage she'd stayed in with her family. A small three-bedroom stone cottage on the outskirts of the town. She'd thought of an open fire and snuggling under a duvet with Lola by her side. But with the evening creeping over the day, she realises how stupid those thoughts were, how stupid she was to come here. There is no holiday cottage waiting empty for them, no pre-booked caravan even.

'We'll find a bed and breakfast like we stayed in last night,' she says, deciding to ask in the shop for directions. She's sure there are plenty to choose from. Less sure that in the middle of summer, in this popular tourist town, any will have a room for them.

Long breath in. Exhale. Food first, she decides.

'Will it have a dog like Luna?' Lola asks. 'I love Luna. I want to get a dog. I'm going to ask Daddy when I get home.' The last words drop to a whisper as though she's wondering if she'll ever go home. If everything goes to plan, Lola will never set foot in that house or this country again after tomorrow.

If it goes to plan.

Emma thinks of the message she received in the car. Everything has changed. They're meeting tomorrow at the port in Birkenhead instead of in Belfast. Despite the madness of the new plan, she badly needs this offered help.

So much has gone wrong already. Emma may not have the same feeling of drowning she felt when she was trapped in the taxi, but she is swimming against the strongest current. Any second now and it will sweep her under again.

Can she trust them? Emma's focus has always been Lola. Keeping her daughter safe. She's beginning to suspect there is more going on than she's being told, and yet if the end result is the same – a life with her daughter, both of them safe – does it matter?

She forces the thought away. 'Let's get our picnic then.'

'With jam tarts?' Lola asks.

'Of course. Lemon jam and raspberry jam,' she replies with a smile as Lola pulls a face.

'Yuck. No. Just strawberry.'

They step inside a small supermarket. The aisles are narrow and the shelves stacked high with everything from dried pasta to icing sugar. The kind of shop people nip to when they've forgotten that one thing. Emma's gaze darts to the ceiling and corners, scanning for cameras.

'What would you like in your sandwich?' she asks as they step to the refrigerated section.

'Jam,' Lola replies.

'I don't think they have jam sandwiches.' She considers buying a loaf of bread and a pot of jam, but then they'd need a knife and it would be messy, and she's not sure yet where they'll be staying. And besides, Lola needs something more substantial than jam. It's her job now to make sure Lola eats properly after all.

'How about cheese?' Emma asks.

Lola shrugs, hugging Ducky close as she starts to suck her thumb.

'I know. We'll get one cheese and one ham and then we can swap and have half of each.' She puts them in a basket, adding crisps and the jam tarts too and then two bottles of water. She wants to get more water so they won't have to shop again, but the backpack is already so heavy, her shoulders bruised and aching from the weight of carrying it the last few days. Wherever they go next, it can't be far.

They join a short line of people queuing for the one and only checkout. There is a TV behind the counter, positioned above a shelf of vapes and matches and bottles of gin. The volume is muted, but she can see it's a news story showing a war-torn country and the destruction of a recent bomb explosion. Emma drops her gaze, feeling a tug of despair. Sometimes it's hard to see the world as anything but something rotten and bad, hard to remember that people like Jenny exist. Kind and caring and funny. Like Haz.

Her conversation with Malik earlier is still humming in her mind. No more calling Haz's phone just to hear his voice. Sometimes she's so angry with him for ending his life. Sometimes she's angry at herself for not trying harder to be a better friend to him, and furious he felt there was no other way.

She knows the feeling. Remembers it from when Roly kicked her out of their home so suddenly, and the solicitor had told her there was nothing more he could do. Lola wasn't hers. She'd gone to the common and waited for hours and hours, day after day, in the hope of seeing Isobel and Lola alone. She'd felt so lost in those days, as though the world had turned against her, turfed out into a barren wilderness and there was no way back.

When Isobel had so cruelly told her that she wasn't Lola's mother, a darkness had spread through her, and she'd blurted out a terrible thing. *'I'd rather we were both dead than he get her.'*

She hadn't meant it. Would never wish her daughter dead. But the words still haunted her.

When it's her turn to pay, Emma smiles at the boy behind the counter. He is young, his face pimpled with acne scars and a fresh outbreak on his chin.

'Excuse me,' she says as she takes her change and loops the carrier bag over her wrist. 'I'm looking for—' She stops suddenly. The boy is looking at her with a curious expression, like he's trying to figure out where he knows her from.

The realisation freezes her. She sees his mind searching for the answer, and all she wants to do is run, but that would only draw more attention. Emma is suddenly too aware of the line of people behind her. How many of them will be scrolling through their social-media feed to pass the next few minutes? How long before one of them sees the alert? She forces herself not to turn and look, hoping none of them have seen her face.

'Don't worry,' she says, moving away so fast that Lola isn't ready. Her little feet trip and her hand knocks against a shelf of sweet packets, sending them scattering and clattering across the floor.

Everyone is staring.

Hurry!

'Sorry,' she manages to say, the word a breathless gasp as she rushes them from the shop.

Outside, her heart thunders in her chest. There is no way they can go to a B&B. No way she can risk anyone seeing her. Not even Jenny. She swallows down her mounting panic and hopes Jenny doesn't see the fake reports. Or if she does, that she won't believe it. The thought is shallow and pointless and quickly swallowed up by the fear of someone reporting her location.

There is nowhere for them to go. Nowhere is safe.

THIRTY-SEVEN

EMMA

The streetlamps flicker on as they hurry through the empty town. Only the pubs and restaurants are open now, and in the distance somewhere is the hum of chatter. Emma pictures a beer garden nearby, tourists and locals enjoying the last hours of a day that promises summer is here at last. The image is incongruous to their pace as they rush along the cobbled street sloping down towards the river. She has a sudden urge to rage and scream. How can there be people in the world laughing, relaxing, *living*, when this monstrous fear is chasing her.

Hurry!

She has no idea where to go, just that she needs to get them away. 'Come on, Lola,' she urges.

'I'm tired,' Lola whines, scared and unhappy.

'Me too. We just need to—'

'I want my mummy,' Lola says then, her tone somewhere between angry and upset. And out of nowhere, her daughter stops, feet rooting to the pavement. Emma is still moving, her hand gripping Lola's. The change in movement causes her daughter to stumble forward. Emma is quick, already whirling around and catching her in her arms before she can hit the pavement.

'You OK?' Emma asks.

Lola nods, startled out of her protest.

'Let's find somewhere to eat our dinner. Then we'll both feel better.' She forces herself to slow down.

A red-brick clock tower comes into view, the white face of the clock glowing 9 p.m. And then the bridge appears, leading across the Severn. On either side of the bridge is a sandy bank and a copse of trees and bushes, thick with dark-green leaves. An idea settles in her head, and it feels like she breathes for the first time since panicking in the supermarket that someone would recognise her.

'Look down there,' she says, pointing to the huddle of greenery. 'Let's make a secret den and eat our dinner in it.'

'It looks scary,' Lola whispers, her gaze moving from the trees to the bridge and the water as she pushes up against Emma's body.

'We'll be safe in there,' she soothes; hopes. Anything is better than being out on the street, or in a shop or a B&B with guests and prying eyes. She pictures a hotel room. The door flying open in the middle of the night, hands snatching at them. No warning. No way of knowing. She needs to be somewhere open; to hear them coming.

'Tomorrow it will all be over,' she says as much to herself as to Lola as they step carefully down the steep path and into the shrubbery.

But will it really be over tomorrow? The message from earlier rushes back at her. She won't think about the details yet. First she needs to get them to the ferry port at Birkenhead, and right now that feels an impossible task. In the comfort of Jenny's car, she'd felt so sure that they'd make it. But now she sees the truth. They have nearly a hundred miles still to travel and her face is all over social media and who knows where else.

Away from the streetlights, it is gloomy and a little menacing. Around them, leaves rustle and water laps against the
bridge. Inside the bushes is a circular clearing with a dirt floor
that looks worryingly well-trodden. Emma spots a pile of
cigarette butts and a discarded bottle of sugary alcopop and
hopes they'll have the place to themselves tonight. They settle
by a tree trunk, Emma leaning up against it as she opens the
food packets. They eat in silence, and it's a far cry from the
happy picnic she'd envisaged. She wants to make it fun, but
there is nothing left inside her. Her heart is still beating too fast,
her mind racing with it.

'Can we go now?' Lola asks, pushing the last of her sandwich away. 'I'm tired,' she adds, dragging out the final word as
she picks up Ducky and holds him close. In the dim light,
Emma sees fresh tears forming in those bright-blue eyes. 'I
want... I want Barnaby.'

'Oh, Lola,' Emma says. She needs to find a way to explain
that there is nowhere to go. That here is the safest place, here
they are hidden, but Lola is so little and so tired, she knows she
won't understand.

'Why don't we carry on the adventure and sleep out here
tonight?' she says instead.

'Here?' Lola's frightened gaze travels across the bare earth.

'Come snuggle against me,' she adds, opening her arms.
'We'll put our jumpers on and be nice and warm.' She's
thankful the summer warmth has finally arrived and it's no
longer cool. There might be a slight chill to the air tonight, but
they'll be fine in jumpers.

The crying starts as soon as Emma pulls the jumper over
Lola's head. Deep, heaving sobs. Watery cries for Barnaby and
Mummy and Daddy and home, until her little girl has worked
herself up into a frenzy and won't be soothed. In the end, Emma
takes her daughter in her arms and holds her close as she says
over and over again, 'I want Mummy.'

I'm right here.

The sadness wells up in Emma. Tears stream down her face too. All the guilt for what she's doing, the pain. This can't be right. This can't have been the only way. What has she done?

Eventually Lola's cries soften and her body relaxes. She falls asleep, pushing Emma's back into the bumpy bark of the tree trunk, but she doesn't move. She won't sleep anyway.

Gently, careful not to wake her, Emma kisses the top of Lola's head. 'I'm your mummy,' she whispers.

She stares into the darkness, unable to stop the memories coming back to her. She remembers the first party Jonny had invited her to after she'd broken up with Damien. Warm rooms and chilled champagne and twenty or so of his friends. Mostly men, but some women too. Not wives or girlfriends though, Emma had noticed.

Everyone had been so welcoming. All of them asking about her degree and what she'd thought about a recent news event, listening to her replies, nodding agreement or gently posing their own opinions. She'd never experienced anything like it before. They treated her like she was smart but were happy to disagree. It was a far cry from her dad's 'got nothing to do with us' mentality whenever she'd broached political topics with him. Or the debates between her fellow students that always seemed to end in hurt feelings and name calling.

The men were mostly of a similar age. Late thirties or early forties, she'd guessed, and all of them had a story to share. It was the kind of group she'd have expected to find rife with misogyny, but they'd all been so friendly, so gracious.

She'd met Roly at that party. He'd had her laughing until tears rolled down her cheeks, telling her stories about their university days when they'd all got *'blottoed'* and had broken into a lecturer's car and pushed it to another car park. *'We kept waiting for him to mention it in class, but he never said a word. Not once.'*

Later, she'd found Jonny sitting alone in the garden with a whisky and cigar. He'd smiled and motioned for her to join him.

'Having fun?' he'd asked.

She'd nodded. *'Your friends are funny, and very nice. Thank you for inviting me.'*

He'd shrugged as though it was nothing.

'Why did you?' she'd asked him, the alcohol making her flirty and brave and comfortable in her own skin in a way she never normally was. *'Because if this is some weird sex ring or something, I'm afraid you've picked the wrong girl. I might only be twenty years old, but I'm not stupid.'*

He'd laughed then. A proper guffaw. *'I can assure you, that's not why I invited you. The truth is, I like to spend time with beautiful, smart women.'* He'd waved a hand towards the house and the party going on inside. *'It's part of my business to host soirées such as this. Good for networking and a safe place for my more private investors to talk. Sadly, in my line of work, they are mostly men, and so I invite beautiful women such as yourself to enjoy my hospitality. It keeps the mood light, and we all enjoy ourselves.'*

He'd leaned forward, and she'd thought he was going to brush a hand over the bare skin of her thigh where her dress had risen up, but he didn't. *'I'm asking nothing from you, Emma. If you have a nice time here, I hope you'll keep coming. If you don't, then I'll wish you well. I'm always clear with my friends that everyone in my home is treated with respect. If anyone crosses a line with you, you must tell me. OK?'*

She'd nodded and looked through the glass doors to the men in their expensive suits and neat haircuts. *'What business are you in?'* she'd asked.

He'd paused for a beat before replying. *'Finance mostly.'*

She'd been about to ask something more, but then the music had started and she'd been invited to dance, and she'd laughed and said yes.

Looking back, Emma can't remember falling in love. Only that it had happened hard and fast and she became intoxicated with it, unable to study like she'd done before. Never turning down a dinner invite, a late-night hotel room, all of Jonny's parties. The third and final year of her law degree had just started and she was barely making it to lectures. When she was, her thoughts had been on the practised way his fingers ran over her body, causing a fiery intensity she'd never experienced with Damien.

A few months passed in that love-filled haze. For the first time in her life, Emma felt seen. Not just for who she was, but for all her potential too. Her dreams felt in touching distance.

Then she'd found out she was pregnant.

THIRTY-EIGHT

EMMA

The two lines on the pregnancy test had shaken Emma's world with the force of an earthquake. She couldn't wrap her head around it. They'd always used condoms. Always. She was only twenty. She still had the final year of her law degree to finish and years more training ahead of her. She hadn't even thought about whether children would be in her future. She wasn't ready to be a mother. She'd cried and raged and cried again. Confused and uncertain and suddenly so lost.

Jonny was the first person she told. His reaction was calmer than hers. *'What do you want to do?'* he'd asked as he'd made her a cup of tea in the kitchen of his house in Belsize Park.

Tears had filled her eyes. *'I don't know. I just... I know I don't want to be a mother right now. I want to be a barrister and live my life before I even think about this. But I... don't know if I can go through with a termination. I'm stuck.'* Her dreams had felt like holding water in cupped hands. No matter how hard she'd tried, she couldn't stop it all slipping away.

'Not necessarily.'

'If you're about to tell me I won't be alone, please don't. We both know what this is.' She'd felt a flash of anger at Jonny as

much as the situation she was in. She'd known what she was getting herself into with the relationship, but he'd been to blame too. How could she have allowed herself to fall so blindly in love?

His silence said everything. Jonny was the kind of man who always spoke out if he didn't agree, and it was not one of those times. She was alone in this.

'What am I going to do?' she'd cried.

'Right now, you're going to do nothing. You're going to go to your lectures and carry on striving for that dream of yours. How far along are you?'

'The test said six weeks.'

'So you'd be due' – he'd paused and she could see the months tick by in his head – 'in August. Whatever happens, you'll be able to finish your degree.'

She'd nodded, glad to have someone thinking ahead when she was cemented in a present she couldn't wrap her head around.

'Don't think about it, Emma. Come over on Friday night and we'll talk again. I'll cook for us.'

She'd nodded and tried to do as he said, focusing on her lectures and essays, but it was impossible. While her classmates left for Christmas drinks and holidays, all she'd been able to think about was the pregnancy. She didn't want to be a mother, and yet she couldn't put a voice to the feeling inside her that she already was.

Jonny had cooked that Friday, just as he'd promised. The house had smelled of garlic and chicken and, despite everything, she'd been famished, and it had been worth the heaving Tube carriage all the way to North London and the icy-cold December air that had whipped her face as she'd walked to his house.

'I have a plan,' he'd said as he'd opened the door. 'Let's go through to the living room. The fire is already going, and I had a

Christmas tree delivered today. Come and see it. We can eat later.'

The soft glow of the lamp light and the crackling fire had reflected in the tree ornaments, had made the room feel cosy and welcoming. She'd slipped off her shoes and tucked her legs under as she'd sat on the sofa, foolishly grateful that Jonny had a plan when all she had was panic and fear.

'I know a couple who are struggling to conceive,' he'd said when she was settled. *'They want a baby desperately. They're good people, and they'd be able to give a child the best life imaginable.'*

'You want me to give the baby up for adoption?' She'd been surprised, not just at the idea but that it hadn't crossed her mind. Was it the answer? A wrenching sadness was already tearing at her just thinking about it, and yet... what about her dreams?

'Why not?' Jonny had continued, staring at her with those sharp eyes. *'You yourself have said you're not ready to be a mother. You've got a fantastic career ahead of you. You'd be throwing it all away. And what kind of life could you give a child right now, Emma? You're not even twenty-one.'*

'I guess, I just... I hadn't thought about adoption.'

'You'd be giving the greatest gift imaginable. And I could make sure you were compensated.'

'Paid, you mean? You want me to sell my baby?'

'I didn't take you for being so naïve,' he'd said, causing a heat to creep over her cheeks. *'It wouldn't be like that. Think about it. You wouldn't be able to start work straight away, would you? Or carry on studying. It would impact your career – only a setback, but still. Why shouldn't you be compensated for that? Pupillage isn't going to be cheap either. Even kitting yourself out in the right clothes will cost you a small fortune if you want to be taken seriously as a barrister.'*

'I... I guess it's worth considering,' she'd found herself

saying. *'How would it work exactly? Is it done through an agency? I'd want to meet them.'*

He'd nodded, smiling. It shouldn't have mattered, but she'd been able to tell she'd pleased him by asking those questions and was glad. *'Of course. But it's slightly more complicated than a straightforward adoption.'*

'Why?'

He'd held her gaze, watching her reaction as he'd told her. *'It's Roly and his wife, Isobel.'*

'Oh,' is all she'd been able to reply.

Jonny had swept her into the kitchen and over dinner he'd told her how easy it would all be. *'It's win-win,'* he'd said more than once that night.

She doesn't remember saying yes to starting the adoption process, only that she hadn't outright refused. It had been so easy to be swept away by Jonny's plans. Every fear had been answered with reassurance.

'My parents will go mad,' she'd said. *'I can't tell them.'*

'Then don't. In fact, don't tell anyone. Hide your bump until you finish your degree and then tell your family you're going travelling.'

'But where will I really go?'

'You can live here.'

'Why are you being nice to me? What's in this for you?'

'I'm a nice man, Emma,' he'd replied, laughing a little as though she'd told a joke. *'Nothing has changed between us. You know that, don't you? I want the best for you, just like I always have. Can't I be nice to my friends and nice to you? This is the perfect solution. Of course I'm happy to help.'*

The months had passed. Still, she hadn't seen Roly again or met Isobel. In a hot week in May, when she was six months pregnant, she'd sat her exams. And the next day, in a baggy T-shirt, with a backpack slung over her shoulder, she'd waved goodbye to her parents and brothers, pretending to head to

Thailand to travel for five months with friends. She'd hated lying but hated the thought of them knowing the truth even more. They'd have convinced her to keep the baby, to shrink her life down to a single-parent world of minimum wage and cheap rentals, and even though she'd loved this baby already, she'd still wanted her dreams so badly it had hurt.

She'd arrived at Jonny's house to a folder of paper. *'It's the adoption paperwork,'* he'd said, handing her a pen and tapping the space for her signature. *'All standard stuff.'* Then he looked at her and even though she wanted to read over every line, she found herself ignoring the three years of her law degree and every instinct she had, and signed her name. That was the last time she saw the folder. Weeks and months later, she'd wonder what exactly she'd signed away.

'Great,' he'd said. *'Now there's been a slight change of plan. I'm having my house renovated next week so you won't be able to stay here after all, but don't worry. Roly and Isobel would love to have you, and it will give you an opportunity to get to know them and settle in for the birth.'*

'Won't I be having the baby in hospital?'

'Of course that's an option. But I assumed you'd rather have it in a comfortable home environment without disapproving midwives.'

Those months in the house overlooking the common with Isobel are blurred in Emma's mind. They'd tiptoed around each other at first, but Emma had soon found she'd liked the woman who would be a mother to her baby. And Roly had been such a doting husband. She could see they'd be the perfect family.

Then Lola was born. A 2 a.m. delivery after hours of pushing, hours more of contractions. The midwife had been a kind and steady presence, but only in the moment her baby girl was born, as Emma had slumped down, spent in every possible way, and watched her scrawny baby placed in Isobel's arms, had she truly understood how much she loved her daughter.

She'd called Jonny the next day, crying down the phone. Asking to see the contract. Surely there was a break clause, a way to change her mind? He'd told her there was nothing to be done. *'It's just your hormones, Emma. Calm down. You signed the paperwork. It's their baby, Emma. Not yours.'*

She should never have stayed on in the house. But she'd overheard Roly suggesting they get a nanny to help out, and she hadn't wanted to leave her baby girl so soon anyway. It was only later, when Roly had kicked her out, that she'd started to think about all that had happened to her, and how much of it had been planned without her even knowing.

Her mind had raced back over the adoption – how quick Jonny had been to suggest Roly and Isobel as parents. With sickening clarity, she saw the first invite to the party, and the heady, love-filled days that followed. How quickly she'd fallen head over heels. How quickly she'd fallen pregnant too. Condoms weren't a hundred per cent, but they were close. Had he tampered with them? Had she merely been a pawn in a business deal of Jonny's?

Now, the holler of shouts in the dark shatters the memories playing in her thoughts. She blinks, her cheeks damp from tears she didn't know she'd cried. Shapes appear in the darkness. A branch, leaves, the dirt ground; Lola snuggled against her. The voices grow nearer. Loud and slurred. Stumbling footsteps. Emma holds her breath, counting the sounds of one, two, three men. Her heart starts to beat so fast she is sure the thudding will wake Lola before the noise of the men does.

Please, please, please go away.

Silent tears roll down her face. She cries for all that happened and all that's still happening. She cries out of fear for a future that feels unknown, and she cries for an exhaustion she thinks will never leave her. Then the voices grow distant again, and the only sound left is the rustling leaves and the lapping water.

She holds Lola close, remembering every kick and movement from her pregnancy. She gave birth to this perfect little girl. She doesn't care about the contract she signed. She doesn't care what the doctors told her, or what the solicitor said after Roly kicked her out. She doesn't care what the faked DNA results said. She is Lola's mother.

DAY FOUR: 9.40 A.M. WEDNESDAY
2ND AUGUST

THIRTY-NINE
ISOBEL

Isobel stares at her reflection in the hall mirror. The black of her top washes her out, but it's loose, hiding the curve of her growing stomach. Her face is pale, and beneath the Charlotte Tilbury mascara and the YSL concealer are eyes that are dark and puffy. She will not cry today. Whatever happens, she will not cry.

Roly's words this morning, as she'd stepped out of the shower, still spin round her head. *'Iz, Owen just called. They've got a location on Lola. He's coming to pick us up in an hour. Get ready.'*

'Where is she?'

'He didn't say, but we're going to get her. We're going to get our daughter back!'

The noise of a car on the road makes her turn to the front door, but it passes without stopping. Where is he? She scoops her hair into a ponytail and tightens the backs of her pearl earrings. They will forever remind her of these dark, torrid days. Tomorrow, she will throw them away, never wear pearls again.

In this house, time has lost all meaning. Minutes have crawled, hours have jumped forward. Only the daily walks on the common and brief exchanges with the dog walker have given her any sense of the outside world still moving forward. This morning, after pulling herself from a fitful sleep with a new kind of energy, determined to take control of her emotions and the situation, she'd opened the curtains to bright sunshine and blue skies. Standing on the common was the same runner in the pink outfit she'd seen a few days ago. She'd looked up at the house, and Isobel had almost waved before realising how stupid that was and turning away.

Three days have felt like a lifetime, but now they've found Emma and Lola. And this time it isn't pretending to drink coffee and sly remarks from Margaret as they wait for news. They're going to get her.

The thought feels almost unreal. Like the fantasies she's had of Lola being home, the memories of her daughter. Will it really be over today? The question makes her pulse thrum through her body, and she fights the urge to cry before telling herself to get it together. There is no time for tears. She has to believe this is it.

'Isobel, what are you doing?' Margaret appears from the landing above and steps with one hand on the banister towards her. She's wearing loose white trousers and a pale-green blouse and cardigan. Her hair is blow-dried into its neat bob with the ends curled under, the ends brushing a sharp jawline.

'Didn't Roly tell you?'

'Tell me what? Is there news?'

'Yes,' Isobel replies, turning to face Margaret as she reaches the hall. And even though Isobel can't be sure, she thinks the woman's gaze strays to her stomach. Just one more day, Isobel pleads to herself. Let her keep this secret just one more day.

Isobel relays Roly's earlier words, and her mother-in-law breaks into a rare smile.

'Thank God.' She heaves a sigh, and even though Isobel loathes so much about this woman and everything she believes, she can't deny that Margaret loves Lola. In a different world, they could've been allies, friends even. They both love Roly and Lola so fiercely, and yet that love is somehow a wedge between them. No matter what Isobel does, it's never right in Margaret's eyes. And even though it shouldn't matter at this moment in time, a fluttering anxiety dances through Isobel for an imagined future where Margaret has her way, and Isobel's beautiful children are shoved off to boarding school and a life away from Isobel's love.

She won't think about it now. Nothing in their future is set. The last few days have been proof of that. Was it really only Sunday that they'd been travelling home from a perfect holiday in Cornwall, Roly's hand on her thigh, that delicious half-smile, not a care in the world?

'You really should've told me immediately, Isobel,' Margaret says with a heavy sigh before turning back to the stairs. 'I'll get my bag.'

A protest forms on Isobel's lips. She wants to tell Margaret, no, she can't come. But she swallows the words. What would be the point anyway? Margaret would never listen to her. It'll be down to Roly to say something. Isobel has no idea what events will unfold today, but the truth they've kept from Margaret will surely be exposed when they arrive at wherever they're going and she sees that there is no police presence. No flashing lights. No uniforms. Just Jonny and his men, and them.

Maybe it won't matter. As long as Isobel has Lola back. As long as she's safe. Lola is all that's ever mattered. That love. That pure, raw and all-consuming love has been the most dazzling light in Isobel's life. Shining bright enough to ignore the shadows and the dark deeds that led them here. And the thing is, the thing that makes the guilt really hit her in the still of the night when she can't sleep – a sledgehammer to her insides – is that she'd do it all again for that love.

If the hours rolled back – the days, the years – she'd change nothing. Even taking Jonny and his dark world on as a client. It scares her sometimes – all the time really. Whenever she sits down at Roly's antique desk to look over Jonny's accounts, seeing those vast sums of money she must move and disguise and hide for him. Always worrying what he'd do if she messes up. She wouldn't change it, because without Jonny, they wouldn't have Lola.

Then there's all that came after. Forcing Emma out of their home when Lola was only eight weeks old. Paying off a technician to fake the DNA tests Emma's solicitor had requested. And worst of all, telling Roly to call Jonny when she'd turned up on the common, knowing it would be so bad for Emma but doing it anyway to protect her longed-for family. What kind of person does that make her? What kind of mother?

The desperate kind, a voice whispers in her thoughts. Desperate. So fiercely, inexplicably desperate to be a mother. There are no words to describe the hollowed-out longing she'd felt after all those failed pregnancy tests. A yearning that seemed to pull her down. A heavy weight she could never shift. Only worsening when she saw other women with their children. Why them and not her? The question ate her up and spat her out – a broken mess.

And that was before Margaret's belittling remarks.

'I had no problem conceiving. Although I was much younger than you when I had Roly and Felicity.'

'You must be doing something wrong, Isobel.'

'You really are letting the family down. Poor Roly.'

Isobel had snapped once, unable to endure her cruelty for another moment. She'd dropped her knife and fork on the dinner plate over Sunday lunch at Huntington Hall after another of Margaret's comments had cut to the quick.

'Actually, Margaret, we're going to adopt.'

She'd only mentioned it to Roly the previous day. A few weeks had passed after the last doctor's appointment, when their final shred of hope had been singed to ash. He'd looked up from his coffee and scrolling on his phone, eyes wide with alarm. They'd skirted around the question of adoption on and off for the last few months. She'd known Roly was reluctant, but he hadn't said no, and so she'd clung to that.

'*You will not.*' Margaret's reply had been loud and harsh and followed the three sharp taps of her index finger on the pristine white tablecloth. '*No grandchild of mine will be adopted. We are of royal lineage from Edward the sixth. Roland, what's the meaning of this?*'

He'd spluttered and backtracked, trying to stay in the middle place of pleasing both the women in his life and always coming down to side with his mother.

'*Let me be clear, Roland,*' Margaret had said then. '*If you adopt a child, I will never accept it into this family, and to ensure the family line, I will remove you from your inheritance. You would no longer be heir to the Huntington estate.*'

'*Mother,*' he'd replied, sounding more scared than she'd ever heard him. '*There is no need for that. We won't be adopting.*'

Isobel had fled from the table, fighting back the tears and the haunting realisation that she'd never be a mother. And without giving Roly the family he wanted, surely he'd leave her and then she'd really be left with nothing. An anxious shell of the woman she'd once been.

The days had passed in a stony silence. She'd been hurt by how quickly he'd sided with his mother. But she'd understood. Being a Huntington was everything to Roly. The truth was, she hadn't known what to say to him. Their relationship had shrunk down to a world of trying and failing, arguing and trying again. All they'd ever talked about was a baby. They'd lost their way, and yet Isobel had started to focus on a new plan. Surrogacy. A child carried by someone else, but still Roly's. She'd been researching how it would work, preparing to talk to him when he'd approached her first.

'*Jonny has a friend in trouble,*' he'd said. '*She needs some help, and I think it could be the answer we're looking for.*'

Then he'd told her about a girl called Emma who was pregnant and wanted to give the baby up for adoption.

'*But it wouldn't be ours. Your mother said—*'

'*Mother doesn't need to know a thing.*'

'*What?*' she'd reeled back, surprised by his words. She'd never known him to defy her before. '*How would that work?*'

'*We lie. We tell her what she wants to hear. That you're pregnant at last. In a few months, we cook up a story of you being unwell and housebound until after the birth. I'll say we've had a leak in the guest bathroom and have plumbers in getting it repaired. You know how she can't stand having workmen in the home. It will keep her away.*'

'*You want me to hide from your mother for nine months?*' And even though it had seemed crazy and impossible, she'd smiled at the thought.

'*It would be more like four or five months, don't you think? You can wear baggy clothes to start with.*'

'*And you're OK with this? The baby not being yours – biologically I mean?*'

He'd pulled her into his arms and kissed her. '*I want a family as much as you do. We'll love this baby like our own, I promise.*'

And even though she'd had a dozen more questions about Emma and how they'd deceive Margaret, Isobel had felt the hope flooding back through her with the force of a tidal wave. What did it matter who this girl was, or even who the father was? There was a baby and it would be theirs. She'd be a mother.

Only once had she broached the subject of the father with Jonny, gently asking if it was his. He'd tipped his head back and laughed. '*I'm just the broker in this, Isobel. The father is inconsequential.*'

And she'd realised then that Jonny's part in this was not kindness; helping a friend in need. It was about money to him, something Roly hadn't mentioned. Had they bought Emma's baby? It was illegal, of course, and yet, just like all the other business dealings of Jonny's she'd seen over the years, she'd pushed the thought to the back of her mind and focused on the only thing that mattered – she was going to be a mother.

FORTY

ISOBEL

The sound of an engine pulls Isobel back to the hallway, and this time when she peers through the window, she sees DCI Watkins climbing out of a silver BMW. She rushes forward, pulling open the front door, halfway to shouting up the stairs for Roly and asking where they're going. Where's Lola?

But before she can do either, the detective is putting a finger to his lips and beckoning her onto the doorstep. She glances up the empty stairwell before stepping outside. The morning sun is warm, the sky an azure blue. Already the common is filling with picnic blankets and families on summer holidays – footballs and frisbees and dogs off leads rushing after thrown tennis balls. It's the perfect paddling-pool day; playing tea-parties and pretending to drink water with grass floating on the top. She wonders if she'll ever look outside to another beautiful summer's day and not think of Lola being snatched away and the terrible things she's done.

She forces the thought away and focuses on the man in front of her. The expensive suit and the sharpest mind she's ever known. A detective chief inspector for the Met, an Oxford graduate, a friend to Roly and all the others who graduated with them. He is risking everything to help them. His career, his reputation. For the first time, she wonders why. Is it really about loyalty to Roly and a bond she can never understand?

No. She is not that naïve. This is, and has always been, about business. And Jonny is at the centre of it all. Suddenly, it's not Emma and her state of mind that sends tendrils of icy fear to every corner of her being. It's this. It's Jonny. His men. It's the uncertainty of what will happen when they reach Emma and Lola.

'What's going on?' she asks, hugging her arms to her body. 'Do you know where Lola is?'

'I'll get to that in a minute,' he says, and then glancing behind her to the open door and empty hall, he pulls out his phone. 'There's something I want you to see.'

'Shall I get Roly?'

He shakes his head. 'We have a new lead, Isobel, on who we think might be helping Emma.'

'It's not Zeen, is it?'

'No. That's the other thing. I spoke to your housekeeper early this morning. She's in a village twenty miles from Manila with poor phone signal. It seems her mother fell ill while you were on holiday and she went to visit.'

Isobel takes a moment to breathe, to process his words. She'd known Zeen had nothing to do with Lola's abduction, but hearing it is still a comfort. She's glad Zeen is far away from all of this.

The detective steps closer, and she catches the deep scent of his aftershave, the smell turning her stomach. She swallows, willing the nausea away as he taps the screen and tilts it towards her.

'What is it?' She swallows again. Her legs are weak from the racing of her pulse. What is she about to see?

'The cyber team went back over the CCTV from

Winchester services when Lola was taken. They sent me something they'd missed the first time around.'

She leans forward, cupping her hand over the top of her eyes, shielding out the sun as she watches. From what she can see, the camera is high up on a building or a lamppost. There is something ant-like about the people as they bustle around parked cars and in and out of the revolving glass doors.

'What am I looking for?' she asks.

'Keep watching.'

Another few seconds pass, and then Isobel sees Emma and Lola exiting the doors, holding hands. Emma is smiling down at Lola. Her little girl is skipping a little, each step tugging at Emma's arm.

How many times had she told Lola to walk properly and stop skipping? She'd give anything to take back that fraught tone she'd used sometimes and skip with Lola. Seeing her look so happy with Emma is a knife in her side. They step off the pavement and across the car park, and the video ends.

'I'm not sure what I'm looking at,' she says, feeling the hurt well to the surface. She grits her teeth. She will not cry.

'Watch again. Look at who is standing outside as they exit the building.'

The video plays again, and this time Isobel watches the people around the doors, seeing nothing of significance. And then there's something that makes her gasp. A familiar figure walking towards the entrance. Someone she would recognise a mile away. The broad shoulders, the confident stride.

'Roly,' she says, the word a breathless whisper. Her gaze shoots to the hall and then back to the screen. What the hell is she seeing? Emma and Lola appear again, but this time Isobel's attention fixes on Roly. He stops in his tracks as they appear and whirls around, changing direction and walking away.

A dawning realisation sweeps through her. Her heart is beating too fast, her thoughts spinning with it. DCI Watkins is telling her Roly is involved in Lola's abduction? She wants to tell him he's wrong. Not Roly. Not her husband, the love of her life. The man she trusts. Except... does she?

Isobel thinks back to that time in April when Scarlett disappeared and Emma started planning Lola's abduction, and her husband's mood was dark and secretive. She'd known he was hiding something from her and had suspected an affair. Could it have been something worse?

Then there's the ease of the lies he's told his mother these last few days. No hesitation, no stammer. He'd been smooth and confident. Practised. She thinks back to all the things she's never asked. His business dealings with Jonny. The deal struck with Emma. The women she's certain he flirts with on his client nights out, and more.

'It was a drunken snog in a nightclub. I promise you, Iz, nothing more.'

She isn't sure his promises mean anything anymore. She's turned a blind eye to so much of their lives and their marriage. Would she even know if he was lying to her?

But why would Roly do this? Why would he help someone take his daughter? Why would he put himself and her and his mother and his close friend through this ordeal? She doesn't have answers.

The video ends and then starts again. 'Look at the moment he turns around,' the detective says. 'He sees Emma and Lola, and then he moves out of their way.'

She shakes her head, still not wanting to believe it. 'He's talking on the phone. Look.' She points to the figure on the screen that is so clearly her husband. 'I don't think he sees them. I think he just hasn't finished his call or something.'

'You really believe that?' He slips his phone into his pocket, his gaze never leaving hers. 'Let's not forget that Emma had access to your car at some point after you took Lola into the services. She took Lola's bag and teddy.'

'Roly left it unlocked when he went to make a call,' she explains.

'That's quite convenient, wouldn't you say? There's also the passports and paperwork missing from your home. Zeen was the likely suspect there, but we've ruled her out.'

Isobel presses the palm of her hand to her forehead. 'Why are you telling me this?' she asks. 'Roly is your friend. I thought you were doing this for him? Why aren't you asking him about this CCTV and the missing files?'

'Because I might be loyal, but I don't like being lied to. I also like to know what I'm walking into.'

'And you really think Roly is involved in Lola's abduction?'

There's a thud of footsteps on the stairs behind her. She's about to turn away, but a firm hand grips her arm, and words are whispered low and fast in her ear. 'Perhaps you don't know your husband as well as you think you do.'

Her mouth gapes. It's the same thought she had just moments ago. She wants to ask what he means, but Roly is by her side, an arm already looping around her. All she knows from the sudden shift in his posture and the smile as he greets Roly is that this is something to be kept between the two of them. Another threat to add to the growing web of lies they're weaving around each other. If there'd been more time, she'd have told the detective that he's mistaken. Roly wouldn't do this. The footage is a bad angle, that's all. And actually, doesn't he start to turn a fraction before Emma and Lola appear? She wishes she could look again. She knows what Roly's like on his calls. She's watched him walk into lampposts and trip up kerbs. He never pays any attention to his surroundings.

But does she really believe that? Roly has been on his phone like always the last few days. She remembers the wounded expression on his face when she'd asked him how he could think about anything but Lola. She'd assumed he'd still been in contact with his clients. But how sure is she?

'Owen,' Roly says, glancing behind him before reaching out to shake his friend's hand. 'You've found Lola?'

'She's in Bridgenorth,' he replies.

Isobel gasps. 'How did she make it so far?' She looks to Roly, expecting to see the same shock pulling at his features, but instead he's frowning.

'How do you know?' he asks.

Before there's a chance to reply, Margaret is upon them too, a white leather handbag looped over one shoulder. 'You have my grandchild? Is this true, DCI Watkins?'

Roly steps to one side so they're all standing on the doorstep, half in, half out. Isobel's gaze is drawn once more to her husband and she thinks of how easily he lied to his mother yesterday. *'Perhaps you don't know your husband as well as you think you do.'*

He nods, playing the role of the diligent detective once more. 'We have, Mrs Huntington. We received a call from a doctor in Bridgenorth early this morning.'

'A doctor? Is Lola OK?' Isobel jumps in.

'As far as we know, yes. The doctor is a local Bridgenorth GP. He told us that his wife was returning from a visit to her mother in Eastbourne and met a woman and her daughter at a roadside services in Portsmouth. According to the doctor, his wife drove them all the way to Bridgenorth. It was only when his wife saw one of our Facebook alerts for Emma that she told her husband. They apparently argued over whether or not to report it. In the end, he called the number in secret.'

The detective rolls his eyes as though this poor woman who helped Emma was an idiot for doing so, and not, as it happens, right to be wary of a fake social-media story.

'Most importantly, it appears Emma trusted this woman enough to divulge her plans. We now know that Emma is travelling to the Liverpool area, specifically to Birkenhead, where she's planning to board the night ferry to Belfast. It leaves at ten thirty tonight.'

A fresh wave of fear grabs Isobel so hard that for a second then another she can't draw breath. 'Did the woman mention if Emma was being helped?'

The detective shoots her a warning look. 'No. Nothing was mentioned.'

Isobel glances to Roly. 'Could it... could it be Scarlett?' she asks.

'What would make you ask that?' There's a coldness to the detective's tone, but she pushes on. She has to know the truth. He's not the only one who wants to know what they're walking into.

'It all feels connected. Scarlett disappears at the same time Emma begins planning to take Lola. Maybe that's because Scarlett's been in hiding, helping Emma.'

'Who is this Scarlett?' Margaret asks. 'How is she connected to Emma?'

They fall silent, all knowing the answer. Jonny.

'It's not Scarlett,' the detective replies, ignoring Margaret.

'How do you know for sure?' she pushes.

'Because Emma has been a fugitive for three days, and we've had numerous sightings and near misses. Scarlett's disappearance has been national news for months. Don't you think that if anyone had seen her, they'd have reported it?'

'What does that mean? Is she dead?'

'I'd really like to understand—' Margaret begins, her voice rising a fraction.

'How about we focus on Lola?' Roly says, and it's clear he wants to move the conversation on. Isobel holds her breath, still waiting for the detective's reply. Is Scarlett dead? And if she is, what does that mean for Emma?

'Can you stop the ferry's departure?' Roly asks, and Isobel

grits her teeth, holding back her need for answers as he moves the conversation away from Scarlett.

'We won't need to. We'll be there ourselves. Emma won't be getting on that ferry.'

'When do we leave?' Roly asks.

'Right now,' is the reply, and Isobel rushes to get her phone and slip on her shoes. She grabs a bag from the back of her wardrobe and stuffs Barnaby inside.

Only when she's sitting in the cool leather interior of the detective's BMW with Margaret beside her and Roly in front, still tapping on his phone, and they've weaved their way out of London, speeding north on the motorway, do the questions return.

How well does she really know her husband? How will this day end?

FORTY-ONE

EMMA

The Stena Line terminal in Birkenhead is a glass structure with a funnel-shaped roof that's like the outline of a ferry. Beyond it, streaked with the rays of the setting sun, Emma can see the top of the huge white boat and imagines the first passengers stepping up the walkway. She can't believe they've made it.

Two days late, exhausted, wrung out, sick of eating sandwiches, achy from walking, stiff from sleeping in the copse last night. But here. Their safety feels almost touchable. Even this morning, when they'd woken to the stop-start trundling of a bin lorry on the high street and a day promising to be sticky and hot, Emma hadn't been sure they'd make it.

'*Morning, baby girl,*' she'd said to Lola, expecting more tears and upset. But her daughter had smiled instead.

'*Sleeping here is fun. Can we do it again tonight, Emma?*' she'd asked.

'*Let's see, shall we?*' She'd wanted to tell Lola that they'd be sleeping on a big boat later, except she wasn't sure they would anymore. It wasn't just a question of whether they could travel the final hundred miles to the ferry port without being recognised. It was the message she'd been sent yesterday, the new plan she didn't like but had no way to stop.

They'd packed up their things, and Lola had skipped around the tree trunk with Ducky in her arms as Emma had slipped on the blonde wig once more. It was ratty and tangled beneath the baseball cap, but she'd felt less recognisable. They'd walked hand in hand through the empty town to the top of the narrow high street, eating the last jam tarts for breakfast as they'd waited for the first bus that would take them to Wolverhampton. From there it was a train journey to Liverpool and a vast domed train station. They'd walked a while then, Emma's heart still racing from the train and the certainty that any second it would roll to a stop and the doors would open, and Jonny would be there.

It took another two buses and a lot more walking before they reached the ferry port in the late afternoon.

'What are we doing here?' Lola had asked as Emma had found a hiding place in a wasteland area beside an empty freight container, near enough to watch the terminal and the car park. They'd settled on the hard concrete and played I Spy as the ferry had arrived and the passengers disembarked. Cars came and went, and in every face she'd expected to see Jonny.

She has no idea what she'll do if he arrives before the help does. There is no busy road, no waiting bus to carry them to safety this time. Nowhere to run. The port is right on the water's edge, surrounded by an industrial area and not much else.

'We're waiting for a friend who's going to keep us safe,' Emma had replied. The answer had caused a tangled knot of indecision to form in the pit of her stomach. There were so many questions and no one to ask. The message she'd sent earlier had gone unanswered.

Are you sure this is the best way?

'*Safe from the monster?*' Lola's voice had been curious, not sad, as though she'd forgotten the fears she'd felt in the last few days. Little legs running, gulping sobs.

'*Exactly.*'

Hours passed. The urgency continuing to claw at her as Lola, bored of playing with her toys and I Spy, settles against her body once more and falls asleep to Emma's story of Goldilocks and the three bears. She holds her daughter close, thinking of all the hugs she's missed. Her thoughts see-saw between relief that it's almost over and fear that it never will be. Will they ever truly be able to stop running?

'*Do you know how easy it would be for me to end you?*' Jonny's voice fills her head.

The memory is vivid. She remembers sitting in his car after Roly had kicked her out of their house when Lola was only eight weeks old. Jonny had been waiting to take her home, driving in silence across London, ignoring her tears and protests, and only speaking when he'd parked outside her parents' house.

She hadn't replied. The question hadn't needed an answer.

'*No one will believe you,*' he'd said then as though reading her mind. His voice had been so fierce that she'd jumped in her seat.

'*Lola is my baby,*' she'd whispered.

'*No. You gave her away. You signed a contract. You have no legal rights over that child.*'

'*That's not true.*' It can't be true.

'*No one will believe you if you make a fuss about this, Emma. And don't even think of going to the police. If you want to see a penny of your money, you'll keep your head down and move on.*'

She'd expected to feel angry in that moment. She'd given more than she knew she had to give. But she didn't want that money anymore. How could she take it? It would forever be tainted with the knowledge that she'd given away her daughter because this man had convinced her with his smiles and charm and always knowing just what to say.

Despite Jonny's warning, she'd been unable to stay quiet. She hadn't gone to the police though. Jonny had too many friends on the force. Instead, she'd hired a solicitor and told him everything, not caring that it was costing all of her savings; not even caring that Jonny might make good on his promise. The solicitor had been willing to help at first. His outrage and support had made her hope for a little while that she'd get Lola back. How stupid she'd been.

'Emma, sit down,' her solicitor had said a month after their first meeting, leading her into a small office with cheap, mismatched furniture. *'It's not good news, I'm afraid.'*

'But the DNA test. You said they'd agreed to it. Do you have the results?'

He'd nodded. *'Their solicitor sent them yesterday.'* He'd held out the piece of paper for her to take.

She'd stared at the squiggles and the words and it hadn't made any sense. *'What is this?'*

'It's the DNA profile of Lola Huntington, and that of Isobel and Roly Huntington. Your DNA is also there at the bottom. What you're looking at is irrevocable proof that Lola is the biological child of both Isobel and Roly. Their DNA is a fifty per cent match to Lola's. Yours is not. I'm sorry,' he'd added.

'But this isn't right. What else can we do? Can we get it retested?'

He'd looked at her with pity in his eyes. *'I don't think they'd agree to that. And quite frankly there is no reason why they should. The lab who ran the test is one we've used countless times before. They're trustworthy and they're thorough. Mr and Mrs Huntington have been quite understanding, but they're asking now for you to leave them alone and seek help for your... confusion. This is not your baby.'*

'*Her name is Lola.*' She'd stood from the chair and stepped to his desk, anger throbbing through her body. This couldn't be happening. She'd cried, shouted, sobbed. '*The results are fake. Lola is mine.*'

'*I'm sorry, Emma,*' he'd replied, and his tone was no longer pitying but filled with disgust. '*But I can't take this any further with you, and I suggest you find a way to move on.*'

She'd gone home to her parents' house and crawled into bed, crying for days, until the need to see her baby had dragged her out again, and she'd waited on the common for Isobel. Not able to believe that these people could do this to her. Were they really such monsters that they'd lie and fake results, and destroy her wholly and completely, steal her baby? The answer was yes. She'd seen it flashing in Isobel's eyes as they'd talked, but the realisation hadn't fully dawned until those hands had snatched her from the street and she knew they'd called Jonny. God, how she'd hated them for that. For everything they'd done to her.

But what could she do about it? Jonny had made good on his promise and thrown her into that hospital. Inside that locked ward she was crazy; a delusional woman obsessed with a baby she'd been hired to nanny for. Only Haz had kept her from losing her mind in that place. From giving up. But then he'd died too, and all the hopes and dreams he'd started to coax back into her had disappeared. She doesn't know what would've happened if help hadn't walked into the florist one day in early January. She'd probably still be there, forcing herself to stay quiet, her life so small, because it meant even though she could never see her daughter, she was safe at least.

'*Emma?*'

The voice had been unfamiliar, but when she'd stepped onto the shop floor, she'd recognised the red-haired woman immediately. That wide smile, the bright-red lipstick Emma remembered from some of the parties they'd both attended.

Scarlett.

They'd only spoken a handful of times in passing. They'd never been friends, and the sight of Scarlett in the shop had sent a bolt of fear through her body. She wouldn't go back to the hospital. She couldn't go back. She'd grabbed the scissors she'd been using to curl ribbon, gripping them tight in her hands. *'Tell Jonny I'm not doing anything wrong.'*

The smile had dropped from Scarlett's face. *'I'm not here with a message,'* she'd replied.

'Why are you here then?'

'Because I'm not really Jonny's friend. And I'm here because I need your help and I think you need mine.'

Three months later, Scarlett was reported a missing person, her face on every newspaper and news channel in the country.

Emma blinks away the memories. What good will it do to think about it now? She shivers. A chill has seeped into her core, as much from the mounting fear as the cool air blowing from the water and the smell of petrol and algae on the wind. Like rotting seaweed.

She checks her watch. It's eight thirty. Her stomach dips, a whoosh of nervous energy. Almost time.

Another minute passes, and then there's a sound behind her. The crunch of footsteps.

Emma jumps, crying out. Someone is here. She turns around, hoping it's shadows, her imagination, but it's not.

'It's OK,' the voice says. 'It's me.'

'Hi,' Emma replies, her hold tightening on Lola. She wants to feel relief, but instead she finds only the wrenching pull of indecision and loss.

'Are you ready?'

Emma shakes her head. 'No.' Tears prick her eyes. She can't do this again. She can't give up her daughter for a second time. She'd promised herself that if she ever got Lola back, she'd never let her go. But she also promised herself she'd do everything to protect her daughter.

'You can have a minute.'

'Thanks.'

Lola stirs then, rubbing at her eyes before opening them. Her face is pale, her hair tangled and wayward. There's a smudge of dirt on her cheek and dried chocolate at the edge of her lips. The shower they'd had at the bed and breakfast in Brighton feels like a long time ago. Emma is sure she looks no better. Her skin is grimy, and she smells bad. At least the wig has gone. Dumped in a bin at the train station. There's no need for it anymore.

Emma kisses the top of her head. 'It's time to go,' she whispers to her daughter.

Tears form and fall down Emma's cheeks in the split second it takes Lola to notice the person standing over them. She and Lola were supposed to catch a ferry to Belfast. They were supposed to stay together forever, but now Emma must do the impossible. She must give Lola up again if she really wants to protect her.

'You'll be safe now,' she says, explaining to Lola as best she can that she has to leave her. Her little girl cries softly, begging Emma to stay with her, but she leaves with the promise of episodes of *Peppa Pig* and chocolate, and Emma takes the bag she's given and tries to convince herself that this was the only way.

FORTY-TWO

EMMA

The car park is empty of passengers as Emma makes her way towards the glass ferry terminal. It feels wrong to be alone. For three days, Lola has been by her side. Her hand feels cold without her daughter's pressed inside it. A tremor starts to rattle all the way to her bones. Each breath she takes is fast and gasping. She should do the breathing exercises Haz taught her, but she knows there's no point. There is no calm for her now. Ahead of her, car doors bang. Then there's movement. Figures step beneath a streetlight.

She sees Isobel first, deathly pale and looking as distraught as Emma feels. Beside her is an older woman Emma has never seen before but guesses from the stories Roly told her, and the arguments she overheard between him and Isobel in those strange months spent in their home, that it's Roly's mother. Emma wonders how much she knows. Why is she here?

She looks to Roly next. His face is pleading, his gaze darting from her to the space around her. One emotion pushes up from all the rest. Hate. She hates these people. They used her as a means to an end. A commodity and nothing more. Destroying her dreams, her hope, her whole world because it suited them to. Because they could.

'Where's Lola?' Roly calls out, his voice filled with the same fear burning inside her. Does he think Lola isn't safe? Did he think she'd hurt her own daughter?

Before she can reply, another car pulls into the car park. She glances behind her and sees it's the black SUV. The sight of it causes another sickening wave of terror. It draws to a stop, blocking her path of escape, as if that was ever an option. Then her feet stop, her heart stops, because there, moving to stand beside Roly, is Jonny.

A voice inside her screams for her to run. But she can't. Fear has bolted her feet to the ground. There is nowhere to go. More doors bang. His men remain silent, keeping their distance – a threatening presence.

'What's going on here?' Roly's mother calls out. 'Roly? Who are these men? Where are the police?'

A tension is building in the air around them, but Roly doesn't reply.

'DCI Watkins?' the woman calls out then. 'What is going on here? Arrest this woman.'

Emma stares at the detective. The hate now sharp and venomous. Isobel and Roly stole her baby; stole her life. She will never forgive them for keeping Lola from her. But still, a part of her she loathes to think about understands their desperation. That need for a child. It can't be much different from the love and longing she has felt all these years. But this man – this detective – is a monster.

'Emma,' he calls out in that same even tone she remembers, as though she's walking into one of his parties, as though he hasn't spent nearly four years ruining her life over and over again. 'Where's Lola?'

Her heart pumps so fast, she can't tell one beat from the next. Her eyes dart left and right. The sun has given up its hold on the day. The orange glow from the streetlights and the terminal is all that is lighting the car park. There is nowhere to run. No escape. But maybe another passenger, a passer-by could help. Someone. Anyone.

There is no one.

His dark eyes find hers and there's a hint of a smile pulling on his lips. He's found her at last. He's won. *'There's nowhere you can go where I won't find you.'*

'Jonny,' she says, staring at the detective. 'Your name is Jonny – isn't that right, DCI Watkins?'

He laughs. Roly makes a noise, but Jonny just shrugs. 'The game is up, Roly.'

'Will someone please tell me what is going on?' Margaret says again. 'Where is my grandchild?'

All eyes land on Emma, but she cannot move her gaze away from Jonny. DCI Owen Watkins. Owen Jonathan Watkins. Jonny to most of his friends – his business associates he's made over the years. Although a few old school friends like Roly still call him Owen. Those who knew him before he became the man he is today.

The name change is a barrier, she's always assumed, between the good and the bad. Between Owen Watkins, respected detective chief inspector at Scotland Yard, and Jonny, the man with all his deals in the shadowy parts of the world most people don't think about beyond crime shows on TV.

'Lola's safe,' Emma replies. 'You can see her once you all admit what you did to me.'

Jonny scoffs. 'I don't remember you being forced into any of it.'

'I was forced into that hospital. You drugged me, remember? You almost killed me.'

Isobel gasps and Emma's gaze flies at her, and the rush of emotion is hurt and hate and so much more she can't even begin to untangle. 'Don't pretend you didn't know what he was capable of. That he wouldn't do that to me.'

Isobel opens her mouth to reply but closes it again. 'I just want my daughter back. Who's helping you, Emma?'

'We'll get to that,' she replies. Although now she's standing here with these people who destroyed her life and stole her child, Emma isn't so sure if anyone is really helping her.

Roly's mother steps forward, an index finger pointed towards Emma, then Roly and then Isobel and Jonny. 'Someone needs to tell me what's going on.'

'Mother.' Roly seems to find his voice at last. 'It's complicated. I was trying to shield you from this, but the truth is... Lola is... I mean to say that Emma is... she was Lola's biological mother.'

'Lola's mother?' A hand flies to the woman's mouth.

'They stole her from me,' Emma says. 'I was' – her gaze moves back to Jonny – 'coerced and manipulated.'

'That's hardly true,' Jonny replies, the smile twitching again.

'You stole my daughter,' Emma cries, and suddenly it's not fear bubbling inside her, it's anger. She'd missed a period and done a test, her mind reeling with the result and the sudden change in her life. Her dreams had been everything she'd ever believed in. She didn't say no when Jonny had first suggested the adoption, even though she'd felt that wrench of loss at the first mention of the word. She'd allowed herself to listen to his plans, to believe the dreams she'd clung to for so many years could still be something.

But when she looks back, she wonders if 'no' was ever an option. When someone like Jonny, with his confidence and his power, asks a naïve and distraught young woman to do something, can they say no? And if they agree, is that really consent? It's a question that has haunted her for years, one she's argued

over time and time again in the imaginary courtroom in her
head.

Margaret drops her hand, her eyes narrowing on Roly. 'I
told you I would never accept a grandchild that wasn't a Huntington. You tricked me, Roly. I can't believe you'd do this to me.'

'It's not what you think, Mother. I can explain,' Roly is
quick to reply, and then he turns to Isobel and shakes his head.
'I'm sorry, Iz.'

'Sorry for what?' Confusion crosses Isobel's face.

Roly looks from Isobel to Emma. 'Tell her.'

'Tell your wife what?' Emma says, emotion cutting into her
throat that she wishes she didn't feel. She draws a shaky breath,
steels herself. 'That I loved you? That her husband made me
fall for him with all his compliments and those perfect dates.
All those messages. Love bombing, it's called. I had no idea, but
I fell for it just like you planned.' She doesn't cry. Won't cry for
this man and what he did.

The second she'd told Jonny about the pregnancy, the affair
with Roly had been over. She'd been too wrapped up in
thoughts of a baby and Jonny's plans for an adoption to mourn
her heartache. It didn't take her long to realise it had been infat-
uation, not love. But it still hurt that Roly never acknowledged
their relationship, never apologised, or asked if she was OK. All
those months she was in his house and he didn't look her in the
eye once. Not until he'd told her to leave.

She's wondered over the years how different it might've
been if it hadn't been Roly she was giving her baby to. Would
she have found her voice to say no during any of the conversa-
tions with Jonny? Roly was Lola's father, and he had the means
to give her the best life imaginable. She'd thought that counted
for something. Now she looks back, she thinks it made it so
much worse, so much more tangled and confusing.

Emma looks at Isobel. The woman who'd tried so hard to be
her friend when she'd arrived on their doorstep six months preg-

nant. Always staring at her growing belly. Asking to feel her bump, gasping as the baby kicked. But turning cold and cruel as soon as Emma dared to love her own daughter.

She is frozen.

'I thought... you might be part of it,' Emma says then. 'The plan to get a naïve young woman pregnant and convince her to give up the baby.'

Isobel shakes her head. Her eyes glisten with tears. 'No.'

'Iz,' Roly says, dragging the name in a pleading tone.

'If it makes you feel any better,' Emma continues, 'I was nothing to him. Was I, Roly? I wasn't even a mistress or a fling. I was a woman to be impregnated and manipulated, wasn't I? You planned it all. You never cared for me.' Her words end in a shout as she finally voices the suspicion she's had all these years about their affair and how quick Jonny was to suggest the adoption.

Roly makes a noise in his throat, a cough and a groan rolled into one, and there is her answer. He looks to Isobel. 'I couldn't risk my inheritance by having a child that wasn't really mine,' he mutters, and there is the answer she's long suspected. She was nothing to these people.

He turns to his mother then. 'I'm sorry I lied to you, Mother, but I didn't want you to know Lola wasn't conceived in wedlock in case that made a difference to you as well. But she's mine. I promise you that.'

Emma bites back the emotion, gritting her teeth to the pain ripping through her even after all these years. God, she was so stupid to fall for it. She takes a long breath in, a longer exhale and steadies her thoughts. She must live in the present. And in this present, the people who did this to her must pay.

FORTY-THREE

ISOBEL

A falling feeling takes over Isobel's body as she stares at the younger woman. Emma is wide-eyed and terrified; hurt and furious. The same emotions clogging her body. For so long, she'd thought Roly had lied to Margaret. Tricked his mother into believing Lola was his child when really they'd adopted her with Jonny's help. But all along, it had been her he'd lied to and tricked. She'd never thought about who the father was. Not after the time she'd asked Jonny if it was him, and he'd told her not to worry.

She pictures her beautiful little girl and knows the truth is glaringly obvious if only she'd wanted to see it. Lola has Emma's huge eyes and cute little nose. But Roly's eye colour – that startling blue – and the wild blonde hair that never stays in place.

'It changes nothing,' Roly says, taking a step towards her, hand reaching out. 'I love you, Iz. You love me. Lola is our daughter. You are her mother.'

Isobel allows herself to wonder if Roly is right. Does this change anything? Then she thinks about the video Jonny showed her on the doorstep this morning. All those calls and messages he's always taking. Deep down she knows there is no more turning a blind eye, no future for them. She stares at Emma's haunted face. The girl looks like she hasn't slept for days. The jumper she's wearing is two sizes too big and swamps her tiny frame. This was not an affair gone wrong; this was a plan to impregnate and manipulate an innocent young woman. How could she continue to love a man who thought that was acceptable?

She thinks of the baby growing inside her now and the life this precious gift will be born into. A life of privilege and Margaret's rules. The right education. The right friends. The right everything. For what? So her children can become like their father who treats people this way? Or like her even, who went along with it? No. She has changed. She won't carry on these lies. She never thought she'd fall pregnant. The doctors all said it was near-impossible. Less than a one per cent chance. But here she is. That less than one per cent. She will do anything to keep her children safe.

Isobel steps back. Only minutes have passed since they climbed out of the car and found Emma alone. It feels like it's been hours. They are so far off course. There will be time to peel back the layers of their lies and deceit in the future. She has her secrets too after all.

Right now, there is only one thing that matters. Keeping Lola safe.

'Where is Lola?' she asks, fixing Emma with a fierce gaze. 'Who is helping you?'

Emma opens her mouth to reply, but the fury is catching hold of Isobel, and she can't wait to hear another lie or denial.

'It's Scarlett, isn't it? She's who's helping you.' Isobel spins to Roly, pointing a finger at him. 'She was another one of your affairs, wasn't she?' The words rush out of her. 'Don't bother trying to deny it. I saw how you were after she disappeared. I thought you'd gone moody on me because you were having an affair, but it was that the affair had stopped, wasn't it? I can't believe I didn't realise it. Scarlett must've wanted to hurt you. That's why she's helping Emma. To get back at you. They knew each other. Did you even think about that before falling into bed with her?'

'Iz, please. I didn't—' Roly starts to say, but Isobel can't hear it.

'SCARLETT!' She screams the name out into the night. 'WHERE ARE YOU? BRING ME MY DAUGHTER.'

She turns to Jonny. Too angry to be scared of this man and what he's capable of.

'You knew, didn't you? You knew it was Scarlett. All those hours you've spent in our house this week. Pretending to Margaret that it was a real investigation.' She rubs a hand over her face. 'Oh my God, you and Roly were pretending to me as well, weren't you? All that talk about Zeen. It was all a lie to protect Roly and your stupid boys' club.'

Jonny's face is hard. The look of amusement has gone. The tension in the air is crackling – the first strike of lightning in a storm.

'Isobel.' There is a warning in Jonny's voice that she ignores.

'SCARLETT,' she shouts again, and the woman's name echoes across the concrete car park.

'Stop it,' Jonny hisses. 'Get a hold of yourself, woman. Scarlett isn't here.'

'You don't know that. She helped Emma abduct my daughter. She could at least have the decency to show herself.' She spins around, hollering her name into the night again and again. She grabs at her bag. 'Where's my phone? We need to call the police. Her poor family think Scarlett is a missing woman. The police are searching for her body. And she's fine. They need to know what she's doing to us.'

'Iz,' Roly says, but his attempt to get her attention is lacklustre. 'Scarlett was just one of Jonny's girls. A friend. Nothing more. I swear it. She came to the parties. I knew her of course, but—'

'Stop this.' Jonny steps forward, and she's not sure if he's talking to Roly or her.

'No.' With a shaking hand, she pulls out her phone. This is it. The end has come for all of them. But in one step, Jonny is on her, a vice-like grip holding her arm. She tries to yank it free and yelps in pain.

With his free hand, he snatches the phone away from her. 'Scarlett,' he growls low in her ear, 'isn't here. You keep asking me how I know, and so I'm going to tell you this one time only. Scarlett is dead. So put your phone away and get a grip.'

Isobel stops moving. All she can hear is the thudding of her pulse in her head. 'Dead?' she whispers. 'How do you know? You can't be sure she's dead.'

He raises his eyebrows. 'Yes, I can, because I killed her. The bitch deserved it. She was a police officer, Isobel. She'd spent years pretending to be our friend, one of the girls I liked to have around to keep the mood light, but she was undercover trying to build a case against me the whole time.'

Isobel shakes her head. She doesn't want to believe it, but there is no reason for Jonny to lie. 'You killed her?' She looks to Roly. 'Did you know?'

'Jonny was protecting his business interests and ours,' he replies.

'Not ours. Yours. I had nothing to do with this.' She wants to back away but forces herself to stay. Tears swim in her eyes. 'Were you there when Jonny killed her? Were you involved?'

Roly shakes his head. 'Of course not, Iz. I could never. But...'

'But what?'

'Scarlett was getting close to me. We'd been flirting for a while, but I was cautious after everything with Emma. I wanted to protect myself and so... I used Mother's private investigator to check her out. He found out she was a police officer.'

'And you told Jonny, knowing what he'd do.' Isobel fills in the rest. This world, these men. How has she been part of it for so long? They really are rotten beneath the glimmering perfect life the rest of the world sees. Deep down, she wonders how much better she really is. She took Jonny's money. She managed his accounts, knowing all the while that she was covering up criminal activities. He had the perfect cover as a detective in the police. Who would suspect a chief inspector of buying and selling drugs and whatever else he did that created that cash she would mark as rent for the properties he owned across London that were never really rented out. She's been blind to so much. For what? Because of love? She really does love Roly. *Did*, she corrects. Already, the feeling is tainted and dark.

'Christ.' Jonny spits out the word. 'Will you two stop this lovers' tiff, or whatever it is. I should never have got involved in this.'

'Why did you?' she asks.

He sighs. 'Several reasons, none of which seem important now. First of all, you needed my help, and that's what I do. It wouldn't have been good for me if you'd had a team of police officers grilling you on your daughter and your past. And I help my friends, especially friends like Roly, who will gladly pay for my time.'

'You're paying him?' Isobel shoots the question at Roly.

He shrugs. 'Nothing comes for free.'

'So it was never about finding Lola?' she asks Jonny, knowing the answer.

'No. But I did need to get my hands on Emma.' His gaze moves to the younger woman. 'I couldn't risk you deciding you'd had enough or running and going to the police to tell them all you know about me and my business, and Scarlett of course. Since you had Lola, you had my leverage.'

Isobel gasps. 'You threatened to hurt my child?' She remembers that day on the common. How scared Emma looked. She'd warned Isobel that Lola was in danger, but she hadn't believed it. 'I'm calling the police,' she says again, but before the words are fully out, Jonny is reaching into his pocket, and when he pulls it free, there is a gun in his hand. She gasps, and it feels like the world stops – a pause button hit.

Her mind can't move on. Her gaze is glued to the shiny metal. A gun. She thinks of the baby inside her. She thinks of Lola, suddenly so glad her daughter isn't here. Her legs are jelly and cement all at once. Barely holding her but unable to move. In the corner of her vision, she sees Emma flinch too.

'Oh my.' Margaret who has stood silent for the last few minutes cries out.

'Now, Margaret,' Jonny says with the reassuring tone he's used this week in their home, pretending to this woman that the search for Lola was an official investigation, instead of him abusing his police powers and using the men stood silently now beside their SUV, 'there is nothing to worry about. You love your grandchild, don't you?'

She whimpers, and for the first time, Isobel doesn't see Margaret with her wealth and her vile opinions, the matriarch of the Huntington estate and all connected to it. She sees a woman who is in her seventies, suddenly frail and scared. But she will not feel sorry for her. So much of this is her doing.

If she hadn't insisted to Roly that their children be his blood, like some antiquated royal nonsense. If she hadn't spent a lifetime filling his head with a puffed-up importance of a surname that meant nothing. If she'd accepted Isobel as her daughter-in-law, allowed her to raise Lola as she wanted, they wouldn't be stood in this empty car park with a gun pointed at them.

'So there's nothing to worry about,' Jonny continues. 'You will keep this little chat to yourself. You will have Lola to raise and care for. And I will deal with this.' He waves the gun between them. 'Because I know it wasn't Scarlett that helped Emma. You're forgetting the missing passports there, Isobel, aren't you? So it can only have been someone with access to your home. And considering that Scarlett didn't have that, and not to mention the fact that she's currently residing under a new patio at one of my properties, I think we can rule her out. Can't we, Roly?'

Jonny turns to face her husband, the gun pointing directly at his chest. Roly's face is white, his mouth slack.

'Steady on, chum,' he says, trying to laugh, trying to be the same old Roly and failing.

In the deadly quiet that follows, Isobel sees the truth about her husband.

FORTY-FOUR

EMMA

Scarlett is dead. Jonny killed her.

Emma closes her eyes for a second, wishing it wasn't true. She'd hardly known Scarlett in her previous life as part of Jonny's world. The beautiful redhead had always been aloof with the other women, always focusing her attention on Jonny and the other men at the parties.

She'd never given her a second thought until the day she'd walked into the florist.

'*I'm not Jonny's friend,*' she'd said. Emma hadn't believed her at first, but then she'd shown Emma her warrant card. '*I've been working undercover for years, trying to nail Jonny and his associates. We know he's heavily involved in a huge drugs operation across London, as well as illegal trading and plenty of other things. But we don't have the evidence to prosecute him,*' she'd explained. '*We've had to be really cautious, because you don't accuse a chief inspector in the Met without the evidence to back it up. Especially one with so many friends in high places.*

'*The investigation has been kept very low-key, but we're running out of time. If I don't get results soon, we're going to have to move on to other cases. I'm taking a huge risk coming*

*here and telling you this. But I know you were close with Jonny
at one point. And I'm hoping you can tell me something that can
help, or if you could testify against him.'*

Emma had wanted to say yes, but what did she know? Only
that Jonny was a monster. She'd told Scarlett everything that
had happened to her, and even though Scarlett had been kind, it
was clear there was nothing she could do. Emma didn't have the
information Scarlett was looking for.

'This is my number,' Scarlett had said, scribbling down a
mobile number on a scrap of paper. *'If you think of anything
else.'*

The next day, Emma had called her and told her something
she thought might help. That was the last time she heard from
Scarlett until her face appeared on the news and Emma had
assumed the worst: that Jonny had found out about her and she
was dead. And she'd known then, she'd have to run.

Roly holds up his hands, spluttering at Jonny. 'Steady on.
What are you getting at, Owen? You can't think I'd help Emma
abduct my own child?'

Jonny no longer looks calm but wild in a way that sends a
shot of fear through Emma. He waves the gun between her and
Roly, and each time she feels herself shrink back. There is
nowhere to run.

Then everything changes.

The silence of the night is shattered. The air fills with noise
and light. Engines, and tyres moving fast. Bright-white head-
lights and the strobing blue of a silent siren as five cars speed
into the car park and jolt to a stop around them.

Emotion overwhelms her. The police are here. The actual
police. Not Jonny and his friends. It's over. It's all over. Tears
swim in her eyes. All she'd wanted was to keep Lola safe. To get
her away from Jonny and his threats.

After Scarlett had disappeared, Emma had been scared.
Terrified. Jumping at every passing car. Convinced Jonny had

got to Scarlett and knew Emma had helped her. He'd be coming for her next. She worried about Lola and that promise from years ago that he'd kill her daughter if she stepped out of line.

She'd been worrying about what to do. Stay quiet? Run? Warn Isobel and Roly. She'd never really considered going on the run with Lola. Not until that day a few weeks after Scarlett's disappearance when someone else had come into the florist looking for her and she'd known Jonny was still dangerous. Only then did she really start making plans.

A car door opens and everything happens at once. More car doors slam, and suddenly there are people everywhere, forming a circle around them. She sees more guns, and the bright-white lettering on the uniform that reads POLICE.

A tremor starts shaking her body. For one awful second, she thinks the police are here to help Jonny. Could they all be on his payroll? Is this the end for her? But then Jonny's men set off running, footsteps pounding the concrete, and two officers give chase, and Emma remembers the woman from earlier that evening. The police officer with the kind smile who'd promised to keep Lola safe and away from harm with an episode of *Peppa Pig* and a packet of chocolate buttons.

They are here to arrest Jonny. This was the new plan sent to her in Jenny's car yesterday. She was no longer to flee to Belfast and wait for help, but to stay and end this once and for all, to confront Jonny and get him to confess everything he's done.

'Police! Everyone stay where you are,' a voice shouts.

'What have you done?' Jonny hisses at Roly.

Roly gives a bewildered shake of his head, still floundering and staring down the barrel of Jonny's gun.

Without moving his aim, Jonny's gaze travels across the faces of the officers. 'I'm DCI Owen Watkins from Scotland Yard. Who's in charge here?'

A man with black hair and a sharp beard steps forward. 'I'm DS Anik Saha. This is my operation.'

'Well, Anik, you're way out of your depth. You've just ruined an ongoing Met investigation. I'll have your head for this. I was just arresting this man and his accomplice.'

He nods to Emma, and she gasps. *Don't let him talk his way out of this.* She remembers Scarlett's words to her that day in the florist. *'You don't accuse a chief inspector in the Met without the evidence to back it up. Especially one with so many friends in high places.'*

'He's lying,' she cries out.

Jonny shoots her a pitying look. 'There's no reason to keep pretending now, Emma. I know you and Roland Huntington planned the abduction of a child.'

The lie is enough to send a sickening wave of reality pulsing through Emma's body. She sees it all unfolding. This man with all his confidence worming his way out of this, carrying on. He'll find a way to pin it all on Emma, just like before. He'll kill her this time. She has no doubt.

'I...' She struggles to find the words. 'It's not what you think,' she says, staring between the officers.

'Owen Watkins,' Anik continues, 'I'm arresting you for the murder of DS Philippa Holloway. You do not—'

Jonny laughs. The sound is calm, relaxed, but Emma can see the fury tightening his features. 'Never heard of her.'

'Her undercover name was Scarlett Peters.'

Jonny pauses. Just a fraction of a second before he's talking again. 'Who authorised this?' he asks so lightly he could be discussing a wrong coffee order. 'I think perhaps you need to reconsider what you're doing here before your whole team is fired.'

'You do not have to say anything unless you wish to do so,' Anik continues, 'but anything you do say will be taken down and may be given in evidence.'

'Evidence?' Jonny scoffs. 'And what evidence are you basing this so-called murder charge on?'

'We can discuss that during your interview.'

'I think, all things considered, I've earned the privilege of hearing the evidence against me now.' He waves the gun a little as though reminding everyone of its presence, as if Emma needed any kind of reminding that the man who manipulated and coerced, the man she has been running from for three days, is dangerous. 'If you want me to come quietly, I'll need to know what you've got.'

A silence falls. There's a shift in the air. Emma glances from Roly to Isobel. None of them dare to move. Anik nods to a colleague with long blonde hair tied in a ponytail. The same woman Emma gave Lola to just an hour ago. The officer removes a phone from her pocket and taps the screen. A second later, Jonny and Isobel's voices ring out into the night. The audio is tinny, but there is no doubt it's them.

'*I'm going to tell you this one time only. Scarlett is dead. So put your phone away and get a grip.*'

'*Dead? How do you know? You can't be sure she's dead.*'

'*Yes, I can, because I killed her. The bitch deserved it.*'

The relief comes then, wild and unstoppable. Emma heaves in a shaky breath. Jonny might be high up in the police force with friends all around him, he might be rich and he might be powerful, but he has confessed to the murder of a police officer, and there is no way he can talk his way out of that. He must realise it too because his pupils blaze with fury.

'There's more if you want to hear it?' Anik says.

Jonny's gaze shifts from the officers back to Roly. 'What have you done? You fool. If you think I won't bring you down with me, you're mistaken. I will drag you and your family through the mud, old chum,' he says, anger accentuating his final words.

'Me?' Roly looks aghast. He mutters something under his breath. Emma only catches the final words. '... up to my neck too.'

An electric charge ripples between them. Emma is certain she can hear the thudding pulses of everyone in the group racing as fast as her own.

Anik takes a step forward. 'Put down the gun, Owen.'

Jonny responds by holding up his free hand in a stop motion. 'Don't come any closer.'

He turns slowly, the barrel moving away from Roly and on to Emma. He stares at her for a long moment. 'You were recording me? Well, well, well. I didn't think you had it in you, little Emma.' His eyes narrow on her as no one dares to move. He shakes his head.

'Gun down, now,' Anik shouts.

Jonny acts like he doesn't hear and instead moves his free hand up to the gun as though about to take aim. Emma's heart is racing so hard, it feels like it will burst out of her chest. It's not her life that rushes before her eyes. It's Lola's and all she has to live for. She thinks of her daughter, hidden away somewhere, safe. That's all she'd wanted.

'This is your last warning, Owen.' Anik takes another step towards them, but it feels like he and Emma and the gun in his hand are stuck in a glass tunnel. No one can stop him.

'You deserve everything that's coming to you.' Emma's voice is stronger than she feels. 'I couldn't let you hurt my daughter.'

He makes a noise. 'Why on earth would I hurt a little girl?'

'You told me you would,' she says. 'You said if I stepped out of line, you'd kill everyone I loved, including Lola.'

Despite the police surrounding them and the guns and the severity of the situation, Jonny still laughs. 'I said that years ago. I was scaring you off, trying to get you to get on with your life. I would never hurt a little girl.'

He's lying. She knows he's lying. 'You threatened her recently too.'

'When?'

Emma doesn't mean to do it, but her eyes betray her as she

turns to look across the group. She sees Roly, still looking as bewildered and scared. But she keeps going, and finally their eyes meet.

Jonny follows her gaze, his head already shaking. 'You?' he calls out.

Isobel stands statue still. She stares back at Emma. Something passes between them in that split second. A silent understanding that despite all of their differences and all that has passed between them, they are united in one thing – protecting Lola.

Then Isobel is nodding and fixing Jonny with a defiant look.

'It was me,' she says. 'I recorded you. And I was helping Emma keep my daughter safe from you.'

FORTY-FIVE

ISOBEL

Her words land, and she watches the surprise form on Roly and Jonny's faces. They have no idea yet how much she's done and all she's capable of. But they will see it soon enough.

'What do you mean, safe from me?' Jonny's face is a scowl of anger. His dark eyes bore into her. But before Isobel can reply, there's another shout.

'Put down the gun, Owen.' Anik's voice is firm, sounding so different from the softly spoken detective Isobel met four months ago. He'd first come to see her at the beginning of April, catching her on the walk home from dropping Lola at nursery.

'Mrs Huntington, I believe you've been in conversation with my colleague, Philippa Holloway?' he'd said, flashing his police warrant card.

'We had one conversation, yes,' Isobel had replied, thinking back to the woman she'd shared a look with across the dinner table nearly four years earlier but had still recognised when she'd knocked on her front door last month.

Scarlett had known Isobel was the money person for Jonny, and she'd tried to convince her to turn on him. But Isobel was hardly innocent and so she'd said no. The woman had promised immunity, but still Isobel had refused. The police officer hadn't understood that it wasn't just her. Roly was one of Jonny's investors. He would not escape unscathed. The Huntington name would be dragged into whatever came Jonny's way. Immunity or not, Jonny would make sure the Huntingtons were dragged down with him. And so she'd given Anik the same answer.

'Like I told Scarlett or Philippa, whatever her name is, I don't want to talk to you,' she'd replied, quickening her pace, wanting to get away. 'I don't know anything. I can't help you. Please leave me alone.'

'Philippa is missing. I'm very concerned for her where-abouts,' Anik had said.

'I've not seen her.'

'Did you tell Jonny or your husband about your talk with her?'

'No,' she'd said, and it was the truth. She might not have wanted anything to do with the woman, but she wasn't about to put her in harm's way either. She hadn't known how far Jonny would go to protect his business and had no desire to find out.

'She left her home on Monday evening to meet with Jonny and your husband. We are gravely concerned for her safety. We believe Jonny may have discovered her real identity and killed her.'

Roly was involved with Scarlett? She'd slowed, her stride faltering. 'You should speak to Roly or Jonny about that then,' she'd replied with an indifference she hadn't felt. Inside, her blood had run cold. Roly had come home on Monday night in a state. He'd been drunk and upset but wouldn't tell her why.

'Right now, we're continuing to use her undercover name in the press so we don't blow the operation. We're hoping one of Jonny's friends will come forward with information.'

'That will never happen. His friends are loyal.'

'Are you?'

'*I don't know anything that can help you,*' she'd lied.

'*If we approach Roly, we blow this entire operation.*'

'*I'm sorry,*' she'd said. '*But I can't help.*' She'd meant it at the time. Even when Anik had pleaded with her, pushing his business card into her hand and urging her to reconsider, she hadn't thought she would.

But Scarlett's disappearance, or Philippa as Isobel now knew her, had got under her skin. She'd obsessed over every news story and Roly's behaviour too. What had happened that night to make him so unhappy so suddenly? If it had only been about a missing woman and Roly's mood, maybe she'd still have carried on as before, turning a blind eye in order to keep her perfect life and her happy home for her daughter. But then something had happened to change her mind.

She'd discovered she was pregnant. The impossible had happened. All those doctors who told her she'd never conceive. All those failed pregnancy tests, and all that she did to Emma to have Lola as her baby. She'd turned a blind eye to how that young woman had come into their lives and whatever deal had been struck between Jonny and Roly. She'd ignored Emma's pleading and done nothing when Roly had told her he'd talk to Jonny and get it sorted when Emma wouldn't leave them alone. She hadn't cared what that meant. All she'd been focused on was that Lola was her daughter and hers alone.

But then another baby was coming. This one conceived by her at forty-four years old. A shock. A miracle. Had they stopped trying too soon? Should they have done more before destroying someone else's life? She will never regret being Lola's mother, never stop seeing Lola as her daughter, her whole world, but discovering she was pregnant changed something. And one of those things was realising all the bad she'd done and wanting to change.

New plans had formed in her mind, and she'd seen straight away that if she was going to do this, if she was going to turn on her husband and a man like Jonny, then she was going to do it her own way.

'*It's not enough for me to give you Jonny's accounts,*' she'd told Anik when she'd called him the following week. '*You have no idea how careful he is. I won't put my whole life and marriage on the line on the chance he can talk his way out of whatever charges you can make stick. The only way this works is if we get him to confess to being involved in your undercover officer's disappearance.*'

'*And you think he'd tell you that?*' Even on the phone, she'd heard the scepticism in his voice.

'*Maybe.*' It was a huge risk. She knew he'd never confess over a bottle of wine and dinner. But she'd worked with Jonny long enough to know that when he was put under pressure, when he was angry and lashing out, he'd say things he shouldn't. It's how she'd known it was drugs he sold. He'd told her once when they'd received a random letter from the Office for National Statistics wanting more information on one of his fictional businesses – the number of employees, the hours they worked, details that didn't exist. '*I'm a drug dealer, Isobel. How the hell do we give them more detail on that?*'

Isobel had known that if Jonny was going to confess, then she'd need to create a high-pressured situation. Put him under stress. And she also had to make sure Lola was somewhere safe. A crazy plan had formed in her head. But if it was going to work, she'd need help from the one person in the world who'd never agree to help her.

Emma.

FORTY-SIX

EMMA

'You think I can't bring you down with me,' Jonny says, his voice a low growl as his gaze moves from Isobel to Roly.

'I had nothing to do with this,' Roly says. 'Iz, what on earth have you done?'

She shakes her head. 'What I should have done years ago, Roly. This man is bad. Do you get that? He does bad things. He's a criminal. He murdered a woman.'

'You bitch,' Jonny shouts.

Emma is aware of the crackling tension, the officers moving closer, the barrel of Jonny's gun. She drags in a lungful of air, suddenly hot and unable to breathe properly in her vest and jumper. She inches a fraction closer to Isobel. For the last few days, her world has been an out-of-control rollercoaster careening towards a cliff edge ever since she climbed out of her car at the roadside services and watched Isobel and Lola walk inside.

Her heart was already racing at lightning speed and she hadn't even walked inside yet. She'd watched Roly, making sure he wasn't following straight away. Then she'd passed by their car as he'd stepped away and she'd seen Barnaby on the back seat. In a split second, she'd reached in the open window and grabbed Lola's beloved bear and bag.

Angry tears blur her vision now. She's shaking all over. Freezing cold. Adrenaline is humming through her body, but she is suddenly so tired. The tears fall onto her cheeks as she closes her eyes. How did it come to this?

She hears Isobel's voice in her head. *'Emma, can we talk?'* she'd said, stepping into the empty florist shop just as Scarlett had done a few months earlier.

'I have nothing to say to you.'

'Please hear me out. I know Scarlett came to see you. You know she's a police officer. She's missing. I think Jonny killed her and he's going to be tidying up any loose ends that can connect him to the woman.'

'Me?' Emma had staggered back, the fear so sudden it was an electric shock.

Isobel had nodded *'And... and Lola.'*

It had felt like Emma had been punched, winded, knocked off her feet. She'd remembered Jonny's threat to her outside the hospital. He'd meant it. She had to keep her daughter safe. She'd been doing it all these years, keeping quiet and hiding from life, but it wasn't enough.

'Why?' she'd asked. *'I mean, why is Lola in danger now? You never believed me before.'*

'Because... he knows I want to leave and stop working for him. He told me Lola was dead if I ever walked away. I'm sorry I didn't listen to you, but I have to keep Lola safe.'

'Oh my God,' Emma had said. *'You have to take Lola and get the hell away from him.'*

'I can't.' Tears had streamed down the woman's face, and even though Emma hated Isobel with every fibre of her being, she'd understood the fear in her eyes. *'He'd find me. He's got police resources and friends everywhere. Besides, Roly would never agree to leaving.'*

'Go without them.'

'But then he and his mother would be looking for me as well as Jonny. I can't just up and leave like that, Em.'

Isobel's shortening of her name had rankled. They'd almost been friends once. Back when Emma was pregnant and Isobel was doing all she could to prove what a good person she was, what a good mother she'd make to Emma's child. She'd called her Em then too and Emma hadn't minded. But now it's all wrong. They are not friends. They never were.

'Why have you come here? What do you expect me to say?' Emma had asked, folding her arms around herself.

'I hope you'll say you'll help me.'

And then she'd told Emma her plan. Step by step. A way to take Lola out of the country and keep her safe. A way to distract Jonny and get him to admit to harming Scarlett.

'I can get money. I have money. I just need your help.'

They'd met the following day at a park, and Emma's heart had filled with undiluted joy at the sight of Lola playing on the swings. Isobel had introduced Emma as one of her friends and the little girl had been so delighted to meet her, telling her all about her love of strawberry jam and pandas, and Emma had felt whole in a way she'd never realised was possible.

'How will you get him to confess though?' Emma had asked. 'He's too smart. He's not going to just tell you what he did.'

'I'm going to mention Scarlett whenever I can. I'm going to say I think she's the one helping you with the abduction. I think if I keep pushing and Jonny loses his temper, then he might let slip what happened to her.'

'What if it doesn't work? What then?'

'Either way, Lola is away from him and safe. I'll meet you in Belfast, and we can start a new life with Lola. I have an old client, someone I worked for at the wealth management company years and years ago, before I met Roly. He said he can get us fake passports, and we can go anywhere in the world. You can be part *of Lola's life, Emma. I... I'm sorry I've kept her from you all these years. I want to make things right.'*

'So let me get this straight. If I agree to becoming a fugitive and be hunted by a man who has already destroyed my life and had me locked up, you'll let me be in Lola's life?'

'Whatever happens, I want you to be in her life. Even if you don't agree to this, I'll find another way to keep her safe somehow and you can see her whenever you want. But you're the only one I trust. You're the only one who will put her above everything else.'

'How do you know I will?'

'Because you're her mother too.'

It had been everything Emma had waited so long to hear. Tears had fallen, and of course she'd agreed.

'When are we going to do it?'

'It needs to be soon. I'm... I'm pregnant, Emma. I'm scared what he'll do to the baby too.'

The news had hit like a stinging slap. It shouldn't have mattered. But somehow it still had. This woman had been so desperate for a baby that she'd stolen Emma's. There was no excuse, except that small part of her that had understood the desperation. And now Isobel had conceived her own child. She'd never needed Emma's.

'I want you to know,' Isobel had said then, *'that I really thought we'd be giving Lola a better life. I didn't realise — No... that's not true. I didn't want to see that you'd been convinced to give up your baby by Jonny.'*

Emma had cried out. *'You think that's all that happened? Don't you know what Roly did?'* And it had been Emma's turn to hit Isobel with shocking news of her own. She'd told her about her affair with Roly and the plan she's certain he and Jonny had made together.

A part of Emma wonders now if they've always been moving towards this point in time, this showdown. Staring at

Jonny's dark wild eyes, she knows he has had a hold over her life for all these years. That her fear of what he'd do has kept her shrunken and silent. She grits her teeth against the hurt and frustration fighting for space in her body. She will not be scared anymore.

'You have ten seconds to put down your weapon or we will shoot,' Anik shouts.

'Let's all calm down, shall we?' Roly says, sounding anything but calm.

'No, let's not.' Jonny's reply rings with malice. 'This ends now.'

'I was trying to protect her,' Emma blurts out, taking another step towards Isobel as the police officers close in.

Jonny's eyes are fixed on Isobel. Emma knows he will not back down, not go easy. But Isobel doesn't cower. She stands her ground, and then to Emma's surprise, a barely there smile touches the woman's lips. Isobel is looking at Jonny with an 'I win' expression that surely she knows will provoke him. Emma wants to shout out, tell her to stop smiling, to turn and run. Does she not realise what this man is truly capable of? But it's too late. Maybe it's that smile or maybe it's the police closing in around them, the knowledge that there is no way out, but something tips Jonny over the edge.

Everything happens at once. There's a scramble of feet and bodies, but it's not quick enough. Without thinking, Emma leaps forward as Jonny fires. Two bangs. One and then the other that rattles her eardrums.

Hot pain sears through her chest, stealing her breath. She feels her legs give way and is powerless to stop herself falling to the ground.

It's over at last.

An inky black skirts at the edges of Emma's vision. She's aware of the commotion around her. Feet moving. Orders being given. The scraping gravel on her face where it's resting on the ground.

Someone is calling her name. It seems to take all her concentration to realise it's Isobel. A second later, she is kneeling beside Emma and clutching her hand.

'We did it,' Emma tries to whisper, unsure if the words reach beyond her thoughts. 'Lola is safe from that monster.'

Every breath causes a sharp pain to strike out from her lungs. She forces her head to move, to turn and look at Isobel. This woman has taken so much from her, but she's also a victim. Jonny has manipulated and threatened her just as he did Emma. And Roly has lied and lied. Isobel isn't like them. Not deep down. She has ignored the bad things happening around her because Lola is her whole world, and she loves her daughter. Emma can understand that. What wouldn't she do for Lola?

'I'm her mother,' Emma whispers as a darkness creeps over her. 'And so are you.'

FORTY-SEVEN

ISOBEL

Isobel squeezes Emma's hand. Her skin is icy cold. 'Yes, you are. You're Lola's mother too. We did it, Emma. You're safe now. Lola is safe.'

She can't stop staring at the body lying just metres away from them. Jonny, a heap of bulk and limbs. He's dead. Gone. He'd fired the first bullet at her – at Isobel – but the second had come from one of the officers, hitting Jonny right between the eyes. A thousand thoughts spin out of control in her head. He'd tried to kill her. She should be dead. Would be dead if it wasn't for Emma jumping in the way.

She hadn't thought he'd shoot. Or had she? Had she smiled at him just a fraction, tempting him to move the gun, expecting the police to get there first? She doesn't know. All she's sure of is that she's alive and he is dead, and this woman lying on the ground saved her. This woman, whose life she ruined, jumped in front of a bullet for her.

Oh God, this is all her fault.

There is movement all around them. Shouting too, but it all feels so distant; muffled. Isobel forces her gaze away from Jonny's body. She looks up from the ground to the blonde police officer who's working with Anik. 'Do something,' she shouts.

It's the same woman who'd walked a dog every day on the common. The same woman in the pink running kit, who'd watched for Isobel to open her bedroom curtains each morning, waiting for a signal to abort. If Isobel had felt she wasn't going to get Jonny's confession, or there was any danger, all she had to do was wave. She almost had once, but there'd been too much at stake.

They'd spoken on the common each day too. A brief moment when Isobel would tell the officer walking a boisterous dog that she was fine to continue. Isobel had tried for days to get Jonny to talk about Scarlett. Always checking the pearl earrings Anik had given her were in place in her ears, each one equipped with a recording device. She'd almost called it off when Margaret had commented on them, certain the woman would know they were fake.

It was pointless though. No matter how often she brought Scarlett into the conversation, Jonny never took the bait. And so she'd changed plans at the last minute. Gambling on this final showdown. Messaging Emma in a hurried moment on the common after sharing her plans with the police officer.

Beside her, Emma's breathing is a ragged gasp.

'It's OK, Emma. Hold on.'

The frantic desperation of the last few days rushes back through her. The search of the services on Sunday. Spending the extra moments in the toilet, giving Emma a chance to take Lola just like they'd planned. Convincing Roly. The abduction really had been her fault. She'd orchestrated all of it. The guilt had been real though, and so had the panic, as a small part of her had wondered if maybe Lola had been taken by someone else. And knowing that even though Lola knew Emma as Mummy's friend by that point, she was still putting her daughter through a huge ordeal. Taking her away from everything she'd known. She'd barely slept; living on a knife edge of adrenaline and fear, trying to find the right moments to push Jonny about Scarlett. Praying he didn't get to Emma or discover what she was doing first.

Every second, she'd expected Jonny or Roly or Margaret to see through the expression on her face to the real emotions running wild, like an unstoppable river, through her body. As soon has Jonny had identified Emma, she'd had to play along, pretending to want the press involved, pretending to want the real police. Playing her part as the anxious mother. How relieved she'd felt when Jonny had messaged Roly to say he hadn't found them yet, but she'd been terrified too, that at any moment he would get them, and Emma wouldn't be able to escape.

She'd been desperate to have Lola back in her arms. Not just home, but home and safe, and those two things were not the same. Lola was not safe in her home. But it wasn't Jonny Isobel was protecting Lola from.

Isobel had lied to Emma on that one. She'd never told Jonny she wanted to leave, and he'd never threatened Lola. She sometimes wondered what he would've said if she had told him she was leaving. He could be so reasonable sometimes and fly-off-the-handle angry other times. She'd never wanted to know what he'd say, but the lie had been easy to tell and easy to believe, so maybe there was some truth in it.

She'd known if the younger woman thought Lola was in danger from the same man who'd hurt her in so many terrible ways, she'd do anything to protect Lola, including helping Isobel. Including abducting a child and putting herself in danger. To Emma, Jonny was a monster. All Isobel had to do was spark that fear in Emma.

The truth would've been too hard to articulate. How could she have explained to Emma that Lola did need protecting, but that the threat was coming from much closer to home – from

Margaret and Roly. She'd watched her mother-in-law lash out and nitpick, forever whispering ideas in Roly's ear. And always, Roly did what Margaret said. Putting Lola in nursery when Isobel felt she was too young. Leaning towards boarding school next. And before that, suggesting Isobel leave her job because his mother thought working was unbecoming for a wife.

When the woman had first mentioned boarding school for Lola at Christmas, a sharp hurt had sliced through Isobel. She'd never agree to leaving her daughter like that. But she'd known that it was only a matter of time before Margaret's *'just something to consider'* comment became a command Roly would follow. After all, her husband was loyal to a fault. He was loyal to his mother. Loyal to his family name. Loyal to his friends. The only thing he'd never been loyal to was her.

Then everything had changed. She'd discovered she was pregnant during Roly's dark weeks of misery. Before she'd found the right time to tell him, she'd overheard Margaret talking to him one day when they'd thought Isobel had been in the playroom with Lola.

'*You must pluck up the courage to divorce her, Roly. She's never been right for you. Just think how much easier life would be if you married a better sort. How happy you could be. And Lola could come and live with me and at St Martin's school. Don't you want your daughter to have the best life?*'

He'd told his mother she was wrong, that he loved Isobel. But there was no warmth or reassurance in those words. Instead, a cold hard reality had started to settle in Isobel. For the first time, she'd realised how precarious her life was with these people. They had money and friends in high places. If Roly decided to divorce her, he could so easily push her out. Under Margaret's direction, Isobel had no doubt Roly would take custody of Lola and find a hundred ways to keep her from seeing her daughter – her whole world.

And it wasn't just Lola anymore. She had her baby to think

of too. A miracle baby no one had ever expected after all the years of failure. Lola was her everything. Her shining light. The new baby already meant just as much to her. There was no way she would let these people take her children from her.

And so the week after Anik had come to see her, the week after Scarlett's disappearance had hit the news and Isobel had overheard Margaret tell Roly that he was unhappy because his wife was making his life miserable, she'd known she needed to act.

She'd approached Emma and made her think Jonny was going to hurt Lola. Isobel had known the only person who would keep her daughter safe was the woman who believed with the same fierce devotion as Isobel that she was her mother.

They'd made a plan, and she'd told Emma about a car she'd leave in Crawley just a few hours from the services that Emma could collect the next day. She'd found the caravan park they'd stay in, and she'd given her Lola's passport and told her about the night ferry to Belfast, promising to meet her there the following day. Promising her a world where she could be in Lola's life forever.

There would've been easier ways for them to escape, to get them out of the country before anyone even realised, but that was never the plan. Isobel needed Emma and Lola to be close, to be chased. She needed Jonny following leads, pressured and distracted so she could push him about Scarlett, record his confession and end him – and with him, Roly too.

Because if she was leaving and taking Lola, then she needed to make sure Jonny wouldn't be trying to track her down. And he would've tried. Would never have stopped, she's certain of that, especially because she was also stealing so much of his money for her new life.

She'd known Roly would never call the actual police, just as she'd known that he and Margaret would want the Huntington name kept out of the press. They'd be so busy trying to avert a scandal, they'd never notice what Isobel was really doing right under their noses. So she'd found a road in Crawley that would be closed. Pretended to leave a car there for Emma to collect, knowing that without it, Emma would be frantic and desperate. She'd be seen and chased by Jonny's men, but she'd also known that Emma would do everything to protect Lola. Whatever it took, she'd never let Lola be caught.

The guilt has half-destroyed her this week. Not just because of what she'd put Lola through, but because only after the plan was in place and Lola was gone did Isobel worry that maybe Emma wasn't to be trusted. It made Isobel the worst kind of mother. But the end result had to be worth it. This was the only way she could think of to start a new life with Lola and her baby, and have the wealth she'd become used to.

Of course, she'd hoped it wouldn't come to a final show-down, but when Jonny hadn't confessed yesterday, and Emma had made it all the way across the country, Isobel had known there was no choice. She'd told Emma to go to the ferry terminal and meet the police there. Give them Lola. Keep her safe. Then walk into the car park and face Jonny.

It had worked. She can hardly believe all her planning had come to this and now Jonny was dead.

A movement on the ground catches her eye. It's a puddle. An inky mess of blood growing around Jonny's head. She is glad he's gone; would've fired that gun herself if she'd had the chance. There's no way for him to hunt her down now. No way anyone will ever know how much money she's stolen from him either.

Now all that is left to do is stop Roly and Margaret too.

FORTY-EIGHT

ISOBEL

Isobel releases her hold on Emma's ice-cold hand and starts to speak, but her voice is lost to the rush of people around her. A paramedic in a bright-yellow jacket appears at Emma's side. It should be Isobel lying there. She should be dead. She must finish this. For Emma as much as for herself. Roly and Margaret must pay. On shaking legs, she stands, casting her gaze around the groups of police officers, and Roly and Margaret both statue still, staring between Jonny and Emma.

'I have the files,' she calls out, her voice loud but shaking too. She reaches into her bag and pulls out an old-fashioned memory stick. It's not all of Jonny's businesses and accounts and money. It's not the ones she's stolen from, but it's most of them.

Anik steps forward. He holds out a hand to take the stick. 'We can do this later, Isobel. Take a moment. Are you OK?'

She shakes her head. 'There's everything on there you need that shows they were involved. Those two.' She turns and stares at Roly and Margaret. Her loving husband. Her mother-in-law. She's been planning Isobel's downfall for so long, but it's Isobel who will win. Margaret who will lose.

Her mother-in-law's hands fly to her chest. 'What do you

mean involved? I have no idea what you're talking about.' Her voice cracks. 'Roland, what's going on?'

'There's no point denying it, Margaret,' Isobel says, fighting back a smile at the sight of her mother-in-law's distress, reminding herself of all the tiny pinpricks of cruelty she has endured because of this woman. 'Your accounts and Roly's are tied up with everything Jonny was doing. It's all in the files. There's no way you didn't know what was going on.'

It's another lie. What's one more anyway? She hadn't had access to Margaret or Roly's trust accounts, no way to get to their money. Even Roly, with all his declarations of love, had never trusted her with that. But she'd found the account numbers in his files, and over the last few months, she'd made sure that money was being funnelled into them. Roly was already up to his neck in Jonny's businesses, as he'd muttered earlier, but it had been easy to add Margaret too.

She was certain that they'd talk their way out of any charges with the right legal team at their side. But it would be enough to distract them. While they were scrambling to prove their innocence and protect the Huntington name, she would slip away with Lola and go somewhere they'd never find her.

'It's OK, Mother,' Roly says, sounding entirely unconvinced. 'Iz, darling, what is all this? What are you doing?'

She stares at her husband then. Oh, how she loved this man. How she'd tried so hard to please him. Even ignoring his womanising and his investments with Jonny. But it was never enough. He would never put her before Margaret. When Scarlett had disappeared and she'd watched him crumble, known he'd been dragged into something with Jonny, she'd realised he'd always be weak, always listen to others over her. That damn loyalty. She'd found out she was pregnant and had wanted to make amends on her past, but it wasn't the only reason she'd done this. The truth was that this new baby meant as much to her as Lola, and there was no way she could let either of her children be taken away from her or manipulated by Margaret.

So she'd gone to see Emma to ask for her help, and Emma had told her Roly was Lola's father.

The news had felt like a bomb detonating. Her heart had shattered, pain in her chest. She'd been shaking her head, not believing, but it was as though a curtain had been drawn back to reveal an ugly truth she could no longer pretend wasn't there.

Not only was Roly the father, but he'd tricked Emma into an affair with a plan to impregnate her. It was sick. It was terrible. It was exactly the kind of thing Roly would do. Thinking only of himself and his family. A means to an end.

None of it mattered now. Her heartache for him would heal. With Jonny's money, she didn't need him anyway. She could provide for Lola, give her the world. And her baby too.

'I'm doing what any mother would do. I'm protecting my children.'

'Children?' Margaret says. 'Who—'

'I'm pregnant,' she replies, touching the small, perfectly formed bump of her stomach and relishing the shock dawning on their faces. 'And you will never see this child,' Isobel hisses, 'or get your claws into it like you've been trying to do with Lola. You'll never see Lola again.'

'How dare you—' Margaret starts to say, her words stopping short as an officer takes Roly's arm.

'Roland Huntington, I'm taking you into custody to answer questions on the murder of Philippa Holloway and your business dealings with Owen Watkins.'

'Am I being arrested?'

'Not at this time. But you will need to come with me, please.'

The blonde officer steps up to Margaret. 'Would you follow me please, Mrs Huntington?'

The woman doesn't move. She's still frozen in place, staring at Isobel with shock and anger and hurt. 'How dare you do this to us?' she says in a voice low and menacing. 'You will not get away with this.'

But Isobel turns away, ignoring the comment. She already has.

She kneels back to the ground beside Emma and takes her hand again. This time fingers squeeze back.

'Emma?' Isobel says, searching her face.

'Hey,' she murmurs, eyes still closed.

'Are you OK?' It's a stupid thing to ask. A sob catches in Isobel's throat that somehow ends in a huff of laughter. It's the shock, she thinks. 'Sorry, of course you're not. I... I can't thank you enough. You saved my life. Jonny was going to shoot me.'

'You weren't given a vest like I was,' Emma says, struggling then to sit up. She pulls down the oversized jumper she's wearing and rubs at the space on the bullet-proof vest where the bullet hit.

'But it could've hit you anywhere and you still saved me.'

'For Lola,' Emma says. 'She loves you so much. I didn't want her to be without you.'

Emma's gaze flicks to Jonny's lifeless body, and she gives a shuddering breath before wincing and clutching at her chest.

They fall silent as another paramedic covers the body. There is the distant sound of a siren, drowned out by the blast of a ferry horn.

'We missed our ferry,' Emma says, and the first sign of tears form in her eyes.

'We can get another one.'

'We?' There is such hope in Emma's eyes that Isobel finds herself nodding. This is the woman who saved her life and has saved Lola from Margaret and Roly's clutches. She hadn't spent much time thinking about what she'd do once she'd escaped with Lola, only that it would be somewhere far away and perfect. New passports, new names, a new beginning. She'd sold the plan to Emma with promises of being part of that life, but it isn't until now that she realises she meant it.

Isobel nods. 'If you want to come with us, yes. But I can't stay in this country. Jonny might not be a threat any longer, but Roly and his family – they'll do everything to take Lola away from me, to stop me seeing her, and stop you as well. There is nothing for us here. I'm going to disappear with Lola.'

'I guess I'm coming then.' Emma smiles before turning to look across the car park. 'Where's Lola?'

At that moment, a car draws up and a door opens. A little girl with wild blonde hair rushes towards them. 'Mummy!' Lola shouts, throwing herself into Isobel's arms.

Emma shuffles away a little, and Isobel catches the hurt on her face. She reaches out her spare arm and pulls Emma into the hug. 'We did it,' she whispers in Emma's ear before landing a dozen kisses on Lola's face, which makes her giggle and squirm.

Isobel doesn't know what the future holds for any of them, what her life will be like, but she has Lola and that's all that matters. They are free.

Emma's words after the gun had fired and she'd dropped to the ground ring in Isobel's head. *'I'm her mother. And so are you.'*

No! The word scratches across her thoughts. She pushes it away before it can take root. She will let Emma into Lola's life. After everything she's done for Isobel – and after Isobel had tricked her – how could she not? Emma can help with the baby; she can help care for Lola.

For now anyway.

EPILOGUE

The man crouches among the tufts of grass on top of the dune. The sand is soft, the kind that he'll find grains of in pockets and folds of clothing for months to come. He does not like sand. But this is a well-paid job and so he doesn't mind much. Cannon Beach's shoreline, seventy miles from Portland on the west coast of America, is picturesque. Dark sand stretching far into the distance. White driftwood that looks like washed-up whale bones. Thin strips of picket fence line the dunes, tilted and barely standing. The sea is a dark blue in the late afternoon sun. There's a nip carrying on the sea breeze. He wishes he'd brought his beanie.

He shifts position, lifting the camera to his eye and adjusting the long telescopic lens. He zooms in on the figures. Two women and a little girl with white-blonde hair. They are all barefoot, shoes discarded in a heap near the path. Jeans rolled up to the calves. The blonde woman moves towards the shoreline. He hears her distant cry of joy and surprise as the cold sea touches her feet. The little girl follows, screaming with delight; laughing.

He snaps a photo of the woman and the child, and as she

turns to hold the little girl's hand, he sees a baby in a pale-blue sleepsuit nestled in a carrier on her chest. He takes another photo.

The other woman has reddish-brown hair that sits in waves on her shoulders. She follows more cautiously, smiling but not running. The little girl beckons her in, and then the two women take a hand each and swing the girl over the waves.

He takes a dozen more photos and smiles to himself. At last, he's found them. The Huntingtons will be pleased. He's found Roly's children for him. They were not easy to find, even with all the budget and resources at his disposal. But no matter. He has found them now. Knows all there is to know.

The older blonde stays home and cares for her baby and the little girl. The younger woman has opened a flower shop next to a deli and an art studio selling driftwood sculpted into the shape of fish. Idyllic, but not for long. Not after what they did to his client. There's no rest for the wicked…

Later, when he's back in his car, he'll open up his laptop, attach the photos to an email and type just two words before pressing send.

FOUND THEM.

A LETTER FROM LAUREN

Dear Reader,

Thank you so much for reading *I'm Her Mother*. If you want to keep up to date with my latest releases and offers, you can sign up for my newsletter at the following link. Your email address will never be shared, and you can unsubscribe at any time.

www.bookouture.com/lauren-north

I have loved the idea of this story since the very second it came to me. I don't think anyone who's read it will be surprised to learn that the seed for this idea began at a roadside service station. My family and I were travelling to the Lake District for our summer holiday. We'd stopped for a break, and I was focused on getting Rodney, our dog, to have some water and to stretch his legs. So when my teenage daughter said she was fine to go to the toilets on her own, I didn't think to stop her.

It was only after she was out of my sight that I looked around at the hundreds of cars and people, and realised that if she was snatched away, it would take us a long time to realise. I immediately gave Rodney to my husband and hurried in after our daughter and all was fine. But when we started our journey again, I began to think about that moment of fear, and how quickly someone could be snatched or even rescued at a roadside services, depending on which side you were on. That moment became Emma, Isobel and Lola's story, and it's been so much fun to bring it to life.

I always love to hear from my readers. Whether it's through reviews, tags in posts, or messages, it never fails to make my day! My social-media links are below, and I can be found most days popping in to X, Instagram and Facebook. If you enjoyed *I'm Her Mother,* then I'd be so grateful if you would leave a review on either Amazon or Goodreads, or simply share the book love by telling a friend.

With love and gratitude,

Lauren x

www.Lauren-North.com

 instagram.com/Lauren_C_North

 tiktok.com/@Lauren_C_North

 facebook.com/LaurenNorthAuthor

 x.com/Lauren_C_North

ACKNOWLEDGEMENTS

Thank you so much to the early readers and bloggers who put so much energy and time into supporting authors. You're the best! A special mention to Teresa Nikolic for always shouting about my books and being so generous with your time for authors!

I dedicated this book to my editor, Lucy Frederick. Lucy – from the first time I pitched this idea, you've been one hundred per cent behind it. But more than that, your vision for it and relentless hard work has elevated this story to something so much more than even I realised it could be. Thank you! And thank you to the entire Bookouture team. So many people have been involved in the publication of this book, so please do take a moment to read the credits page at the back.

A huge thanks also to my agent, Amanda. You never bat an eyelid when I suggest another book idea or a schedule that seems nearly impossible. Your faith in me is such a boost! Thanks also to the whole team at LBA.

While wading through the structural edits of *I'm Her Mother*, I stumbled across a Facebook support group called Write MAGIC. The Zoom motivation and camaraderie saw me through so many hours with this book. Thank you to the dedicated team who run it and all those who've cheered me on for another ten pages and ten more.

If it isn't completely obvious by now, writing is not the solitary existence some believe it to be. It's a team effort with Amanda, Lucy and Bookouture all part of my team. But also on my team are my friends. I count myself incredibly lucky that there are too many names to mention here. So to my X friends, my village friends and my school mum friends and uni friends, thank you for reminding me of a world outside of my stories.

I've taken a healthy pinch of creative licence to create this story, but I'd also like to thank Matt Carney for his help answering questions on ANPR and policing.

I'd also like to thank Merry Anslow for proof reading this book, and all her input on ideas for the next one.

There are a few names I would like to mention. Louise Beech and Charlotte Duckworth, you remind me that we're all in this together and keep me going through the harder times. Thank goodness for WhatsApp voice notes. Lesley Kara, you are such an amazing woman. I'm so grateful to have you as my friend. And of course Nikki Smith, Zoe Lea and Laura Pearson – I say it every time, but talking to you is so often the highlight of my day. Thank you for cheering me on and distracting me, for all the guidance and support and love you give me. Roll on, Harrogate!

My work schedule when I wrote and edited this book was quite mad. And while I wouldn't have it any other way, I have been at my desk so much that I need to give a very special thanks to my family – Andy, Tommy and Lottie. Your belief in me, and support, your understanding and encouragement, keeps me going. Escape rooms, cat cafés, dog walks and action films really are the best reason to take a break. You are always the best reason!

PUBLISHING TEAM

Turning a manuscript into a book requires the efforts of many people. The publishing team at Bookouture would like to acknowledge everyone who contributed to this publication.

Commercial
Lauren Morrissette
Hannah Richmond
Imogen Allport

Cover design
The Brewster Project

Data and analysis
Mark Alder
Mohamed Bussuri

Editorial
Lucy Frederick
Imogen Allport

Copyeditor
Donna Hillyer

Proofreader
Laura Kincaid

Printed in Great Britain
by Amazon